HEART
QUEST

## More to Love

HeartQuest brings you romantic fiction

dation of biblical truth.

tery, intrigue, and suspense

e heartwarming stories of

en of faith striving to build

at will last a lifetime.

Quest books sweep you

into the arms of God, who longs for you

and pursues you always.

∽◆∾

*Song of a Soul*

# LAWANA
# BLACKWELL

*Romance fiction from*
Tyndale House Publishers, Inc., Wheaton, Illinois

**www.heartquest.com**

Visit Tyndale's exciting Web site at www.tyndale.com
Check out the latest about HeartQuest Books at www.heartquest.com

Copyright © 1997 by Lawana Blackwell. All rights reserved.
HeartQuest edition published in 2004 under ISBN 0-8423-7229-6.

Cover illustration copyright © 2004 by Robert Papp. All rights reserved.

HeartQuest is a registered trademark of Tyndale House Publishers, Inc.

Scripture quotations are taken from the Holy Bible, King James Version.

This novel is a work of fiction. Names, characters, places, and incidents are either the product of the author's imagination or are used fictitiously. Any resemblance to actual events, locales, organizations, or persons living or dead is entirely coincidental and beyond the intent of either the author or publisher.

**Library of Congress Cataloging-in-Publication Data**

Blackwell, Lawana, date

Song of a soul / Lawana Blackwell.
p. cm.— (Victorian serenade ; 4)
ISBN 0-8423-7965-7 (pbk.)
I. Title.   II.Series: Blackwell, Lawana, date   Victorian serenade ; 4.
PS3552.L3429S66   1997
813'.54—dc21                                                                                  96-47577

Printed in the United States of America

10   09   08   07   06   05   04
8    7    6    5    4    3    2    1

*To Andrew*

*Your tender heart and sense of humor
make living in the same house with you
a pleasure. May your love for God bring
you even more joy in the years to come.*

*Song of a Soul*

The song of my soul
since the Lord made me whole
has been the old story so blessed
of Jesus who'll save
whosoever will have
a home in the haven of rest.

*Henry L. Gilmour*

# Prologue

## March 12, 1868

I N a Covent Garden backstage dressing room, mezzo-soprano Clarisse Pella winced as a hairpin scraped her scalp. "I've hurt you, ma'am?" the girl gasped, her eyes wide with horror.

"No." Clarisse angled her face in the mirror to study the hairpieces mixed in with her own glossy black curls. "Pin them in tight. I do not want them coming loose onstage."

When the girl was finished, Clarisse got up from the dressing table and studied her reflection in the cheval glass in the corner. The plum-colored velvet dress she was wearing boasted a tight, square-cut bodice, a low-pointed waist, and long sleeves puffed up at the shoulders. Except for the heavy stage makeup, Clarisse strongly resembled portraits she had seen of sixteenth-century Spanish royalty. She would be playing the part of Eboli tonight, a princess in King Philip II's court. The role called for great beauty and coloratura, and even at the age of thirty-five, Clarisse still possessed both.

"Is this your first time to sing in London, ma'am?" asked the girl, who stood off to the side watching. Clarisse gave her a long-suffering smile and reminded herself that the girl was hired for her hairstyling genius, not for her knowledge of opera.

"I have sung everywhere," she answered. Tonight's debut of Verdi's *Don Carlo* would be only one of dozens of operas in which she had performed during her eighteen years on the stage. She walked back to the dressing table and took a sip of water.

In a few minutes, the stage manager would call for her. Already she could hear the orchestra tuning up, and voices buzzed as the nobility and gentry were being ushered to their seats. Queen Victoria was to be in attendance, she had heard. But Clarisse was not the least bit nervous. She had sung for royalty all over Europe.

A knock sounded at the door, and she signaled for the hair-dresser to open it. It was too early for the call to go onstage, and for fear of affecting her voice, she did not allow flowers in her dressing room from well-wishers and admirers. She set down her glass and eyed the door curiously. A young boy stood there, trying to see past the six inches of opening the girl allowed.

"Signora Pella is busy," the girl told him. "What do you want?"

"I've a telegram for her, miss. I was told I could bring it to her here."

*Probably congratulations from Cecilio for beating Adelina Patti out of this part,* Clarisse thought, smiling to herself. "Let him give it to you. I've time to read it."

The girl obeyed and closed the door again. When she turned back to Clarisse, her face had suddenly gone white as chalk. "I-I'm sorry, ma'am!"

"What is the matter?" Clarisse demanded. Then she looked down at the envelope the girl was holding. Its borders were black.

Trembling, the hairdresser asked, "Should I fetch someone to be with you while you open it?"

Clarisse stared at the envelope. All she could think about was what an opportunity this would be for Faye Donatello, her understudy. On opening night, the opera critics were out en masse, hungry for fodder to use in their newspaper columns. An understudy who assumed a starring role on opening night would be the talk of all England the next day—provided she possessed the talent to give a strong performance. Miss Donatello had such a talent, Clarisse knew, with youth and beauty to match.

It wasn't fair, she thought, that a mere understudy would set the standard by which all future performances of the role of Eboli would be measured. Critics could be fickle, even to famous prima donnas . . . and just what if Faye Donatello gave a better performance than she?

"Signora Pella?"

Clarisse looked up at the girl's face. "Put it on my dressing table. I will read it afterwards."

"But it's got black—"

Clarisse ignored the cold chill that snaked up her spine. "Then three hours will not make any difference, will it?"

# 1

July 7, 1883

EDMUND Woodruff IV rubbed his throbbing temple
and glared across his desk at the young man seated
before him. *Why do our children have the power to grieve
us so?* he asked himself, though he already knew the answer.
Love was the shackle that had so far kept him from throwing
his hands up in resignation. Even if, at twenty-one, his youngest son was too thickheaded to see where his folly would ulti-
mately lead him, Edmund still felt an obligation to intervene
and point him in the right direction.

*But this is the last time. I'm getting too old for such aggravation.*

"Sir?"

Edmund looked up as Gregory's voice cut into his thoughts.

"I would just like to say—," his son began, looking as contrite as he always did when called on the carpet. But Edmund
was not willing to listen to the young man's excuses just yet.
He held up a silencing hand and continued to glare.

The tragedy was that Gregory had the potential to go as far
in life as he desired. The brightest of Edmund's six children,
he had made excellent marks at Owens College in Manchester
before being expelled for scandalous behavior two years before.
And easily he was the most handsome man in Walesby, for his
dark hair and intense blue eyes, combined with the aristocratic

lines of his face, drew attention everywhere he went. *It would have been better if he had been ordinary looking,* Edmund thought. Good looks were a curse without the character to go with them.

Finally, he cleared his throat. "What possessed you to lock a cow in the vicar's house?" he asked in a remarkably calm voice for his state of mind.

Gregory had been sitting there in rigid foreboding since being summoned into the study. Now a lightning-quick twitch played at the corners of his mouth.

"So, you're still amused by your little prank!" Edmund snapped, and the vein in his temple throbbed harder.

Gregory's face blanched. "I'm not, sir."

"Then answer my question."

"My friends—"

"Oh, I've no doubt your friends wagered you into it. How much money did this idiocy earn you?"

This time Gregory's handsome face went crimson in an attempt to look indignant. The effect was spoiled, however, when he could not meet his father's eyes. "It wasn't a wager."

"How much?" Edmund demanded.

After some hesitation, his son mumbled, "Ten pounds."

"You will give that to the vicar for the inconvenience you've caused, along with your sincere apology."

"Yes sir." Though Gregory's eyes were still lowered, there was an easing of his posture, a relief that the worst was over. "I'll do that right away."

"Not quite yet."

"Sir?"

Edmund took a deep breath. "The examinations for

Cambridge are next month. I have arranged for you to take them."

"Cambridge?" Now the young man looked up at him with a dazed expression. "But I don't want to——"

"You're going to enroll in the university, or I will purchase you a commission in the army. Either way, you will not stay in Walesby and shame your family any longer."

"Father, please. Just give me one more chance."

"That's the problem, Gregory. I've given you too many chances already."

The color came back to Gregory's face. "And if I don't choose to take the exam? You would force your own son into the army?"

Edmund sighed, the heaviness in his heart far worse than the pain in his head. "I would force my son to become a man."

~

After leaving his father's office, Gregory walked outside to the garden, where his mother usually sat with her embroidery. Sure enough, she was there in her favorite spot—between the goldfish pond and a bed of blue larkspur—her matronly frame bent over a hooped canvas in her lap. At his approach, his mother looked up at him and smiled.

"Gregory."

She said his name, as she did all of her children's and grand-children's names, in a tone that resembled a verbal caress. Gregory's spirits lifted. Surely, if he were careful about it, he could convince her to talk his father out of this latest insanity.

He sat down on the bench beside her. "What are you making?"

"A sampler for little Frances's nursery." Frances was her latest grandchild, his older brother Jeremy's daughter, who had just been christened the month before. Holding up the fabric, she pointed to an elephant she had just embroidered around the letter *e*. "Each letter of the alphabet will represent an animal."

"That will be nice," he said, feigning interest. "But tell me, what animal could you possibly find for *x?*"

"Xiphosuran."

Gregory had to laugh. "There's no such thing."

"Yes, there is, although I'm not sure if I'm pronouncing it correctly. It's another name for a horseshoe crab."

"You're going to put a picture of a *crab* on a baby's sampler?"

She shrugged her shoulders. "It's either that or have little Frances go through life believing there are only twenty-five letters to the alphabet. At any rate, it will be a most attractive crab, I assure you."

Gregory smiled, secure in the knowledge that he could always put his mother in a good mood. Now was the time to work on her maternal instincts, he told himself. He would have to hurry if he were to make the start of the faro game at The Cat and Fiddle in a little over an hour.

He peered off into the distance with what he hoped was a melancholy expression and breathed a sigh that was heavy but not too theatrical. "I will miss our talks, Mother." Actually, it had been weeks since he had last sought her company—when the bill for the dozen new shirts he had ordered had reached his father's hands, and he had needed an ally.

His mother put the canvas back down in her lap. "And so will I, dear." Her voice was shaded with sadness, but she didn't ask what he was talking about. It wasn't a hopeful sign. If Mother already knew what was going on, that meant she had been in on the decision—or had already been convinced by Father to see things his way. Gregory knew he would have to be careful with his presentation.

"I do wish I could make Father understand how sorry I am about my past actions," he began, heaving another sigh.

"Have you told him?"

The sympathy in her voice gave him some hope. "I have," he replied. He hung his head and allowed his shoulders to sag. "But he still wants to send me away."

After a protracted silence, his mother shook her head. "The university will be good for you, Gregory."

"But you don't know how lonely it was for me in Manchester."

"Oh, I don't recall that you were *that* lonely."

Gregory looked up at her, startled. Surely Father, who usually shielded her from the most indelicate incidents, hadn't told Mother about that bit with the daughter of a smithy.

"I'm not proud of what I did," he said, lowering his head again. He dared not take out his watch, but he wondered what time it was. If he left soon enough and rode Spartacus, his father's fastest horse, he could still easily make the game. "I wish I could prove to you and Father how badly I wish to change my ways. Just one more chance would mean so much to me."

His mother touched his shoulder, and Gregory stifled a victorious smile. He knew he could win his mother over— she always had been a soft touch.

She patted his shoulder gently. "You can prove it by doing your best at the university, Son."

~

### October 3, 1883

In London, nineteen-year-old Deborah Burke closed the catch on her trunk for what she resolved would be the last time. "If

I've forgotten anything, I'll just have to write Mother and ask her to send it," she told her younger sister Theresa. "I'm worn out from packing."

Theresa, one year Deborah's junior, drew a wool wrap of bright chartreuse from the open armoire. "Won't you need this?"

Deborah winced and then glanced at the door. "I suppose Laurel would notice if I left it behind."

"I imagine she'll be up here checking the room an hour after you're gone," Theresa replied, covering a giggle with her hand. "But just because you pack it doesn't mean you have to wear it."

Their youngest sister, fourteen-year-old Laurel, had decided to make all of her Christmas gifts last year—a touching gesture and a sweet idea. Unfortunately, she was attracted to colors that could be seen for miles. *It could have been worse,* Deborah thought. *She might have used the same wool she chose for Father's muffler.* She smiled inwardly at the thought of the garish fuchsia scarf. But like a good father, he gamely wore it during nippy weather and pretended to love it.

"You're right, of course," Deborah sighed. She took the wrap, folded it, and unlocked her trunk one more time.

Later, as she sat with her family in the dining room, she realized with a pang of regret that it was the last dinner she would share with them until Christmas. Lucy, the cook, had prepared Deborah's favorite dishes for the occasion: chicken-and-leek pie, braised shrimp, and Welsh rarebit, with treacle tarts and marmalade pudding for dessert.

"Lucy has boxed up several jars of apple chutney for Miss Knight," her mother told her. "She doesn't want you to show up empty-handed."

Deborah had grown up taking for granted the bond between her mother and the cook. Until she visited in the homes of some of her school friends, she had assumed this kind of relationship to be the norm. She traded smiles across the table with her mother, whose green eyes were so much like her own and whose honey-colored hair had only recently begun to show traces of gray.

Before marrying Father, Mother had been a servant herself, which was why she treated the household servants as people instead of property. Now she was a successful portrait artist, whose works were commissioned by such eminent people as Octavia Hill and Lord Randolph Churchill. But Mother would tell anyone who asked that her most prized works were the portraits of members of her own family, which occupied places of honor in the sitting room.

A lump came to Deborah's throat. She had been so eager to begin her tutoring with Signora Pella that she hadn't given much thought to how she would miss her family. Now the reality of her imminent departure struck her full force, and she blinked back tears.

"I'm surprised Lucy hasn't convinced Deborah to stow a roast goose away in her trunk," her father said from the head of the table. When Deborah looked over at him, he raised an eyebrow as if to say, *Are you all right?*

She smiled back and nodded, but the lump still remained. Though her father drew curious stares from strangers out in public, she thought him the most handsome man alive. The warmth and intelligence in his brown eyes made up for the severe scars on the right side of his face, wounds from the Crimean War. She had inherited her dark brown hair from him, as had Laurel, while Theresa's hair was light, like Mother's.

Father was the one who had made the arrangements for her voice lessons from the famous Clarisse Pella, now retired from the stage and residing in Cambridge as the wife of Lord Payton Raleigh. Ten years ago, Deborah and her family had attended a performance of Verdi's *Aida* at the Opera Comique while on holiday in Paris. Deborah, who was already showing promise with her choral lessons at school, had sat in teary-eyed absorption, caught up in the spell of Signora Pella's clear mezzo-soprano voice.

At that moment nine-year-old Deborah fell in love with opera and determined that she must one day become the weaver of such musical spells. With a recommendation from her school music teacher, she auditioned for and was accepted by the Royal Academy of Music in London. She proved herself a dedicated student. As a young woman, while most of her friends were giving their attention to soirees and fashions—and later, to finding suitable husbands—Deborah was spending two hours a day going over the scales. And her hard work paid off. She made her mark in the academy's opera productions, starting out in the chorus and progressing to larger parts.

Then last spring, a few months before graduation from the academy, she auditioned for and won the role of Amneris, the same role that Clarisse Pella had once played, in the academy's production of *Aida*. Deborah felt that she had reached the pinnacle of her dreams—how could she aspire to anything greater than playing the role that Signora Pella had so magnificently brought to life? But as the performance ended and the curtain calls went on, she discovered that this was not an end but a beginning. There was no place more exciting to Deborah Burke than the boards of the theater. Opera had become so much a part of her soul that she couldn't imagine life without it.

Upon graduation, most students of the academy began a life

of auditioning for the London opera houses. The majority of them would begin with parts in the choruses while waiting for that one big part that would establish their careers. That had been Deborah's plan, too, although she felt she still had much to learn to reach the perfection she desired. Hopefully, the polishing of her craft would continue with maturity, experience in various small roles, and her own vocal practice at home.

Then one day her father approached her with a letter he had received from Clarisse Pella. He had been secretly writing to the great diva for over a year, detailing Deborah's progress and asking if Signora Pella would consider taking her on as a student. He had kept his plan a secret from Deborah so as not to raise false hopes, especially since Signora Pella never answered his letters. When she finally did answer, it was in response to Father's account of how splendidly Deborah had performed in *Aida*.

*"I will give your daughter one month,"* had been her succinct reply. *"If she is as promising as you claim, I will continue to teach her."*

Father's news brought an abrupt, though joyful, change to Deborah's plans. She would be taught by the very woman who had so inspired her a decade before!

Once the lessons were finalized, Father wrote to a friend of his late mother's, Helene Knight, to ask if Deborah might board with her. The eighty-year-old spinster—blind, but still in good health—replied that she would be delighted to have a young guest in her house and wouldn't dream of charging board.

~

"Did you pack your green wrap?" Laurel sat at the table next to Mother. Her intense tone of voice drew Deborah back into the present.

Ignoring a nudge from Theresa's foot, Deborah smiled at her youngest sister. "It's the first thing I'll see when I open my trunk."

After supper, the family sat around the game table in the library and played *vingt-et-un*. Except for Laurel, who had a strong competitive nature, everyone cared more about enjoying each other's company than actually winning. The laughter and good-natured banter that marked these family times struck a bittersweet chord in Deborah's heart.

"Are you getting tired, dear?" Mother asked when Deborah had grown quiet for several minutes.

Deborah smiled and shook her head. "I'm packing away some memories for later."

Her mother reached for her hand. "I pray you won't be too homesick."

"I suspect Signora Pella won't allow me the time," Deborah reassured her, although she knew better. She and her sisters had enjoyed opportunities to travel extensively, but always accompanied by their parents. Her father, Adam, had been in his late thirties when Deborah was born. He was a strong believer in family, even sending his daughters to day schools here in London when the trend among the wealthy was boarding schools. *We didn't have children so that we could send them away,* was his philosophy. *They'll be gone soon enough.*

For the first time Deborah allowed herself to consider how difficult this must be on her parents. If Signora Pella accepted her, for at least the next two years she would only be coming home for short visits at Christmas and Easter. She looked around the table at the faces that were so dear to her. Was her ambition worth the price she would pay?

Then she recalled the silence in the Opera Comique after

Signora Pella had finished the powerful scene in act 4 where Amneris pleads for the life of Radames. During the song, the audience had grown as still as death, as if each listener had become part of the ensuing drama. A hush had descended—to breathe, even, was to be reminded that they were merely spectators. But after several seconds, the clapping of one pair of hands broke the stillness, joined by another, then another, until the walls of the huge auditorium vibrated from the applause and shouts of "Bravo!"

It would be worth the pain of separation.

~

"Would you care to walk with me for a bit?" Father said to Deborah when the game was over and Mother and the other girls had gone upstairs to prepare for bed. She took his arm, and they went outside to the garden. The quarter moon on the southern horizon, combined with a crusting of stars overhead, gave a lustrous hue to the deep lavender of the anemones.

Father cleared his throat as they walked along the cobbled path. "I've never been to Cambridge in all of my travels," he began, "but all university towns are basically alike." He gave her a crooked smile. "Well, maybe Oxford is just a wee bit better."

Deborah smiled back. She supposed that the Oxford-Cambridge rivalry would always be part of him, even though he had graduated over thirty years ago.

"Unfortunately, Signora Pella didn't use good judgment in marrying a Cambridge man," Father went on, then stopped himself and smiled again. "I'm just joking now, you know. You'll like the excitement of a university town."

"I'm looking forward to seeing it."

11

"But I want to warn you of something."

"Warn me?"

He stopped walking and turned to her, his tone growing serious. "You're a beautiful young woman, Deborah. There will be hundreds of young men who will compete for your attention. Most will be gentlemen, but a good number will be cads."

"But just in Cambridge, of course," she couldn't resist teasing. "Surely there aren't any cads at *Oxford.*"

He chuckled and shook his head. "I'm serious," he protested. "It's the cads that give parents nightmares and ruin young girls' lives."

"Surely you don't think I would be interested in anyone like that, do you? Besides, I'll be too busy with my music to socialize."

"You have to allow yourself a little free time. There is such a thing as balance, you know. But getting back to the cads . . . sometimes they're hard to recognize, especially when you're so young."

Deborah nodded. "Like the wolf in sheep's clothing."

"Exactly," he agreed. "I must remind you that you've not spent a lot of time with young men. Discernment is more important to you now than it has ever been."

*He's worried that he won't be around to protect me any longer,* Deborah thought. "I'll be careful," she whispered around the lump in her throat.

Father absently patted her hand, but his scarred face still wore an anxious expression. "Being careful isn't enough, Deborah. You'll need to listen to the still, small voice of the Spirit. And you'll only be able to hear it if you stay close to God."

He stopped walking and turned his face up to the night sky. The great oblong constellation of Andromeda was easily recognizable directly south of the five stars of the Cassiopeia constellation.

"Beautiful, isn't it?" Father said.

"Yes," she answered. "It makes me feel so small."

"Me too, sometimes." He turned to her and smiled. "The Scriptures say that the heavens declare the glory of God. Your incredible talent was given to you for the same reason. But the temptation will be there to allow your talent to declare its *own* glory, to put your music ahead of God. You must constantly be on guard to see that doesn't happen."

Deborah marveled at how well her parents knew their daughters. Sometimes, especially while studying a new role, she found herself allowing every waking thought to be taken up with music, with no room for anything else. Afterward, with a contrite heart, she always resolved that she would never again consign God or her family to second or third place. But then . . .

"I will remember that," she promised her father, squeezing his arm. "And I know that you and Mother will be praying for me."

"Will *continue* praying for you," he corrected gently, his eyes shining. "You've been in our prayers every day for nineteen years."

~

### October 4, 1883

Gregory Woodruff slumped in his seat and stared gloomily out the window of the moving coach at the red-brown ironstone cottages of Walesby sloping down to the river Rase. He had never felt any appreciation for the charm of his picturesque village, but he would not give his mother and father the satisfaction of pleasant conversation. He caught them watching him with worried eyes and smiled inwardly. If they wouldn't change their minds about sending him away to Cambridge, at least he could ruin their morning by sulking. It was a small victory, but as he was still tied to their purse strings, it was the only one he could afford.

He pretended not to hear his father clear his throat, looking up only when his name was finally spoken. Reluctantly he tore his eyes from the window. "Sir?"

His father and mother exchanged glances, and for the first time it struck Gregory how old and tired they looked. *Has Father's hair been that gray all along?* he mused. And had he been too busy to notice the lines along his mother's forehead? For a brief moment he felt a surge of remorse, wondering if their concern over his antics had aged them as much as time had. But no doubt their incessant worrying over the family name and the spending of money "responsibly" had played a hand as well.

"I've written to inform your aunt Helene that you'll be in Cambridge," his father said. "You will remember your promise to pay a call every Sunday, won't you?"

Gregory's heart sank. Yes, he had promised, but just so that his parents would stop reminding him about how his mother's blind old aunt would someday be leaving her considerable fortune to her great-nephews. Even as he had made the promise to his father, however, he had figured that an afternoon now and then was enough.

"*Every* Sunday?" he said in a voice just a shade too close to a whine. To Gregory, there was no greater torture than boredom. Bad enough that he would have to submit to the tedious, rambling lectures of the dons at the university—but

14

whatever did he have in common with an old woman? He couldn't even remember her since his last visit to Cambridge had been when he was a tot of only two or three.

He regretted his protest immediately, for his father again launched into the familiar discourse about the joy his visits would bring to Aunt Helene and how it would be good for him to be accountable to someone older and wiser, who cared about his well-being. Gregory focused his eyes on his father's face and pretended to listen, while allowing his mind to carry him back to the going-away party his friends had given him at The Cat and Fiddle two days before. After a few seconds, however, his ears picked up the word *money,* and he allowed himself to be drawn sharply back into the present.

"I beg your pardon, sir?"

His father looked a trifle irritated, but he said after a short pause, "Mr. Ambrose Cornell is the solicitor who will be handling your expense money. His office is located on King's Parade."

Gregory nodded, his spirits lifting considerably.

"You will be allotted five pounds monthly," his father went on, shifting his hands on the cane he had propped between his knees.

Just then the wheels underneath them hit something in the road, causing the coach to lurch sharply. Gregory barely noticed, for the jolt to his insides was far greater. *Five quid?* Why, his allowance at Owens had been three times as much! "You must mean five pounds per *week,*" he corrected his father.

"Per month. That's more than most wage earners have to provide for their families. Your meals and housing have already been taken care of, as well as your books. And I can't

15

see how you would possibly need any more clothes, after what you've spent on them this past year."

"But *five—?*"

His father's jaw tightened. "I'll not finance your gambling and carousing this time, Gregory. If you don't think you can manage, there is always the army. You'll thank me one day for—"

"Edmund," Mother interrupted finally, putting a gloved hand on Father's knee, "we won't be seeing Gregory until Christmas."

"All right." Father stared across at him for a second and then exhaled heavily. "Eight pounds monthly. When we get to the station, I'll write you a note to give to Mr. Cornell." He held up a hand as if heading off any arguments that Gregory might offer. "As long as I receive no disturbing reports from you. *And* as long as you visit your aunt Helene faithfully."

Suddenly Gregory realized that this cloud had a silver lining. Why hadn't he thought of it before? He straightened in his seat. *Aunt Helene has plenty of money. . . .*

"But don't you even think about begging from Aunt Helene," his father's voice went on, crushing Gregory's rush of optimism. "I've already written her that she's not to give you any financial assistance. Hopefully with less money to waste, you'll stay out of places where you don't belong and concentrate more on your studies."

Gregory sighed inwardly and slumped in his seat again. He wouldn't be drawing the fifteen pounds he had gotten while at Owens, but he knew it was useless to press for more. Besides, he had over seventy pounds warming the inside of his purse, money he had won last week. The way his luck at cards was going lately, he could easily turn that into much more once he investigated the gaming opportunities at Cambridge.

His father was watching him with an air of expectancy, so Gregory forced himself to assume a grateful expression. "I won't give you cause to regret it, sir."

# 2

THE Eastern Counties Railway locomotive pulled into Cambridge Station at two o'clock on Thursday afternoon. Deborah Burke, inside one of the first-class coaches, brushed the wrinkles from her olive cashmere traveling suit and pinned on her straw bonnet at an angle. When the conductor swung the door open, she shouldered her valise, picked up her reticule, and stepped down onto a single platform, roughly a quarter of a mile long and crowded with people.

Father had warned that the autumn term, called Michaelmas, was about to begin for the twenty colleges that made up Cambridge University and that there would be a crush at the depot. She was not prepared for this, however. Passengers from the train—most of them college-aged men but also a goodly number of young women—held reunions on the platform and vied noisily for the limited number of porters.

*How will I ever recognize Miss Knight's driver?* she wondered, scanning the faces in her immediate vicinity. A harried-looking porter pushed his way past, muttering, "Sorry, miss," when Deborah attempted to get his attention.

She would have never admitted this to anyone, but she halfway wished she hadn't talked her father and mother out of accompanying her. "I have to grow up sometime," she had reminded them, excited about the prospect of going off by herself for the first time.

Loud laughter erupted from a group of people close by, but the sound caused an ache at the pit of Deborah's stomach. How was it possible to feel so lonely in such a crowd?

"Need your trunk, miss?" came a voice to her right ten minutes later when she had almost given up hope of finding a porter. She turned to find a red-whiskered, burly man, an empty hand truck before him. Deborah gave a sigh of relief and followed him to the baggage car.

Finally, he had her trunk loaded on the hand truck. "Got a carriage?" he asked, revealing snuff-stained teeth.

"There should be one waiting for me," she told him. Pushing the trunk, he made his way around the depot to the front, with Deborah in his wake again. The front of the depot was almost as busy as the platform had been. Lining the street were at least two dozen vehicles: hackneys, coaches, hansoms, and private carriages. Half were being loaded with passengers, trunks, and miscellaneous baggage, and the other half seemed to be waiting. But which one had been sent for her?

"I've got to get back to work." This came from the porter beside her.

*Think like an adult,* Deborah told herself. Mother had sent her photograph to Miss Knight's housekeeper and even included a description of Deborah's traveling suit. She wasn't doomed to spend the rest of her life at the Cambridge depot, no matter how much it seemed that way at present. Turning to the porter, she said with an authoritative politeness that would have made Father proud, "I assume my carriage has been delayed, sir. Where would you suggest I wait until someone comes for me?"

He nodded and pushed the hand truck over to a cast-iron bench against the station front wall. It had only one other occupant, an older gentleman who looked as overwhelmed as Deborah was beginning to feel. The porter set Deborah's trunk down next to the bench, pocketed the florin she extended to him, and disappeared into the crowd.

There was nothing to do but sit and wait. The gentleman on the bench beside her smiled, tipped his derby and leaned closer to say something, but Deborah couldn't hear him over the shrill blast of the final boarding whistle behind her. She did not wish to appear rude, so she nodded back, hoping that she hadn't just agreed to run away to a desert island with him. *Now you're getting silly,* she told herself. But silliness was all that stood between her and the tears that were threatening.

*At least the crowd seems to be thinning,* she thought. That would make it easier for Miss Knight's coachman to spot her. Ten minutes later her prediction seemed to be coming true, for fewer people bustled about in front, and about half of the carriages were gone. Then a shrill whistle sounded in the distance, growing louder until it dwarfed all other noises. Another train was arriving. Deborah let out a dismayed sigh.

In the relative quiet that followed the arrival of the train, the man who had been seated beside her rose. "My wife and daughter have arrived," he explained, tipping his hat and hurrying toward the platform. Although they had hardly spoken, Deborah felt an acute sense of loss as she watched him disappear through the doors of the depot building. So far, he and the porter had been her only acquaintances in Cambridge.

Was it going to be like this all day? New groups of people

21

were beginning to spill out through the depot doors. Perhaps Miss Knight had misunderstood her arrival time. Deborah considered hiring a carriage, for the address was in her reticule, but what if her driver came in the meantime? The back of her throat seemed stuffed with cotton. She swallowed and felt a burning in her eyes. *You will not sit here and cry like a helpless mollycoddle!* she ordered herself, then shouldered her valise and got to her feet.

~

The best thing about being tall, Gregory Woodruff decided as he stopped to gather his bearings on the crowded railway platform, was that it was easy to get attention. *You just need the right signal,* he thought. He drew a half crown from his pocket, held the coin up in the air between two fingers, and was approached within seconds by a middle-aged porter.

"Fetch yer trunk for you, sir?" the porter shouted above the noise while pocketing the coin.

Gregory nodded and shouted back, "There's another tanner in it if you hurry!"

Five minutes later, with the porter wheeling his trunk, Gregory shouldered his way through the mass of people toward the depot. He hadn't been here since he was three years old, but he remembered the hackneys lining Devonshire Road out front. He would have enough time, after stashing his belongings into some stuffy hall smelling of old wood and older books, to see what extracurricular diversions Cambridge offered. Surely there would be *something* to take his mind off the fact that the only place in the world he wanted to be less than here was in the army.

On the other side of the depot, Gregory headed for the first

unoccupied hackney he spotted. He was making good head-
way until he tried to edge his way between a post and
a woman standing with her back to him. On her left side,
a reunited family was caught up in embraces and chattering.
It would be useless to try to push through them.

"Excuse me," he said impatiently. Why was there always
a woman in the way when he was in a hurry? Men decided
where they needed to go and then went there or got out of
the way. But women seemed to having nothing to do but
place themselves as obstructions.

When she didn't move, Gregory repeated his words more
loudly. The woman jumped slightly and turned, and Gregory
found himself looking down into the greenest eyes he had
ever seen. She was young, he noticed right away, and stun-
ningly beautiful, with clear skin and a shapely mouth set into
an oval face.

"Oh, f-forgive me," she stammered.

Her voice sounded oddly thick for someone so young and
feminine, and Gregory took another look at her eyes. *She's
about to cry,* he thought.

Gallantly he removed his hat and slipped the porter another
coin to go ahead and find a hackney. "May I be of assistance,
miss?"

Instant relief came over her face. She dabbed her eyes with
the finger of a white crocheted glove and motioned toward
the queue of vehicles. "A driver is supposed to fetch me here,
but I've been waiting for almost an hour now."

"Is that so?" Suddenly Cambridge didn't seem so bad if
this young woman were a sample of the students at the two
women's colleges. Gregory flashed her a reassuring smile and

reached for the valise on her shoulder. "Here, let me hold that for you."

She seemed hesitant to let go of it at first but then passed it over to him. "Thank you. It was getting heavy."

Encouraged by the confidence she was placing in him, Gregory said, "My porter just happens to be finding a hackney. Shall I take you where you need to go?"

"You are very kind, but I would rather wait for a little while longer."

"Then I'll wait with you," Gregory told her. He held up a hand to ward off her protest. "I'm in no hurry. You have a trunk?"

She glanced past his shoulder. Gregory turned and peered through spaces between the passersby, spotting a trunk at the side of an occupied bench.

"Yours?" When she nodded, he said, "I'll have the porter go ahead and load it onto my hackney . . . just in case."

"No, thank you," she answered with a tight smile. "I'm sure my ride is on its way here."

Gregory understood. He had even expected her refusal of his offer. It was part of a script that every well-brought-up female in England was forced to memorize at her governess's knee. A young lady is to be wary of a gentleman she has just met, even if she is hanging by a branch from the side of a cliff. By accepting his offer of assistance too quickly, she would be perceived as a brazen woman. Better to fall from the cliff than allow that to happen!

Now, *his* part of the script was to assure her that he was only being chivalrous because of his obligation as a gentleman and an Englishman to do so—that he would do the same for anyone, even someone not as beautiful as she was.

"I should think that, after an hour, your ride isn't coming," he persisted, affecting a grave look of concern for her well-being. "And once we let the porter go, it may take a while to find another. I strongly suggest you allow me to have him load your trunk onto my hackney."

It startled him when the young woman turned to him, her cheeks spots of crimson, and held out a hand for the valise. "Sir, you will do no such thing. And I must ask you to leave me alone."

*You're moving too fast, you idiot!* Gregory reprimanded himself. Handing over the valise, he put a hand up to his chest and allowed himself to look stricken. "I do beg your pardon, miss." His mind reeled for an explanation and came up with, "It's just that you remind me so much of my younger sister . . . Claudia. I would hope that someone would assist her if she were to find herself in your predicament."

For a moment she looked confused, then her expression softened. "I suppose I'm not as grown-up as I thought," she sighed. "This *is* intimidating. I've never traveled without my parents."

"Ah, no wonder you looked so lost." He gave her his best reassuring smile. "And you seem very grown-up to me. But here I am, frightening you by acting so forward."

"No, you weren't forward," she said quickly, returning the smile. "I appreciate your kindness. I just misunderstood."

"No offense taken," Gregory told her. A woman carrying two white Persian cats moved between them, then he stepped back to the young woman's side. "But at the risk of sounding forward again, you really shouldn't be here alone. It would ease my mind if you would at least allow me to keep you company while you wait."

25

"But your hackney . . ."

"Will be happy to oblige me," he finished for her. "I'll just step over and have a word with the driver."

After a moment's hesitation, she nodded. The driver of the hackney did agree to wait, pacified by the promise of an extra half sovereign for his trouble.

"Surely my carriage will be here any minute," the young woman said as Gregory took her valise again. They walked together to stand near her trunk, as the closest bench was still occupied. She turned to him, her green eyes earnest. "And again, I'm grateful for your help."

For the first time in his life, Gregory was at a loss for words. He stared into the emerald-colored eyes and wondered at the strange, protective feelings they elicited from him. He was no longer the black sheep of his family, but a gallant knight, a bastion of chivalry, the rescuer of young ladies. *She would have been in tears by now without me.*

The gratitude in her expression turned into puzzlement, and he realized he was staring. "Huh?" he said, blinking.

"I was thanking you for your help."

"Oh, my pleasure. Are you from London?"

"Yes," she answered, obviously impressed. "I didn't realize the accent showed."

"It doesn't," he told her, then confessed that he had glanced earlier at the timetable on the depot wall. Women were always charmed by disarming honesty. "The London train arrived half an hour before mine."

She laughed—a rich, melodious sound—and he joined in with her. "And where are you from?" she asked.

"Walesby." When she gave him a blank look, he smiled and

said, "It's a small village . . . about eighty miles north. Are you here to attend one of the women's colleges?"

She shook her head. "Private music lessons."

"Oh? Do you play the harp or something?"

"Opera." She held out a hand. "I'm sorry. I haven't introduced myself. My name is Deborah Burke."

Gregory took her hand and gave a quick bow over it. He was about to tell her his name, then remembered the trouble he had gotten into at Owens College. After being expelled, he had berated himself many times for giving the girl his real name. All her father had to do was go to the university authorities, and he was out.

Still, some nagging voice inside—what remnant of conscience he still possessed—reminded Gregory that there were times when he had longed for the companionship of a decent young woman. One who could make intelligent conversation and respected her person enough not to allow herself to be used. He knew instinctively that this Miss Burke was such a woman and imagined himself bringing her home to meet his family. How impressed his mother and father would be over someone like her!

But then the hedonistic part of his nature took over, the part that loved the thrill of a chase. *Well-bred or not, she's still a woman.* And he had yet to pursue one who hadn't eventually succumbed to his charms. The aristocratic ones usually took a little longer, but that only added to the excitement of the challenge.

Gregory knew, from the covert and sometimes overt stares he received from females everywhere he went, that he was a cut above handsome. And he could tell by the way this

Deborah Burke's emerald eyes looked into his, that she was of the same opinion. *And she's feeling lost and alone!*

"I'm Fred Tarleton," he said, giving the name of one of his best friends back home. After all, he would need an identity he could always remember, no matter what his state of sobriety.

Encouraged by the obvious admiration in her expression, he decided it was time to press on. After all, her ride could appear at any minute, and any chance he had would be lost. "I have enjoyed our accidental meeting, Miss Burke. I wonder if I might call upon you some time?"

He was disappointed at the look that crossed Miss Burke's face—a return of her earlier wariness. She gave a regretful shake of her head. "I'm sorry, but I will be very busy with my music lessons."

"Too busy?" To his chagrin, he recognized the whine in his voice that he sometimes still used on his parents. He cleared his throat. "Surely not too busy to go for a walk now and then."

"I'm afraid so."

*She's just being coy,* he thought. The most tiresome part of the "don't allow familiarity with strangers even if hanging from a cliff" rule was that young women thought they had to refer to their scripts again and again, just in case there was any doubt as to their being well-bred ladies. "Oh, come now," he wheedled.

"Miss Burke?" Suddenly a boy of about thirteen years of age stood in front of them. He was clad in a fustian shirt and brown corded pants that were caked in places with equally brown mud. "Are you Miss Burke?"

Obviously startled at the appearance of the boy's clothes, she hesitated before replying, "Why, yes I am."

"And who are *you?*" Gregory demanded, taking a protective step in front of her.

The boy doffed his billycock hat, revealing a shock of brown hair as curly as a watch spring. "Name's Thomas, sir. I'm the lady's driver."

The opportunity to play the knight in shining armor was once more being handed to Gregory on a silver platter, and he intended to make the most of it before this Miss Burke disappeared from his life as quickly as she had entered it. "You don't look like any liveryman I've ever seen." He turned to the young woman and said in his most solicitous voice, "Do share my carriage, Miss Burke. I can take you wherever you're going."

He was stunned when his gallant offer was met with a frown of annoyance as she stepped around him to face the boy. "You're my driver?"

The lad gave a self-conscious nod. "I'm a gardener, actually. Mr. Henry—he's the liveryman—was supposed to fetch you, but one of the horses stepped on his foot when he was hitchin' them up. Mr. Darnell—he's the head gardener, you see—said I had to go for the doctor first." Frowning down at one of his mud-caked sleeves, he added, "Sorry about the dirt, Miss. I was digging up a rosebush when it happened."

"Oh, dear. I'm sorry."

"Mr. Henry wears good stout shoes," the boy said with a shrug. "He's likely all right, but they wanted the doctor to see him, just in case." Darting a bemused glance at Gregory, he said to Miss Burke, "You've got a trunk?"

When she turned to indicate the trunk behind her, the expression on her face was of someone who had just been rescued—a direct assault upon Gregory's pride. "It's over there. I'll find a porter to help you load it."

She turned and politely held a hand out to Gregory. "Thank you for your kind assistance, Mr. Tarleton," she said as they shook hands. Before he could say anything in response, she took her hand away and lifted it to signal a passing porter.

Gregory watched with clenched teeth, while Miss Burke followed the boy over to a finely appointed black brougham trimmed in silver and drawn by two Welsh cob horses. *She wasn't that attractive anyway,* he told himself, lapping at his wounds like an injured dog.

But his heartbeat quickened when she turned to face him again. She was actually walking back in his direction!

"Mr. Tarleton?"

*Don't look too eager, old chap.* He knew she would regret her snootiness once she realized that she might never see him again. Gregory raised a nonchalant eyebrow. "Yes, Miss Burke?"

She smiled sheepishly and pointed to the valise he was still holding. "I almost forgot my bag."

~

Seated in the carriage, Deborah seemed to feel Mr. Tarleton's eyes on her back as she waited for Thomas to climb into the driver's box. Surely she was imagining things—*surely he's not standing there watching me.* But she wasn't certain enough to turn around and look.

She wasn't quite sure exactly when she had begun to suspect he was one of those cads Father had warned her about. And perhaps she was judging him wrongly—discernment was still a fairly new concept for her. Still, there had come a point when his presence made her uneasy, in spite of his handsome looks.

Thomas clucked to the two horses, and the barouche started moving. She took in a deep breath and settled back into the seat. *Well, it doesn't matter, does it?* she thought. *I'll never have to see him again.*

# 3

S AINT Andrew's Street!" Thomas shouted over his
shoulder. Deborah watched the traffic, as busy as that
of any street in London. She supposed it would lighten
once the university term began. Presently the carriage turned
to the right onto a street called Thompson's Lane and followed
it to the end before turning to the right again. Deborah caught
the name *Park Parade* on a street marker hanging from a pole
beside a corner lamppost.

Above the cobbled street, massive sycamores and elms on
each side met in an arch, creating a tunnel of green. Behind the
trees Deborah could see a row of stuccoed four-story terraced
houses, all in pastel hues and trimmed in white, with glazed
porches supported by decorative ironwork. On her right were
more terraced houses, these of red brick under slate gray roofs.

"That one's Miss Knight's," Thomas said, twisting around
to tell her as the carriage slowed in front of the third house
on the left. He drove the carriage past, then took two left
turns into a mews running behind the row of houses. When
the brougham stopped at a carriage house and stable, a man
clad in work clothes appeared.

"You're supposed to help th' lady out at th' front door," he grumbled at the boy as he lowered the step at the side of the carriage.

"Oh, I forgot!" Thomas, now on the ground looking up at Deborah, exclaimed. "I never drove anybody before."

Deborah smiled down at him. "Please don't worry. I wanted to see the back of the house, too."

"Sorry about sendin' Thomas for you in thet state o' dress," the older man said, extending a work-roughened hand to help Deborah down. Slightly stoop-shouldered, he appeared to be in his late forties, with thick shoulders and arms, and sideburns running down from sparse brown hair to a square jaw. It was obvious from the stains at the corners of his lips that he was partial to snuff. "I never learnt to handle th' horses, and the doctor says Mr. Henry's got a broken toe."

"A broken toe!" Thomas came around to the side.

"Now you see why I don't like horses. Even th' tame-lookin' ones . . . they're allus waitin' for a chance to clout somebody with their hooves."

Deborah watched as the two figured out the best way to get the trunk out of the boot of the carriage and into the house. *The man must be Mr. Darnell, the head gardener,* she surmised.

She looked around. Only thirty feet or so of court extended beyond the terrace, but what was there was impressive. Marigolds, zinnias, asters, and scarlet sage, their hues grown more intense with the autumn nip in the air, abounded in orderly chaos, while chrysanthemums and dahlias bloomed with reckless heed to the season. It struck Deborah to wonder why a blind woman would care about having so many colorful flowers, then she chided herself for the thought. *She can still touch and smell them.*

"Miss Burke?"

Deborah turned to find a thin, middle-aged woman standing in front of her. A blue poplin dress covered a frame as erect as that of a palace guard, and graying brown hair was drawn into a topknot. The ring of keys dangling from the side of her apron signified that she was the housekeeper.

"I'm Mrs. Darnell," the woman said, and a smile softened the severe lines of her face. She was not a handsome woman in the classical sense, but her brown eyes were framed beautifully with long, thick eyelashes.

*Mrs. Darnell.* At first the name didn't register, but then Deborah glanced back toward the carriage. "You're . . ."

"He's my husband, all right." She nodded, still smiling. "We met while in service here. I was just a parlormaid then, and Mr. Darnell was the assistant gardener. Would you like to come inside? They'll get the trunk up to your room sooner or later."

She shepherded Deborah through the ground-floor terrace doors into a hallway. An open door to the left revealed a dining room holding a table, sideboard, and chairs of rich mahogany, with a deep crimson flocked wallpaper above the wainscoting. Farther down was a small lobby, which opened into a grand staircase lit by a stained-glass lantern. "The parlor and entrance hall arc at the front," said the housekeeper. "I'll show you all of that later. The missus will want to meet you now."

The steps led down as well as up, and Deborah supposed that the kitchen and servants' hall were down in the basement. She followed Mrs. Darnell up to the first-floor landing, past an anteroom on the left, to a door at the rear of the house.

"Miss Burke is here, missus," the housekeeper announced from just inside the door. She moved aside and motioned Deborah into a spacious drawing room. The walls were paneled in warm oak, the furniture well used, and the atmos-

33

phere redolent of comfortable old leather. In one of three damask upholstered Queen Anne chairs arranged by the fireplace, an elderly woman was seated. She held a crochet hook in one hand and a nearly completed dresser scarf in the other.

"Ah, Miss Burke," the woman said, transferring the hook to her left hand so that she could hold out her right in Deborah's direction. She sat with finishing-school erectness, her cloudy blue eyes set into a face that looked as soft and wrinkled as old flannel. Her white hair was braided behind the high collar of a gray-and-white checked dress whose single ornament was an ivory cameo at the neck.

Quickly Deborah walked across the Brussels carpet to take her hostess's hand. The skin felt soft and cool, drawn tight against fragile bones. "Please call me Deborah. And I must thank you for your kind hospitality."

"Oh, it is I who must thank you . . . Deborah," Miss Knight said with a smile, giving the girl's hand a gentle squeeze. "It will be so pleasant to have a young person in the house. Do have a seat, will you?"

While Deborah chose one of the other chairs, her hostess wove the hook through the newer part of the scarf, set a skein of ivory-colored thread in the middle, and rolled it up in her lap. "You didn't expect me to be crocheting, did you?"

"I *am* a little surprised," Deborah had to admit.

"It keeps my hands busy and my mind occupied." An almost impish smile came to the woman's face. "And if I make an error . . . who is going to tell me?"

From where she still stood just inside the room, Mrs. Darnell declared that her mistress's handiwork was just fine. "I still wear the wrap she made me." The housekeeper chuckled. "Would you like an early tea, missus?"

"Yes, please," Miss Knight answered. "I'm sure our young guest is ready for some refreshment." After Mrs. Darnell left, the older woman turned her face in Deborah's direction. "I trust that your father and the rest of your family are well?"

"Very well, thank you," Deborah told her.

"Your father's mother, Hyacinth, and I were lifelong friends. Some of my fondest memories are of the tea parties we would give for the servants' children on her family's estate in Horncastle."

"Weren't you distantly related?"

Miss Knight smiled. "We claimed to be fourth or fifth cousins—something like that—but actually there was no blood relation. One of my aunts was married to one of her cousins." A shadow passed over her face. "Yes, I was so saddened to hear it when Hyacinth died. She had married and moved away to Gloucester, and I had moved here with my brother, August, when he took a fellowship at King's College. But we kept in touch faithfully through the post. The first and last time I met your father was at his mother's funeral. That was before he went off to Oxford."

Then, in an obvious effort to lighten the mood, the older woman smiled again. "Adam was a most handsome young man, as I recall."

"You *saw*—," Deborah began before embarrassment clamped her lips shut.

"Yes, I could see back then." There was no sign in Miss Knight's voice of her having taken offense. "I assumed you were aware of that. No wonder you were surprised to find me crocheting. You see, I only began losing my sight some seventeen years ago."

To Deborah, nineteen, that seemed like an eternity. How did one show sympathy to a blind person? "I'm so sorry," she said.

"Sorry?" There was a pause, and then Miss Knight nodded her understanding. "Oh, you mean about my blindness." She smiled. "I've lived for eighty years now, and enjoyed over fifty years of sight. How can I feel any way but blessed?"

"You have a remarkable outlook," was all Deborah could say.

"Have I? Well, I suppose wisdom does come with age." Changing the subject, she said, "Tell me all about your music lessons. I have heard of Signora Pella—how exciting for you!"

Deborah straightened in her chair. "I'm to be her first student, and I believe it's because my father was so persistent. But she's only taking me on a trial basis."

"A trial basis? And how long will she give you to prove yourself?"

This was the part Deborah didn't like to think about. "One month."

"That doesn't seem like very long."

"She told my father that she doesn't want to waste time with anyone who has mediocre talent."

"I see. A perfectionist." Her colorless eyes seemed to stare directly at Deborah now. "And you believe your talent is not mediocre."

Deborah sighed. "I'll find out in a month."

"Your lessons begin tomorrow?"

"Yes, but I'm not certain for how many days a week. Signora Pella wrote that she would decide that after she met me."

A parlormaid dressed in black alpaca and a white lace cap showed up with a tray of tea and sandwiches and biscuits. She was a heavyset, middle-aged woman with kind hazel eyes, a bulbous nose, and ginger-colored hair peeking from her cap. Miss Knight affectionately addressed her as "Bethina."

"Most of my servants have been with me for years and years," Miss Knight said to Deborah as the maid set down her tray and put a clean cloth on a marble-topped table to the right of her mistress's chair. She shook her head when Deborah offered to help bring the table between her chair and Miss Knight's.

"Been movin' this table for years," she said, giving Deborah a grateful smile. "Can't leave it in front of the missus, here, or it might get in the way."

"You mean I'm so clumsy that I'll trip over it, don't you?" Miss Knight said with feigned sharpness.

"It happened once before," the maid answered back, sending a meaningful nod to Deborah.

"Ten years ago!"

It was obvious to Deborah that the two had had this conversation many times before and were merely going over well-rehearsed lines. She sat up on the edge of her chair, then made a closer observation of the drawing room. One thing she hadn't paid attention to at first was the lack of vases, statues, and other ornaments. Even her mother, who found amusing the current trend for as much decorative clutter around as possible, had several favorite pieces set about here and there.

"You're rather quiet over there, Deborah," Miss Knight remarked as the maid poured their tea into two Wedgwood cups.

"I'm just taking in everything," she answered.

"You must be wondering why the surroundings are so austere?" The elderly woman smiled again. "Several years ago I realized that it was heartless to keep bric-a-brac in every nook and cranny for the servants to have to dust and polish, since I could no longer see any of it."

"That was very thoughtful of you."

Miss Knight waved a spindly hand. "We've consigned such decorative pieces to the front parlor—but in cupboards, so they only have to be dusted once a year or so. I probably should go ahead and parcel them out to the family, but so many of my memories are connected with them. Even though I can't see them, it comforts me to know that they're still with me."

"You should ha' seen the fight me family had over me mother's things," Bethina said over her shoulder on her way to the door. "You'd think they was the crown jewels. Didn't know me sisters-in-law could be so greedy."

Deborah smiled and took a nibble from a cucumber sand-wich. "You have family in Cambridge?" she asked Miss Knight.

"Not since my brother died ten years ago. Walesby is where the rest live, over in Lincolnshire. I have one niece—Oriel—but she has six children and at least a dozen grandchildren now. I haven't been to visit them since I lost my sight, but occasionally Oriel and Edmund—her husband, of course—come to see me. Their sons all attended Owens College, where Edmund's brother is a provost."

*Walesby?* When the word hit her ears, Deborah wondered where she had heard it before. Then it dawned upon her. *That man at the train station.* Was it just a coincidence that she would hear the name of a town she'd never heard of from two differ-ent people in the same day?

"In fact, Oriel's youngest should be arriving in Cambridge any day now. He's promised to visit me every Sunday after chapel."

"What is his name?" Deborah asked. She held her breath and waited for the answer.

"It's Gregory. Gregory Woodruff. The last time I saw him, he was a boy of three, and I'm so looking forward to becoming reacquainted with him."

Relieved, Deborah took a sip of her tea. The man at the train station had been named Tarleton. *Frank . . . no, Fred.*

"I believe we'll both enjoy his company," Miss Knight went on. "As I remember, all of Oriel's children were particularly delightful when they were small. In fact, I have a photograph of them." Motioning in the direction of a pianoforte against the wall, she said, "Would you mind fetching it for me, dear?"

Deborah set down her cup and walked over to the piano. Its only ornament was a silver-framed photograph, slightly faded by time. She came back to her chair with it and peered down at six children of assorted ages standing in front of a vinecovered gazebo and looking stiff and ill at ease for the camera. The youngest was dressed, as was the custom, in a frock but wore a boy's cap instead of a bonnet like his two older sisters wore.

It was impossible to discern any resemblance to the man at Cambridge Station, or to anyone else for that matter. *Not the same name,* Deborah reminded herself, and she relaxed a bit.

"They are lovely children," she said, setting the frame on the table next to the tray. She smiled and reached for a ginger biscuit. "I'm sure I will enjoy meeting your nephew."

The next thirty minutes passed in pleasant conversation. When Bethina came in for the tray, Miss Knight had the parlormaid ring for an upstairs maid. "I know the journey has worn you out, dear, and you're eager to get unpacked and settled. You've been most kind, indulging an old lady with her ramblings."

Once the table was moved again, Deborah leaned over to take her hostess's frail hand. "I can't tell you enough how much I appreciate your having me here."

Miss Knight held her head erect and smiled. "Just don't allow me to monopolize your time. You must concentrate on your voice lessons so that Signora Pella will keep you for longer than a month."

Another servant, who appeared to be in her midthirties, entered the room. "Miss Burke is ready to go upstairs?" she asked in a Kentish accent.

"Yes, Avis," Miss Knight answered, her face turned in the maid's direction. "I trust you will help her unpack?"

"I've already begun to do so." She turned to Deborah. Dark, gray-green flecked eyes were set in a heart-shaped face, and the chignon behind her cap was as yellow as ripe corn. She stood at least five inches shorter than Deborah's five foot three, but her petite body was evenly proportioned. "I hope you don't mind my goin' ahead without you."

"No, not at all," Deborah said, smiling back as they walked to the door together.

"It's a lovely green shawl you've got up there, by the way. T'was the first thing what caught my eye when I opened the trunk."

Deborah looked closely to see if she was jesting, but it was obvious the woman was totally earnest. "Why, thank you. You must borrow it sometime."

Avis put a hand to her cheek. "Oh, but I mustn't!"

"I insist. My sister would be pleased to know that others were enjoying her handiwork."

At the staircase, Deborah started up slowly out of consideration for the maid, until she found herself outdistanced by three steps. On the second-floor landing they walked past a water-closet door to a guest room at the back of the house.

"Just two bedrooms on this floor," Avis said, stepping back so that Deborah could enter first. "Miss Knight's is at the front, and yours here, of course. We got indoor plumbin' eight or nine years ago," she added proudly. "On each story, too, even the basement. We're probably the only servants in Cambridge who don't have to use washstands and chamber pots."

The bedroom was every bit designed for a woman, from light rose-colored bed curtains and draperies to hand-stenciled borders above maroon wallpaper. Decorative items such as botanical prints, a Japanese screen, needlework footstools, small inlaid tables of lacquered black, and lots of assorted crocheted lace or embroidered cushions added warmth and coziness.

"It's very nice," Deborah said, turning around to take in all of the details.

"Isn't it though?" Avis went right to the open trunk, which was still half filled, and took out a skirt of raspberry batiste shot with blue threads. As she helped Deborah hang her clothes in a huge armoire, she told her about the occupants of the house and grounds. "There are two guest rooms on the floor above this one. Bethina and I and Gwen—she's the kitchen maid—live on the top story, and Mr. and Mrs. Darnell and Mrs. Reeves, the cook, have rooms in the basement. Thomas and Mr. Henry are above the carriage house, although Mr. Henry will likely have to move into the basement until his foot is all well."

She paused long enough for a quick breath and went on. "We had twice as many people in service here ten years ago,

41

some who came here to work when the missus moved here with her brother, but as they retired on their pensions, Miss Knight didn't see the need to replace them, except for hirin' Thomas out in the garden. There ain't that much to do, to take care of the missus. Not a lot of fancy things lyin' about no more."

"Yet this room is so lavishly furnished."

"Well, because it's a guest room, of course. All the guest rooms are nice, and there was once a lot of company to use them. But now her friends are either passed on or too old to travel." The maid snapped a blue poplin dress in the air to take out some of the wrinkles and went on. "We were all excited to hear about you bein' a singer and all. I never knew any real singers before. Maybe could you sing to us sometime?"

"I'm flattered you would ask."

Once the unpacking was done and Avis was gone, Deborah removed her bonnet and changed from her traveling clothes into a housedress of bronze beige with satin kilting. It would be wise to rest from her journey, as Miss Knight had advised, but she knew it would be impossible to relax. Too many changes had come in such a short period of time, with still more to come. She pulled a chair over to the window, sat down, and stared out at the smoke curling over rooftops in the distance and at the garden below.

The maid had called her a *real* singer. Deborah had never thought of herself in that way during her many years at the academy. If a person went to school to study law, he didn't become a "real barrister" until his education was finished. Even her performances on stage had been tied in with her schooling. *And here I am to take more lessons.*

More lessons. And with the woman she had patterned her

life after. If her voice wasn't up to Signora Pella's ideals, she would return to her family in shame. A shiver ran down her arms, and she crossed them in front of her, hugging them close to her body. *O Father,* she prayed silently, *help me to be worthy of her.*

# 4

MATTHEW Phelps paused at the stoop of a converted, red brick terrace house set among other such buildings on King's Parade. Just as he was taking a set of keys from his coat pocket, a loud *bang!* overhead caused his heart to jump in his chest. When his pulse calmed down again, he frowned up at the sign, now dangling from its post by one chain.

Though he stood at six foot three the last time he measured, Matthew wasn't tall enough to work on the sign without something to stand on, so he let himself into the office and took a sturdy chair from the foyer. It was a simple matter to twist the hook into a new place in the weathered oak, and he had it repaired in no time. *That'll hold you for a while,* he thought.

He hopped down from the chair and eyed his handiwork. *Ambrose Cornell, Solicitor of the Law,* the sign said in what must have been ornate lettering at one time. Now at least half of the gilt had worn away from the carved letters, and the remainder had turned a greenish brown.

"Looks to me like you oughta get a new chain," came a familiar voice from behind him. Matthew turned and gave a nod to Lucas, the boy who picked up the post twice a day for the businesses on King's Parade.

"It's not the chain," Matthew answered affably, reaching for the stack of envelopes and tucking them under his arm so that he could bring the chair back inside. "The wood is wearing away around the hook."

"Then you oughta tell your Mr. Cornell that he needs a new sign. One day it's going to drop on somebody's head and kill him flat." He tapped his right temple. "Might even be me, and I wouldn't appreciate that one bit."

Matthew peered up again at the sign, which now hung in subdued obedience. He had mentioned the need for a new one to Mr. Cornell weeks before, only to have the project deferred to Mrs. Cornell. That put a crimp in things then and there, for his employer's wife was extremely forgetful about anything not having to do with her pet bulldog, Royce. *I suppose I should remind her,* he told himself, wincing inside at the thought. It was so difficult to carry on any sort of conversation with Mrs. Cornell.

"Might even be *your* head, Mr. Phelps," the boy went on, picking up steam. "Just because you're a big feller don't mean your head can't crack open like anybody else's."

"I'll mention it again," Matthew reassured Lucas, then picked up the chair again. Once inside, when he went to wipe away the dust from his shoes with his coat sleeve, he noticed how frayed the cuff of his shirt sleeve was—and this was his best shirt. *Got to get a new one,* he told himself, walking over to drop the envelopes on his desk. *Can't go losing my job for looking shabby.*

Ever since leaving Trinity College three years ago at the end of his third term, he had been working for Mr. Cornell, who lived with his wife on the two floors upstairs, Matthew had dreamed of becoming an engineer, just as his father had been,

and giving up his education was one of the hardest things he'd
ever done.

But watching his brother, William, waste away had been
harder. Matthew had become responsible for the boy five years
ago, when their widower father had been killed in a railway
tunnel cave-in during construction. Their mother, frail and delicate but determined to have a family, had died from apoplexy
only days after William's birth. Thus, at the age of seventeen,
Matthew found himself using his savings to keep twelve-year-
old William in school while he himself prepared for his first
year at the university. But a year later William came down with
some rare cancer of the blood. When it became obvious that
the boy was dying, Matthew took him to a costly sanatorium in
Bath, where the hot springs were touted to have healing quali-
ties. Their modest inheritance was used up quickly. Matthew
sold their cottage on Warkworth Street and moved into a two-
room flat on Hobson Street, eventually dropping out of Trinity
to take the first position he could find. During the next seven
months he sent every extra penny he could to Bath and went
heavily into debt, but still his brother died.

Now Matthew couldn't even dream of going back to
the university, at least not in the foreseeable future. Even if he
were to enter as a sizar, which would mean earning his tuition
by performing menial chores for the more well-off underclassmen, there was still the matter of his remaining debts. One thing
Father had impressed upon him—besides a love of engineering—was that a man of honor paid his debts as soon as possible.

The thought of William brought an old, familiar emptiness
to his chest. He closed his eyes and pictured the boy sitting on
a bank of the Cam, just days before going away, lifting a frail
arm to wave as Matthew and the rest of the university rowing

team shot by in sculls. Excitement and pride had given William a glow that made him look almost healthy that day. It would have devastated the boy to know that Matthew had left Trinity College because of him, but Matthew had taken great pains to keep this information secret. Still, all his sacrifices hadn't saved his brother.

He swallowed hard. He would do it again without hesitation, this much he knew. At least William's last months had been spent under the solicitous care of well-trained doctors and nurses, with the best medical care possible. He had to believe that.

A noise jarred him back to the present, and he turned to see Mrs. Cornell, wearing a bright fuchsia dress, coming down the staircase. Her head was full of curling papers, and her pet bulldog, Royce, waddled down the stairs behind her. "Oh, good, you're here!" Her face was flushed with excitement, a sharp contrast to the bored expression on the dog's wrinkled face.

Matthew got up from his chair and walked over to the bottom step. "Mrs. Cornell, the sign—"

"Here . . . take Royce," she said, thrusting the animal's leash into Matthew's hand. The dog signaled his displeasure with a low rumbling in his throat.

"Now, Royce, behave!" She shook a finger over the animal's pug nose and gave him a look of mock severity, then leaned down to stroke his short grayish brown fur. "He's such a beast before his morning tea."

*He's a beast after his tea as well,* Matthew thought. To actually voice such a thought would put his job in jeopardy, for Mrs. Cornell considered her pet more human than animal.

"Mr. Cornell is just opening up his newspapers," Mrs. Cornell said, opening her husband's office door. "But I just couldn't wait to find a place for this." She disappeared into her husband's office, then came out seconds later carrying a huge canvas framed in dark wood.

"Here, let me get that," Matthew offered, walking over to where she was standing. She gave him a grateful smile and traded the painting for the dog's leash.

"It was delivered last night," she said, beaming. "A birthday surprise for Mr. Cornell. The moment I saw it, I knew he would love it. It's as if the artist knew Royce personally!"

Matthew leaned forward so that he could see the canvas in his arms. Not quite believing his eyes, he turned it around and held it in front of him. Seven dogs of different breeds sat upright in chairs at a table playing . . . *poker!* Matthew's mouth gaped in amazement. And true, the bulldog in the foreground looked exactly like Royce, except that Royce never smoked cigars to Matthew's knowledge. Tea was his only vice, besides having an obvious dislike for Matthew.

At a loss for words, the young man looked up at Mrs. Cornell. His employer's wife stood there watching him with an expression as eager as a child's at Christmas. "Well, what do you think?"

"It's . . ." He forced a benign smile. "Quite interesting."

"Isn't it though?" she gushed, dimpling genteelly. "It's by an American artist, a Mr. C. M. Coolidge. He's very popular in the States, I hear."

"Incredible."

"My very words when I first set eyes upon it!" Her mouth dipped into a frown, and she sent a reproachful glance toward the staircase. "Only, Mr. Cornell doesn't want it in his office. He says it would distract him from getting any work done."

"Oh, well," Matthew consoled. "He *is* very fond of Royce."

49

Mrs. Cornell pursed her lips in thought, reaching down to scratch between the dog's ears at the same time. "You're suggesting he doesn't want it hanging in his office because he *likes* it?"

After a brief hesitation, during which Matthew kicked himself mentally for being drawn into another family dispute, he said, "It's . . . possible. Legal work calls for a great deal of concentration, you know."

"Why, of course, the dear man!" Relief washed over her face. "The same reason he doesn't want *my* portrait in there."

Matthew swallowed and pretended to study the painting again.

"You know," Mrs. Cornell said, "I was going to bring it upstairs for the parlor, but since my husband likes it so much . . ." She put a plump finger up to her cheek and studied the walls of the outer office.

"There!"

Following where she was pointing, Matthew's eyes latched upon the wall some twelve feet behind his desk, where a Constable landscape had been hanging for the three years that he'd worked here. "There?"

Mrs. Cornell nodded. "That way, he can see it every time he comes out of his office, yet it won't be a distraction while he's working." To the dog she cooed, "Isn't that right, Royce?"

Royce voiced no objection, and Matthew realized there was only one way to hurry Mrs. Cornell along so that he could begin his work. "Would you like me to hang it for you?" he offered. At least it would be behind him.

"Now? Why . . . yes. That way Mr. Cornell will be surprised when he comes downstairs."

He went to it immediately, relieved to find that the same

hook that the Constable had been hanging by would hold the newer painting. "What would you like me to do with this one?" he asked her.

"Oh, just prop it behind the bookshelves until I find a new place for it upstairs. I'll send Henry down for it after he's finished serving Mr. Cornell his breakfast." She stayed around to admire the new acquisition for another five minutes, holding Royce's front end up so that Matthew could indeed see that the bulldog could have been the model for the painting.

When she was finally gone, Matthew returned to his desk and began sorting through the correspondence that Lucas had delivered. He was halfway through this task when he heard the front door open. He looked at the grandfather clock in the corner. Only a quarter past eight. Mr. Cornell never scheduled appointments before nine o'clock . . . not until he'd had two cups of coffee and read *The Cambridge Chronicle* from front to back.

"May I be of service?" he asked the young man who walked in from the foyer.

The visitor stopped in front of Matthew's desk. "This is Mr. Cornell's office?"

"Yes, it is. I'm his assistant, Matthew Phelps."

The young man nodded, put both hands in his pockets, and looked around the room. He would have been strikingly handsome if not for the puffiness beneath his bloodshot eyes. His white flannel suit, the mark of a university man, was well tailored, yet hung limp and wrinkled from his shoulders, as if it had been slept in.

"I do so admire an office with tasteful furnishings," he said mockingly, squinting his eyes at the painting behind Matthew.

Though he agreed with the man's opinion, Matthew sighed

and wondered if he was ever going to be allowed to get to work. "May I be of service, sir?" he repeated.

The visitor blinked, confirming Matthew's suspicion that he was slightly inebriated. "You're not really a clerk here . . . are you?"

"I am," Matthew replied. He could tell what the young man was thinking. Most first-time visitors to Mr. Cornell's office were more subtle about covering their astonishment. Matthew had inherited an imposing frame from his father's side of the family, and four years of rowing teams at public school and then at the university had developed muscles in his broad shoulders. His big hands seemed awkward holding a pen or pencil, and he was aware that he looked as if he would be more at home behind a plow than behind a desk.

"I wish to speak with Mr. Cornell," the young man said.

Matthew glanced at the clock again. "Mr. Cornell will be down shortly." Motioning to the chair across from his desk, he said, "If you would care to have a seat, perhaps I can help you, Mr. . . ."

"Woodruff," he replied. He flopped into the chair and peered over at the staircase. "How shortly? I'm in dire need of a nap."

*A bath wouldn't hurt, either,* Matthew thought, then estimated out loud. "Thirty . . . forty minutes at the most."

"I don't suppose you'd be a good lad and fetch him right away, would you?"

*A "good lad"?* Matthew smiled to himself wryly and allowed the condescending request to pass. "No, sir. Not unless it's an emergency."

Scratching his stubbled cheeks, Mr. Woodruff said, "Then I suppose I'll just have to wait. That is, unless you can help me."

*I've only been offering for the past five minutes.* Matthew gave the man a polite nod. "I'll try."

"I'm here to pick up the allowance my father has arranged."

Matthew nodded as the name finally registered. He took a ledger from a desk drawer. "Is your father a Mister Edmund Woodruff?"

*"Sir* Edmund Woodruff, actually."

"My apologies." Matthew leafed through the ledger, through the names of other wealthy university students whose fathers had arranged monthly allowances in the hopes of enforcing *some* long-distance restraints. He found Gregory Woodruff's name, then took the cash box key from his waistcoat pocket.

"I assume you would rather have the five pounds in cash?"

Mr. Woodruff shook his head and deposited a crumpled piece of paper on Matthew's desk. "My father upped it to eight pounds. I've his note for Mr. Cornell."

"Very well," Matthew told him. "But I'm afraid I can't release the extra three pounds to you until my employer authorizes it." He glanced at the clock again. "Twenty minutes at most."

The young man shrugged his shoulders. "Oh, very well. We must have our little rules if we're to keep civilized, mustn't we?" he said in a cynical voice.

"It's only this first time. After that, I can give you the whole eight pounds without authorization."

Yawning, the young man looked around the room. "Would you have any coffee around?"

"I'll be happy to get you a cup from the café down the street," Matthew offered. When he received no answer, Matthew became uncomfortably aware that Mr. Woodruff was staring across the desk at the frayed edges of the cuffs that

stuck out from his coat sleeves. He fought the urge to move
his arms down to his sides.

"Mr. Woodruff?" he finally said.

"What?" The young man waved a hand. "No . . . no, thank
you. I'll get some later."

Matthew nodded and opened an envelope from the stack
of correspondence. Drawing out a check for Mr. Cornell's
services, he picked up his pen to post it in his ledger when
he became aware that Mr. Woodruff was still staring.

"Is there something more I can do for you?" he asked,
wishing that Mr. Cornell would forego the second cup of
coffee this once and come on downstairs. Back when he was
a student at Trinity, Matthew had never noticed how obnox-
ious some of the wealthier students could be. But back then
he had been one of the mainstays of the rowing team. One
could be forgiven for being middle class if one had athletic
prowess. When he'd had to leave school and was plunged
almost instantly into poverty, former teammates would pass
him in the street without any sign of recognition.

*Oh, well . . . just a few more minutes.* Then he would only
have to see this Mr. Woodruff once a month. It would be
a simple matter of handing the young man his money and
bidding him good day.

~

Gregory Woodruff smiled to himself, quite in awe that the
solution to his problem regarding Aunt Helene would come
so unexpectedly. The obvious answer pierced through the
fogginess of his alcohol-steeped mind like a lightning bolt
piercing a cloud.

Aunt Helene hadn't seen him since he was a tot and likely

wouldn't recognize him even if she still had her sight. He rested an elbow on his knee and rubbed his bristled chin. Why not hire someone to take his place on Sunday afternoons?

The clerk seated in front of him appeared to be close to his own age, twenty-three. They shared the same coloring, too; the blue eyes and dark hair. Not that it mattered a great deal, but just in case one of the servants or someone else were to describe him to Aunt Helene, it couldn't hurt.

True, the man behind the desk sat taller in his chair and appeared to outweigh him by some two stone, but how would anyone at Aunt Helene's know anything about his physique?

*You've lost your mind!* he told himself. Then he pictured himself sitting in a stuffy parlor on his only free day, listening to an old woman drone on and on about her life. A shudder went through him at the thought, and he studied the clerk again.

Having never worked a day in his life, Gregory was ignorant of wages and such, but judging from the frayed cuffs, this man was obviously near the bottom of the wage scale. Surely someone like this would be only too happy to earn some extra money.

A moment of uneasiness seized him, a brief flash of conscience, but it was gone as quickly as it had come. Surely he would be doing poor old Aunt Helene a favor by finding someone to take his place. Surely if he went himself, he wouldn't be able to mask the boredom that would come out in his voice. *After all, I'm not an actor,* he thought. It would only hurt Aunt Helene, make her feel as if she were a burden, if she sensed that he longed to be elsewhere. Hadn't he heard, somewhere, that blind people had a greater sense of perception than seeing people?

But someone *paid* to be there would have good reason to

pay attention, even make conversation. He realized with a start that he was still staring at the worn cuffs of the clerk. It wouldn't do to offend someone so potentially useful, so he turned his face away and pretended to study a bust of Socrates on one of the bookshelves.

*Should I ask him now?* Gregory wondered. Surely it would take some time to talk anyone into pulling off such a deception. He glanced over at the staircase. Once Cornell came downstairs, he wouldn't likely get another chance this morning.

*Tomorrow is Saturday,* he reminded himself. If he didn't find someone soon, he would be stuck in the role of attentive nephew for the remainder of his years at Cambridge. It wouldn't work to find a replacement *after* his aunt had heard his voice and her servants had seen him. He cleared his throat and looked at the clerk again. The fog had completely dissolved from his mind, replaced by a sharpness that had served him in good stead in the past. "Did you say that there is a café down the street, Mr. . . . ?"

The clerk looked up from some papers with a bemused expression. "Phelps. You would care for some coffee after all, Mr. Woodruff?"

"No, thank you." Gregory glanced at the staircase again. "Have you any idea how late it stays open?"

Mr. Phelps's face was thoughtful for a second and then he answered, "Until ten o'clock, I believe. It closes earlier on Sundays."

"Splendid." Before the clerk's attention could be drawn back to his work again, Gregory leaned forward in his chair and propped both elbows on the desk. "And what time do you leave this office?"

The clerk cocked his head as if he hadn't heard correctly. "I beg your pardon?"

"When do you stop working?"

After another pause, he replied, "Seven."

Gregory smiled. "No doubt you're wondering why I wish to know."

The clerk put down his letter opener. "The thought does occur to me."

"Because I would like for you to meet me there this evening—at the café. I'll even buy your supper."

An immediate wariness came across Mr. Phelps's face. "I'm sorry, but—"

"I've a job to offer you," Gregory cut in, rushing his words. "Three or four hours every Sunday afternoon. You do have Sundays free, haven't you?"

Gregory's words did nothing to ease the suspicion in the clerk's expression. In fact, he was shaking his head. "Thank you for the offer," he said politely, "but I'm afraid I'll have to pass."

Footsteps sounded from above, and Gregory scooted to the edge of his chair. "Don't tell me you can't use an extra five and eightpence." It was more than he had intended to offer, considering how meager his allowance was, but he had neither the time nor the energy to look for someone else.

A flicker of interest sparked in the clerk's narrowed eyes. "Are you serious?" he asked, folding his arms across his large chest.

Gregory grinned. "Serious as taxes."

"I absolutely refuse to become involved in anything illegal, Mr. Woodruff."

"Perfectly legal, my good man," Gregory replied, steepling his fingers on the top of the desk. "In fact . . . you would be performing a very worthy service."

# 5

FRIDAY afternoon Miss Knight insisted that Deborah forget her plan to use hired carriages to take her to her lessons at Signora Pella's. "I only use my carriage for chapel on Sundays," the woman had said. "Besides, Thomas needs the experience now that Henry is off his feet."

After a light lunch of consommé, bread, and cheese with her hostess in the dining room, Deborah changed into her best dress, a black-and-plum grosgrain silk with an elaborate bustle. Her hair, freshly washed last night, trailed down in ringlets from a black narrow-rimmed hat made of chantilly net and velvet. Thomas gave her a bashful grin when she stepped out to the mews to meet him.

"You're even prettier than you were yesterday," the boy said, and then blushed at his own audacity. "I mean . . ."

"I *was* in rather a sorry state then," Deborah told him, holding out a hand so that he could help her up into a trap, drawn by a chestnut-colored horse. She gave him a smile when he got up in the seat next to her. "And I do thank you for the compliment."

The afternoon air was invigorating, cool enough to bring color to her cheeks as the carriage ambled down Queen's Road. Even the horse—"Chester," according to Thomas—

had to be kept on a tight rein to keep him from breaking out
into a gallop. To the left, the river Cam slid lazily past the
different colleges' back lawns, called the "Backs" by the
Cambridge natives. A faint breeze stirred the long, drooping
branches of willows that grew along the lush green banks.
Students taking advantage of their last free days before Monday
classes laughed and called to each other from punts—narrow,
flat-bottom boats that were steered by means of a long pole.
Deborah even found a temporary respite from her anxiety
about meeting Signora Pella. How could a person feel anything
less than optimistic on such an afternoon?

"How long have you worked for Miss Knight?" she asked
the boy beside her.

"Almost a year," he replied, his eyes still on the reins.
"I was twelve when I was hired."

"Have you family in Cambridge?"

"My mother." He turned to Deborah, and it seemed his
eyes were shining. "She makes hats for ladies. The fanciest
hats in Cambridge."

"You don't say!"

"Has her own shop on Petty Cury."

"How interesting." Deborah smiled back at him. "I can
tell you're very proud of her."

He gave her a strained smile and turned his attention back
to the horse. He was silent for the rest of the time, leaving
Deborah to wonder if she were imagining the discomfort she
could feel coming from him now. Presently Thomas reined
the horse into Sidgwick Avenue in Springfield, at the southern
end of the Backs.

The entrance to the Raleigh estate was through a pair of
iron gates, past a rustic lodge, and along an extensive carriage

drive. A stone bridge arched over the west bank of the Cam and led to a symmetrically arranged seventeenth-century mansion of mellow red brick. Enormous English oaks stretched out their branches over a lawn where statuary, encircled by beds of flowers, interrupted the flow of the landscape.

Deborah sat motionless when the trap came to a halt in the forecourt, her former nervousness returning with a vengeance. While her family was wealthy and lived in a fine house of the Italianate style, she couldn't imagine a single family, other than the queen's, living in such an imposing house. *Why, there must be at least a hundred rooms,* she thought. She looked down to brush a wrinkle from the skirt of her dress and wondered how she could feel so dowdy all of a sudden, when she had felt so fashionable just an hour earlier.

"Miss Burke?"

Deborah started and turned to Thomas, who was waiting at the side of the carriage. "I'm sorry," she told the boy as she got to her feet and took his outstretched hand. "I'm just a bit overwhelmed."

"It's a grand sight, all right," he agreed as he helped her out of the carriage. He gave her a reassuring smile, but then turned his face to the house and gave a low whistle. "I'm glad it's you that's going in there and not me."

Just then it occurred to Deborah to wonder where the boy would be while she took her lesson. Before she could ask, he volunteered that Miss Knight had instructed him to wait. He waved at two approaching livery servants, and Deborah realized that she was on her own.

*You've traveled all over the Continent,* she reminded herself, squaring her shoulders as she walked toward an elaborately carved oak door. *You're well educated. You've even performed on stage. There is no reason to be intimidated just because she lives in a palace.* Her bravado weakened a bit when an imperious looking butler answered her ring. He stood ramrod straight and waved away Deborah's card with a white-gloved hand.

"You are Miss Burke, I presume?"

"Yes—" She almost said *sir,* but caught herself. *Your family loves you,* she thought.

"Lady Raleigh is expecting you." He turned crisply on his heel and led her first through an imposing hall paved with stone, then through an inner hall lit by a glazed dome. Through a doorway to the right they came to a huge sitting room with marble Corinthian pillars, heavily carved cornices, fine furniture, and in one corner, a grand piano. The walls were high, at least twelve feet, and over the fireplace hung a portrait of Lady Raleigh wearing a costume from her Paris debut in Verdi's *Rigoletto,* the role that had made her famous.

"Please make yourself comfortable," the stoic-faced butler said, indicating with the fluid motion of one hand a velvet-upholstered French settee behind a rosewood tea table. "Lady Raleigh will be here shortly." He stood at attention until she had taken a seat and then turned on his heel and left.

Alone in the huge room, Deborah could only sit there and stare at the portrait of Lady Raleigh. She looked close to Deborah's own age, and the artist had managed to capture a self-assurance that hinted the young person on the canvas was aware that she would one day become a great diva. *Will she think I have talent?* Deborah asked herself for the hundredth time.

"Miss Burke."

She turned to where a surprisingly petite woman stood in the doorway.

"Lady Raleigh?" Deborah said, getting to her feet.

"You may address me as Signora Pella," the woman answered with only a trace of an Italian accent. She came over to offer a slender hand. "That was the one concession I demanded of Lord Raleigh when I married him. Unless we're at court, mind you, for you British love your protocol."

She was simply but elegantly dressed in a black velvet gown with a pearl-and-amethyst pin at the throat and wore a single gold bracelet upon her wrist. Smooth olive skin stretched over high cheekbones, and glossy black hair was fastened with a tortoiseshell comb at the nape of her slender neck. Deborah knew from following Clarisse Pella's career that she must be nearing fifty years old, but the only signs of age about this woman were webbings of fine lines about the corners of her slate gray eyes.

"My husband at the time, the Marquis de Crozat, commissioned that portrait," she said, turning to stare at it. "I was so unsure of myself back then."

*"You?"* Deborah asked in amazement.

"I would have cut out my tongue before allowing anyone to know it. And I got over it quickly once I became aware of how devastating fear is." The eyes appraised Deborah with an unwavering stare. "You must avoid any emotion in excess, Miss Burke, good or bad, for they exhaust and injure the voice."

Without further ado, Signora Pella walked over to the piano and sat down on the bench. "Come stand here." Deborah hastened to comply, taking a position adjacent to where Signora Pella sat. The diva struck the A below middle C and held it. "Without using your chest voice, let me hear you now."

Clearing her throat, Deborah sang the low note. There was no expression on Signora Pella's face as she went up the scale, one note at a time, ending two octaves above middle C. The last four notes were an enormous strain, but Deborah held them as long as possible.

"You had some difficulty with those last notes," Signora Pella observed.

"I'm sorry," Deborah said, feeling the heat in her cheeks. "I've neglected my scales for the past few days while preparing for my trip . . . and I'm a little nervous now. But when I've practiced and warmed up, I can hold them much longer."

Surprise crossed Signora Pella's elegant features. "But why would you want to, Miss Burke?"

"Why?" Deborah gave Signora Pella a helpless look. *Because you wanted me to,* she thought. No doubt she would have attempted to sing the highest note on the piano keyboard if the great diva had instructed her to do so.

"You have the perfect range of a mezzo-soprano," Signora Pella went on when she didn't receive an answer. "Surely you are aware of this."

"Well, yes, but . . ."

"It should make you happy."

"Yes, of course." Deborah gave her a grateful smile. "Thank you."

"But at the academy, the coloratura sopranos received most of the accolades. Yes?"

Now Deborah glanced away. She had never admitted to anyone how frustrated she would become for failing to sustain the highest notes, when they came so easily to some of the other young women at the academy.

"Does the cello feel inferior to the flute and piccolo?" Signora Pella asked. "You have no doubt heard of Cornelie Falcon in your studies, haven't you?"

"Only that she lost her voice and had to retire early."

"Early?" Signora Pella shook her head regretfully. "She was only a child, twenty-six, when she left the stage. But she tried to force a glorious mezzo into registers too high for it. In those days, it was thought that the higher a woman could squeal, the better."

With a nod toward her portrait on the wall, she said, "I was almost caught up in that way of thinking, too, but fortunately my tutor, Rafaele Bernardo, would have none of it." She turned back to Deborah and raised an eyebrow. "And now, mezzo-sopranos with a mastery of coloratura are in short supply and in great demand on the stage—this I know for a fact. So be proud of your mezzo, Miss Burke . . . as I was of mine." She replaced her fingers on the piano keys. "Now, some trills and runs."

Deborah straightened and took a deep breath from her abdomen. She tried to lose herself in the music, so that her voice would stay as light and flexible as possible, and began to feel a confidence that she was doing well. But when Signora Pella finally closed the piano, the diva's expression was as stoic as her butler's had been. Although she knew it was childish, Deborah couldn't stop herself from asking, "Do you think I have talent, Signora Pella?"

"Talent?" The older woman, now on her feet, looked surprised. "Surely you didn't come here to find out if you had talent. You would not have lasted six months in the academy without it."

"Yes, but—"

"Talent is not so rare, Miss Burke. There are people sweeping the streets of the city every morning who may possess incredible talent and not even be aware of it. What you are really asking is, can I train your voice so that you will become a great diva of the stage, as I once was. Am I correct, Miss Burke?"

The question seemed so ruthless, yet Deborah knew the answer—had known the answer for years. She nodded. "Yes."

Signora Pella's eyes glittered. "Ambition is nothing to be ashamed of. If you have ambition enough to do as I teach you, anything is possible."

A maid came into the room bearing a tray and brought it over to the tea table. "Come, we will have something to soothe the throat," Signora Pella said, motioning Deborah over to the settee. The maid poured, but out of the spout came a steaming clear liquid instead of tea.

"Hot water with a good dose of lemon," Signora Pella said, balancing her cup and saucer on the arm of the settee. "Clears the throat after singing."

Deborah took a sip and tried not to wince.

"You will become used to the taste." She dabbed at the corner of her mouth with her linen napkin. "No tea or coffee from now on, and especially no wine or spirits. You must limit your sweets as well. Fresh fruit for dessert, and only in moderation. *Mi capisce?* Do you understand me?"

"I understand," Deborah answered. "And I will do that." She would have agreed to eat hay and drink pond water had the diva demanded it.

"Your lessons will be every afternoon, except for Sundays. Warm up your voice before you come so that you will be ready to sing when you get here. In addition, you will practice your scales for one hour every morning and night. You have studied Italian, yes?"

"I have."

"Are you familiar with *Don Giovanni?*"

"I've heard of it, but never . . ."

"That is good. I will not have to go back and remedy what the academy has taught you. Tomorrow I will give you the libretto—read it two or three times, then you must set to work on memorizing the words for the part of Zerlina. Never mind the music—we will study that when you have the words perfectly."

Deborah nodded, still unable to believe that she was actually to be tutored by the great Clarisse Pella. *Three months ago, I would have never even dared to dream this would happen.* The wonder of it all brought tears to her eyes. "I will do anything you say," she said, dabbing at her cheeks with her napkin.

Signora Pella frowned and lifted a warning finger. "Emotions, Miss Burke."

~

"What was the house like?" Thomas asked her as the trap took them up Queen's Road. "I mean, the inside."

"It was beautiful," Deborah answered. "But . . ." She paused, recalling the feeling that had come over her upon entering the sitting room, and even later during the lesson. She had been too anxious about her voice to pay it more than a passing thought, but now that the house was behind her, she realized what she had felt. "Empty," she said.

"A house that rich and no furniture?"

"Not *that* kind of empty. It just didn't feel like home."

The boy gave her a confused look. "But it's not your home."

"Yes, of course." She shrugged and smiled at him. "It didn't feel like anybody's home."

~

The Café Aeneas, Latin for "excellent," was situated in a convenient location across the street from the grounds of King's College. After leaving the office that evening, Matthew Phelps paused to look into the window. Underclassmen filled almost every chair at every table, throwing their energies into enjoying the remaining days before Monday's classes would begin.

It was Matthew's practice, ever since having to leave Trinity College, to avoid the haunts of the university students. Envy could be as sharp and destructive as any knife, and he couldn't see the point of exposing himself to it any more than necessary. *One day you'll be a student again,* he reminded himself— but he had trouble believing it lately.

A flash of motion caught his eye. He moved closer to the glass and noticed Gregory Woodruff, waving and mouthing something from a corner table. With a shave and a fresh flannel suit, he looked much more presentable than he had that morning, and Matthew decided that Mr. Woodruff must have had his nap. Again Matthew considered walking on by. Judging from what little he knew about the man's character, he was aware that the evening would likely be a waste, but he had nothing better to do. And he was curious.

"I took the liberty of ordering cottage pies," Mr. Woodruff said after Matthew had taken a seat across from him. "But then, perhaps you would rather I had waited and let you make your own choice? No doubt this is a rarity for you . . . a nice place like this."

Matthew toyed with the idea of leaving. Instead, he poured himself a cup of tea from the pot on the table. "I haven't always been poor, Mr. Woodruff," he said. "And frankly, I rather resent your condescending tone."

"Oh, do forgive me! I certainly didn't mean any offense."

He looked honestly distressed, seated there with a hand up to his heart, and Matthew shrugged his shoulders and mumbled that it didn't matter. A waiter appeared and set two pies before them, with side dishes of hot mustard pickles and tiny pearl onions. Matthew took in a whiff of his pie. It smelled heavenly and had a top layer of golden-toasted potatoes. Picking up his fork, he took a small, unhurried bite. He would rather die than allow Mr. Woodruff to see how welcome a respite he was providing from his usual supper of potato or cabbage soup and barley cakes at a small but cheap pub close to home.

"I can't help but wonder how you've found yourself in your present circumstances," began Mr. Woodruff, who had yet to touch his food. He immediately held up a placating hand. "No offense intended, mind you, but I could tell this morning that you've an educated background."

"Debts," was the only explanation that Matthew cared to give.

"Oh." Mr. Woodruff gave an understanding nod. "Unlucky at cards, eh?"

"No."

Mr. Woodruff waited expectantly, as if anticipating the rest of the story, then shrugged and picked up his fork. "This is quite tasty," he remarked after downing a good-sized portion of the pie. "I never got around to eating today, so I didn't realize how famished I was."

Matthew nodded his agreement that the food was indeed good, then sat back, waiting for the explanation of why he had been invited here. After Mr. Woodruff had consumed half of the pie, he dabbed his mouth with his napkin and got down to business.

"I wish to hire someone to pay a call upon an elderly woman—my mother's aunt—every Sunday afternoon. As I said this morning, it's worth a half crown every week to me."

"Five and eightpence is what you said," Matthew corrected.

Clearing his throat, Mr. Woodruff said, "Yes, of course. Five and eight. My mistake."

"But why?"

"Because I don't want her to be lonely."

*There is more to this than he's willing to let on,* Matthew thought. "I'm afraid I don't understand. Why don't you visit her yourself if you're worried about her?"

Mr. Woodruff's eyes darted away for an instant before he replied, "She's expecting me to visit her every Sunday, and I just haven't the time. I'm to be enrolled in some rigorous legal courses at Pembroke, you see, and shall be very much absorbed in my studies."

Matthew shook his head and wondered if the man across from him had napped too long. Having spent three terms at the university himself, he was fully aware that no course of study took up every waking minute of a student's time. "If your aunt is expecting you, she will hardly be satisfied with calls from a complete stranger. And I assure you, there will be ample time to study if you put your mind to it."

"Yes, of course." For several seconds Mr. Woodruff sat there silently drumming his fingers upon the tablecloth, his glazed expression fixed upon something just over Matthew's shoulder. Assuming that the matter was all settled, Matthew pushed away his half-eaten pie. Throughout the day he had foolishly entertained the idea of an extra guinea every month, and even though the money had never touched his hands, he was feeling a definite sense of loss. It would have gone a long way toward paying off his debts.

He was just about to take his hat from the seat of the chair adjacent to his when Mr. Woodruff spoke again.

"You see, I've always been a little on the selfish side."

"I beg your pardon?"

Embarrassment washed over his face. "I simply do not wish to have my every Sunday tied up with paying calls. I haven't seen her since I was a tot and wouldn't recognize her if she were sitting at the next table."

Matthew couldn't help but send an automatic glance sideways. The table closest to theirs was occupied by four joking and laughing university-aged young men—and not one elderly woman.

"Aunt Helene is blind and wouldn't even know the difference," Mr. Woodruff went on. He leaned forward on his elbows, his blue eyes intense. "You would be doing her a great service. She would never have to know."

Matthew could hardly believe his ears. "You're suggesting I pretend to be you?"

"Why, of course. How else would she accept my not coming? You said yourself that you would be a complete stranger to her."

"That's the most preposterous plan I've ever heard in my life. How could I possibly convince your aunt that I'm her nephew?"

"Quite easily." Reaching into his coat pocket, he drew out and unfolded three sheets of paper. "You see, I spent the whole afternoon writing down everything you should know about my family." He held up the first sheet of paper for Matthew's inspection. "A bright chap like yourself could have this memorized by Sunday."

Matthew recoiled from the paper held out toward him as if it were a vial of poison. He slid back his chair and regarded the man with a level gaze. "Thank you for the meal."

"Please don't leave yet." The man's expression was almost

pitiable, his voice suspiciously close to a whine. "You're my only option."

*Just get up and leave,* Matthew told himself. Still, some morbid curiosity held him to his seat. "And why is that? There should be hundreds of poor wretches in Cambridge willing to take you up on your offer."

"That's just it. I can't pick some beggar out of a doorway and expect him to pull it off. You've been educated . . . I can tell." He leaned on his elbow again. "But the most important thing is, I don't know anyone's character yet, save yours. My aunt is quite well off and, of course, defenseless without her sight."

"It's good of you to care."

Mr. Woodruff glanced up sharply at the sarcasm in his voice. "Give me credit for some scruples, Mr. Phelps. I wouldn't want to hand someone an open invitation to steal from someone in my family. He has to be honest."

"Honest?" Matthew couldn't help but smile. "How ironic that you're looking for someone with *that* qualification to dupe a poor old woman. Besides, how can you be sure that I wouldn't steal from her as well?"

Mr. Woodruff rubbed his forehead wearily. "The cash box in your desk. Your Mr. Cornell wouldn't trust you with it if you weren't honest."

"And that is why I must turn down your offer." Matthew pushed out his chair and got to his feet. "It's not for me to lecture you, but we don't fully appreciate our families until we're without them. Thank you again for supper."

Mr. Woodruff's face grew desperate. "Half a sovereign every week—that's two quid a month you're looking at."

"Good day to you."

Weaving his way around the other tables, Matthew walked out into the bracing night air. Only a few early stars could be seen through a shroud of clouds, and a sliver of moon hovered above the delicate stone pinnacles of King's College Chapel. You could hardly go anywhere in Cambridge without seeing some reminder that it was a university town. *I should move away from here,* he thought as the familiar ache returned to the pit of his stomach. What ties did he have to the city now? Why suffer through this torment, having to pass the same ivy-covered halls that he used to walk through with books under his arm? *I could move to London . . . perhaps even find a better position.*

"You know," came a voice at his elbow, "the funny thing about all this is that my aunt would likely enjoy your company more than she would mine."

Amazed at the persistence of this man, Matthew turned to stare. Mr. Woodruff smiled apologetically and tipped his derby. "I'm a rather shallow person, if the truth be known. Having a good time has been my only goal for as long as I can remember. What can I possibly have to say that would interest an old woman?"

"Perhaps she would like someone just to listen?"

"Yes." Mr. Woodruff's shudder was visible. "Then what does it matter who does the listening?"

Matthew gave another longing look at the outline of the college buildings across the street. *I would certainly be a better listener than anyone as self-centered as Woodruff would be,* he told himself, aware that he was rationalizing and despising himself for doing so. Still, an extra two quid a month would pay off his debts in half the time.

*Don't think,* some voice inside his head urged. *Just do it.*

Suddenly he turned to the well-dressed man beside him and

held out a hand. Mr. Woodruff looked confused and made a motion to shake the offered hand, but Matthew shook his head and pointed to his pocket.

"Your family history," Matthew said in a flat voice.

"You'll do it?" Mr. Woodruff dug eagerly into his coat pocket.

*He'll just find someone else if you don't.* "Yes."

"I can't tell you how much I appreciate this," Mr. Woodruff said as he handed over the papers. "Oh, and one more thing." While Matthew waited, he pulled a purse from his waistcoat pocket. "I don't wish to offend you, but you should buy a new shirt."

Matthew could feel the heat creeping up his neck toward his ears.

"If one of the servants tells Aunt Helene that your shirt is . . . well, not new, she may wonder about it." He pressed a half crown into Matthew's palm. "It can come out of your first week's wages."

Closing his fingers around the coin, Matthew turned on his heel to walk home. *I hope you're not watching me from heaven, William,* he thought. How crushed would his brother . . . his family . . . be to witness the depths to which he had just sunk?

There had been a time when he would have walked away from Mr. Woodruff at the first mention of his dubious scheme. His parents, devout Presbyterians, had raised him and his brother in an atmosphere of faith in God, and his father had continued to do so even after Mother's death. Matthew came to be a believer himself at the age of eleven. But the death of his father, and later, William's sickness, had dealt a blow to his convictions. Still, he'd had enough faith left to pray that his brother would be healed.

When that did not happen and William died, something died inside Matthew as well. He never yielded to the temptation to turn his back on God completely, but he did stop praying, and his increasingly sporadic appearances at church ceased altogether. He still believed in eternity and could dredge up some gratitude for his salvation on the rare occasions when he thought about it. But he no longer believed that God cared about the here and now. How could he, when God had allowed everyone Matthew had ever loved to slip away from him? All he had left was a loneliness that turned his days into mechanical motion and his nights into sleepless longing.

Only one thing mattered anymore—getting his education and becoming an engineer. If he hadn't had this goal, he would have found another. A person had to have some excuse to keep on living.

~

After a supper of baked mullet, pickled cabbage, and baked potatoes, Deborah visited with Miss Knight for a little while, then went upstairs to start a letter to her family. She had decided that she would write a little every evening, recording her day-to-day activities and thoughts. Her family would be interested in knowing everything about her new life, and she would have a nice, long letter to send every week.

"Signora Pella is demanding," she wrote. "But I believe she thinks I have potential."

Her eyes began to smart.

"I think of you often. Please tell Laurel that I keep the wrap she made draped across my chair so that I can remember her every time I look at it."

It was true. The green wrap didn't seem so ugly anymore.

There was a soft knock, and Avis walked into the room. "Would you like me to draw you a bath, Miss Burke?"

"I'll do it myself in a little while," Deborah answered. "But thank you."

"Indoor plumbing is a wonder, isn't it? I don't never take it for granted. No more luggin' buckets of hot water up the stairs from the kitchen." She made a face. "No more emptying chamber pots."

Deborah had to smile. "You seem to see the bright side of everything, don't you?"

"It's because I can still remember the house I used to work in," the maid replied with another grimace. "Up and dressed by six and never in bed before eleven. I forgot what it was like not to be tired all of the time. Most of the other servants here started out the same way, so we all know how good we got it . . . workin' for the missus."

She stopped and gave a self-conscious grin. "I tend to rattle on and on, Miss Burke. It's a bad habit."

"I like talking with you." Suddenly Deborah remembered her earlier curiosity about Thomas. "Avis, what do you know about the boy who drove me from the station?"

"Thomas? Only that he came here last year, lookin' for a job. Mr. Darnell's back was out, and he happened to need help with the garden for a little while, so Mrs. Darnell hired him. They took a liking to the boy, and he's a hard worker, so they asked Miss Knight if they could keep him on."

"He told me his mother owns a millinery shop."

Avis nodded. "Aye, that she does, but none of us has ever been there. It's in a fancy-priced part of town."

"Why would he be going around town looking for a job, then?"

"You know, I asked him that myself."

"You did?"

She nodded again. "He said he doesn't like hats."

# 6

O N Saturday morning at breakfast, Deborah asked
Miss Knight if she could use the piano in the sitting
room to determine pitch for her practice session.

"Would it make you uncomfortable if I sat in there and
listened?" the older woman asked wistfully.

"If it does, I've no business on the stage," Deborah told her.
"I would love an audience."

It turned out that she had a larger audience than expected,
for servants drifted in and out, pausing to listen for a while
before going about their duties. Despite their pleased expressions, they all seemed confused, and finally Bethina put their
question to Deborah.

"What kind of songs are you singing?" she asked bluntly.
"There ain't any words to them."

Deborah had to smile, then explained that she had been
going over the scales, not singing any song. The maid looked
so disappointed that Deborah offered to sing a few bars from
her part in *Aida*. "The words are Italian, though," she warned,
and the maid waved a hand.

"Just so they're words, and not all that la-la-la. At least
they'll mean *something,* even if I don't know what it is."

"I'll tell you what they mean," Deborah offered. "An

Egyptian princess is pleading for the life of a man who has been falsely condemned for treason. You won't understand the words, of course, but you *should* be able to understand the emotion, no matter what the language."

She sat up straight, curled her fingers over the piano keys, and imagined herself as Signora Pella, standing center stage, mesmerizing a hushed audience. Striking an F-sharp chord, she began to sing:

> *"Ar-bi-tri del tuo fato*
> *Pur dell'ac-cu-sa or-ré-bi-le. . . ."*

She became lost in the story as the music poured from her throat, until she was no longer Deborah Burke but Amneris, daughter of the king of Egypt, pleading for the life of Radames, captain of the guard, and the man she loved. Her audience may have been one old blind woman and three servants, but they represented anyone who loved opera.

When she finished, the hushed silence in the room and the glistening in Bethina's eyes told her that she'd done well.

At her music lesson, however, all the confidence she had felt that morning dissolved as she was put through an intense exercise in scales and arpeggios. After her years of training, breathing from the diaphragm came naturally to Deborah. But no teacher at the academy had ever demanded that she draw out her notes for as long as Signora Pella demanded.

"Sustain, sustain!" the diva would cry, the expression in her slate gray eyes daring Deborah to do otherwise. By the time the lesson was over, Deborah walked over to drop onto the settee, her lungs aching from the effort.

"You are using muscles you've never used before," Signora

Pella consoled as they sat with their cups of steaming lemon water. "You will learn, with practice."

"Was it that difficult for you?" Deborah groaned.

The diva smiled. "When I began studying with Rafaele Bernardo, I had never heard of the diaphragm. Sustaining the sound meant singing it until you were out of breath and then taking in one huge gulp of air. The maestro . . . he was so demanding. With his hands digging into my arms, he would cry, *'Senti!* You will not take a breath until I give permission!' I was fifteen years old, I must tell you, and in terror of the man."

"And you learned how?"

"With months of hard work. But when I was finally able to control my voice and sustain, I knew that I would have a great career. So the terror and intense study were worth it." She looked up at her portrait, and a shadow passed over her face. "And then sickness took away what I studied so hard to obtain."

Deborah didn't know what to say. She had grieved when she read the newspaper accounts four years ago of how a near-fatal bout of pneumonia had scarred the diva's lungs, leaving her with little ability to sustain her voice and bringing to a halt a spectacular thirty-year career.

"It must console you that you had thirty years," Deborah finally ventured, hoping she didn't sound trite.

"They seem as only a day now," Signora Pella said sadly.

"But you have such wonderful memories. . . ."

"What can memories do but mock me now? They cannot bring back my voice. Music was what I lived for, the reason I had for rising in the morning."

"The *only* reason?" Deborah felt compelled to ask. As much as she herself loved music, she couldn't imagine feeling that it was the sole motivation for life. Was that the chasm that separated the prima donna from the talented but ordinary singer?

As she watched, a wistfulness stole into Signora Pella's expression. "Oh, sometimes there was love," the diva replied, seeming to fix her eyes upon something in the distance. "But that failed me, just as my voice eventually did. You see, the only two men I have ever loved were never completely attainable."

Abruptly Signora Pella put her cup down on the tea table and rang the silver bell that was on the tray. "Merrit will fetch your wrap and show you to the door. I will see you Monday, Miss Burke."

~

Upstairs in her boudoir, Clarisse lifted the lid from an Oriental carved teakwood chest and knelt down beside it. Colorful playbills, photographs with curled edges, yellowing telegrams, and scripts lay inside—memorabilia chronicling thirty years. She picked up an envelope by the corners, and it rattled as she pulled out the flap. A rosebud, brown and dry, lay inside—one of the many she had worn in her hair during her four seasons of performing in *Carmen* at the theater Lyrique in Paris. She put it back down and carefully unfolded the veil she had worn in Gounod's *Romeo et Juliette,* at the Opera House in San Francisco. *Why wasn't I aware how quickly the time was passing?* she asked herself. She had taken for granted that she would sing opera until the day she died.

Digging deeper into the stack, she pulled out a yellowed playbill featuring mezzo-soprano Maria Malibran as Desdemona in Rossini's *Otello.* She sat back on her heels and touched the portrait on the playbill. Dark Mediterranean features, so like her own, stared back at her. "You died the year I was born,"

Clarisse whispered. "So young, *mià sorèlla,* yet you were the fortunate one. You still had your music when you died."

Maria Malibran was a Romantic icon in Italy and had been an inspiration to Clarisse all of her life. It was said that the young woman possessed such a rare degree of vocal agility that she could rouse an audience to rapture. Sadly, she was thrown from a horse at the pinnacle of her career, dying at the age of twenty-eight. So many times during a performance, while walking the same floorboards that Maria had walked, Clarisse had felt her presence, urging her on to a perfect performance.

"And now *I* have become an inspiration to young women," she said softly. "The same way you were to me." This Deborah Burke had techniques that were still undeveloped, despite her time at the academy, but she had tremendous talent and the potential for greatness. *What's more, I believe she has the tenacity to push herself toward that greatness,* Clarisse thought. And the tenacity was as important as talent, for she had met too many lazy, talented people in her life.

She set the playbill reverently on top of the heap. When she had finally sent a reply to Mr. Adam Burke's letter, she had done so without quite knowing why. She had little patience with young people, especially those who aspired to become great singers. Europe was full of them. And she certainly had no need for the money, for Lord Raleigh, her fourth husband, was willing to pay dearly for the trophy he had acquired by marriage.

During today's lesson, Clarisse discovered why she had agreed to teach. If her performing days were over, she could at least live them vicariously through someone else. She would shape this Miss Burke's voice, molding her into her own image. Then, with the experience and contacts she had accumulated during her career, she would lead the young woman to greatness and fame. The prospect of reaching for that sparkling star again, even through another person's life, brought tears to her eyes, and she wiped them on the back of her hand. Now, once again, she had a reason to wake up in the mornings.

~

In his room over the carriage house, thirteen-year-old Thomas Sully woke up Sunday morning at his usual time. He stretched, sat up, and peered out the window just above his bed. An orange glow lit up the sky to the east, and it looked as if there would be no rain for at least the better part of the day.

Quickly he washed his face, pulled on his trousers and shoes, then exchanged his nightshirt for the blue checkered shirt he wore on Sundays.

Miss Knight's other servants would be assembling in the servant's hall in an hour, but Thomas hadn't the time today to spend dawdling over breakfast. Perhaps he could wheedle a bit of bread and cheese from Mrs. Reeves if she was in a good mood. Just to make sure, he stopped to snatch a pink Christmas rose from a bed on the terrace, ignoring a blue jay's screeched warnings overhead.

The cook, a stout Irishwoman with dimples in her pink cheeks, was at the worktable slicing bacon. She raised her head when Thomas walked into the kitchen.

"I've got to drive Miss Knight to chapel . . . ," he began, shifting his feet as he stood before her. "So I need to tell Mother that I won't be going to church with her today."

"And you think you can bribe me out of an early breakfast with that posy!" she exclaimed. Gwen, rolling pastry dough at the table, stopped long enough to grin at him.

Thomas flushed, as was his habit whenever Mrs. Reeves scolded him. "I—"

"Oh, don't go stammerin' on," she fussed, taking the flower from his hand. "I've a house full of people to feed." The cook turned to Gwen and put her hands on her ample hips. "Have you any of them pear tarts ready?"

Gwen nodded, crossed over to a cooling table against the brick wall, and scooped up two of them in her hand.

"May as well give him another for his mother," Mrs. Reeves said in a voice colored with both irritation and affection. "Wrap them in a clean cloth, or the lad will be shovin' them into his pockets."

To Thomas she said, "You'd better have thet towel back here by this evenin', or you won't be settin' foot in my kitchen again. Now, get on out of here before I set you to work in the scullery!"

"Thank you, ma'am!" Thomas said, then dashed out of the room. On his way down Bridge Street he ate one of the tarts, careful to rewrap the remaining two in the cloth. He quickened his pace. He would have to hurry so that he could be back in time to drive Miss Knight and the others to chapel in the brougham.

After he had walked two blocks down Trinity Street, he turned to the east, leaving the stately buildings of Trinity College for the worst slum in Cambridge. Set between Sidney and Trinity Streets, it was a place where jerry-built tenements listed toward the streets, and piles of garbage and pools of reeking filth accumulated in the hollows of the disjoined pavement. Sunlight rarely penetrated here, and profanity was the dialect spoken by young and old alike.

Because of the early hour, only a few loiterers now lurked

about the stagnant streets. He tucked his bundle securely under his arm. Even a couple of pear tarts would be temptation for thieves. He came upon a great maze of narrow, crooked paths, crossing and intersecting in labyrinthlike passages. His eyes darting from side to side, Thomas threaded his way through an extraordinary tangle of dark alleys, only the corners marked by flickering lamps jutting from the ebony walls.

He wound up at a dreadful paved court flanked by a rotting corpse of a house. Thomas approached a glass-littered stoop, watching his feet with care, for it wouldn't do to ruin the soles of his good shoes.

No one answered his first knock, so he tried again, then frowned bitterly at the torrent of oaths coming from the inside. The door opened with a rattle of wood and squeak of hinges, and there stood a tall, thin man wearing only a filthy pair of corduroy breeches held up by frayed braces. He held the blade of a pocketknife in a defensive position but lowered it when he saw who was there.

"So, the brat's come to call on 'is mummy," the man seethed through greenish teeth, scratching the stubble on his cheek. The pupils of his eyes were the color of ashes, the whites bloodshot and jaundiced. "Why can't you pick a more decent hour to go 'bout disturbin' folks?"

"And good morning to you, too, Orville," Thomas said with sarcasm as he passed the man in the doorway. A rat scurried by Thomas as he moved through what had, in more genteel times, been a front parlor to the next room. There, on a sunken wreck of a four-poster bed sat a woman in a torn nightgown, her hair matted about her shoulders. Dull green eyes blinked, and then a smile came to her sallow face.

"My Thomas," she whispered, holding out skeletal arms.

Thomas went right to her. It was painful to embrace her, for his mother seemed to grow thinner and more fragile every time he visited. Sitting down on the bed next to her, he drew out the bundle from under his arm. "I brought you some breakfast," he said, folding back the cloth so that she could see the tarts.

She seemed to look right through them. "Not hungry. Maybe later."

"All right. I'll just put them here under your pillow so the rats don't get them. Don't forget about them." He looked around for something to wrap the tarts in, but every bit of cloth that he could see was filthy. The pillowcase itself was no cleaner but stained and grimy. He decided he would have to risk the anger of Mrs. Reeves and leave them wrapped in their clean cloth. That done, he produced an amber bottle from his pocket. "It's cod-liver oil," he explained, setting it on a dust-covered bedside table. "It cost me half a crown, but I hear that it's good medicine."

"Thank you, dear," she said, not looking at it. Her tone was distracted now, and she watched over his shoulder for something.

"You shoulda given 'er the half crown." Orville came walking into the room. "She needs money worse."

"I've got some money," said Thomas but not to Orville. Digging in his pocket again, he brought out a florin and three shillings and pressed them into her hand. "It ain't much 'cause I had to buy the medicine. But I'll bring more next time. I'm gettin' a raise for not taking my Tuesday afternoons off until Mr. Henry gets better."

She merely smiled at him, then looked over at Orville with a pleading expression. "I don't feel well."

"It's coming," he answered in a gruff tone. He stood at a table, holding a spoon over the tiny flame of a little brass lamp. Intently he stirred the contents with a match stick.

"You're only making her sick with that!" Thomas snapped at the man.

Orville raised a threatening eyebrow. "Maybe you plan on doin' something about it?"

Ashamed, Thomas lowered his eyes and berated himself for not having the courage to knock over the foul brew. The last and only time he had done so, Orville had beaten him so savagely that he had limped for weeks afterward.

He hated being so short and runty for his age. It made him feel helpless to see the hold that this man had over his mother and to know that he could do nothing to change things. Even if his mother had somewhere else to go, she would not leave Orville.

"It's just not good for her," he tried again.

"Then why don't you try takin' it away from her?" the man sneered. Carefully he poured the opium into a pipe, then brought it over to the bed.

"Please don't, Mother!" Thomas begged.

But his mother's trembling hands reached for the pipe without hesitation. Her dry, cracked lips lapped about the rough wood and drew in the poison.

Thomas swallowed past the lump in his throat and wondered how just four years could have ravaged his mother's beauty so completely. Doreen Sully had once been a milliner with an exclusive little shop on Petty Cury. The stylish members of the upper classes kept her so busy with their business that she had once had three girls working for her at one time. While she had not had much time to devote to Thomas, she'd made sure that he went to school when he would much rather have spent his time running about in the streets.

Thomas hated Orville with a passion, but he couldn't blame the downward spiral that his mother had taken on him alone. There had been other men before Orville, men who bought his mother jewelry and trinkets and promised chateaus in France. Which man had introduced his mother to opium, he didn't know, but he hoped with all of his heart that the black-guard was dead.

Thomas's eyes began to sting. His mother had finished with her pipe and sat there, oblivious to his presence, staring out into space. There was no use staying. Leaning over to kiss her sunken cheek, he said, "I'd better go back now. I've got to drive Miss Knight to chapel." She didn't answer.

Orville caught up with him at the door and grabbed his arm. "I want to talk wi' you, brat."

Thomas shook off the arm, although he knew he risked a beating. "I've nothing to say to you."

"You stay and listen," the man growled. "Yer mum needs to be in one o' them sanatoriums."

"She needs you to stop giving her that pipe is what she needs."

Lowering his face closer to Thomas's, Orville gave him a threatening leer. "If I take it away from her now, it'll kill her. At a sanatorium, they can make sure that don't happen."

Although still suspicious, Thomas wanted to believe so badly that he took some hope in Orville's words. "Then let's take her to one . . . right now!"

The man frowned and shook a lock of oily dark hair from his forehead. "And who's gonna pay for it?"

"How much does it cost?" Thomas asked, his hopes fading fast.

"More than you can earn diggin' in the dirt."

"But I don't know if I can get a better job at my age."

"You don't need a better job. You just need to work smarter at the one you've got."

"I already work hard. What do you mean?"

A grin spread across Orville's face, revealing chipped, stained teeth. "I mean . . . yer workin' for a rich old lady. Seems to me like you could pick up something valuable once in a while."

"You mean . . . steal?" Thomas gave an adamant shake of the head. "I never stole anything in my life."

"Well, ain't you the one with the hoity-toity ideals!" Orville spat, hooking his thumbs into his braces. "They'll be good comfort to you when yer mother's passed on!"

Thomas felt his eyes burning. "I don't even go in the house much, except the servants' hall and sometimes the kitchen."

"That's all?"

Thomas nodded.

Leaning so close that Thomas could smell his fetid breath, Orville said, "Well, what if you was to take a little walk in the other parts o' the house . . . maybe at night?"

"I'd get the sack."

"Only if you got caught." He nodded toward the other room. "Seems like a boy's mum would be worth takin' the chance."

This time the tears did come to Thomas's eyes. Deeply ashamed, especially with Orville standing there watching him, he wiped at them with the back of his sleeve. He wanted to act like a man, but sometimes it was so hard to be thirteen and have no one to help him with decisions. His mother was the most important person in his life, but how could he agree to skulk around Miss Knight's house at night? If he got caught with something valuable in his hands, he could be sent to prison. Who would help his mother then? Certainly not Orville, for Thomas had no doubt that he would eventually be on his way, just like the men before him.

"What d' you say, lad?"

Thomas lifted his chin and glared at Orville. "I say if you really wanted her to get well, you'd get a job, too. Then we could both save up the money!"

Orville's laugh sounded wheezy, like some animal. "And who would take care of your dear mum?"

Thomas knew the real reason the man did not find work. Besides being lazy, he was just as addicted to the drug as was Thomas's mother. No doubt once he was gone, Orville would be firing up the pipe again.

"I'm not going to steal," Thomas finally answered, taking a step back from Orville in case he decided to swing his fist. "But I'll try to figure something out."

Orville's yellow eyes narrowed. "Well, while yer trying to figure it out, try to figure out what yer gonna do without a mother one day! She ain't gonna last too much longer the way she is!"

"Don't say that, Orville." Thomas gulped, circling around to the door. He dashed through it and ran as fast as he could out of the slum, until his side began to burn and he had to lean against a lamppost to catch his breath. The streets were busier now with vehicles and pedestrians, and the first deep strokes from Trinity were setting off the morning chorus of bells. For some reason, the sound always filled Thomas with an inexplicable sadness. He thought his heart would burst. Here he was, surrounded by people in one of the great cities of England, and he felt more alone than he ever had in his life.

~

Deborah, dressed for chapel in a skirt of cream serge and a vest and tunic of royal blue serge, went to Miss Knight's room to see if her hostess needed help. Avis and Bethina were already ushering the older woman out the door.

"Good morning, Deborah!" her hostess greeted, a smile wreathing her wrinkled face. She wore a maroon dress, trimmed with rows of black cording, and a bonnet of burgundy velvet. "These two are telling me I look like a princess. What do you think?"

Deborah traded smiles with the two maids flanking their mistress and answered, "All you need is a tiara."

They descended the stairs together and went out to the brougham, where Thomas stood waiting beside Chester and another horse, a gray-speckled gelding named Prince. Deborah greeted the boy, then drew in a whiff of sweet alyssum and wondered if she were the only person to notice that flowers always seemed to smell sweeter on Sunday mornings.

Gwen, the kitchen maid, was already seated in the carriage. The girl had a wide gap between her front teeth and dark brown hair under a flower-trimmed straw bonnet. She leaned down to extend her hand to Miss Knight as Thomas and Avis helped her up into a seat. After Deborah had taken a place beside her hostess, she watched Bethina settle into the seat beside Gwen.

"It's a fine mornin' for the drive," Avis said, then lifted a hand and turned to go back into the house.

"I've taken her place, haven't I?" Deborah asked Bethina,

for there was no more room in the carriage. *Why didn't I consider that earlier?*

The maid shook her head. "Avis goes to Saint Giles's with Mr. and Mrs. Darnell. It's just a short walk up to Chesterton Lane. You could see th' steeple if it wasn't for the houses across the street."

"It's a new church—only ten years old or so," Miss Knight said. "But I've been attending King's College Chapel since my brother and I moved to Cambridge and couldn't bear to change."

"Mr. Henry drives us—when his foot ain't broke, and Thomas goes to church with his mum," Gwen offered. "Saint Andrews, over by her hat shop. And Mrs. Reeves is Catholic. Her cousin fetches her for Saint Clement's."

"We're rather scattered on Sunday mornings," Miss Knight told her. "But it does my heart good that all of my household are faithful in worship."

King's College Chapel was a high rectangular building with delicate-looking stone pinnacles. Thomas tied off the horses to a post along King's Parade and helped the women alight. "You're coming in with us, aren't you?" Miss Knight asked the boy.

"I should stay with the horses," he said uneasily.

"The horses are fine." She felt for his shoulder and rested her hand upon it. "I feel badly enough that we've prevented you from going to your own church."

The boy shrugged and came with them, but Deborah couldn't help wondering at his hesitancy. Surely the chapel wouldn't be too different from what the boy was used to. She herself had been raised Methodist but had no qualms about accompanying her hostess to Church of England services. *As long as the same gospel is preached,* she thought.

The five of them filed into a pew close to the back, with Bethina leading Miss Knight. Gwen stepped back to allow Deborah to sit beside Miss Knight, but Deborah realized that the two servants were used to sitting protectively on each side of their mistress and shook her head. "I'll sit here with Thomas," she whispered.

Three-quarters of the congregation appeared to be young men, students from the university, wearing black coats with high collars. Quite a few in the near vicinity turned to give Deborah covert—and sometimes bold—glances, but she pretended not to notice. When she was seventeen, she had gone through a stage of fanciful daydreams and romantic notions, only to find that they were affecting her concentration upon her music. She was in Cambridge to study opera. There would be time enough for other things once her career was established.

The congregation rose and began singing as the organ played the first notes to the "Gloria Patri." Deborah joined in as well, careful not to raise her voice to its full operatic crescendo. She could have easily drowned out the voices of everyone around her, but Mother had taught her years ago that there was a difference between making a joyful noise and showing off.

The congregation was in the middle of "Come, Thou Almighty King," when Deborah realized the boy standing next to her was not singing but simply staring into his open hymnal with a miserable expression.

"Are you all right?" she asked, leaning down to whisper. He turned his face up to give her a solemn nod and then began moving his lips to the words of the hymn. *He looks as if he's lost his last friend,* Deborah thought.

Later, when the congregation was seated and the chaplain was stepping up to the pulpit to begin the litany, she caught a motion from the corner of her eye. She automatically glanced to her right, just in time to see Thomas brush a tear from his cheek with a finger. Not quite sure what to do, Deborah touched his arm. The boy pretended not to notice.

"'Praise ye the Lord; sing unto the Lord a new song,'" the chaplain read. "'And his praise in the congregation of saints. . . .'"

~

Thomas Sully, never having set foot in a church before, wondered how much longer the service could go on. Although he knew that God lived everywhere and could see everything, Thomas hadn't considered that God knew about the struggle going on inside of him until he walked into the chapel.

How offended God must be to have a boy who would very likely steal from his employer—for he could think of no other way to help his mother—sitting in one of his churches. If lightning were to come down from heaven and strike him on the spot, Thomas thought that he wouldn't be surprised. He watched the rows of people in front of him with envy. How wonderful it must be to live as a normal person with normal responsibilities. Actually, lightning from heaven would be a relief. At least it would put him out of his misery.

# 7

MATTHEW Phelps ran sweaty palms down the sides of his best fawn-colored trousers and adjusted the cuffs of his new white shirt before reaching for the chain connected to Miss Knight's doorbell. *You've gone and lost your mind,* he told himself for the hundredth time since the evening before. The sound of footsteps on the other side of the door almost sent him flying, but then the door opened, and a maid with ginger-colored hair stood there looking at him.

"Gregory Woodruff," he told her, producing from his waistcoat pocket one of the cards that the real Mr. Woodruff had given him.

The maid's face brightened as she waved away the card. "You don't need that," she said, opening the door still wider. A hallway stretched out behind her, leading into the recesses of the house. Matthew knew that once he left the safety of the doorway, there would be no turning back. *Leave while you still can!* he ordered his leaden feet, but they refused to budge in any direction. "Are you sure this is a convenient time?" he asked, stalling the inevitable.

"A convenient time?" the maid echoed, hazel eyes sparkling. "I should say so, Mr. Woodruff! The missus has been

expectin' you." She backed away from the door, holding it
with one hand and waiting for his entrance. Matthew stepped
past through the threshold and followed with the enthusiasm
of someone being led to his own execution.

The night before, during the hours he'd sat up to memorize
Gregory Woodruff's family history, he had refused to allow
himself to form a mental picture of Miss Knight. Thinking of
her as some faceless, formless entity had made the task before
him somewhat easier. Yet for some reason, he wasn't surprised
at the appearance of the frail-looking woman in the parlor
chair.

"Gregory?" she said, turning sightless blue eyes in his direction. The hope in her expression moved him with pity, and
he wondered if there were a more despicable reprobate in
England than himself. *Only the real Gregory Woodruff,* he
thought. But only by a narrow margin.

Again he was tempted to excuse himself and bolt. "A mistake," he could say. "I'm actually here with a message from
your nephew. He has a bit of a fever today and says that he'll
be here next week."

"Gregory?" Miss Knight repeated.

Matthew turned to deliver his just-composed lines to the
maid, but she nodded encouragingly at him and inclined her
head toward Miss Knight, a signal that he should step closer
to the elderly woman.

"Aunt Helene," Matthew mumbled, walking over to
where she sat. A beatific smile lit her face as she held out
a hand. After a second of hesitation he took it in his own,
careful not to squeeze her fragile fingers too hard.

"I'm so happy you came to see me," she said in a surprisingly steady voice. The maid, hovering close, offered him a

chair adjacent to Miss Knight's. But he could not move yet, for she still held his hand in a frail but firm grip.

"Please let me touch your face, dear boy," she said wistfully, as if afraid he might refuse. He leaned closer, and she laid her other hand lightly against his cheek. "How wonderful it is to have family here."

Matthew blinked, startled to feel wetness upon his eyelashes. "I . . . it's good to be here," he stammered.

"Now, sit please, and talk with me."

He folded his long limbs into the chair but felt so guilty that he couldn't allow himself to settle comfortably. He sat on the edge, both feet flat on the ground, his elbows propped against the arms at rigid angles. It seemed that Miss Knight was waiting for him to speak, so he inquired about her health.

"Very well, thank you," she replied, smiling in his direction. "I don't feel like one would suppose a seventy-year-old woman should feel."

"If she did, she wouldn't tell you," the maid cut in with a wink at Matthew. "She's just like my mum's sister was. Aunt Maud would rather take poison than complain about anything." She turned to Miss Knight. "Are you ready for tea, missus?"

"Yes, Bethina. And some lemon water for Miss Burke. She should be coming downstairs soon."

*Miss Burke?* Matthew thought, his mind groping for some remembrance of that name on Gregory Woodruff's list.

"The poor dear has a lengthy opera to learn, so she's spending some time with that now," Miss Knight said to him. "She's quite interesting. I believe you'll enjoy meeting her."

*Has to be someone Woodruff doesn't know about,* he decided.

"How is the rest of the family, Gregory?" she asked. Although he pitied the old woman for her blindness, Matthew was glad she couldn't see the redness he could feel coming over his face. It was time to earn his salary, so he cleared his throat and edged forward even more so in his chair.

"Well, you know that Jeremy has another daughter," he told her, despising the smoothness of his voice.

"Oh, yes," the woman said, clasping her hands together. "Frances. Your mother wrote when she was born. And who does the child favor? Is she as sweet-tempered as her brothers and sisters?"

Cursing Gregory Woodruff under his breath for not supplying this detail, Matthew groped for an answer. "My brother *claims* that she smiled at only three weeks of age," he finally said. Matthew knew practically nothing about infants and hoped that the statement he'd just made wasn't too outrageous.

"The little angel! And how many does that make for Jeremy and his wife? Four?"

"Five, counting the twins." Relieved to be back into territory he'd studied for, Matthew wondered if his conscience would be so badly seared when all of this was over that he would no longer be able to distinguish the truth from lies. Gregory Woodruff could be in Cambridge for three years, he thought. Three years of deception! Could he keep this up for that length of time? Why didn't he consider that before?

"Ah, yes, the twins," Miss Knight said. "What a blessing . . . so many little ones in the family." A shadow fell over her face, and Matthew felt a surge of pity for her. Was she regretting having had no husband or children? But this was apparently not on her mind, for she then said, "Gregory, I am aware that your father insists you spend Sunday afternoons with me. I do hope that doesn't distress you. There must be so many other things a young man would rather be doing."

"Distressed? Not at all, Miss . . . Aunt Helene." His pulse jumped at the slip of the tongue. Fortunately, she hadn't seemed to notice. "I wanted to come anyway."

She shook her finger at him, a little smile on her face. "You're a dear boy for saying that, even though I know better. Do tell me about yourself. Are you looking forward to attending the university?"

"Very much so," Matthew answered, and for at least this once he could speak the truth.

"And you'll do quite well, I'm certain. It's often wise to give yourself time to mature so that you can appreciate your education. So many young men are pressed into a field of study before they have the faintest idea of where their interests lie. Which college will you be attending, Gregory?"

"Pembroke."

"And what *are* your interests?"

"I wish to study law," Matthew lied.

"Ah, law. Like your brother Kenneth."

"Yes." Matthew relaxed just a little in his chair. At least Gregory Woodruff had been thorough in describing his family members.

He heard a footstep and automatically glanced to his right. A young woman stood framed by the doorway.

"You must be Mr. Woodruff," she said. "I'm Deborah Burke."

Remembering his manners, Matthew got to his feet and shook the hand she was offering. She was quite beautiful, with green eyes framed by dark eyelashes and dark brown hair tied at her neck with a yellow ribbon. Her brown calico dress was without ornament, save for carved ebony buttons, yet she looked as if she had just stepped from the pages of *Godey's Lady's Book*.

"Please, take your seat again," she said as she settled in the other Queen Anne chair.

Miss Knight smiled in the direction of the young woman and said, "Miss Burke is the young lady I spoke of earlier. She will be my houseguest for a while." She turned to Matthew again. "I've told her everything about you that I can remember . . . but it has been awhile, so you must update us."

"I'm afraid my life isn't very interesting," Matthew said. It was his second truthful statement since entering this house.

"Oh, modesty can be so tedious," Miss Knight sighed, yet gave him an affectionate smile to show that she was merely joking. Changing the subject, she said, "Miss Burke here is being tutored by Clarisse Pella. Have you heard of Signora Pella?"

Matthew nodded, then remembered that she couldn't see him. "Yes, I have. She married Lord Raleigh a couple of years ago, didn't she?"

"Why, yes, Gregory," Miss Knight said. "How did you know that?"

Too late he realized his mistake, for someone who didn't live in Cambridge wouldn't likely know about Lord Raleigh. "I heard . . . someone mention it. I believe it was on the train." To deflect attention from his discomfort, he turned to Miss Burke. "You are studying opera, then?"

She answered that she'd only had two lessons with Signora Pella so far. "But I graduated from the Royal Academy this summer. I wanted some more intense study before auditioning for roles in the London theater." It was obvious from the way her eyes lit up as she spoke that she loved music.

The maid came back in with a tray. Ignoring her protests, Matthew got up to help her place a table in the center of the three chairs. He noticed, after the tea and Miss Burke's hot water were poured, that the young woman declined to put any of the chocolate biscuits on her plate, just three small tomato-and-cheese sandwiches. "Signora Pella is rather strict," she told him when she became aware that he was staring at her plate. "No tea or sweets."

"For how long?"

She tilted her chin thoughtfully for a second, then answered. "Why, I suppose for the rest of my life. Or for as long as I want to sing opera."

"I'm sorry."

"Oh, there are worse things to give up." She shrugged, then smiled at him. "I'm actually beginning to like the taste of lemon water."

After the maid came to take away the dishes, Miss Knight asked her to leave the table in place. "Would you care for a game of dominos?" she asked the two young people.

"Crocheting . . . and now dominos?" Miss Burke asked, an eyebrow raised in surprise.

The old woman smiled. "Mr. and Mrs. Darnell and I play in the afternoons. I can feel the dots with my fingers."

The maid brought over a wooden box from the chimney-piece and handed it to Matthew. "Would you like to divide them up, Mr. Woodruff?" she asked.

"Of course." He was amazed, once the game was under-way, at how easily Miss Knight remembered the values of the dominos that were played once she'd had a chance to touch them with her fingertips—a testimony to the sharpness of her mind as well as her other senses.

Matthew was also surprised to discover, halfway through the game, that he was having a good time. Now that the questions about "home" were fewer and farther between, he could allow himself to relax a little and push away from his mind the thought that the hospitality, though genuine, was misplaced.

They were in the middle of a discussion of favorite novels, when Miss Burke snapped a domino into place on the table and asked him, "Have you read *Treasure Island?*"

"Why no, I haven't," he answered, straightening in his chair. "I've been wanting to though." His Sundays, since William died, had been spent at the Cambridge Free Library, but there was a long waiting list for the recently published novel.

"My parents gave me a copy before I left," she told him. "But I've only had time to read the first chapter, on the train. I'll be glad to lend it to you when I've finished . . . if you don't mind the wait."

He thanked her, flattered that such a beautiful, self-confident woman of the upper class would care to make such an offer to a lowly clerk. *It's not you she's offering it to,* he reminded himself, deciding at that moment that he hated Gregory Woodruff.

"You know, that is what I miss the most," Miss Knight said. Miss Burke looked at her. "Reading?"

"I once had quite a collection of good novels, but I donated them to Newnham ten years ago. That's the women's college, you know, and the new library was desperate for books. Mrs. Darnell kindly reads letters and the newspaper and a bit from the Bible each day to me, but I hunger for a good story now and then."

"I'll be happy to read to you," Miss Burke told her.

"Oh, dear." Miss Knight put a hand up to her withered cheek. "I despise hinting, and here I am. . . ."

"But I would love a chance to pay you back for your hospitality."

The old woman looked grateful but gave a firm shake of her head. "You do that every time you allow me to listen to you sing. You have an opera to memorize, and besides, it can't be good for your voice to be reading aloud."

"Why don't you allow me?" Matthew found himself offering. "I could read for an hour or so every Sunday, since . . . I'll be here anyway."

Miss Knight's smile became almost radiant. "You wouldn't mind, Gregory?"

"No, I would enjoy that." He meant it, too. Perhaps providing Miss Knight with a long-denied pleasure would atone, in some small measure, for his treachery.

Miss Burke turned her face toward him with something resembling admiration in her green eyes, evoking a strange ache in Matthew's chest. How long had it been since a woman looked at him in such a way?

Oh, he supposed he was handsome enough, judging by the coy glances that were often directed his way—from eyes that seemed to lose interest once they took in the cheapness of his clothing. But the way Miss Burke had just looked at him was different. Not coy or flirtatious but something much better. It was as if she had just decided at that moment that she *liked* him.

"Why don't you start with my copy of *Treasure Island,* since we're all eager to read it?". she suggested. "The three of us could enjoy it at the same time." Her smile faltered just a little, and she looked at Miss Knight. "That is . . . if you don't mind my sitting in."

"Mind? Why, I shall be crushed if you don't," Miss Knight answered. "And I'm sure Gregory feels the same way."

*He would be crazy if he didn't,* Matthew thought. "Of course I do," he said aloud, trying to keep his voice casual. He glanced at the clock on the chimneypiece and was shocked to realize that he had been in Miss Knight's parlor for almost three hours! Even if he were supposed to be a member of the family, there was such a thing as wearing out one's welcome. Standing, he thanked "Aunt Helene" for allowing him to visit.

She beamed in his direction and extended a frail hand, which he put to his lips. "You don't know how it does my heart good for you to visit, dear boy."

The sincerity of her words brought a lump to Matthew's throat. "You don't know how good it is to hear you say that," he said in return. He bade farewell to Miss Burke, returning her smile as he shook the hand she extended.

"I'll see myself out," he said with a mixture of reluctance and relief. At least today's lies would soon be over.

"Oh, Gregory." Miss Knight's words stopped him at the parlor door, and he turned around.

"Yes, Aunt Helene?"

"I forgot that you haven't a carriage here. You must allow Thomas to drive you back in the trap."

Matthew protested that the walk was good exercise, but she was adamant. "And you must show him where to fetch you at Pembroke next week, so he can drive you both ways."

Bethina came into the room just then, and Miss Knight asked her to lead him to the carriage house and find Thomas. Fifteen minutes later Matthew was sitting in a trap, allowing a boy who looked barely old enough to be driving around town to deliver him to Pembroke College, from where his walk home would be doubled.

"You're studying law?" the boy suddenly asked as the horse trotted down Thompson's Lane.

Matthew looked sideways at the boy, realizing from the voice that he was a little older than he appeared to be. And the dark hair sticking out from the edges of the billycock cap reminded him of his brother. *He's probably the same age William was when . . .*

"Yes," he replied in answer to the question, for the deception had to go on a little longer.

The boy glanced at him as if he had something to say, but then he turned his attention to the horse again. At the second glance in his direction, Matthew said, "You have something to ask me?" He was immediately sorry for the sharpness in his tone, for it wasn't the lad's fault that his walk home would be doubled.

"It–it's about the law," the boy said after some hesitancy.

"I haven't even started school yet," Matthew said. The boy looked so disappointed that he felt compelled to add, "But why don't you ask me anyway? I may happen to know the answer."

Another pause, and then, "Can boys be sent to prison?"

Though there was a space of about four inches between them, he could feel the tension coming from the lad. "Yes, they can," Matthew replied, then added, "But only if they're convicted of a crime."

His reassurance had the opposite effect than he had intended, for the face beside him paled. Matthew thought of William again. "You know, I've a . . . friend who is a solicitor. Why don't you tell me exactly what's wrong, and I'll see what he advises?"

"Nothing's wrong," the boy was quick to say, his eyes unwavering from the reins.

Matthew decided to be direct. "Are you in some kind of trouble?"

"No sir. It's a friend of mine."

"What has your friend done?"

"Nothing." The boy chewed on his lip for a second and said, "But someone is tryin' to get him to . . ." He looked at Matthew again. "Can he go to prison if a bigger person makes him do something bad?"

"Your friend, you mean," Matthew said gently.

"Yes sir."

"Well, I suppose that depends. Why don't you tell me what it is your friend is being forced to do, and I'll find out for you."

After still another hesitation, the boy shrugged his wiry shoulders. "He ain't that good a friend. Just someone I know. I don't really care what happens to him." As if to emphasize his point, he stretched his lips into what looked more like a grimace than the smile he'd intended.

Impulsively, Matthew put a hand on his shoulder. "It's possible that I can help your . . . friend if he'll allow me."

This time the boy shook his head. "I just wonder about things," he said with a flat voice. "He'll have to take care of himself."

~

"You would like Miss Knight's nephew, Gregory Woodruff," Deborah wrote in her continuing letter home. She had spent a couple of hours picking her way through *Don Giovanni* for the second time, and she was ready for a break.

*He came by for a visit with her today, which speaks volumes about the goodness of his heart. Although he seemed shy and rather nervous at times, he also seemed to enjoy Miss Knight's and my company. His reluctance to talk about himself was refreshing when so many young men feel they have to impress you with their sporting exploits and social status.*

*Oh, by the way, next week Mr. Woodruff will begin reading to Miss Knight and me from the* Treasure Island *that you gave me. I stay so busy with my practices and learning the opera that Signora Pella assigned, that it will be nice to have an opportunity to relax and visit with two very pleasant people on Sunday afternoons.*

When she was finished with the day's entry, she opened the lid to the writing table and put the letter inside. Wiping her pen, she recalled the dread she had felt when she first went downstairs to meet Miss Knight's nephew. She had already committed herself to participating in the Sunday visits—and what if he'd turned out to be like that man at the train station? After all, Father had warned that college towns had more than their share of cads.

It occurred to her to wonder, then, if the two knew each other. Walesby was a small town, the man had said. What if they were even friends?

She replaced the lid on her ink bottle and dismissed the thought. People tended to seek out friends who shared the same convictions and general way of looking at life. The two men might know each other, but it was impossible to imagine them being anything but acquaintances, for in character they were poles apart.

As she dressed for bed, Deborah became aware that she was spending an inordinate amount of time thinking about a person she had only just met. *You should be concentrating on your music,* she reminded herself, *not on Gregory Woodruff—no matter how charming he might be.*

# 8

ONDAY afternoon Matthew was filing some correspondence and legal papers when Gregory Woodruff walked into the office, dressed in white flannels and a straw boater hat. "My lectures are over for today," he said, picking up a small globe from the top of the oak filing cabinet. He gave it a spin and held it up to watch. "Stuffy lot, these Cambridge people. It's going to be a long three years, I'm afraid."

Matthew put the remaining papers under his arm, closed the drawer, and took the globe from the man's hands. "Mr. Cornell bought that in Florence," he said, replacing it on the cabinet. "It's not a toy. What do you want?"

"What do I want?" Mr. Woodruff raised a warning eyebrow. "You've developed a rather cheeky attitude for someone in my employ."

"You have the liberty to dismiss me at any time," Matthew replied, and Mr. Woodruff's posture immediately assumed a more humble stance.

"I just came in to hear about your visit yesterday. Didn't intend to get in the way."

"Well, you *are* in the way. My employer doesn't pay me for social visits."

"All right, all right," he said, holding up a hand in a placating gesture. "Just tell me about your visit with my aunt, and I'll leave."

Matthew sighed and shook his head.

"What's wrong?" Mr. Woodruff asked, an edge of panic in his voice. "You did go, didn't you?"

"I went."

"And . . . ?"

"She believed I was you."

He let out a breath. "You had me worried there."

"She's a dear soul," Matthew told him. "And she doesn't deserve what we're doing to her."

"We aren't going to go through all of this again, are we? You agreed to—"

"And I'm going to keep my agreement. But to be frank, Mr. Woodruff, the less I see of you, the better."

"Ah, but I assume you're interested in being paid, aren't you?"

Matthew wondered how he could have forgotten that, when the only reason he had agreed to do this was for the money. Humbled, he gave a tight-lipped nod, and the man before him grinned and pulled his purse from his pocket.

"I'm not even going to deduct the money I already gave you for the shirt," Mr. Woodruff said magnanimously, holding out a half-sovereign note. "Regardless of your low opinion of me, I'm extremely pleased that you were able to pull it off."

It would have taken him two weeks to earn as much working here in the office, but Matthew couldn't bear to thank the man for it. And the thought of having to go through this every week was too much. He pushed the money into his waistcoat pocket and said, "From now on, why don't you just pay me monthly, when you come to collect your allowance?"

Mr. Woodruff touched the brim of his hat. "Whatever you wish."

When he was gone, Matthew opened the drawer again and resumed his filing. He wondered, as he worked, what Gregory Woodruff would say if he knew about his aunt's houseguest, Miss Burke. No doubt he would be interested.

*But he's not going to find out about her from me,* he resolved.

~

Clarisse Pella came into the music room on Tuesday afternoon wearing a simple wrapper of burgundy cordeliere. She wore no jewelry, not even on her fingers. Her hair was drawn back tightly into a simple chignon, and her complexion was colorless save for violet shadows under her eyes. Without a word of greeting she walked over to sit at the piano, struck the middle-C note, and gave Deborah an expectant nod. There was nothing Deborah could do but sing the note on her way to the piano, then stand there for the rest of her scales.

"Signora, is something wrong?" she asked the first time she was given a moment to catch her breath.

"Wrong?" The diva's slender fingers curled up on the piano keys. "Why are you concerned with something that doesn't concern your music? Now, the scales again."

Signora Pella was merciless this time, making her sustain the notes until she felt her lungs would collapse. After thirty minutes of this, Deborah shook her head. "Signora, I have to rest."

"Rest, then!" the diva exclaimed, slamming the lid shut over the keys. "It is just as well."

"I want to sing," Deborah said, her eyes smarting, "but I'm only human!"

The diva looked up with a shocked expression in her slate gray eyes.

"I'm sorry, but . . . ," Deborah began.

"I apologize, Miss Burke," Signora Pella sighed, in a tone that suggested great weariness. She rubbed her forehead. "And now you must go home. We will begin anew tomorrow."

"Is there some way that I can help you?" Deborah offered, but hesitantly. Surely the pedestal that Clarisse Pella occupied was out of her reach.

"No," answered the diva, but she studied Deborah thoughtfully. After several seconds, she said, "Perhaps you should know, Miss Burke. You must understand why it is necessary to be a strong woman if you are to survive in the world of the theater."

She got up from the piano bench and motioned for Deborah to follow. Together they went up one flight of a gleaming mahogany-and-marble staircase, past dark portraits of reproachful ancestors. The boudoir they entered was lavishly furnished with brocades and velvets in warm colors, intricately carved furniture, and fine Brussels carpets.

"Leave us," Signora Pella said to a housemaid who stood at a table with her polishing cloth, her work interrupted. When she was gone, the diva went over to a huge teakwood trunk and opened the lid. She knelt down beside it and began rummaging through the contents. Deborah, still standing just inside the doorway, didn't know what was expected of her now, so she ventured to go over and kneel beside the diva. Her eyes widened at the accumulation before her, all chronicling an outstanding career on the stage.

"You've saved everything . . . how wonderful!" she breathed.

Signora Pella gave a distracted nod, then brought out a small photograph album, its leather cover embossed with the image of a peacock in full plumage. She sank back on her heels on the carpet, and Deborah reluctantly did the same, though she would have longed to spend hours looking through the trunk. Her bustle billowed out behind her as she tucked her gown around her legs, and she watched while Signora Pella, a frown of concentration furrowing her brow, leafed through the pages of the album.

"Patrizia Este," the diva finally said, passing the book over to her. Deborah looked down at the page she was indicating. Four yellowing photographs were mounted on the page, faces that she didn't recognize until she looked closer.

"That is you?" she asked Signora Pella and received a nod for an answer. She studied the photograph again. Two very young women stood holding hands and smiling in front of a rose trellis, their white-lawn dresses in the hoopskirted style of the mid-1850s. One she now recognized as Signora Pella.

"This is Madame Este?" she asked, pointing to the other young woman. Of course Deborah had heard of Patrizia Este, who still graced stages in Europe and the States. "She was your friend?"

Signora Pella let out a most unladylike snort. "We were on an outing in Naples before rehearsals were to begin for *Nella Mattinata*. She had just returned from making her formal debut in New York, and I had gained recognition in Italy and France, so we were evenly matched as far as fame is concerned."

"Clarisse Pella and Patrizia Este on the same stage," Deborah said, studying the photograph again. "I never knew that you had worked together. I would have loved to have been there."

"No one was there."

Deborah looked up at her. "No one?"

"Patrizia Este left for London three days before opening night, without even the courtesy of informing the young composer, Michel Alrigo . . . who went bankrupt and soon after committed suicide. She had no understudy, you see, and the production had to be canceled."

"Why did she leave?"

"She had been offered the leading role in Bellini's *La Sonnambula.*" Signora Pella gave Deborah a significant look. "You know, of course, it was this role that won her worldwide recognition."

"But how could she break her contract?"

"Ah, this was the genius of Patrizia Este. She had it written into her contract that she would not sing under conditions that were detrimental to her voice." Signora Pella shrugged. "That summer it rained almost every day in Naples. Had it not rained, she would have claimed that the weather was too dry."

Deborah could only shake her head, disappointed in this revelation about a performer who was still admired by thousands of people. "Surely she found out about the composer's suicide. How could she live with herself after that?"

"I do not know. I never again accepted a role that would put us on the same stage."

"It would be a hard thing to forgive," Deborah admitted, even though she had been taught from her childhood that forgiveness of others was one of the basic tenets of a Christian life. "I don't think I've ever heard of anything so selfish."

"Selfish?" Signora Pella tilted her chin. "What do you mean?"

Stunned by her tutor's tone, Deborah gaped at her and stammered, "Well . . . leaving Naples."

"But she was offered a much better role and had a way to obtain it. I would have done the same thing."

"Surely not!"

The diva gave her a sharp look. "One thing you must learn, Miss Burke, is that if you don't seize the opportunities handed you, someone else will. If Patrizia Este hadn't found a way to make that London debut, perhaps the one who took her place would now be enjoying her fame."

An argument came to mind about keeping one's word, but Deborah did not voice it. Clearly, it was a debate that she could not win. "Then why . . ."

"Why did I not want to work with her?"

"Yes."

"Because I would have been forced to relive my old hatred, and it would have affected my voice."

The answer sounded oddly clinical, yet the tone did not match the bitterness in Signora Pella's slate gray eyes. Confused, Deborah shook her head. "But why did you hate her if you would have done the same thing?"

Signora Pella's expression darkened again. "I was in love with Michel Alrigo. I left my husband because of him and believed that he felt the same way about me. When Patrizia Este left, I would have happily consoled him, but he could barely look at me. It turned out that he was smitten with *her.*"

Leaving Deborah holding the album, Signora Pella raised herself to her feet, walked over to a settee of tufted gold velvet, then leaned over to pick something up from one of the cushions. She returned with what looked like a crumpled piece of newspaper.

"This was delivered to me in the post this morning," she

said, both hands carefully smoothing out the folds in the paper. "Unsigned, but I know who sent it."

Deborah took it from her. It was a page from *The London Times,* dated two weeks earlier. She scanned the column titles until Signora Pella pointed an impatient finger at the words in bold print:

> **Patrizia Este's First Stop on Transcontinental Tour**
> It was predicted to be a tremendous success, if Frankfurt was to be any measure. One week of sold-out performances at double the usual ticket rate, to witness the forty-seven-year-old prima donna performing arias from her past engagements. "I wish to dedicate this opening night to someone whose memory still inspires me to sing my best," Madame Este said with a radiant yet sad expression. "Michel Alrigo."

Deborah lowered the page. "You believe Madame Este sent you this?"

"Who else would stoop so low? She wishes to flaunt to me that she is still able to perform, and to rub salt in the wound, she uses poor Michel's name." Signora Pella's jaw became a sharp line, and her mouth drew tightly together as if she were biting on something bitter. "You know, it is almost a relief to me that I can no longer sing, for now I am free to hate her without the worry of damaging my voice."

Deborah sat there, stunned that Madame Este, someone she had perceived as larger than life, would stoop to such pettiness. But her disappointment in Signora Pella was even more acute.

No, she had never suffered the hurt that Signora Pella had suffered and hopefully never would. But thirty years was too long to keep bitterness sealed away in one's heart, no matter what the cause. The diva's hatred was like a seed that had been covered with a protective shell to keep it from affecting her performances. Now she seemed almost happy that she finally had the freedom to nurture it and allow it to grow.

And how could anyone of integrity condone breaking a contract and bringing a production to ruin, just to advance one's career?

*I wanted to be just like her for so long,* Deborah thought. *I imagined that anyone with a voice that beautiful would have a beautiful soul as well.* Then she realized what was wrong. It went back to the discernment Father had described. *She doesn't know God.*

She watched as Signora Pella took the newspaper, stalked across the room, and threw the crumpled ball into the fireplace. "Now you see why you must put everything you have into your training." Her eyes were filled with intensity. "And you must seize every opportunity you have to advance, no matter what the cost. There can be only so many prima donnas of the stage."

Deborah felt the usual stirring in her chest at the diva's last words, an overwhelming desire to become one of those privileged few. But surely it could be done without compromising one's values along the way. Signora Pella and Madame Este had soared to heights most singers could only dream of, but at *what cost to others?*

*Ask her if any of this will matter in eternity,* a voice inside Deborah urged. But the words would not come. Although the pain of her burning conscience was great, her fear of offending the diva was greater. Then a sobering thought came to her: *I'm already compromising my values.* When had she ever been afraid to tell someone of her faith in God?

Ashamed of her cowardice, she lowered her eyes to the open album she still held in her lap. A photograph on the opposite page caught her attention: two small children, obviously twins no more than three years old. They were posed in front of a photographer's screen depicting the seashore, dressed in identical nautical-style clothing, with ribbons in their fair hair. In such a poignant pose, their huge eyes somber, they seemed much too serious for their tender age. Deborah wondered if it was due to timidity before the camera. They held child-size parasols casually over opposite shoulders, pressing in together as if seeking comfort from each other's presence.

"Here, give me that."

Suddenly the album was taken out of her hands, and Deborah watched as Signora Pella put it back into the trunk and closed the lid.

"I must rest now," the diva said. "I will ring for a servant to show you out."

"I don't mind showing myself out."

Signora Pella shrugged on her way to the door leading to her bedchamber. "As you wish," she said over her shoulder. "Be here half an hour early tomorrow. We have no time to waste."

~

The next afternoon, as soon as Signora Pella came into the music room, she folded her arms and stared critically at Deborah. "What is the matter with you? Are you sick?"

"I didn't sleep well last night," Deborah answered, stifling a yawn.

The diva frowned. "Please do not tell me that you're infatuated with some young man. Your music should be . . ."

Suddenly Gregory Woodruff's warm blue eyes flitted across

her mind, but she pushed the thought away. "No, Signora. . . .
I was ashamed of myself."

"Ashamed?" An eyebrow was lifted. "For what reason?"

*Tell her,* Deborah ordered herself. She forced herself to
meet the diva's critical eyes. "For not saying anything to you
yesterday."

"We spoke yesterday." Signora Pella let out an impatient
breath. "Either explain yourself or let us begin the lesson,
Miss Burke."

"I have wanted to be like you for so long," Deborah blurted
out. "But yesterday I . . ."

"You pitied me." Signora Pella's tone grew razor sharp.
"Is that what you are trying to say, Miss Burke?"

"No, not pity. I feel compassion for your bitterness."

"Don't you think I have a right to be bitter? I can no longer
sing, and my former friends mock me."

"My father has a right to be bitter as well . . . and he was
for years, Signora. His face was badly scarred in the war, and
people stare at him. His fiancée even rejected him out of
embarrassment. But when he allowed God to take away his
bitterness, his life changed dramatically."

Her lips tightening, Signora Pella said, "And you feel it is
your duty to ask me to do the same, yes?"

Deborah swallowed, wondering how saints like John the
Baptist had ever had the boldness to stand by the river Jordan
and preach. *I can't even speak to Signora Pella without sweaty
palms.* But she passionately believed in what she was saying
and knew that she wouldn't be able to live with herself until
she had said it all. "I . . . care about you and wish you could
know the difference that God can make in your life."

"Miss Burke." The hostility in Signora Pella's face was

gone, replaced by something even worse . . . boredom. "You are not the first to suggest that I should embrace religion—"

"Not *religion,* Signora. Christianity is a relationship—"

A silencing hand went up. "Whatever it is, I am not interested. Your concern for my well-being is touching, but I will be furious if you come in again looking as you do now. I have warned you about excessive emotions." She motioned toward the piano, a signal that the lessons were to begin.

"And as for your God," Signora Pella added on her way to the bench, "I do not wish to have this conversation again. Music has been my god for all my life. It is too late for me to desert it now."

"But I'm not talking about deserting your music," Deborah persisted as she stood in her usual place at the side of the piano. "Music . . . our talents . . . are gifts from the very God who wants you to become his child."

"I have indulged this talk for long enough, Miss Burke." The diva's gray eyes smoldered. "If you wish to continue lessons with me, you will concentrate upon the music and not upon things which are none of your business." A finger struck A below middle C, bringing an end to the discussion.

~

That evening in Miss Knight's drawing room, when Deborah had finished practicing her scales, she told her hostess about what had happened at Signora Pella's. "She refuses to let go of her bitterness long enough to take hold of something that would add some meaning to her life."

Miss Knight nodded sympathetically. "It's a sad thing when that happens."

"I wanted so much to persuade her to become a Christian. But I failed."

"And how did you fail?"

"Well, she didn't want to listen to me."

The older woman gave her a sad smile. "You mustn't blame yourself, Deborah. Signora Pella has a free choice in the matter, as has everyone else."

Absently tracing a finger around the design on the damask upholstery of her chair, Deborah sighed. "I suppose so. But I'll never have another chance. From now on, she says, I mustn't speak to her about God."

"Then you must respect her wishes when you're in her home. But your life can still be a powerful witness. Allow her to see God through you."

"I hope she does," Deborah replied. "But I'm afraid I'm far from being a perfect Christian."

A brief smile touched the older woman's lips. "I wouldn't trust the person who said that he was. But if *I*, blind as I am, can see the Father in you, then so can Signora Pella."

~

"You should go see the Fitzwilliam Museum sometime," Thomas said to Miss Burke on the way to her lesson the next afternoon, as the trap fell in line with the traffic of Queen's Road. "It's got some of them mummies from over in Egypt."

She looked interested. "Perhaps we could leave the house early one day and have a look at them. If Miss Knight doesn't mind your taking the carriage out early, that is."

"I don't think she'll mind. The missus is the one who told me about the mummies. They were in the newspaper."

"Then we'll have to plan it one day," Miss Burke replied, smiling.

Thomas found that he enjoyed driving Miss Burke to and from her singing lessons. He knew the city, and she made him feel bright whenever she asked him questions about the buildings and landmarks they passed. Yesterday he even took a different route home, just to be able to show her the seventeenth-century sundial decorating the First Court at Queen's College.

While she was at least six years older than his thirteen years, Thomas found himself feeling strangely protective of her. Perhaps because she reminded him a little of his mother, back in the early days when she was so beautiful and happy. If only someone had cared enough to protect his mother from the men who had led her down the path of ruin, perhaps she would be selling hats again and making him laugh at night over their suppers with her stories of the peculiarities of some of her customers.

The thought of his mother made Thomas's eyes start to burn, and he pretended to turn his head to watch a group of five university-age men cycling past in the opposite direction. *She's got to go to that sanatorium,* he told himself, squeezing the reins so tightly that his nails dug into his palms. His mother's appearance grew worse every Sunday. How much longer could he expect her to live unless something drastic was done?

"Thomas . . . are you all right?"

Thomas turned to nod. "Yes, miss."

Miss Burke studied his face. "Sometimes you seem so sad."

"I do?" He forced a smile. "I was just thinking, that's all."

"About your mother?" she said after a worried pause, and Thomas gaped at her. *How could she know?*

"Pardon me for prying, but I watched you in chapel last

124

Sunday," she said, her green eyes fixed upon his face. "I was told that you're used to attending your own church with your mother."

"Yes," he muttered while his mind worked to figure out what she was getting at.

"Well, I could easily walk to church with Avis and Mr. and Mrs. Darnell. Then there would be room in the carriage for your mother. I don't think Miss Knight would mind your fetching her—if your mother wouldn't mind coming to chapel with you. At least you'd be together."

Touched by her thoughtfulness, Thomas pretended to consider her offer. There was no way out of it except to lie, though, and he knew it. "My mother only likes to go to Saint Andrew's," he told her. "She understands about my not being there with her. It's only until Mr. Henry gets better, anyway."

"But you must miss her."

"I still go visit her. Early, before chapel."

"Oh, I didn't realize that. Well, I'm glad." Miss Burke smiled at him, then turned her attention to the road in front of them, and Thomas let out a quiet sigh of relief that she didn't pursue the matter. Still, he wished he hadn't had to lie to her—or to anyone else at Miss Knight's for that matter— for they were kind to him. But how would he ever have obtained a job had he admitted that his mother was an opium addict, living with a man who was not her husband? And now he was caught in the lies of his own making, just like a fly in a spiderweb.

A chill snaked down his spine. He was a liar, soon to become a thief. It occurred to him that all of his efforts were going to be in vain, that it was too late to save his mother, but he shook the thought from his mind. He had to try.

~

That afternoon Signora Pella was more demanding than she had ever been, but she did not mention the disagreement they had had the day before. Remembering Miss Knight's advice, Deborah took even the harshest criticism with a respectful attitude.

She was in the middle of a scale when Signora Pella rose from the piano bench and motioned for her to come closer. When Deborah did so, the diva put a finger under her chin and raised it.

"Make a yawn for me, *per favore.*"

It took Deborah several seconds to comply, and she felt rather sheepish doing so, but when she was finished, Signora Pella gave a satisfied nod.

"When you breathe during a performance, there should be a yawning feeling that opens the throat," she said, smiling and shaking her head when Deborah was seized by another yawn.

"I'm sorry," Deborah told her. "But thinking about yawning makes me . . ."

"I know," replied Signora Pella, covering a yawn with a hand herself. She sat back down at the piano and held her fingers poised against the keys. "I don't mean for you to actually yawn upon the stage—that would be a disaster. But put your hand up to your throat as you sing the next scale and see if you can feel it opening wide."

Deborah sang, obeying her teacher's instructions, and was rewarded with another nod. "Remember not to show the teeth," the diva added as she played the sixth scale. "Singing is natural—the face must be kept loose."

*I'm doing everything wrong,* Deborah thought miserably as the practice went on, and she was stopped for more corrections.

But when they sat with their cups of hot lemon water, Signora Pella surprised her by saying, "I am very pleased with your progress, Miss Burke. You have an incredible voice."

"I have?" The relief came out in a sigh.

"And I am impressed with your attitude while being corrected. Very mature for someone of your age."

Deborah smiled and thanked her but did not voice her thought. *It's God in me that you see, signora.*

~

Saturday night Thomas lay in bed in a sweat until he heard the midnight chimes from Magdalene College. It had been easy to lift Mr. Henry's house key from his tool kit, which was still in a cupboard in the tack room. No doubt the liveryman hadn't thought the key necessary while he was temporarily staying nights inside the house. At the terrace door he took off his shoes before taking the key from his pocket. His teeth were chattering violently, and his hands trembled so that it took him three tries to open the door.

Down the hallway he crept, running his hands along the wainscoting in the darkness. He stopped at the parlor door to turn, cock his head, and listen. The only sound was the pounding of his heart against his rib cage, and his shallow, wavering intakes of breath. Satisfied that no one was moving about, he turned the knob and pushed open the door, one inch at a time.

Only when he was inside the parlor did he realize he'd not thought to bring a candle. There was nothing he could do about it now, for he would have sooner walked barefoot on glass than make this trip a second time tonight. He edged his way along the wall to the bay window, then slowly pulled apart the heavy curtains. They allowed in enough light from the streetlamps so that he could at least see the doors to the giant cupboard that dominated the wall opposite the fireplace.

On his way across the room, he prayed under his breath that the cupboard wouldn't be locked, then gulped at the realization that he was praying for God to help him commit a crime. *Think about what you've got to do,* he ordered himself. The first cupboard door that he tried wasn't locked but squeaked so loudly that he eased it back and opened another one. Even though light came in from the window, it was too feeble to allow him to see the contents of the cupboard shelves. He allowed his hand to hover over the top of the middle shelf, figuring that something from the back wouldn't be missed. Slowly he brought his hand down, until his fingers touched something resembling smooth china. Tracing the top of it with his fingers, he realized by the pointed ears that it was a figurine of a cat. He lifted it straight up so as not to topple anything that might be around it. It was heavier than he had expected. Switching the statue to his left hand, he unfastened his top buttons so that he could tuck it into his shirt.

The trip back to the mews seemed to take longer as he inched his way along, straining his ears for any sound from above or below. Had he been caught on his way *to* the parlor, he would perhaps have been able to come up with some kind of explanation, but not on his way back with ill-gotten gain in his shirt. A picture crossed his mind of disappointment and hurt on kindly Miss Knight's face. *I'll save up and buy her a new china cat one day . . . when Mother's well.*

~

The statue turned out to be white marble with shining green stones set into the eyes. Orville snatched it out of Thomas's hand the next morning and brought it up to his face to squint at it. *"Real* emeralds?"

"I don't know," Thomas answered.

"Looks like it to me!" Orville grinned, clapping him on the shoulder. "You turned out to have some sand after all, didn't you?"

"I can be back here after chapel," Thomas said as he shrugged off Orville's hand. "We can take Mother to the sanatorium."

"Not so fast."

"But you *said* . . ."

Orville gave a wheezing cough and then scowled down at him. "If you think this little pretty is gonna get yer mum into a good hospital, you better think again. It's gonna cost money for her to stay there."

"But Miss Knight has nice things—it's probably valuable. You can sell it, can't you?"

"It's a start all right, but it ain't gonna be enough. Take another little walk through the house and bring me something else next Sunday . . . and we'll see."

Thomas felt his knees go weak. "I won't do that again, Orville."

"Oh, methinks you will," the man replied and pointed a grime-stained finger in the direction of the back room. Thomas gaped at him, then flew past him through the doorway. His mother lay on the pillow, oily brown hair in strings about her head. She was breathing—he could tell by the shallow movements of her sunken chest—but she stared up at the ceiling with an uncomprehending expression.

"Mother?" Thomas whispered, putting a hand up to her

cheek. Her lips made a faint movement, but the glazed eyes did not even blink.

"Makes a boy figger out what's important . . . seein' yer mum like that," came Orville's cloying voice from behind him. Though his vision was now blurred by the tears in his eyes, Thomas turned around to glare at him. Orville stood there, leaning against the doorframe, picking his teeth with his pocketknife.

"I'll see you next week," he said, looking solemnly past Thomas at his mother in the bed. "Be sure to have somethin' with you."

# 9

SUNDAY afternoon Matthew left his flat to walk the seven blocks to the corner of Trumpington and Pembroke Streets, where he was to wait for Thomas. The boy turned up almost precisely at two o'clock. After a solemn "Hello, sir" to Matthew as he climbed on board the trap, Thomas began guiding the horse and carriage back into traffic.

"Looks like rain later," Matthew said in a feeble attempt at starting a conversation. Thomas merely glanced up at the sky and nodded. "I hope you don't have to drive me back during a downpour," Matthew went on.

"It's all right. I'll put up the hood."

Silence again, until Matthew said, "How is your friend?"

The boy kept his eyes on the reins. "My friend?"

"The one you asked me about. I would really like to help him, if I can."

"Oh, he's all right now." Thomas gave him another one of his grimacelike smiles. "Just fine."

Matthew decided to give up trying. It was obvious that something serious was still bothering the boy, but he couldn't help someone who wouldn't allow him to. *It's just as well,* he thought. *I've enough troubles of my own.*

But in spite of his resolve to mind his own business, he found himself saying, as the carriage stopped in front of the house on Park Parade, "You know, William, I've always been good at keeping confidences."

This time the boy looked at him. "William?"

"Thomas, I mean." Matthew gave the boy a sad smile. "I once knew someone named William. You resemble him somewhat."

"What happened to him?"

"He died."

Thomas brought the gig to a halt in front of the carriage house but made no move to climb down. He turned to Matthew with a curious expression. "Was he as old as me?"

"How old are you, exactly?"

"Thirteen."

"William was a year older."

"And how did he die?"

"Cancer." Matthew swallowed, then looked straight into the boy's eyes. "What I'm trying to say is that if you were to need my advice, it would go no further. And I know a solicitor who would probably agree to help you."

"My friend, you mean," the boy corrected quickly.

"No, I mean *you.*"

The boy's bottom lip trembled, and for a brief moment the expression on his face softened into indecision. But it disappeared as soon as it had come. "Thank you, sir," he replied in a flat voice. "But nobody can help me."

"You don't know that." Matthew pressed.

The boy's only response was a shake of the head. "I know that."

~

"'It was already candle-light when we reached the hamlet, and I shall never forget how much I was cheered to see the yellow shine in doors and windows; but that, as it proved, was the best of the help we were likely to get in that quarter. For— you would have thought men would have been ashamed of themselves—no soul would consent to return with us to the "Admiral Benbow."'"

Matthew glanced up from the pages of *Treasure Island*. Miss Knight sat back in her chair, her chin tilted, an absent expression on her face. " Are you tired of listening?" he asked gently, in case she had drifted off to sleep.

Without changing her posture, the elderly woman smiled. "Just watching the pictures in my mind, dear. You make the story come alive."

He smiled back, even though she couldn't see him. "I used to enjoy reading to—" Matthew realized what he was saying just before "William" could escape his lips.

". . . some of the nieces and nephews," he finished, taking a deep breath in an effort to quell his hammering heart. He looked over at Miss Burke. She sat leaning her head back against the chair cushion, her eyes closed. *Asleep,* he thought, grateful that neither woman had appeared to notice his near slip of the tongue.

Miss Burke stirred and opened her eyes, catching him in the act of staring at her. She gave him a sheepish smile and stretched her arms.

"I wasn't asleep . . . honest. It's just so relaxing to sit and listen to a story. I haven't been read to since I was a child."

"I think that Mr. Stevenson would be crushed to hear his adventure described as relaxing," he teased.

Miss Burke laughed, a sound as rich as velvet. "I shall deny ever saying that if you tell him," she said, causing Miss Knight to laugh as well. Silence ensued, the comfortable quietness of enjoyable company. Matthew found himself wishing that he could sit there with them forever.

"I think we should give Gregory a chance to rest his voice," the elderly woman said after the moment had passed. "Let's just sit and visit for a while. But you will continue next time where you left off, won't you?"

Promising that he would, Matthew looked at the clock and realized that again he had stayed for almost three hours. "I must be going," he said, rising from his chair.

"Must you?" asked Miss Knight, as if she sincerely wished he wouldn't leave.

*She thinks you're her nephew,* Matthew reminded himself. *She would ask the same of the real Gregory Woodruff.* It was the family bond, not anything about his personality, that made her want him to stay longer.

"I don't want to be selfish and take you away from your studies," she went on, "but wouldn't you care for a quick game of dominos? I do enjoy your company so much."

Touched by the longing in her voice, Matthew said, "A *quick* game of dominos?"

She raised an eyebrow and smiled. "It *could* go quickly . . . if you both wear blindfolds. Then we would be evenly matched."

"I believe we're already evenly matched." This came from Miss Burke, who got up to fetch the dominos while Matthew pulled out the table. "I'll have to pass it up this time, though, as much as I would like to stay. Signora Pella wants some lines memorized by tomorrow. But shall I ask Mr. and Mrs. Darnell if they would like to play?"

Miss Knight turned her face toward Matthew. "Do you mind, Gregory? They're quite good."

He replied that he didn't mind at all, although he found himself greatly disappointed that Miss Burke had to leave. *She wouldn't give you a second thought if she knew what kind of person you are,* he reminded himself. *She's miles above your class, anyway.*

The domino game turned out to be more fun than he had thought it would be—in fact, more fun than he had had in a long time. Mr. Darnell was a crusty soul who reminded Matthew a bit of his father, and Mrs. Darnell showed the most skill at the game. She won easily, then told Matthew that "Miss Knight doesn't like us to hold back," as if she felt the need to explain.

"The challenge keeps my mind sharp," Miss Knight added. "And I do win on rare occasions. Shall we play again?"

Before anyone knew it, Bethina was in the doorway, announcing that supper was ready. "We've set another place for Mr. Gregory," she said to Miss Knight.

Matthew was on his feet at once. "Thank you, but I must be going. . . ."

He was outnumbered, though, and soon found himself following the two of them to the dining room.

~

Deborah lay across her bed, still absorbed in *Don Giovanni,* when a knock at the door caused her to jump to her feet.

"Oh, I'm sorry!" she said as Avis stuck her head through the doorway. "I forgot about supper. I'll go down right away."

"There's no hurry, miss," the maid assured her. She stepped into the room and closed the door behind her. "I'll help you change your frock if you like."

Deborah frowned down at the wrinkled skirt of her violet-gray challis gown. "I shouldn't keep Miss Knight waiting."

"You won't keep her waitin' long. Bethina fetched the missus and her nephew just a minute ago. They were caught up in a game of dominos and forgot, just like you did."

Deborah paused halfway across the room. "Mr. Woodruff is still here?"

A wry smile touched Avis's lips, and she hurried over to the armoire. "He's on his way down to the dining room now, I would imagine. I noticed quite a lovely frock the day I helped you unpack. Why don't we get you into it?" She opened the door and pulled out a gown of amethyst organdy.

*Why, she's matchmaking!* Deborah thought, incredulous. Still, her fingers flew along the length of buttons running down the front of her dress. Her suspicions about Avis were confirmed when, after she'd changed dresses, the maid looked at her and pursed her lips.

"Your fringe needs fluffin' up with the brush," she said, scooping up a brush from the dressing table. "Why don't you have a seat, and I'll be done quick as a wink."

Deborah obeyed. Not only did Avis rearrange the fringe upon her forehead, but she untied the ribbon at the nape of Deborah's neck and brushed her thick dark curls. "Now, I saw a comb in your jewelry box that would look better with your dress," the maid said, lifting the lid to the silver-filigree box on the table.

Finally Deborah could stand it no longer. "Avis, what are you doing?" she asked the maid's reflection in the mirror.

"Me?" The brush stopped moving in her hand. "Why, brushing your hair."

136

"Would you be doing that if Mr. Woodruff weren't down-stairs?"

"No, miss," was her matter-of-fact answer as she resumed work on Deborah's hair.

"Then why are you doing it now?"

Avis merely gave her an amused look.

Folding her arms in front of her, Deborah said, "You're doing this because of Mr. Woodruff, right?"

"Why, I suppose I am," the maid answered, as if the notion had never before occurred to her. She gave one final stroke of the brush and then stepped back to admire her handiwork. "Now, you look as lovely as a new calf. You'd best hurry on down to supper."

"Avis, I appreciate your watching out for me, but I want you to understand I didn't come to Cambridge looking for a beau."

"Of course you didn't, Miss Burke." The maid's gray-green eyes were smiling. "But you can't have enough friends now, can you? And Mr. Gregory is such good quality. Bethina is fond of the young man, and I know the missus dotes upon him. In fact, everyone in the house is impressed with his manners."

"Of course he's very pleasant, but . . ."

"We never know what the future's got waitin, do we?"

"Yes, but . . ."

"And surely it can't hurt to look your best at any time, can it?"

There was no time to argue. Besides, Deborah had to admit to herself that she rather liked the way she looked. *And it would be rude to go downstairs with wrinkled clothes,* she reminded her-self. She got up from the dressing bench and gave Avis a warn-ing look.

"I'm not going to go down there and flirt with Mr. Woodruff.

I appreciate how kind he is to his aunt, but as I said, I'm not looking for a beau."

"Of course you aren't, miss," Avis answered, that maddening smile still playing at her lips. "Now, you'd best be headin' downstairs so you won't keep them waiting."

Sure enough, Miss Knight was at her usual place at the head of the dining-room table, with her nephew adjacent to her on the opposite side. He stood when Deborah came into the room and took a step around the table to pull out her chair.

"Oh, please sit down," she said, reaching the chair and pulling it out before he could make his way to her. After seating herself, she turned to Miss Knight on her left. "I do apologize for being late. I lost track of the time."

The elderly woman smiled in her direction. "We only arrived ourselves a moment ago, dear. Isn't it wonderful that Gregory could join us?"

Deborah lowered her eyes to the place setting in front of her, then became irritated at her sudden bashfulness. *It's not his fault that Avis and Bethina have fanciful ideas,* she reminded herself, lifting her chin to smile at him. "I'm glad you were able to stay, Mr. Woodruff."

"Thank you, Miss Burke."

At the head of the table, Miss Knight shook her head. "Would you two mind doing an old woman a favor?"

"Of course not," Deborah and Mr. Woodruff replied at the same time.

Miss Knight sighed. "Forgive me for saying so, but I'm beginning to find it tedious to hear you young people address each other so formally. Now that you'll be spending Sunday afternoons together, why not use your given names?"

Deborah eyed her hostess suspiciously. Surely it had to be

a coincidence—Avis fussing over her appearance upstairs, and now this request. But there was nothing but innocence on Miss Knight's face as she sat there waiting for an answer.

"If I'm meddling too much . . . ," Miss Knight began, but Deborah reached over to pat her hand.

"Of course. It *is* silly to be so formal week after week." She smiled at the man across from her. "Isn't that so, Gregory?"

"I agree completely," he replied, but he had to swallow before adding, "Deborah."

"Now, see?" the old woman said, beaming. "I just know you two are going to become good friends."

"To friendship," Deborah said, lifting her water goblet. "Who won the dominos match?"

Gregory smiled, his blue eyes filled with quiet humor. "Mrs. Darnell, both times."

"One day I shall insist upon the blindfolds," Miss Knight said.

Bethina brought in a tureen of blue-and-white jasperware and dished out a clear chicken-and-leek soup to start the meal. "Missus?" she said when finished.

"Yes, Bethina?"

"It's the boy, Thomas. He's down in the servants' hall, worryin' over if he should have the trap ready after supper."

"Oh, dear. I didn't even think to send word to him that Gregory was staying."

"Mr. Darnell told him," Bethina reassured her.

"How good of him." Turning to her nephew with a worried expression, Miss Knight said, "I've never sent Thomas out after dark. Do you think he is too young to . . ."

Gregory touched her arm. "I'll walk up to Bridge Street and flag down a hansom. I don't think he should be out, either."

139

"Are you sure, dear? Because he could harness up the barouche and Mr. Darnell could accompany him for the ride back."

"That's too much trouble. It's only a short way to Bridge Street." He turned to Bethina, who was waiting just inside the door. "But please tell Thomas . . ."

He hesitated as his eyes met Deborah's. *What is wrong?* she wondered.

There was something familiar in his expression, something that she herself had felt before. Concern for the boy? *I'm not the only one who wonders about him,* she thought. *Does he know something that I don't?*

"Yes, Mr. Gregory?" Bethina asked at the door.

"Just thank him anyway for me, please."

After the three shared pleasant conversation over a main course of turbot with lobster, Miss Knight turned and said, "I wish you could stay for the rest of the evening, dear Gregory, but I shall worry if you're out looking for a hansom too late."

"They don't run all night, sir," added Bethina, who had come in with Gwen to clear the dishes. "One time my sister's boy, Eston, had to walk all the way from Sidgwick to Newmarket because he waited too long to flag a hansom. It took him two hours to get home."

Gregory smiled at her and pushed out his chair. "If you'll excuse me for leaving so soon after the meal . . ."

*If you don't ask him what he knows about Thomas now, you'll have to wait another week,* Deborah thought. Rising from her own chair, she said, "I'll walk you to the door, if you don't mind." She caught the look that Bethina and Gwen exchanged but ignored it.

"Of-of course not," Gregory stammered. He went around

140

the table to Miss Knight's chair, leaning down for a kiss on the cheek. "Good night, Aunt Helene."

"Good night, you dear boy," she told him, her face wreathed in smiles.

Once Avis was at Miss Knight's side, Gregory walked over to Deborah and offered his arm. She did not look at either maid as they walked out of the room.

The two walked down the hallway without speaking, passing the staircase and winding up in the entrance hall. "I would like to ask you about Thomas . . . the boy who drives you," Deborah said when she was sure they were out of earshot of any of the servants. "You seemed a bit worried about him earlier."

"Shall Mr. Darnell secure you a coach, sir?"

They both turned their heads to see Mrs. Darnell standing there with a derby and umbrella. Gregory thanked the house-keeper for his things and reassured her that he could find the cab on his own, then waited until she was gone to say to Deborah, "Would you mind if we talked about this outside? That is, if it's not too chilly for you."

"Why don't we see?"

He opened the door and ushered her out into the night air. The branches of the sycamores and elms lining the street hid most of the light of the stars and moon, but streetlamps along the walkway shed enough light for propriety's sake. Though the air felt heavy with humidity, it was comfortably cool after the arid heat of the dining-room fireplace.

"Would you like my coat?" Gregory offered.

"Thank you, but I'm fine," she told him. "I didn't feel I should ask you about Thomas in front of your aunt. I wouldn't want to worry her."

"That's a wise idea." He nodded appreciatively, and

Deborah wondered if all young men were as concerned about their loved ones as Gregory Woodruff.

"Thomas drives me back and forth to my lessons," Deborah went on. "Sometimes there is such a sadness about him—I assumed it was because he missed his mother. But then he assured me that he still sees his mother. When you seemed concerned about him in there, I wondered why."

"I don't know the boy well at all, Miss Burke . . . Deborah." He gave her a little smile. "It may take me a while to get used to using your first name."

"You don't mind, do you?"

"Oh, not at all," he said quickly. "I rather like it."

"So do I," she told him. "What about Thomas?"

He shrugged uncomfortably. "I don't know if it's my place to mention anything."

"So you've noticed something."

Hesitating for several seconds, he replied, "Something."

"Please tell me," she urged.

Again there was a silence, broken only by the hissing of the streetlamps and the ringing of a set of hooves upon the cobblestones. Gregory motioned toward the steps. "Why don't we sit?"

"But your carriage . . ."

"Please . . . not *you* as well," he groaned, which made her laugh.

"No one wants you to have to walk home," she told him, still smiling. "That's why everyone is rushing you."

"Well, that's exactly what I plan to do," he replied with a smile. "It's good exercise, and I've a good umbrella if it happens to rain."

*He has such a nice smile,* Deborah thought, then forced her mind to return to the subject at hand. *Ask him what you came to ask,* she told herself as they sat down on the top step. *He probably has to study, and you're wasting his time.*

"Regarding Thomas again," she said, gathering the skirt of her dress behind her knees. "Would you mind telling me what you've noticed?"

He stared ahead at a streetlamp. "All I feel at liberty to tell you is that it appears the boy might be in some kind of trouble."

"Trouble?"

"It seems he doesn't want anyone who lives here to know about it. And it doesn't sound good."

"What can I do to help him?"

After a thoughtful silence he said, "I suppose you should just be kind to him. Show him that you're willing to listen if he's ever willing to confide in you. Trying to force him to confide in you may work the opposite way . . . which is likely why he would barely talk to me this afternoon."

Deborah sighed. "I'll do my best."

"But don't be hurt if you make no progress," he warned. "I believe the only reason he mentioned anything to me is that I'm not connected to the household."

"But you *are* connected. You're Miss Knight's nephew."

"Yes," he said quickly. "I mean . . . I don't live here."

Deborah nodded. "I'm sorry for Mr. Henry—he's the coachman here whose toe was broken—but it's good that Thomas has to drive you on Sundays. Perhaps he just needs to get used to you."

"Perhaps so."

Suddenly she realized that she was keeping him from going back to Pembroke. Gentleman that he was, he wouldn't leave her sitting there alone. She reached for the wrought-iron railing beside her, but he was immediately on his feet and extending a hand.

"Please allow me," he said, and helped her to her feet. He did not look her in the eyes as he did so and let go of her hand as soon as she was standing under the portico.

How curious it was that he seemed to be stricken with bashfulness in her presence. Her self-inflicted discipline of practice and schooling had not allowed much time for socializing with young men in the past. Somehow she had naively assumed that men never battled the occasional bouts of timidity that some women suffered.

"I do appreciate your speaking with me about Thomas," she told him.

At last his eyes met hers. "It's good of you to be concerned. Not many people would take the time to worry over a servant boy."

"Well, my family has always had a heart for servants. My mother was a maid-of-all-work before she married my father."

"I didn't know that," Gregory said, his expression surprised. "I would be interested in hearing how that happened."

Deborah smiled and looked out at the dark street. "It's a very long story. I'll have to tell it to you when you're not pressed for time."

He looked strangely reluctant to leave. "I have the time right now. That is, if you have."

"Are you jesting? I'll make time to talk about my family if you like. But we should sit down again." She settled back onto the steps, making sure that the hem of her dress covered her ankles. "My mother was taken in at thirteen by a couple whose occupations were extortion and blackmail. . . ."

"Blackmail?"

"One was a murderer as well." She went on with the story of how her mother, Rachel, had escaped that sordid life and ended up as an artist married to Adam Burke. When Deborah finished some twenty minutes later, Gregory shook his head.

"She must be an incredible person."

"Of course I think so." She smiled. "And what about your parents?"

"My mother is a good woman, just like Aunt Helene," he answered, then held out his hand to help her to her feet again. "I should be on my way now. I hope you have a good week."

"And you as well," she replied, startled at the warmth that came out in her own voice. He seemed just as surprised as she and glanced away.

"Good evening, Deborah."

"Good evening."

He walked down the steps, but at the bottom he turned back around and looked up at her. There was an air of expectancy about his posture, and Deborah wondered if he had thought of something else to say. "Gregory?" she asked.

Lifting the handle of his umbrella to point at the door, he said, "You shouldn't be standing out here alone after dark."

"Of course." She gave him an appreciative smile, but for some reason that she couldn't fathom, she felt strangely disappointed.

~

The tenements grew shabbier and shabbier as Matthew walked east down Market Street toward Hobson Lane—still, his neighborhood was clean compared to the squalor of the slums directly north of him. The fine mist that had started five

minutes ago turned to a light rain, and he opened his umbrella to keep from ruining his coat and hat.

*You're insane to keep doing this!* he thought. Then he recalled
how lovely Deborah had looked, standing there at the top
of the stairs. It was fortunate she hadn't been able to read his
mind as he stared up at her, for he had briefly imagined what
it would have been like to bound up the stairs like some mad-
man, take her in his arms, and kiss her.

# 10

THE remainder of October slipped away like steam from a kettle. Since that day when Signora Pella had taken Deborah upstairs and shown her the newspaper column, her practices became longer and even more intense. But she was beginning to develop a confidence in her technique that she hadn't even been aware she was lacking. Even Signora Pella, still as demanding as ever, now gave her more and more words of approval.

For all the time she spent at the estate, however, she had only seen Lord Raleigh once. He came into the music room one day to bid his wife farewell, and from the gist of their brief conversation, Deborah gathered that he was leaving for London to participate in a series of meetings with other members of Parliament.

He was older than Deborah would have imagined him to be, but in his frock coat, top hat, and gloves, he cut a digni-fied figure. After a brush of his lips upon Signora Pella's hand and a quick bow over Deborah's, he headed for the door again. Signora Pella seemed to take this in stride, for her fin-gers immediately resumed the scales before her husband had even made it out of the room. So different from her parents' marriage, Deborah had mused, and rather sad—though the two of them didn't seem to mind.

As willing as she was to put herself through the rigors of her training, Deborah found herself looking forward to Sundays. For one thing, she found the worship services uplifting and encouraging. Now that she was used to the ceremony of the chapel worship services, which were more formal than the Methodist church her family attended in London, she discovered she could experience the same quiet communion with God as before.

Thomas was not driving anymore and had started going back to church with his mother a week ago. Mr. Henry, who still hobbled about with a cane, had endured enough of his enforced rest and resumed his duties as liveryman. She saw little of the boy now and had begun to wonder if he were avoiding her. The few times she did see him, he was polite but hurried, avoiding any personal questions.

Deborah had finally taken her concerns about Thomas to Mrs. Darnell, who called the boy in and spoke with him at length. Later, she told Deborah that the boy denied that anything was wrong. "Boys get a bit out of sorts when they get that age," she said. "I don't think there's anything to worry about."

And now that Gregory was being driven on Sundays by Mr. Henry, he had no clue either as to whatever Thomas's trouble was. *"We've both offered our help,"* Gregory had reminded her. *"Hopefully he'll remember that if he ever gets into serious trouble."*

A second reason for Deborah's impatience for Sundays to roll around were the afternoons spent in the drawing room. As much as she loved her music, she found it refreshing to relax and take her mind off opera for a while. Miss Knight and her nephew were pleasant company, and it was good to have someone with whom to converse after a week of no-nonsense instruction from Signora Pella. Sometimes they would play dominos, sometimes just talk, but always Gregory would read aloud from *Treasure Island*.

"I believe he finds as much pleasure in the reading as Miss Knight and I do from the listening," she wrote to her family.

"Every so often he will glance over at his aunt to see if she is enjoying the story. Whenever he reads the part of Long John Silver, he does so in a gruff voice that always makes her smile."

After Avis and Bethina had continued to make pointed remarks about what a good beau Mr. Woodruff would make for some young woman, Deborah had been forced to confront the two maids and demand that they give up all notions of matchmaking "We're friends . . . nothing more," she told them. "Can't a woman enjoy a man's company without talk of beaus and romance?"

To her relief, Avis had shrugged and replied, "All right, miss. But don't be blamin' me if you find out later you've missed out."

"I won't blame you," Deborah told her.

"I have a sister, Trudy, who was too picky, too," Bethina warned. "She ended up marryin' a poor tallow-chandler in Hereford when she was forty years old, just so's she wouldn't be alone."

"I'll stay away from tallow-chandlers," had been Deborah's reply.

~

On a Wednesday, the last day in October, Deborah had been at Signora Pella's for less than an hour when the butler walked into the music room and stood just inside the doorway.

The diva motioned for Deborah to finish the aria she had been instructed to sing, then turned impatiently. "Yes, Merrit?"

"A Madame Gauthier requests to see you, your ladyship," he said, advancing with a card extended in his gloved hand. "Shall I have her wait in the drawing room?"

As soon as the name was mentioned, Signora Pella paled. She ignored the card and got up from the piano. "No, bring her in here. And send for tea." When he had given a courtly nod and was gone from the room, Signora Pella turned to Deborah and said in a caustic tone, "He knows very well who she is. My husband's servants find it amusing to play childish games with me. It would serve them right if I discharged every one of them and started again with new ones."

"Should I leave?" Deborah asked, glancing at the door.

"Leave?" An expression of something akin to fear washed over the diva's face. "No . . . please stay." She walked over to stand next to the settee, motioning for Deborah to take one of the adjacent upholstered chairs. Merrit came back through the door a minute later, accompanied by a petite, well-dressed woman and two delicate-looking boys of about four years of age—twins, dressed identically in navy cheviot suits.

"Mamma," the woman said, her brown silks rustling as she crossed the room to give Signora Pella a quick embrace. She bore a striking resemblance to the diva, save the auburn tint to her dark hair.

"Felicienne." The diva smiled and turned to look at the boys, who stood together just inside the doorway, holding hands in a pose that seemed strangely familiar to Deborah. "How precious!"

The woman turned to smile proudly at them. "Merle . . . Julian . . . come over and meet your grandmamma."

They stopped eyeing the room and walked closer, bringing another smile to Signora Pella's face. "So precious," she cooed, yet made no move to draw closer to them. "You have grown so much since your christening."

"Thank your grandmamma," Madame Gauthier instructed gently, and they complied in unison.

"Such obedient children!" Signora Pella turned back to her daughter. "Your husband is with you?"

"Oram went on into the city to telegraph Lord Prescott. Hunting season, you know. We're to stay a fortnight there."

"Surely ones so young will not be following the foxes!"

Madame Gauthier smiled at the shock upon her mother's face. "Of course not. But it's time they learned about what goes on, Oram says."

With each passing moment Deborah felt like an intruder upon this reunion. In everything she'd ever read about Signora Pella's life, she had never heard any mention of a daughter. And it had obviously been years since they'd seen each other. Should she assume that Signora Pella had changed her mind about her staying and unobtrusively take her leave?

Just then the signora turned to her. "This is Miss Burke . . . my student."

The look the woman gave Deborah was one of surprise but not unfriendliness. "So, you are giving lessons?" she said to her mother.

"Only to Miss Burke. Others have asked, but I've neither the time nor the patience for more than one."

Deborah stepped forward, leaning slightly over the tea table to offer Madame Gauthier her hand. "Your boys are so well behaved."

Madame Gauthier glanced at the children and then smiled at

Deborah. "Thank you, but at the moment they're quite overwhelmed by the new surroundings. I brought their nanny
along . . . just in case."

Two maids arrived with trays, and Signora Pella motioned
everyone to the settee and chairs. "The boys must sit by their
grandmamma," she said, taking a place in the middle of the
settee. Coaxed by their mother, they walked over to sit on
opposite sides of the diva. Deborah took her cup of water and
lemon from the maid and watched as Signora Pella helped her
grandsons manage their cups of milk and plates of biscuits.

"You have been taking lessons for long?" Madame Gauthier
asked from her chair, studying Deborah over the rim of the
teacup.

"For the past month," Deborah replied. Then suddenly
she realized that the trial period had passed without the diva
mentioning anything about the lessons not continuing.
Although it came as no surprise because her lessons were
going so well, it was still a relief. "Do you live in England?"

Madame Gauthier shook her head. "Paris . . . where I was
raised. But my husband is half English. And you?"

"London. My family still lives there."

"You are not married, then?"

"No, I'm not."

"Miss Burke is married to the opera at present," Signora
Pella said from the settee. "There will be time for other things
later."

Madame Gauthier looked over at her mother and opened
her mouth but then, seeming to reconsider whatever she
had been about to say, pressed her lips together again. After
another sip of tea she said to Deborah, "You must forgive my

bold questions. My father says I have always had an inquisitive nature."

Deborah smiled back. "My father tells me the same thing. In fact, I'm bursting to ask you something about your sons."

"You are wishing to know how I tell them apart, yes?"

"You must have been asked that before."

"Many times." She gave a little shrug. "It's an understandable question. So many people have never seen identical twins."

"Actually, I'm one of those people," Deborah confessed.

"Yes? Well, to answer your question . . . a mother knows. The shape of Merle's face is different from his brother's. And Julian has a birthmark on his right shoulder."

Deborah shook her head. "Amazing."

"You should have seen my sister and me," Madame Gauthier went on. "Noelle was her name. We kept the servants in a constant state of confusion, we were so alike. And we were naughty enough to play tricks upon them."

"You are a twin as well?"

"I *was,*" she corrected, a sadness washing over her face. "It often runs in families, you know. Unfortunately, my sister died of scarlet fever when she was ten years old."

"I'm so sorry," Deborah breathed, unable even to imagine how she would have felt had one of her sisters died. *The photograph in the album,* she thought. *That had to be her and her sister.* She recalled how the two girls in sailor clothes had looked so dependent upon each other. Even now, it seemed that Madame Gauthier's hurt was still raw.

"Thank you," Madame Gauthier said softly. "She died in my father's arms."

A terrible sigh came from Signora Pella's direction, and

Deborah shifted her gaze over to the settee. The diva had stopped fussing over the two boys and was looking at her daughter, her gray eyes dull with the memory.

"It was a terrible thing to happen, and it took me years to get over it," she murmured.

"But still you were able to sing, weren't you?"

Signora Pella's lips parted in surprise. "You have no idea how I *grieved* for her."

"No doubt it helped your dramatic parts on the stage." Though her voice was kept low, no doubt for the children's sake, Madame Gauthier's tone was now laced with undisguised sarcasm. "Why allow such a sorrow to go to waste, yes?"

The diva's nostrils flared. "What would you have had me do? Giving up the opera would not have brought her back!"

"Of course it wouldn't have. Besides, you never had her in the first place. How many times did you visit us, Mamma? Three? Four?"

"How can you say such things to me?" Signora Pella gasped, two crimson spots flaming upon her cheeks. The twins stared up at her with uncertain faces, the one on the left looking as if he would burst into tears any minute. Seemingly oblivious to anyone's presence but her daughter's, Signora Pella held a hand to her throat and said, "Your father was penniless when I married him, Felicienne—gaming debts had left him with nothing but his title. My career gave you everything that most people only dream of having! Things *I* grew up without! Schools . . . clothing . . . servants . . . you had it all!"

"Yes, I had it all," Madame Gauthier answered in a voice full of irony. "By the way, Mamma," she said, "everyone else calls me Lecie. Noelle gave me that nickname when we were tots, and no one else has called me anything else since. No one who has been with me long enough to know that, of course."

Signora Pella's face went white as tallow as the two stared across at each other. When one of the children began to whimper, Deborah got to her feet and walked around the settee over to the other side.

"Why don't we find our coats and take a walk?" she whispered, stooping down to offer her hand to the one who was upset. He looked at his mother and began to wail, and Madame Gauthier rose from her chair.

"Thank you, but that is not necessary," she said, touching Deborah's shoulder. She opened her arms to both sons, then knelt down to embrace them. "It's all right," she soothed, pressing their heads against her shoulders. "Mamma and Grandmamma had a disagreement, that's all."

Signora Pella stared down at her family, her face still ashen. "You are staying the night?" she asked in a small voice.

Madame Gauthier seemed to struggle with a response for a second, then shook her head over her whimpering son's shoulder. "I think it would be better if we stayed in Cambridge."

The diva opened her mouth, closed it again, and nodded. "Perhaps you will come through again on your way home?"

"Perhaps," she answered, but to Deborah the tone sounded doubtful.

In the quiet that ensued, Madame Gauthier brought her sons back to her chair with her and sat down, and Signora Pella sank back into the cushions of the settee. She turned to give Deborah, who was still standing awkwardly at the end of the settee, a weak smile. "Please, have a seat again, Miss Burke. We will resume our lesson later."

Wishing she were anywhere but in this room, Deborah

obeyed. How could this woman even think of a singing lesson, when her daughter would soon be walking out of her life again?

"Your father is well?" Signora Pella asked Madame Gauthier presently.

"Quite well. He spends most of his time with his vineyard."

"That is good."

*Small talk,* Deborah thought. *Safe and unemotional. Anything to keep from sitting there and trying not to look at each other while they wait for Madame Gauthier's husband to return.*

Ten minutes of this passed, with the pauses between their sentences growing longer and longer, until finally the butler announced Mr. Gauthier. He was a fair-haired man with a well-trimmed beard, who swept into the room and gathered his family, pausing only long enough to brush a dispassionate kiss on Signora Pella's cheek.

In the hurry to leave, Madame Gauthier did not introduce her husband to Deborah but turned just inside the doorway to say, "It was good to make your acquaintance, Miss Burke." She then turned her face to Signora Pella. "Good-bye, Mamma."

Signora Pella lifted a hand in farewell and opened her mouth, but no sound came out. *Go after them!* Deborah urged under her breath, her stomach in knots from the tragedy of it all.

The diva did not follow, but after several seconds she turned to look at Deborah. Her eyes were shining with unshed tears, her expression grim. "Shall we resume our lesson, Miss Burke?" At the piano, Signora Pella hit middle C, beginning the aria again, and Deborah obediently began to sing. After only five or six notes, the piano went silent.

"Your voice is flat," the diva said, staring up at her. "Why is that?"

Deborah swallowed around the huge lump in her throat. "I just wish that . . ."

"Are you going to lecture me on how to be a good mother, Miss Burke? or perhaps about God again? No doubt there is *much* someone so young as you can teach me." Before Deborah could even frame an answer, Signora Pella closed the lid over the keys.

"Leave now, Miss Burke. Come back when you are serious about singing."

~

"I don't think I've ever fully appreciated you until this day," Deborah wrote to her mother that night. "Your art is so important to you, yet your family has always mattered more than anything. I recall how we demanded so much of your time when we were small, and you freely gave it. Surely there were times when you felt frustrated at not being able to paint as much as you would have liked."

She stopped writing and chewed on the end of her pen. Painting was just as demanding an art as opera. Why had Signora Pella allowed her art to consume everything else in her life, and Mother had not?

Deborah thought about her own passion for music, her longing to walk in the footprints of past prima donnas. Was there a danger of becoming just like Signora Pella? Such a thought was a horror to her now, at nineteen. But as her ambition grew, would she find herself discarding the things that were most important, a little at a time—as one tosses away worn clothing?

*Lord, please give me the wisdom never to allow that to happen,* she

157

prayed. *Help me always to recognize and appreciate the important things in life, even if they have nothing to do with music.*

~

"Oh, Mr. Phelps, dear . . . ," Mrs. Cornell's voice cooed from the top of the staircase, just as Matthew was hanging his hat and muffler on the brass stand near the front lobby. "Would you be so kind as to help me this morning?"

Matthew cringed inside but gave a brief bow to the woman clumping down the staircase. She was wearing a wrapper of claret red with huge white spots and a scarf over her curling papers—and, as usual, Royce lumbered along behind her.

"What may I do for you, Mrs. Cornell?" he asked respectfully.

"Latimer's gout is giving him grief this morning, and I don't think I should demand that he walk Royce," she replied. Latimer was the Cornells' butler, who seemed to have a very convenient case of the gout, for Matthew had often seen other servants pressed into Royce's service. He eyed the dog, who responded by baring his teeth. Never had *he* been asked, though.

"Mrs. Cornell," he began with utmost tact, "today is the first of the month. Students from the university will be in for their allowances all day. I really should prepare the ledger before the office opens."

"Oh, Royce will have you back in time for all of that," the woman said, smiling indulgently. She gave her pet a scratch between the ears and an admonishment to "be nice to Mr. Phelps," then straightened and handed Matthew the leash.

"Latimer usually walks him down to Benet Street and up

the loop. Now, don't allow him to get too winded, dear. He's not as young as he used to be."

*Nor am I,* Matthew thought, but could do nothing but nod. He took a step toward the hat rack, but the dog sat on the floor and would not budge.

"Come on, old fellow," Matthew coaxed.

"He only likes to be called by his name," said Mrs. Cornell, leaning down to shake a finger at the dog. She raised her voice to the pitch of a three-year-old and said, "Royce, you have to go with the nice Mr. Phelps. Mother will become very angry if you don't."

Royce, after giving Matthew a malevolent look, finally got to his stubby legs, stretched, and took a step. Once he got moving, he started trotting for the door and gave a low growl when he had to wait for Matthew to put his hat back on and wrap his muffler around his neck.

King's Parade was busy with vehicles in spite of the early hour. Butchers' traps rattled by with their quick little ponies. Dray horses pulled yellow milk carts that looked like Roman chariots with big brass churns of milk clanking in back. Shire horses with fetlocks plodded in front of great corn wagons in from the country. Across the street to his right, undergraduates in their Norfolk jackets and dons with the wind in their gowns headed for lectures at King's College.

As he followed the dog from lamppost to lamppost, Matthew found himself wondering if Deborah were awake yet. She had told him that she practiced both mornings and evenings. Was she singing at this very moment?

While he knew practically nothing about opera, he had once taken William to a traveling production company's performance of *The Mikado* at the guildhall, and they had both enjoyed it. Perhaps one day Deborah would be performing there. *If she ever does, I'll buy a front-row seat, no matter how much it costs,* he thought, then immediately realized the impossibility of such a dream. Deborah would look down from the stage, see the look of adoration on his face, and know how smitten he was with her. Better to skulk in a dark gallery seat, where feelings could easily be hidden.

The month of October had been the most wonderful, horrible time in his life, his visits to Park Parade both tortuous and blissful. Miss Knight's care for his well-being filled some space inside that had been empty since his mother's death. And Deborah's rich laugh could make him smile anytime, no matter how dark his thoughts. Her beauty and intelligence—even her wit—were so compelling that it was all Matthew could do to keep from staring at her during his Sunday visits.

Just ahead on the left, a beggar sat in front of the alley between two buildings, his ragged legs splayed in front of him. Matthew had seen him many times before and knew that he slept in a piano crate inside the alley. A distasteful stench of body odor and old gin wafted toward Matthew, and he gave a tug on the dog's leash to move closer to the street. Royce would not yield to the pressure of the leash, however, and pulled his way to the alley to investigate. The beggar's mouth stretched into a cavernous smile. "Nice doggy," he slurred, extending a shaky hand.

Royce froze, lowered his jaw as if poised to attack, and let out a low rumbling in his throat. "Royce! No!" Matthew exclaimed, this time giving a great heave on the leash. The dog turned to glower at him but obeyed and trotted over to the other side of the walkway.

"Sorry, old chap," Matthew told the beggar, tossing over a

loose shilling he'd dug from his coat pocket. Breathing easier, he continued the walk but kept a closer eye on Royce.

*You were an idiot to become infatuated like some schoolboy,* he told himself as his thoughts returned to Deborah. *Nothing can come of it.* He could not continue playing the part of Gregory Woodruff forever. And if she ever found out that he had deceived her, she would hate him. And rightly so.

Late that afternoon, just before it was time to close the office, the real Gregory Woodruff came in to collect his allowance. He wasn't alone but had a buxom woman on his arm. Her cheeks were caked with rouge, and she giggled almost incessantly.

"My father wrote to tell me that he sent a letter to Mr. Cornell raising my allowance to ten quid," the man said.

Matthew nodded and took the cash box key from his waistcoat pocket. "We received the letter."

When it came time for Mr. Woodruff to hand Matthew his payment for the Sunday visits, he beamed and said, "My father is delighted over the attention I'm giving my Aunt Helene. You're doing a splendid job, my good man. I should have hired you to go to my lectures at Pembroke as well."

"I'm not your good man," Matthew replied as he pocketed the notes.

"My . . . touchy, aren't we?" Mr. Woodruff mocked, lifting his chin in a priggish manner toward the woman on his arm. She burst into a fresh spate of giggles. "Well, keep it up any-way. I'll see you next month."

~

"I am expecting a guest this weekend," Signora Pella said, rising from the piano bench after Friday's lesson. "So we will resume on Monday. But I would like you to practice twice as long tomorrow to make up for the lost day."

For a fleeting second, Deborah's spirits lifted in the hopes that Signora Pella and her daughter and grandchildren would be spending time together after all. *But she said "guest,"* Deborah reminded herself right away. One person. And besides, Madame Gauthier and her family were likely on their way to Lord Prescott's at this time—wherever that happened to be.

How strange that after Wednesday's emotional scene, practice had resumed as usual the next day. Had years of keeping her emotions under tight rein given Signora Pella the ability to turn them on and off at will?

Deborah realized suddenly that her tutor was frowning at her.

"Woolgathering is an unproductive use of time," Signora Pella said sternly.

"Ah . . . yes," Deborah answered. "I'm sorry. And I'll practice twice as hard tomorrow."

# 11

SUNDAY morning Thomas had to pound on the door to his mother's tenement for several minutes before a bleary-eyed Orville finally answered.

"What d' you want, brat?" the man let out with a belch of sour breath.

"It's Sunday."

Orville scratched the stubble on his face. "Oh . . . Sunday."

"How is Mother?" Thomas asked, pushing his way past the man in the doorway. But Orville's hand snaked out and grabbed the boy's arm with a surprisingly firm grip.

"Let's see what you got first."

Thomas opened his coat and took out a miniature china clock. It was trimmed in gold and could be wound with a key on the back. As it had for the past three weeks, the delight on Orville's face made Thomas think of the sorrow that would be on Miss Knight's when she discovered that some of her keepsakes had been stolen.

Again he started for the back room.

"Wait . . . I got to talk wi' you."

"What about?"

"Yer mum. She ain't here."

Thomas jerked away and ran to the open doorway. The bed was rumpled but empty. "Where is she?"

"She's in a sanatorium, brat. That's what we planned on, didn't we?"

"Why didn't you tell me?"

"Oh, that would ha' been a pretty picture, me showin' up at yer nice lady's house."

"Well, where is she?"

Orville licked his snuff-stained lips and glanced away for a second. "Northampton."

"Northampton? Why so far?"

"She needed to be in a good 'un. I hear this place is the best. And after I wired them, they sent one o' them fancy coaches to fetch her."

"But I can't go see her in Northampton!" Thomas cried.

Taking a step closer, Orville said, "Well, what's more important, brat? Yer gettin' to see her, or her gettin' well?"

"I—" Thomas hung his head. He was ashamed to admit it, but Orville was right.

"Besides," Orville went on, "they won't allow her to have visits just yet, or I'd be there wi' her meself." A note of warning crept into his wheezy voice. "But they won't keep her in there when the money runs out. Just 'cause she ain't here don't mean you get to stop yer Sunday visits."

His heart was a lump in his chest, but Thomas nodded. He turned to stare at the bed again, as if by sheer will he could make his mother materialize there. Out of nowhere a horrid thought popped into his head. *She's dead.*

He swallowed and looked up at Orville again. "What's the name of the sanatorium?"

"The name?" Orville shrugged. "I never went to school like *some* people. Don't recall the name."

"Then how did you know about the place?"

Orville's yellowed eyes narrowed. "Somebody told me about it. I got friends, y'know. I sent a wire, and they came out with the coach, like I said." Taking a step closer, he reached into his wrinkled trousers for his pocketknife, flipped it open, and began picking his teeth. "You're beginning to bore me, brat. Get on out of my way."

Thomas walked all the way back to Chesterton Lane with his head lowered and his hands in his pockets. Miss Knight and the rest of the household were still at church—where he was supposed to be, with Mother.

He hadn't set out to deceive Mrs. Darnell last year when he was hired as a gardener's assistant to Mr. Darnell. But when the housekeeper had told him, "You'll have every Tuesday afternoon off," she had added, "Sunday mornings, too, so you can go to church. You're welcome to come with any of us if you like."

How could he admit that he had never even seen the inside of a church, when it was obviously so important to this household? He needed this job with its more than decent salary. So he gave Mrs. Darnell a casual nod and said, "I go with my mother," figuring that would be the end of it.

He hadn't stopped to consider that he was then trapped in his lie and would have to stay away from the house on Sunday mornings, whether or not his mother was able to receive his visits. On the days he couldn't visit with Mother, he usually walked over to the Backs and sat on the bank to watch the punts glide by on the river Cam, or spent twopence on a horse-drawn bus over to the railway station to watch the trains arrive and leave.

Today, however, he stood outside on the terrace thinking that the house had never looked so empty as it did now. Surely Orville had been telling the truth. As corrupt as the man was, he seemed to care *something* about Mother. And surely no human could be capable of so horrible a lie with so casual an attitude.

The thoughts whirling around his head were too much for Thomas. Even though it was midmorning, he longed for the oblivion of sleep. He climbed the narrow staircase leading to his room above the stables. There had to be some way of finding out if Orville had told him the truth. As much as he didn't want to hear that his mother was dead, he still had to know.

*O God, please help me,* he prayed for the second time in his life.

~

"'If we had been allowed to sit idle, we should all have fallen in the blues, but Captain Smollett was never the man for that. All hands were called up before him, and he divided us into watches. . . .'"

"Gregory," Deborah whispered, leaning forward in her chair. He stopped reading, lowered his book, and looked at her. Deborah pointed at Miss Knight, whose white head rested against the side of her chair, her mouth slightly open.

"Asleep," she mouthed, and he nodded.

"What should we do?" he whispered back.

She slipped out of her chair and pointed toward the door. "Bethina." Motioning that Gregory should stay with his aunt, Deborah stepped into the hallway. She knew that Bethina, ever protective of her mistress, would be somewhere on the same floor. She found the maid in the adjoining anteroom, a basket of knitting on her lap.

"Should I carry her up to her room?" Gregory whispered when Deborah and Bethina walked into the drawing room together.

The maid shook her head. "She might wake up. I'll sit here with her." She shooed them out of the room. "The weather's warmed up a bit since yesterday. Don't even need your cloak, I expect. Why don't you two sit in the garden for a spell?"

Turning to Gregory, who stood beside her in the hallway, Deborah said, "Would you like to do that?"

His blue eyes lit up. "Would you?"

Deborah nodded, and while he waited in the hallway, she ran upstairs for a wrap. Impulsively she grabbed Laurel's green one—her sister would love hearing that she had worn it while sitting with a young man in the garden.

~

In the drawing room, Helene Knight eased her ear away from the side wing of her chair. "Bethina?" she murmured.

"I'm here, missus," the maid answered.

"Are they gone?"

"I sent them out to the garden."

Helene smiled. It had been obvious from the sound of their voices that the two young people had become interested in each other. But she was just as certain that they wouldn't consider leaving her out of their Sunday afternoons.

*You should have been an actress,* she told herself. It had been so easy. She had almost ruined the whole plan, though, for she had felt tears welling up in her eyes when she heard her

nephew offer to carry her up to her room. *He's such a considerate young man . . . and she has a lovely character. It would be nice
to have her in the family.*

~

Deborah and Gregory sat in a swing hung between posts in
the center of the small garden. The weather was cool and clear
and Deborah drew her wrap closer about her arms as a breeze
stirred the fringe upon her forehead.

"I don't know if my voice has gotten any better," she said
in answer to his question about her lessons, "or if spending
time in such intense study has simply given me a confidence
that shows when I sing."

"I would like to hear you sing," he told her.

"I'm always happy for an opportunity to show off. Next
Sunday, if you're still willing to subject yourself to a performance."

Gregory smiled. "Gladly." A self-conscience silence eased its
way between them, and Deborah stared at a viburnum shrub
off to their right. Its scarlet, russet, and yellow foliage ran
together like the colors of an Oriental screen. After a while
Gregory broke the silence. "What is Lady Raleigh like?"

"Well, for one thing . . . she doesn't care for that title."

"She's called Clarisse Pella at home, too?"

Deborah nodded. "She's an incredibly demanding teacher,
but that's what I wanted when I came here."

"So you plan to stay for a while."

"As long as she's willing to teach me. Of course, there will
come a point when I'll have to start trying out for parts on
stage."

"Of course," he agreed. "It always puzzles me to hear of

people who have spent most of their adult lives accumulating degrees but still balk at going out into the real world to apply their studies."

"I don't think Signora Pella would allow that to happen, even if I were so inclined. She speaks often about my making a mark upon the stage."

"How encouraging that must be to you."

"Yes."

He must have caught the note of uncertainty in her voice. "You aren't sure?"

"No . . ." She hesitated and searched for words to explain what had only been a vague, unsettling feeling before. "I'm grateful to Signora Pella for pushing me so hard, and when she speaks of the fame and greatness out there for me, I must confess I get very excited."

"Then why do you have doubts?"

"I wonder if the price of success will be too dear for me." She turned toward Gregory. "I don't want to wake up one day and find that I've traded the things that matter for fame upon the stage."

Suddenly Deborah realized she had her hand on his sleeve, and she quickly moved it away. "Excuse me."

"I didn't mind," he said, then cleared his throat. "What has Signora Pella given up?"

Deborah found herself telling him about the reunion the diva had had with her daughter. "It was as if they were nearly strangers to each other. Worse than strangers, for there was still a bond of love there that had been damaged too many times."

"I've seen that before," Gregory said, his face sad. "Family is so important. Yet so many people take theirs for granted."

"But how do they become that way, Gregory? Do you

think that some people are born with a lesser capacity for love? Or could *anyone* end up like my tutor—myself included?"

~

Matthew felt torn between being touched that she would ask his opinion and being painfully aware of his own inadequacy. He spent his weekdays filling out ledgers and filing legal documents and his Sundays pretending to be someone else. What did he know about the world in which she lived? And certainly he was the least qualified to give her advice on matters of conscience.

*But you know about family,* a voice inside him said. "I don't claim to know everything," he finally told her, "but I don't believe anyone is born with a lesser capacity to love."

"Then people like Signora Pella are made."

"I believe so. A little at a time, by almost imperceptible degrees. I'm sure her earliest goals were not to become a neglectful mother and have a loveless marriage."

"Then how can I be sure I won't become like her one day?"

The analytical part of his mind, the part that found the study of engineering so fascinating, came into action. "I would suggest that you plan ahead *now,* while your career is still at the early stage."

"I like that." She nodded. "So I should set a goal not to neglect the things that are most important."

"Well, I would suggest a different tack," he answered gently, lest he sound condescending. "I have always believed that positive goals are more effective than negative ones."

"What do you mean?"

He thought for a few seconds and then answered, "Suppose two equally skilled chess players are sitting down at the board.

One is telling himself over and over, *I'm not going to lose this match!* Meanwhile, his opponent is thinking, *I'm going to win this match.* Which do you think has a better chance of winning?"

"The second, of course." Admiration shone in Deborah's green eyes that would have overjoyed him had he deserved it. "Very good analogy, Gregory. And so my goals should be positive as well."

"They would be easier to remember." He got up from the swing and walked over to a nearby azalea bush. After taking one of the small, brownish-green leaves, he moved over to a circle of gravel surrounding the birdbath in the center in the garden and picked up a handful of large pebbles.

"I've always enjoyed visual aids," he explained self-consciously as he sat down next to Deborah again. "Hold out your palm, like this." When she did so, he placed the azalea leaf on her palm. "This is your career as an opera singer. You've the talent for it, you've trained for it for years, and it's important to you. But is there anything else that is more important?"

"God is," she replied without hesitation. "My salvation . . . my spiritual walk."

Her answer pricked Matthew's conscience. There had once been a time when he might have answered the same way. "And if you had to choose between God or opera . . . ?"

"I would choose God." She averted her eyes. "I hope you don't think I'm trying to sound pious. I'm not nearly as mature a Christian as I would wish to be. But God has been part of my home since my earliest memories, and I cannot imagine a life that ignores him."

Matthew took one of the pebbles from his other hand and

171

held it up. "This will represent God, then, and your spiritual life." Placing it upon the leaf in her palm, he asked, "And is there anything else more important to you than opera?"

"My family." Again without hesitation. "I can't imagine life without my parents and sisters."

"Again, if you had to choose . . . ?"

"My family is more important."

He placed the second pebble upon the leaf. "Is there anything else?"

After a thoughtful silence, she looked down at the pebbles and leaf and said, "There isn't now, I don't think. But shouldn't I include things that will be important to me in the future, like a husband and children?"

"That's a very good idea," he said, ignoring the heaviness in his heart at the reminder that her future wouldn't include him. "And *before* you even marry, so that your goals will be established by the time they come along." He held up a third pebble. "Your future family."

After he'd set that pebble on the leaf, he carefully took her wrist and held her hand out in front of her. "We've a good breeze about, but it's not blowing the leaf away. Why is that?"

"Well, because of the pebbles."

He nodded. "Now, indulge me if this sounds silly, but let's say the breeze represents the pressure that will surely come as your career flourishes."

"Pressure?"

"You know, pressure to make decisions based solely upon what is good for your career. If you stay determined to keep opera in its proper place, anchored down by the things that matter most to you, there is no danger of becoming like Signora Pella."

Staring thoughtfully at her hand, Deborah said, "The pebbles keep the leaf from flying away, yet they don't cover it entirely." She directed a smile at Matthew. "Meaning . . . I can enjoy *all* of the things that are important to me. As long as I keep them in their proper places."

Matthew reached out to remove the leaf, allowing the pebbles to roll into her palm. "Now let's put the leaf on top. In this arrangement, your career is the most important thing." She held out her hand again. The breeze lifted it away almost immediately.

"Now your career takes off, perhaps even in a more spectacular way, but leaving behind the things that matter most."

Deborah studied the pebbles in her hand for a second, then closed her fingers around them. "I believe I'll keep these," she told him, a thoughtful smile curving the corners of her mouth. "A reminder."

~

The pebbles felt cool and smooth against Deborah's palm. How pleasant it was to sit out here with Gregory. *Having a brother must be like this,* she thought. A young man with whom she could be comfortable and talk easily, without having to suffer through the swaggering—or stammering—flirtations of a hopeful suitor.

"I'm not surprised you feel so strongly about family," she told him while the swing drifted in a lazy to-and-fro motion. "It's so obvious from the time that you spend with your aunt."

"I enjoy spending time with her. She's a kind woman."

"A dear," Deborah agreed. "You should have seen how excited she was before your first visit."

Gregory looked down at the hands he had folded upon his knee. "She was?"

"Indeed so." The memory of her first day in Cambridge came back to her, how she had worried that Miss Knight's nephew might be the man she'd met at the train station. "You know, I met someone else from Walesby my first day here." She tried to keep any distaste from her voice, just in case the two men happened to be friends. "At the station."

"Yes?"

"Do you happen to know a Fred Tarleton?"

"Fred Tarleton?" He shook his head. "I don't believe I've ever heard the name. What did he look like?"

"He had your same coloring, actually. But not quite as . . . tall." She had started to say "broad shouldered" but decided that it might not be proper. "Quite handsome at first glance, but . . ."

A faint shudder caught her shoulders at the memory of the way the man had looked at her, and she decided that she had given him enough thought. "I'm glad to find out that you aren't friends," she said as a final word on the subject. "He was rather odious. You have too much character to have anything in common with someone like him."

Before Deborah could say anything else, Gregory got to his feet. As he reached down to steady the arm of the swing, his expression took on a curious mixture of uneasiness and reluctance. "It's time I should be going."

"Have I embarrassed you?" she asked, recalling the timidity that seemed to come over him whenever he was given a compliment.

He offered a hand to assist her out of the swing, a bleak smile on his face. "Of course not, Deborah. But you are much too generous in your assessment of my character." With that, he touched his hat in farewell.

~

After going out to the carriage house to tell Mr. Henry that he would prefer walking home today, Matthew set out on foot toward the southeast.

Obviously the man Deborah had met at the railway station was Gregory Woodruff. He recalled Miss Knight's remarking that her houseguest had arrived on the fourth of October, the same day her nephew was supposed to have arrived from Walesby. There had been some distaste in Deborah's voice when she spoke of him, which was another clue. She was too sensible to bear two minutes with Woodruff.

But why would he have given her another name? And how could he have met her without finding out that she would be staying with his own aunt? Matthew had known men like him at Trinity College. They gloried in their womanizing, the competition between them as intense as that of organized sports. Someone as beautiful as Deborah would have been an irresistible target for such a person as Gregory Woodruff.

Unable to figure out the man's motives, he shrugged off the matter. He had better things with which to occupy his mind. *He's nothing but a weasel anyway.*

On Market Street, he had to step around some garbage that had been thrown into the street from one of the tenement windows—potato peelings, old tea leaves, and fish bones from the looks of it. At the same time, some voice deep inside him asked, *If Gregory Woodruff is a weasel, what are you?*

~

On Monday afternoon Deborah was led by the ever-phlegmatic Merrit down Signora Pella's entrance hall. She could faintly hear two people, a man and a woman, speaking in Italian as they neared the sitting room. *Lord Raleigh must be back from London,* she thought.

Following the butler inside the room, she found Signora Pella seated upon the settee with a huge man beside her. He looked strangely familiar, with his brown-and-gray beard, balding head, and thick round spectacles. Deborah tried to remember where she had seen him before.

"Miss Burke, your ladyship," Merrit announced, standing at attention just inside the doorway. The diva waved him away.

"Come here, Deborah," Signora Pella said, her face radiant. It was the first time she had ever used Deborah's given name. "I want you to meet someone!"

The diva's smile was infectious, and Deborah smiled back. "Yes?"

"Cecilio Giuseppe, meet my student, Deborah Burke." The big man set his cup of tea upon the tea table, grunted as he got to his feet, then enveloped Deborah's hand in a great paw that was surprisingly soft.

"I am pleased to meet you, Miss Burke," he said.

Deborah gaped back at him in a most unladylike manner. "You lectured at the Royal Academy two years ago!"

"I believe I did," the man said with a chuckle. "But certainly you were not there. I would have remembered such a beautiful face."

"Now, Cecilio," cautioned Signora Pella with mock severity. "You will frighten away my young student." She nodded

toward one of the chairs across the tea table from the settee.
"Sit down, Deborah. Signor Giuseppe has a wife back in
Rome, but he feels that if he doesn't flirt, he hasn't the right
to be called Italian."

"I played the part of Elizabetta in the Academy's production
of *Distinti Saluti* last year," Deborah told the composer after
taking a seat. "And your *Pericoloso* is my very favorite opera."

Seated again, the composer turned to Signora Pella with a
broad smile. "And where did you find such a delightful creature, Clarisse?"

"She found me, *caro*. Or at least, her father did." To
Deborah, she said, "Signor Giuseppe had plans to leave this
morning, but I persuaded him to stay another day. You have
warmed up already, yes?"

"Why, yes."

The diva became all business again, getting to her feet and
motioning for Deborah to do the same. "Then we will show
him what you can do, *va bene?*"

"All right," Deborah answered, joining her at the piano.
Stage fright had never been a problem for her, yet she found
herself as nervous as the first time she sang for Signora Pella.
The diva gave her no time to collect herself but struck a chord
on the piano.

"From *Don Giovanni*. Zerlina's solo in the second act," the
diva commanded.

*"Ve-drai ca-ri-no, Se sei bui-ni-no . . . ,"* Deborah began,
careful not to allow her self-consciousness to interfere with
her ability to sustain the notes. *Pretend you're in Miss Knight's
drawing room,* she thought, drawing herself up to her full
height. She closed her eyes and imagined that, instead of a
famous composer, Miss Knight and Bethina sat there with

177

rapture on their faces. Soon she was completely lost in the song, and then Signora Pella changed keys, ordering her to sing one of the arias from *Carmen*.

After two more arias it was over, and from his place on the settee, the composer was nodding at her, his smile almost as wide as Signora Pella's.

"You are correct, Clarisse!" Signor Giuseppe exclaimed. "She will make a perfect Rosalie. And her beauty will have all of Venice wondering from where she came. You must bring her for auditions in mid-January."

Everything was moving too quickly for Deborah. Venice? What auditions? And who was Rosalie? But before Deborah could voice any of her questions, Signora Pella stood, her hands upon her hips.

"What do you mean, *audition?*" she demanded from the composer.

Signor Giuseppe sighed and shook his head. "A mere formality, *Bella*. I dare not exclude the part of *Rosalie* from the auditions. Bishop Vico, my most generous patron, has asked me to consider his niece for the role."

"Surely she hasn't the talent that my student has!"

With a visible shudder, he answered, "She has a lovely voice . . . *sì?* But she lumbers about the stage like a cow. If I tell the bishop that his niece is not appropriate for the role, he will feel personally insulted. *But* . . . if I allow her to audition with others, she will be only one of dozens who do not win the part."

"Who is Rosalie?" Deborah finally managed to ask.

The big man grinned. *"You* are Rosalie."

"Come, Deborah," Signora Pella said, returning to the settee. "We have much to discuss."

Speechless again, Deborah returned to her chair.

"As you can tell, Cecilio and I have been friends for most of our lives," the diva began. "I have starred in three of his operas as well. *And* I have his newest one here." She lifted a pasteboard-bound book from the tea table. In everything that had transpired during the last half hour, Deborah hadn't even noticed it there.

"Your latest opera?" she breathed, as Signora Pella handed it over to her.

Signor Giuseppe laughed. "To me, only a newborn baby is a more beautiful sight than a newly finished opera."

Opening the pages of the opera on her lap, Deborah read aloud, *"Isabella."* Still not completely sure of how this connected with her, she looked up at her teacher again. "You want me to audition for a part?"

Signora Pella put a hand upon the composer's shoulder. "Didn't you hear Signor Giuseppe? He assures you the part of Rosalie Carlino."

"Now? But my lessons . . ."

"Your lessons will continue, but you are more than ready for this role. And we have eight weeks to learn it completely, so you will be better prepared than anyone else auditioning for the secondary parts."

In spite of the little voice inside telling her that she was not quite ready for a lead part, Deborah felt a surge of disappointment. "Secondary parts?"

Signora Pella smiled affectionately. "You are so much like me, Deborah. The secondary part I'm speaking of is second only to the three leads: Adelina Patti's, Virginia Roche's, and Piero Lorenz's parts."

The thought of sharing the theater boards with three of the

most famous names in opera set Deborah's pulse to pounding at the base of her throat. She took a deep breath and ordered herself to calm down.

"Cecilio has read to me the part of Rosalie Carlino," the diva went on, "and I am convinced that it is the kind of role that will make a star of the one who sings it. Adelina and the others, they have been in opera for decades. Everyone knows what to expect of them, and, yes, they will receive the customary accolades. But it is the fresh, new singers that will arouse the most curiosity. You have the looks and the voice for this. Show what you can do, and Venice will bow at your feet."

The mental scene that her teacher's words evoked caused Deborah's heartbeat to race even more. She looked from one face to the other. "Do you think I am ready?"

"You are ready," Signora Pella replied. "And by the time *Isabella* has finished its European run, you will have been trained—by me—well enough to go on for lead parts."

"I know my family would come to Venice to watch me perform," Deborah said dreamily. How proud they would be, sitting in the audience. She turned to Signora Pella again. "You would come to Venice as well?"

The diva and Signor Giuseppe exchanged amused smiles. "Why, of course. You are my pupil. And it would be unthinkable for a young woman your age to move to Venice without a chaperone."

"And you really believe I'm ready?"

Signora Pella's gray eyes were sparkling now. "Shall we say, you will be ready once you learn your part." She nodded toward the book in Deborah's lap. "But we have our work cut out for us for the next two months. Take this home and read all of Rosalie's lines. Then come an hour early tomorrow."

"Yes . . . yes, I'll do that." Deborah hugged the pasteboard book to her chest and got to her feet. Sidestepping the tea table, she offered her hand to Signor Giuseppe. "Oh, please don't get up. And thank you so much for this opportunity. You won't regret it—I'll study night and day!"

"What did I tell you?" Signora Pella said to the man beside her, as Deborah clasped her hand next.

"She will be a perfect Rosalie," the composer agreed.

"Now, go," Signora Pella told Deborah affectionately. "Signor Giuseppe and I have many plans to make regarding our stay in Venice."

"Of course." Deborah nodded over her shoulder and moved toward the door. The butler opened the door just as she reached it, and she fairly floated through it. As she followed him down the inner hall, she couldn't resist saying, "Isn't life wonderful, Mr. Merrit?"

He turned his head just enough to lift a stoic eyebrow at her. "I beg your pardon, Miss Burke?"

"Never mind," she sighed.

Suddenly, out in the entrance hall, she remembered her reticule. She must have left it in the sitting room, still lying across the arm of her chair. She halted in her tracks. "Oh, dear."

"Miss Burke?" The butler turned again, impatience clearly written across his face.

"My bag—I've forgotten it. Would you mind holding this?" Before he could say another word, Deborah dropped the opera into his arms, turned, and started back toward the sitting room. As she started to open the door, it occurred to her that perhaps it would have been more appropriate for Merrit to fetch the reticule. But she was here now, so she might as well get it for herself.

She had taken only a few steps into the room when her eyes fixed on Signora Pella and Signor Giuseppe, locked in an embrace, their lips together.

"I'm s-sorry!" Deborah stammered, backing toward the doorway. "My reticule . . . I'll get it tomorrow . . . sorry."

Signora Pella gave her an exasperated look, as Signor Giuseppe moved away a bit but kept his arm around her shoulders. "Come now, it is there on the chair—don't you see it?"

Deborah numbly moved toward the chair, keeping her eyes averted from the two faces.

"Oh, don't get so flustered, you naive child! Cecilio and I are old friends. Surely you have seen friends exchange a kiss before!"

"Yes—of course." Apologizing profusely, Deborah fled the room. *But friends don't kiss like that!*

~

*They're Italian,* Deborah reminded herself, seated beside Mr. Henry in the trap. Everyone knew that Italians were passionate people. Why, so much of the world's great music and artwork came from Italy. And as the diva had said, they were old friends. *Can't friends be passionately fond of each other?*

But they're both married, she thought. Would Signora Pella have kissed Signor Giuseppe so ardently if Lord Raleigh had sat across the tea table from them? or Signor Giuseppe's wife, for that matter?

"Are you all right, Miss Burke?" the driver asked after a while.

"Me?" Deborah gave him a smile that she didn't quite feel inside. "I'm fine, thank you. And you?"

He looked puzzled but nodded. "The same."

*Why are you so morose now?* Deborah asked herself. *Just ten minutes ago you felt like dancing! What will your family say when they learn that you're going to Venice?*

"I'm going to have a part in a new opera," she said to Mr. Henry. Speaking the news rekindled some of her earlier enthusiasm over it and required less effort for her to smile. *How Signora Pella acts in her own house has nothing to do with my career. I'm going to forget what I saw.*

"That's right fine," Henry said, but with a small grimace of distaste added, "'Course, I don't care much for that kind of music. All that screechin' and howlin'—it just ain't natural. And why can't they sing in English, like regular folk?"

Deborah laughed and held the book tighter. "I can't do anything about the language, but I promise to remember not to screech or howl." She imagined herself, standing upon the stage of the Teatro La Fenice, and her spirits grew even lighter. In fact, she had half a mind to stand up in the carriage and shout her news to the world!

On her way through the mews and house, she told every servant she passed. Even Thomas paused from pruning a grape-vine to give her a quick smile. Miss Knight was in her usual place in the drawing room, with Mrs. Darnell reading the newspaper out loud from one of the facing chairs. The house-keeper stopped reading when she caught sight of Deborah, and Miss Knight laid her crocheting down in her lap.

The older woman turned her face toward the doorway. "Is that you, Deborah?"

"It's me." Deborah walked over to the group of chairs and

slipped into the one Gregory usually took on Sunday afternoons. She gave an apologetic smile to the housekeeper. "I'm
interrupting your reading."

"It's time my voice had a rest anyway." Mrs. Darnell
smiled back, then lifted a cup from the saucer she had
balanced on the arm of her chair. "Shall I send for some
lemon water?"

Deborah thanked her anyway and turned to Miss Knight
again. "I'm going to audition for a part in a new opera."

"You are?" her hostess said, clasping her hands together
in front of her. "When, dear?"

That was when it struck Deborah that she would be leaving
Cambridge much sooner than she had planned. "In nine weeks,"
she answered. Hesitating for a second, she added, "I'll spend
a week with my family; then I'll be going on to Venice."

A look of sadness passed over the old woman's features,
but still she smiled. "Well, you'll certainly win any part you
try for. Don't you agree, Nelda?"

"Most certainly," the housekeeper answered. "But we'll
miss having you here with us."

"I will miss you as well," Deborah told them both. "Everyone has been so kind and encouraging. I wish I could bring
all of you with me."

"Thank you, dear," Miss Knight said. "We will just have to
make the most of the eight weeks that we still have you with
us. But Sundays won't be the same."

*Gregory!* The Sunday visits had become such a part of her
that Deborah hadn't even considered that they would be ending. For the second time since walking in on Signora Pella, she
felt a heaviness in her chest.

"They won't be the same for me, either," she said, getting

to her feet. She impulsively embraced Miss Knight and then Mrs. Darnell. "Thank you both for being happy for me."

Minutes later, when she had gone to her room to freshen up for supper, Deborah went over to the window seat and peered through the glass. The garden looked peaceful in the early evening twilight. Mr. Darnell and Thomas were heading toward the gardening shed with their tools, probably finished with the day's work and ready to wash up for supper. Her eyes followed them until they closed the door of the shed behind them, then turned back to the empty swing in the center of the garden. She could almost feel Gregory's hand upon her wrist steadying her hand as she held out her palm with the pebbles and leaf in front of her.

*This is a wonderful opportunity,* she told herself, pressing her forehead against the glass. *Besides, I knew I would be leaving Cambridge one day.*

The swing moved just a little, nudged by an evening breeze that stirred the leaves of the viburnum shrub. *I just didn't know it would be so soon.*

~

"We mustn't be selfish," Helene said that night. She sat in front of her dressing mirror while Avis brushed her hair. Uncoiled, it reached down to her waist. While it would have seemed odd to most people that a blind women would sit at a mirror, it had been her habit to do so for years before losing her sight. "This opera will be very good for her career."

She could hear the sound of pillows being plumped at her bed and then Bethina's voice. "But that means she and Mr. Gregory have only got eight more visits to be together."

185

"And you can't be falling asleep every Sunday afternoon," Avis added as she pulled the brush through Helene's hair.

"Of course I would love for them to be together," Helene told them. "But if that is God's will, then he'll allow it to happen. We can't keep interfering in their lives."

She heard Bethina's heavy tread coming across the carpet to join them at the dressing table. Before the parlormaid could speak, Helene warned her, "And don't go telling me you have a cousin who ended up alone because no one cared enough to meddle, Bethina."

"No cousin o' mine," Bethina said thoughtfully. "Unless you count Elvie . . . and she never wanted a man about, anyway. But what about Ruth?"

"Ruth?" This time it was Avis speaking, and the brush paused for a second. "Who is she, someone else in your family?"

After a chuckle, the maid replied, "No, not my family. Ruth from the Bible. It pleased God for her to marry Boaz, didn't it?"

"Yes," Helene replied patiently. Bethina usually managed to come to the point after a while. "I'm sure it did."

"Well . . . didn't Naomi help the good Lord out just a bit?"

After a moment of thoughtful silence, Helene said, "Avis?" The brush stopped again. "Makes sense to me, missus."

Helene gave a sigh, then smiled. "What do you suggest we do?"

~

"Oh, good. You remembered to bring the opera." Signora Pella's no-nonsense greeting the next day displayed again her remarkable capacity to stay focused upon the lesson . . . no matter what had transpired the previous afternoon.

After the lesson, they shared lemon water on the settee, and the diva's slate gray eyes fairly glowed when she spoke of the Venice *appartaménto* she had inquired about just this morning. "I have stayed there twice before. It has a lovely terrace and is near the Teatro La Fenice."

It suddenly occurred to Deborah to wonder about the financial burden of moving to Venice for an undetermined amount of time. "The apartment . . . train passage . . . ," she said. "Should I ask my father to lend me some money until the salaries are paid?"

Signora Pella smiled. "That is not for you to worry about. Did you think Signor Giuseppe would ask us to go to Italy and not provide for us?"

"That is very generous of him."

"*Sì*. He is a most generous man."

"You and I will live there alone?" The question was out of Deborah's mouth before she had time to think about what she was *really* asking.

"We will have a maid and a cook," the diva answered casually, but her eyes narrowed just a bit. "Why do you ask?"

"I was just curious," Deborah murmured. She could say no more—indeed, she could not even formulate the questions that were beginning to stir in her heart.

# 12

THOMAS knocked upon the door of his mother's tenement Sunday morning with a trembling hand. He had almost been discovered in the house last night. Hearing Mrs. Darnell talking to herself as she padded down the hallway, he had ducked under the staircase and waited there, shaking, for what seemed like hours before having the nerve to let himself out again. He'd spent a sleepless night, tormented by thoughts of his mother's grave and Orville's glowering face, but even that hadn't been enough to send him back into the house. And now he had to face Orville's wrath and his own shame for betraying his mother.

When there was no answer after a second knock, Thomas tried the door. It wasn't locked, and he pushed it open. Making his way through the accumulation of filth in the front room, he heard the snoring before he saw Orville in the bed. The sounds coming from the man's wide-open mouth were like the rattle of dry leaves, and the stench of his breath was almost unbearable.

"Orville . . . wake up," Thomas said, shaking his bare shoulder. Orville sputtered but resumed his snoring. Then Thomas noticed the opium pipe on the mattress next to him.

He felt the inside of the bowl. It was still warm and coated with a dark residue that he wiped on his trousers.

For the moment he breathed a sigh of relief. But Orville wouldn't sleep forever, and when he did wake up, he would be furious at Thomas for failing to bring something from Miss Knight's house. *At least I didn't forget to bring my salary,* he thought, looking around the room for somewhere to put it. He caught sight of Orville's shirt lying on the floor and picked it up by a cuff with two fingers. Laying the shirt over the seat of the only chair in the room, he took the coins out of his trousers pocket and arranged them on top, where Orville would have to see them when he got dressed. Surely Orville would realize where they had come from and would use them to help Mother.

As he walked away from the tenement, his hands shoved into his pockets, Thomas tried to think of a place where he could spend the rest of the morning. He had taken a chance last week by going back to Miss Knight's early, before church services were supposed to be over. If someone had stayed home ill, he could have been seen. He needed his job more than ever and couldn't risk being found out as a liar.

So deep was Thomas in his thoughts that it came as a bit of a shock to discover that his feet had been keeping time with music as he walked. He stopped and cocked his head. It seemed that the music came from the south, in the vicinity of Market Street. He could recognize the brassy sound of a trumpet and the deep thumping of a drum, but there were other sounds, too, from other instruments with which he was not familiar.

He had nothing else to do, and the music was compelling, so he found himself turning his steps to the south. The music grew louder as he traveled the length of run-down business buildings along Market Street. Presently he came upon a gathering of men, women, and children standing on the sidewalk listening to the songs of a band he could not see. Most of the people blocking his view wore the unmistakable badges of poverty—worn seams, patches, and frayed cuffs. Thomas looked over their heads at the building the crowd was facing. Salvation Army was printed in white letters on a red banner that ran the width of the building. Underneath was another red-and-white banner displaying the words Food and Shelter.

Curious, he decided to try to make his way through the gathering to the front so that he could see the band. Being short and runty had its advantages—most people seemed to think he was much younger and allowed him to worm his way through. Finally he stood in front, only two or three feet away from a group of six men and one woman, all wearing dark coats with small metal shields affixed to the front. The woman played a flute, one man beat both sides of a huge drum, two played trumpets, and the remaining two played instruments that Thomas had only seen in photographs—brass instruments, much larger than trumpets and with curved bodies.

The band played three more songs. Thomas had never heard of any of them, but one of them sounded like the chimes of the bell tower above Saint Michael's. When they were finished, there was a mixture of applause and puzzled murmuring from the crowd, until one of the trumpet players held up a hand and asked to be allowed to speak.

"Good morning to you, ladies, gentlemen, and children," he called out, smiling. "We would like to invite you to worship services inside and a hot meal afterwards."

At the mention of the words *hot meal,* a murmur of approval ran through the crowd, but it was the phrase *worship service* that caught Thomas's attention. He'd had enough of worship services the two times he drove Miss Knight to chapel, so he turned to leave. But evidently he was the only one with such a plan on his mind, for the crowd pressed in toward the doorway as one body.

"Excuse me," he said over and over, but he was like a small fish swimming against a strong tide. He finally decided that it was a useless, smothering chore to try to escape, so he allowed himself to be swept inside. Once everyone was seated in an orderly fashion, like the worshipers had been at King's College Chapel, he would simply get up and walk out.

He managed to find a seat at the end of one of the middle pews, then twisted around to peer over his shoulder at the people coming in through the doorway. Obviously he was going to be there for a while, so he began to study his surroundings. The room was larger than he would have imagined, with two rows of ten to twelve pews. The walls had been freshly painted in a light green color, which made the room look a little less ancient. In one corner, a cast-iron stove fought a futile battle against the brisk air wafting through the open doors. Thomas knew that, with a crowd this size, the room would warm up quickly once the doors were closed . . . but he didn't intend to be here.

After another glance over his shoulder, he turned to the raised platform at the front of the room, where a man stood by himself. The man wore the same black coat the players in the band had worn, but on each side of his collar was pinned a gold *S,* and one arm held a black Bible at his side. He seemed to be older than Miss Knight's nephew but, despite his thinning hair, much younger than Mr. Henry and Mr. Darnell. There was a slight smile at his lips, as if he were happy at the number of people filling the room, and his eyes were crinkled at the corners.

Just as Thomas turned around to look for a way of escape, he became aware of someone watching him. He glanced back at the platform and locked eyes with the man holding the Bible. *I know you're not comfortable here,* the eyes seemed to say from across the room. *But please stay.*

Thomas tore his eyes away and looked over his shoulder. The room was full of people, with a dozen or so men standing in back behind the pews. One of the band players was in the process of closing one of the double doors.

*Now or never!* Thomas told himself. He jumped to his feet and hurried down the aisle toward the doors, half expecting a hand upon his shoulder. No one stopped him, but he could still feel the man's eyes watching him, begging him to stay.

He dawdled on the way home to kill time, stopping to watch a group of boys chase a can down the street with sticks. *There's nothing for me in there,* he told himself. Even with the band out front and the plain building, the place was still a church. Church was for good people, not for boys who skulked through houses at night to steal. The man who had watched him from the platform would have likely worn a different expression had he known.

~

Matthew Phelps, on his way to Pembroke College to meet Mr. Henry, gave in to an impulse and stopped at a vendor to buy two bunches of hothouse violets. As he made his way farther down Trumpington Street, he pushed his derby down around his ears, wishing he'd brought his muffler as well. The pleasant nip in the air would turn into an insistent chill as the afternoon wore on. He considered asking Mrs. Darnell if there were a spare muffler about the house that he could launder and return next week but immediately discarded the idea. *You don't really belong there,* he reminded himself. But for just a second, he had taken for granted that he did.

It struck Matthew suddenly that he now lived for Sundays. For one afternoon every week, he had a maternal influence in his life as well as the friendship of a young woman whom he admired more than anyone. Today he would enjoy the moment and save self-recrimination for the remaining six days. *But still, you can't be borrowing things,* he thought.

He took a step out into Pembroke Street and was soon rewarded with the sight of the approaching trap. For a fraction of a second he thought Mr. Henry had gotten shorter; then he realized it was Thomas at the reins.

"I thought you didn't drive anymore," Matthew said after swinging up beside him.

Thomas gave a twitch of the reins, and Chester pulled the trap back into the steady flow of carriages and wagons. The boy seemed even more withdrawn and preoccupied than he had the last time he'd driven. "Mr. Henry's brother is visiting at the house."

"Well, I'm glad," Matthew told him, meeting Thomas's cautious glance with a smile. "We haven't talked for quite a while. How are you doing?"

"Fine," he said with a shrug, then gave Matthew another hesitant look. "Can I ask you something, Mr. Gregory?"

"Of course." Matthew was careful to keep the surprise out of his voice, lest the boy retreat to his usual uncommunicative shell. "What would you like to know?"

"Have you ever known anybody who was put in a sanatorium?"

An emptiness came over Matthew, but he pushed it aside. "Yes, I have."

"Will they tell you if someone's in there?"

"What do you mean?"

"I mean, if I post a letter asking if someone I know is there, will they answer it?"

"I don't see why not," Matthew answered. But on second thought, he had to amend his answer. "Of course, the person would probably have to be a close family member."

Instead of looking satisfied, Thomas seemed even more anxious. "Do you know how to find out if there's a sanatorium in Northampton?"

"Northampton? I'm sure there's a way." In fact, he was more than sure, for when William had needed care, Matthew had researched almost every sanatorium in England. He couldn't quite remember hearing of one in Northampton, however, but in the three years since William's death, one could have been established. "Would you like me to make some inquiries?"

Relief washed over the boy's face. "You would do that?"

"I would be happy to. Who are you trying to find out about?"

A curtain seemed to drop over Thomas's expression as he busied himself with reining the trap into the lighter traffic of Bridge Street.

"Thomas," Matthew said, once the carriage was moving at a steady pace again. "Look at me."

Thomas turned his face toward him, and they locked eyes. Tears gathered upon the boy's lashes. Moved with compassion,

Matthew set the violets in the small space between them and held out his hands. "Here . . . let me have the reins."

"But I'm supposed to—"

"I haven't driven a carriage in years. I would enjoy doing it." After the reins had been surrendered to his hands, Matthew turned to the boy again. "You're thirteen years old, right?"

"Yes sir."

Matthew's voice softened. "Don't you think you've shouldered this burden by yourself long enough?"

Thomas wiped his eyes with the back of his hand, his bottom lip beginning to tremble.

"Why don't you tell me what's wrong? You can trust me not to tell anyone without your permission."

After a lengthy silence, broken only by the street noises, the boy whispered, "It's my mother."

"You're mother is the one in a sanatorium?"

He nodded and wiped his eyes again. "I think so. In Northampton."

It was on the tip of Matthew's tongue to ask what was wrong with his mother, but something told him that that particular question could wait. There was something wrong here if the boy couldn't share the news of his mother's interment with the rest of Miss Knight's household. From what Matthew had seen on his visits, Thomas was treated very well there. Surely he would want their help and compassion in such a time as this.

He recalled, suddenly, the question Thomas had asked on that first Sunday that he drove. *"Can a boy be sent to prison, even if someone bigger is making him do something bad?"* Somehow, his question had to be connected to the circumstance of his mother's being in a sanatorium.

With the mews just up ahead, Matthew knew that Thomas

would disappear as soon as the carriage was put away. He pulled on the reins, slowing the horse to a walk. "Why don't you tell me the rest, Thomas?"

There was a longing in the boy's expression, but he shook his head. "I can't," he said firmly. "But when you find out that address . . ."

Matthew sighed. It was useless to press him for any more information. At least he'd made some progress. Perhaps when Thomas saw that he could be trusted with this matter, he would feel more free to confide in him in the future. "I'll send it to you. Or would you rather me write the letter for you and send it on to the sanatorium?"

"I'll write the letter," the boy answered as the trap turned into the mews. "You'll remember not to tell anyone?"

"I won't tell a soul. You can count on that."

At last a glimmer of hope crept into the boy's expression. "Thank you for your help."

Matthew smiled and handed him the reins. "Anytime, Thomas."

~

Gwen let him in at the terrace door. After she took his hat and admired the flowers in his hand, and they exchanged comments about the autumn chill in the air, she motioned down the hallway. "Would you like to show yourself upstairs?"

Matthew's heart grew lighter with each step he took up the staircase. He could hear the low murmur of voices just outside the drawing room. The door swung open before he could knock, and Bethina gave a startled little jump at the sight of him. "I was just goin' down to fetch the tea tray, Mr. Gregory," she said, her hand upon her heart. "I expected you'd be here any minute, but I didn't know you was just behind the door."

"I didn't mean to frighten you." Matthew entered the room to find Miss Knight and Deborah seated in their chairs near the fireplace, both faces turned in his direction.

"I hear the sound of my favorite nephew," Miss Knight said as he approached the two women, but then she put a hand up to her mouth. "Oh, my—I shouldn't have said that. You won't tell any of your brothers, will you?"

The words touched Matthew's heart, even though he was painfully aware that he had no right to the compliment. He leaned down to kiss the older woman's soft cheek. "I'm honored that you would think so, and no, I won't tell." He couldn't resist sending a wink to Deborah and adding, ". . . unless I'm really angry at them, of course."

Miss Knight smiled and wagged a playful finger. "Oh, I know that you'll do nothing of the sort. Have a seat, dear. Deborah has some exciting news."

He moved over to shake the hand that Deborah extended to him. She was wearing a dress of bottle green, which enhanced the emerald of her eyes, and he wondered how she managed to look even more beautiful from week to week. "You have?"

"Yes," she replied.

Her lips were smiling, but there seemed to be some hesitancy in her eyes. He took his chair, his chest suddenly tight with foreboding. *She's leaving.*

"I'm going to audition for a new opera in Venice . . . on January sixteenth."

"Venice?" he said, mentally counting the Sunday afternoons until then. *Nine weeks?* Listening to Deborah give the details, he sat there with a benign smile and tried to be happy for her.

It was what she had studied for, her life's goal. She deserved this opportunity. *Besides, what future did you have with her?*

He realized then that Miss Knight had said something. "I beg your pardon?" he asked.

She gave him a sad smile, as if she could read his disappointment. "I said, what a shame it is that Deborah has seen so little of our fair city. I feel like such a neglectful hostess."

"Now, Miss Knight," Deborah told her, "my stay here has been most pleasant. I never expected you to entertain me."

"I know, I know. But I'm going to have so many regrets when you're gone." The old woman sighed. "There is a concert at the guildhall Tuesday night . . . the Cambridge Symphony Orchestra. I would love for you to hear them."

Before Deborah could answer, Miss Knight turned to Matthew and said, "And you haven't been to one yet either, have you, Gregory?"

He had, in fact, been to two or three, back when his father and William were alive. But, of course, he couldn't tell her that. Miss Knight apparently took his silence for a negative answer. "I just happen to have tickets. Why don't you go together?"

Deborah and Matthew exchanged self-conscious glances, then Deborah said to the older woman, "Wouldn't *you* like to go with Gregory?"

"Or you and Deborah should go," Matthew said quickly.

"I've been to dozens and dozens, dear." Miss Knight turned her face in Matthew's direction. "It's such a pleasant outing, Gregory. And you both work so hard with your studies. It would make me so happy if you both would consider going."

*The more time you spend with her, the more it's going to hurt when she's gone,* Matthew warned himself. He looked at Deborah, who was staring at the flames licking against the coals in the fireplace. The tightness in his chest felt almost suffocating. *Two months . . . and then I'll never see her again.* She would be successful on stage, he was certain. One day she would marry someone with Gregory Woodruff's credentials . . . but with more character. Perhaps even a lord or a duke. And her Sunday afternoons in Cambridge would become only memories for her, consigned to become fodder for occasional pleasant dreams.

"Would you like to go, Deborah?" He could no more stop himself from asking than he could sprout wings and fly. And he almost felt that he *could* fly when she looked up at him and smiled.

"That sounds lovely, Gregory."

~

The concert was to begin at eight Tuesday night, and Mr. Henry was to meet Matthew in front of Pembroke at five past seven. Miss Knight had invited him to come early for supper, but he'd had to tell her that he would be busy until seven. Of course he didn't tell her that his position at Mr. Cornell's office would be keeping him occupied until then.

Knowing that he wouldn't have time to go home, Matthew brought his toothbrush and comb, his newest clean shirt, and the black coat he had worn at his brother's funeral so that he could freshen up after work. Fortunately, Pembroke College was only four blocks south of the office, and he was able to make it there a good two minutes before Mr. Henry appeared. He was surprised to see the man driving the barouche instead of the trap but realized that the liveryman had had to hitch up the horses for the ride to the guildhall.

As Matthew settled in his seat and the carriage started

moving again, he realized that he hadn't even considered the fact that he and Deborah would be riding in a carriage together for the first time. Should he sit next to her, he wondered, or across from her in the facing seat? *Across,* he decided at once. This was not a courtship, nor could it ever be one, so there was no use pretending that it was.

Mr. Henry pulled the horses to a stop in front of the house, climbed out of his box, and let down the step. "I'll wait for you here, Mr. Gregory," he said. Matthew patted his waistcoat pocket to make sure that the paper with the address was still there, then asked Mr. Henry where he could find Thomas.

"Most likely helping clear the supper dishes in the servants' hall," the liveryman answered. Matthew considered asking Mr. Henry to give the boy the address but decided against that right away. While the man would probably not even unfold the note, and if he did, wouldn't know what to make of the address inside, he had promised confidentiality to the boy. *I'll just have to wait 'til I have a chance.*

Avis answered Matthew's ring at the door with a sparkle in her eyes. "Miss Burke's on her way downstairs. The missus says not to come up and see her, that you should leave right away so's you won't be late."

He heard light footsteps, and Deborah appeared in the hallway behind the maid. "Good evening, Gregory."

Avis smiled and backed away, and Matthew took a step forward to take Deborah's outstretched hand. She looked as regal as a princess in an evening dress of blue satin trimmed with colored embroidery on lace. A velvet choker and sapphire pendant graced her slender neck, and when she turned so that Avis could help drape a silver-colored wrap around her shoulders, he noticed that her dark brown hair was pulled back into a charming arrangement with silk flowers of all colors.

"Bethina is getting the tickets from Miss Knight's dresser," Deborah told him.

"Don't Miss Burke look nice?" Avis said, staring up at Matthew with an expression that demanded, *Say something!*

"Very lovely," he murmured. . . . *Beautiful,* he thought and then managed at least enough presence of mind to let go of her hand and remove his top hat.

Bethina came down the hallway, breathing heavily. After exchanging amused glances with Avis, she handed two tickets to Matthew. "Make sure they say 'guildhall,' Mr. Gregory. It'd be awful if you showed up at the place with two skein wrappers."

As he checked the tickets and slipped them into his waistcoat pocket, he felt the paper again. The boy would likely be asleep by the time they returned. Should he ask one of the maids to give him the message? Suddenly it dawned upon him why Bethina had asked him to look at the tickets. *She can't read!* Drawing the note from his pocket, he asked if she would give it to the boy.

"Just something I looked up for him," he told her casually.

"I'll go do that right away," she replied, pausing only long enough to give both of them a maternal smile. "You look so lovely together."

They said good-bye to Avis, and then he helped Deborah into the waiting carriage out front. He took the seat across from her, as he had planned, and felt a measure of sadness when she seemed relieved.

~

Deborah's suspicions that Miss Knight was a partner in Avis and Bethina's romantic intrigues had been confirmed when the older woman insisted that she and Gregory attend the concert together. She had harbored a faint suspicion that he might be in on the plan as well, but it evaporated when he took the seat across from her.

Yet after that relief came a twinge of disappointment, for she recalled how nice it had felt to sit next to him in the garden swing.

*It's good that I'm leaving soon,* she thought. Once in London, she would be caught up again in the world of music and family, and these schoolgirl notions would fade away. There would be plenty of time for beaus and courtship later, when she had made her mark upon the stage.

Then a shiver came over her, and she drew her cashmere wrap tighter. *I'm going to miss him.*

"Are you warm enough?" Gregory asked, staring across at her with a concerned expression.

She nodded and smiled. "I've never seen you in a top hat."

"I've never seen myself in one either," he answered, smiling back at her. "I just bought it yesterday. I feel rather like a banker."

"Well, you look very dignified."

"And so do you," he said and then winced slightly. "You know, I've never been good with compliments. What I mean is, you look . . . well, you know . . ."

She knew. She could see it in his eyes just before he looked away.

~

They were both surprised when, at the guildhall, an usher led them down a passageway and up a flight of stairs to a box at the right of the stage. Eight chairs with maroon velvet-padded

203

backs and seats were lined up in two angled rows. After looking at their tickets again, the young man motioned to two
chairs in the center of the back row. "I didn't even notice
those were box-seat tickets," Gregory told her after the usher
disappeared behind the curtain. "I wonder where everyone
else is?"

Deborah looked at the empty row of chairs in front of
them. Though the orchestra was already warming up on the
stage, and the theater was filling up fast, these were still empty.
Suddenly she recalled the look that Bethina and Avis had
exchanged at the door. *Miss Knight bought all of the tickets in this
box.* She was dead sure of it and could just imagine the three
of them now, congratulating each other upon their scheme.

"*Symphonie Fantastique* is what they're performing tonight,"
Gregory said from beside her. He held the program the atten-
dant had given him out where she could see it. "By Hector
Berlioz. Have you ever heard of it?"

"Vaguely. It's about a musician who is in . . . love . . ."
*Can't you even say the word without blushing?* she thought as she
felt warmth creeping up her cheeks. ". . . with the woman
who appears in his dreams. Whenever you hear the flute, the
oboe, and the clarinet together without the rest of the orchestra, the music represents her presence."

The auditorium grew dim, and the English horn began an
opening solo. Seated there beside him in the darkened theater,
Deborah tried to pay attention to the trills and swells as the
other instruments joined in, but her mind kept returning to
the fact that they were sitting so close that she could feel the
faint pressure of his arm against her sleeve.

And he was thinking the same thing. She didn't know how
she could tell because she had no experience with such things,

but she knew. The timpani drums caused her heart to pound against her rib cage, and the violins brought up a bittersweet longing for something that she didn't have.

"This must be the part where she appears in his dreams," Gregory whispered from beside her as the three instruments began a haunting melody.

She turned her face to whisper that it was and found herself entranced by the tenderness in his expression as he listened to her answer. It required great willpower to make herself turn her eyes to the stage again. Even then, the orchestra could have been playing music–hall ballads for all she knew, for her mind was still upon the man beside her.

*You're acting like a heroine in a penny novelette!* she chided herself. *Are you going to swoon every time you're alone with a man?*

She straightened in her seat and forced herself to listen to the music just as the thought crossed her mind: *Gregory Woodruff is not just any man.*

Suddenly she became aware of his presence again. She turned to say something casual to break the intense emotion that threatened to overwhelm her, and he turned his face to her at the same time. Their eyes met, and they sat there staring at each other. While the melody played on, a slender, delicate thread began to form between them, drawing them together.

"Deborah," he whispered, just before his lips met hers. His kiss was as gentle as his eyes, and she put a gloved hand up to touch his cheek.

And then he backed away, his face filled with horror. "Oh . . . I'm sorry!"

As the first instant of shock wore off, Deborah turned away from him. Her cheeks were on fire, and her pulse hammered furiously against the base of her throat.

"Forgive me, Deborah," he was saying, his hand upon her shoulder, but she could not turn to look at him. "I had no right to do that."

*Why did you back away?* she wanted to demand of him, but a lady would never ask such a question. In the novels she had read, a woman's first kiss was magical and wonderful, and the man didn't look at her afterward as if she were some kind of monster. She felt rejected and . . . cheap.

"I'd like to go home now," she whispered with her back still turned to him. "Please ask Mr. Henry to meet me in the front."

He would not leave, though, and increased the gentle pressure of his hand upon her shoulder. "Please listen to me. You're the last person in the world I would want to hurt."

*Then why did you look at me that way?* she demanded silently, but pride only allowed her to answer, "You didn't hurt me. It didn't mean anything." In the long silence that followed, she knew that those words had stung him. *Good!*

"It meant everything to me, Deborah," he whispered, then moved his hand from her shoulder. "If you only knew how much."

The vulnerable sincerity in his voice touched something in her heart, and she wheeled back around to face him before he could get up from his chair. "If it meant everything . . . then . . . why did you pull back? Why did you look at me that way?"

Pain washed across his face, and tears were clinging to his lashes. He drew in a ragged breath. "Because I don't deserve to even be here with you."

His modesty, which had once been so charming, now irritated her. "How can you say such a silly thing?"

"Because it's true. You don't know anything about me."

Gregory was on his feet before she could even imagine what he was talking about. "I'll come get you when Mr. Henry has the carriage up front. Please accept my apologies again."

After he disappeared through the curtain, Deborah clamped her jaw shut tight and gave her attention back to the orchestra, determined not to allow the incident that had just happened to spoil her evening. *I hope he breaks his neck on the stairs!* she thought.

The trio of wind instruments began their ethereal passage again, only adding to her melancholy. Never, not even in the Cambridge station, had she felt so alone in her life. *What's wrong with me?* she thought, feeling tears sting her eyes as she pressed her gloved hand against her mouth. *It was just a kiss. Women get kissed all the time.*

Gregory was back shortly, offering his arm to her as they descended the stairs. She shook her head and kept her face away from his as much as possible so he wouldn't know that she'd been crying. Mr. Henry sat at the reins of the barouche just outside the front of the theater. After helping Deborah inside, Gregory stepped back and gave her an apologetic look. "It's not far from here. I'll walk."

*Go ahead then . . . walk!* she thought, satisfied at the sight of his hands shoved into his pockets. *Anyone without the sense to bring a topcoat and gloves deserves to be cold.* But she ended up saying, "You don't have to do that, Gregory."

He shook his head and lifted a hand to wave. "Take care, Deborah."

*I'm not even going to think about him when I get to Venice,* she thought, ignoring the raw ache in the back of her throat as the barouche moved north. *I'll probably even forget what he looks like.*

# *13*

"THAT was a haunting melody," Miss Knight commented the next evening as Deborah got up from the piano in the sitting room. "Was it from the new opera you're learning?" Deborah nodded.

"You sounded like you was goin' to stop and cry any minute," Bethina added. She began dabbing at her eyes with the end of her apron.

*That was acting, Bethina,* she thought as Gregory's face flitted across her mind. *I'm all cried out.* She forced all memories of last night out of her mind and smiled at both of them, her audience for the evening practice session. "I thank you both for listening."

Deborah frowned at the libretto in her hands. Signora Pella had insisted that she bring it home with her every night so that she could have additional practice for the part of Rosalie and become acquainted with the whole opera.

"What did the words mean?" Bethina asked.

"Oh, the usual unrequited love," Deborah said flippantly, and the maid scrunched up her face.

"Un-re . . ."

"Unrequited," Miss Knight prompted gently. "You know, when someone's love isn't returned."

209

The maid gave a knowing nod in her direction. "That happened to a sister o'mine. She wouldn't eat, just drifted around the house, pining away to almost nothin' because the young man wouldn't give her the time o'day." When Bethina noticed the expression on her mistress's face, she became defensive. "Well, she did. When you have ten sisters, somethin's bound to happen to at least one o' them."

Turning to Deborah again, the maid asked, "Is that what happens in your opera?"

"Something like that," Deborah answered, then decided that it was time to excuse herself to study upstairs. As she climbed the stairs, her thoughts returned to the scene she witnessed in Signora Pella's sitting room. *If only you hadn't left your reticule lying about,* she told herself. *You would still be walking on clouds right now.*

~

"Have you finished reading the whole libretto of *Isabella?*" Miss Knight asked Deborah over luncheon on Friday.

Deborah stopped making idle swirls in her suet pudding with her spoon and looked up. "Just last night."

"Would you mind telling it to me?"

"Are you sure you care to hear it?"

"You know how much I love stories," the elderly woman assured her.

"I'm sure you would like this one, then. It's very well written." Putting down her spoon, Deborah took a deep breath. "It takes place in Sicily during the thirteenth century."

"Ah, yes. The island was ruled by the French."

Deborah could only gape at her. "How did you know?"

"You're forgetting that my brother was a history lecturer at

210

Saint John's," Miss Knight answered with a bit of a smile.
"I read every book in his library."

"You should have taught."

Her hostess gave a shrug of her slender shoulders. "Oh,
I would have loved it. But in those days, there were no
colleges here for women."

"What a shame," Deborah said, the pity for this bright
woman overshadowing her dilemma about the opera.
"All of that knowledge gone to waste."

"Oh, it wasn't wasted, dear. It brought enjoyment to me
and gave me something to talk about at the dinner table with
my brother." Her expression grew reflective, and Deborah
wondered if she were traveling back into her memory to a
more pleasant time. After several seconds Miss Knight broke
out of her reverie and smiled. "I'm sorry, dear. Please go
ahead with your plot."

"Well, the three main characters are a Sicilian, General
Renzo; his wife, Antonietta; and daughter, Isabella. General
Renzo often meets with other Sicilian officers at an inn to
plot the massacre of a group of French soldiers known as the
Sicilian Vespers."

Miss Knight nodded thoughtfully. "Is Isabella's part the one
Signora Pella wants you to audition for?"

"No," Deborah sighed, pushing away her bowl of porridge.
"I'm to play Isabella's lady's maid, Rosalie, whom she confides
in. You see, Isabella is in love with a young French soldier."

"Does she know that her father is plotting against the lives
of the Vespers?"

"She does . . . and is torn between her love for the soldier
and her devotion to her family and country."

"Ah," Miss Knight said. "And so the young woman must make a very hard decision, one way or the other."

"But Isabella isn't aware that her soldier flirts with Rosalie every time she brings him a message from her mistress. Rosalie's part is minor, but Signora Pella is positive that it will give me the acclaim that leads to leading roles."

The older woman smiled. "Your family must be very happy for you."

"Well . . . I haven't written to them about it yet."

"You haven't?"

"I've tried, but I can't bring myself to pen the words on paper."

"Is that why you've seemed so sad lately?" Miss Knight said gently.

Deborah searched the blank eyes across from her. What amazing perception her hostess had, even without her sight. *You have to talk to someone about this,* she thought. She simply could not keep her confused feelings to herself for much longer.

But how could she tell a godly woman like Miss Knight the ugly suspicion that persisted in her mind? What had Signora Pella said that day back in October? *"The only two men I have ever loved were never completely attainable."* One of the men, Michel Alrigo, had loved someone else. Was the second man Cecilio Giuseppe? And if so, was Signora Pella's plan to accompany her to Venice so that assignations could be easily arranged between herself and the composer? Who would question a teacher who felt compelled to chaperone and continue teaching her only pupil?

*Surely Signor Giuseppe wouldn't assign me a role that I couldn't perform well,* Deborah reminded herself. *He has too much at stake.* If she were to allow the moral or immoral actions of others to influence the choices she made for her own life, she may as well give up opera and join a convent.

"I don't think I can talk about this just yet," she finally told the older woman. "But I believe I may soon be faced with one of those hard decisions . . . like Isabella."

"And it has to do with this particular opera."

"Yes. I want this more than anything, but . . . something just doesn't feel right."

Miss Knight nodded. "Then I will pray for you, that God gives you wisdom to make your decision . . . should it come to that."

"Thank you," Deborah said, reaching for her hand. "That means more to me than you can know."

"Why don't we do something special this evening? There is a wonderful French restaurant in town that I have heard of for years but have never dared to try."

Deborah had to smile at her hostess's thoughtfulness. "You don't have to do that."

"But it would do us both some good, don't you think? I haven't been out to eat in over a year."

"Then let's go. I could use an outing."

"I could even send an invitation to Gregory, asking him to meet us there."

"Please don't," Deborah said quickly.

Sadness came over Miss Knight's aged face, but she nodded. "All right, Deborah."

The only explanation Deborah had given her hostess for returning early from the concert three nights ago was that she wasn't feeling well. By the time she got home, it was the truth. She wasn't sure if her hostess could sense that there was

213

some trouble between her and Gregory, but she was thankful not to have to answer questions. Even Avis and Bethina had restrained themselves from asking, although Deborah could see in their eyes that they were eager to know what was going on.

She went upstairs to brush her teeth and fetch her cloak before leaving for her lesson. As she opened a drawer to take out a pair of gloves, the three pebbles caught Deborah's eye from the top of her dresser. She thought of how Gregory had looked when she last saw him, standing there in front of the guildhall with his hands in his pockets, trying to hide the fact that he was shivering as he watched the carriage move away. *Why can't I stop thinking about him?*

Still, the object lesson he had taught her with the pebbles had given her perception about her music. She took a handkerchief from the drawer, tied the pebbles inside, and tucked the bundle into her waistband. As she studied with Signora Pella today, perhaps it would help to have a reminder of what was important.

~

"Will Lord Raleigh be accompanying you to Venice?" Deborah ventured to ask when the lesson was over. She had exchanged quick greetings with the man in the hallway and felt greatly relieved to know that he was home.

Signora Pella's cup of lemon water never wavered on the way to her lips. After she had taken a sip, she shook her head. "My husband has matters of state to attend." She set her cup down on its saucer with a *click* and fixed her eyes upon Deborah's. "And now I suppose you would like to know if Signora Giuseppe will accompany Cecilio . . . am I correct?"

Deborah's mouth gaped at such bluntness. "Well . . . he could be there for months. Won't she miss——?"

"Signora Giuseppe does not travel. She prefers to stay in Rome and coddle her grandchildren." The last sentence was delivered with just a bit of a sneer. "And now, Deborah Burke, I must ask *you* some questions."

"Y-yes?"

"Why do you study opera?"

"Signora Pella, you know why. And I *want* to go to Venice and perform."

"Ah . . . but you have moral reservations. Because you saw me in the arms of Cecilio."

Deborah hesitated, then nodded.

"Well, allow me to ask you another question," the diva said. "If an opportunity to sing is handed to you upon a silver platter, what concern is it to you if your composer and tutor are lovers? What has it to do with your performance upon a stage? In the Teatro La Fenice, no less! Do you intend to examine the morals of every person with whom you will be working for the rest of your life?"

Shocking as Signora Pella's words were, it was a relief to hear the truth out in the open instead of having suspicion trouble her conscience in the still of night. "Of course not," Deborah mumbled back.

"That's a relief to hear! Because if you do, you'll become like that cow Jenny Lind, and all of your training will have been wasted."

Deborah cringed at the reference. Jenny Lind, the toast of Europe and the States thirty years ago, had left the stage after becoming a Christian, declaring she was weary of struggling to keep her morals from being undermined. Until now, Deborah had never understood what she had meant. "But my going to Venice is . . ." She couldn't finish, not with the diva's gray eyes staring as flat and unreadable as stone.

"Is allowing Cecilio and me an opportunity to be with each other. That is what you are thinking?"

Deborah realized that she was squeezing the empty china cup in her hand and set it back on the tray before she could break it. "Isn't it?"

"And is *that* why you think that you were chosen for the part?" An indulgent smile softened the diva's expression, and she lifted a slender hand to touch Deborah's shoulder. "So, *cara,* we have caused you to doubt your talent, have we? But do you really believe that the great Cecilio Giuseppe would assign a novice to any role just for his personal indulgences? You will shine upon that stage, I assure you."

The disarming words left Deborah groping for a reply. Before she could collect her thoughts, however, Merrit was escorting her with an umbrella through a light rain to the trap.

*If my actions make it possible for two people to sin . . . even if I don't participate in the sin, do I bear some of the guilt as well?* she wondered as the carriage sloshed through puddles in the street. Why did everything have to be so difficult all of a sudden? *Show me what to do, Father,* she prayed, half afraid of what the answer would be.

~

Sidonie's was located in a building of pink brick with pepperpot bay windows and set among some exclusive shops on Petty Cury. As Henry tethered the barouche's reins to a carriage post that evening, Deborah caught sight of The Fashionable Woman millinery shop across the street. From what she could see of the displays in the dark bow windows, it looked quite exclusive.

"Thomas's mother's shop is across the street," she said, leaning forward to tell Miss Knight.

"Oh?" The elderly woman turned to her left as if she could see it. "Is it open? I would love to meet her."

Deborah told her that it wasn't, and Miss Knight looked disappointed. "Mrs. Darnell sent her an invitation to have Christmas dinner with us last year and Easter this year, but both times she declined to come."

"Thomas says she is always very busy," Deborah reminded her, keeping to herself the thought that surely a mother could find time to meet her young son's employer. *No wonder Thomas seems so lost sometimes.* She recalled the strained civility between Signora Pella and her daughter. Obviously not all mothers nurtured their children the way hers had, and with that knowledge came disillusionment. *Is my mother the exception to the rule?* How could a mother be too busy for her own children?

The restaurant was doing a brisk business when Deborah led Miss Knight through the door, and about a dozen people waited in the lobby for tables. The maître d', a short Frenchman with a heavy mustache, took one solemn glance at Miss Knight's sightless eyes and escorted the two through a maze of filled tables to a small one in back. "Not one of our best tables—too near the kitchen," he said apologetically as he pulled out the chairs.

"It's fine," Deborah told him with a grateful smile. "And much better than having to wait."

He glanced at Miss Knight again before placing a menu in front of Deborah. "My sainted mother was blind as well," he said with the tenderest of voices.

"No doubt she was very proud of you," Miss Knight said, smiling in his direction.

His eyes glistened. "Ah . . . but I can only hope so."

When he was gone, Miss Knight leaned forward and commented to Deborah on what a nice man he was. "But I believe he assumes you're my daughter."

"I would take that as a compliment," Deborah said warmly.

"You are too kind. It is I who would be complimented." A waiter came to the table and after consulting with Miss Knight, Deborah ordered *piments doux farcis* (stuffed sweet peppers) for the older woman and *maquereau au groseilles vertes* (mackerel with green gooseberries) for herself. The young man seemed perplexed but did not comment when Deborah ordered hot water with lemon juice to go along with her meal.

When he was gone, Deborah asked Miss Knight, "Does a time come in your life when you don't have to agonize over every major decision?"

Concern touched the old woman's wrinkled face. "Are you sure that you wouldn't want to tell me what's wrong, Deborah?"

"I just can't—not yet." Deborah realized as she spoke that she was not as afraid of shocking the older woman as she was apprehensive of what her advice might be. What if Miss Knight cautioned her not to go to Venice, and she decided to go anyway? She would have the extra burden of knowing she had disappointed such a dear woman.

Miss Knight smiled gently. "I understand. Have you asked God to show you what to do?"

"Yes. More than once."

"Then be patient, Deborah. Wait for his answer."

~

"And so it is his theory that Shakespeare didn't actually write the works that are credited to him," Kendall Hudson, one of the four undergraduates seated at Gregory Woodruff's table, went on. "And you know, it stands to reason—"

"The dons have been saying that since my father was in school," Stanley Parrish cut in with a knowing expression. "They like to stir the green boys up with a bit of controversy. . . . But I don't think they believe it themselves." He turned to Gregory. "Don't you agree?"

"Why don't you ask me if I care instead?" Gregory yawned. "He didn't leave a farthing of his royalties to me, so he could have gotten his horse to write them, and it wouldn't affect my life."

A rumble of wine-sodden laughter went around the table, except from the lips of Kendall Hudson, who raised his chin and said in an injured tone, "I suppose people who don't take their studies seriously have all they can do to keep their minds on the contents of their purses."

"Oh, that's not all my mind stays on," Gregory said, amidst another rumble of laughter. Bored with it all, he leaned back in his chair to signal the waiter to bring another bottle, when he caught sight of a familiar face across the room. The shock cost him his balance, and he had to grab the chair next to his before tipping his own.

"Careful, old chap," warned Hunter Perkins. Perkins said something else that caused the others to laugh, but Gregory had no idea what it was, for his eyes were still upon the young woman he had met at the railway station.

*What was her name?* he asked himself, cursing the six glasses of wine that were now set to work at dulling his wits. She was

speaking to a woman seated adjacent to her and looked even
more beautiful than she had that day. He wondered if he
should walk over and introduce himself again. Surely she
wouldn't be offended if he begged her pardon and confessed
that he had forgotten her name. *You used Fred's name,* he
recalled, thankful that the wine had at least allowed him to
remember *that*.

"Hey, Woodruff . . . you going to finish your meal?" came
a voice from his table, but he waved it away. The young
woman's companion was speaking now, and for the first time
Gregory looked directly at her. She was quite elderly, he realized, and there was something odd about her. Squinting his
eyes, he  studied the way she seemed to gaze out past the
young woman as she spoke. And then she lifted a fork to her
mouth, slowly, deliberately, without even looking down at her
food. *Why . . . she's blind,* he told himself in wonder. But not
only that, she looked strangely familiar.

He thought hard for several seconds until the haze envelop-
ing his mind parted. *The portrait in the morning room,* he recalled
suddenly. *Aunt Helene!*

In a flash his wits cleared. She *had* to be his aunt. How
many blind old women could there be in Cambridge who
resembled a portrait hanging in his house? Relief washed over
him like a tonic, and he started pushing out his chair to go
over and speak to them.

*You idiot!* he told himself, halting where he sat. What was
he to do . . . waltz over and introduce himself as Fred Tarleton
and take a chance on the young woman snubbing him again?
Any advantage he had over being related to Aunt Helene was
gone, for he certainly couldn't use his own name. He could
just see the letter his aunt would send to Father then!

"Woodruff . . . who's that girl you're staring at?"

"I'm busy," Gregory grunted. The young woman was helping Aunt Helene to her feet. He turned in his chair and followed them with his eyes through the restaurant. When they
were no longer in sight, he got up from the table and walked
over to the bay window in front, careful to stand behind one
of the open curtains. One of a group of four matronly looking
women occupying the table closest to the window stared curiously at him through her lorgnette. He leered at her with an
exaggerated wink, then chuckled to himself at her shocked
expression before turning back to the glass.

In the amber light of the gaslamps he could see a man—
obviously a livery servant—and the young woman helping
Aunt Helene into a barouche. From the familiarity with
which the two smiled and chatted with each other, it was
obvious they knew each other well. He took a second look
at the barouche just as it passed in front of the restaurant.
That same carriage, black with silver trim, had come for the
young woman at the railway station that day.

*She's staying with Aunt Helene!* he thought, pressing his forehead against the cold glass. *All this time . . . she's been staying
with my aunt!*

After the barouche was out of sight, he shoved his hands
into his pockets and walked dejectedly back to his table,
where his friends accosted him with questions about the
young woman he had been watching.

"Nobody special," he told them. *What's the use?*

"Don't tell me it was the old woman you were gawking
at!" Hunter Perkins hooted, causing the other two to dissolve
into laughter. Gregory spun in his chair to grab the lapels of
the man's coat.

"Don't be saying things like that," he growled. "That old woman is my aunt!"

"Your aunt?" Hunter's eyes were wide as saucers, and he held up his hands in a placating gesture. "Sorry, Woodruff . . . how was I to know?"

Gregory let go of his lapels and slumped over his newly poured glass of wine. "Forget it."

"Anyway, that's good for you, eh?" Stanley Parrish said carefully. "If the young lady's an acquaintance of your aunt . . ."

"Won't do me any good," Gregory answered before draining his glass. Then it occurred to him to wonder why Matthew Phelps had never mentioned that his aunt had a houseguest. *Of course,* he thought, turning his head again to look at the empty table where the two women had sat. *He's smitten with her himself.*

~

Matthew stepped out of the office Saturday evening and almost bumped into Gregory Woodruff. "Excuse me," he said, trying to sidestep the man.

Woodruff blocked his path again. "I've got something to discuss with you."

"Haven't you anything better to do than harass me? Study, for instance?"

"Yes . . . all right," Woodruff said, taking a conciliatory step backward. His tone changed to a more affable though slightly pitiful one, and he motioned in the direction of the Café Aeneas down the street. "May we talk about it over supper?"

*I might as well get this over with,* Matthew thought. He didn't fancy the prospect of Gregory Woodruff skulking around the office doorway every evening. He shrugged his shoulders and said, "That depends. Are you buying?"

"Of course."

"Then we'll talk."

This time Matthew ordered his own meal, choosing two entrees, soup, bread, coffee, and a treacle tart for dessert. If he was going to suffer Woodruff's odious company, he might as well be compensated in some way.

After he had given his own order to the waiter, the man shot Matthew a critical look across the small table they shared. "I should think that with the money I'm paying you, you wouldn't act like a starving man when you get a free meal."

Matthew smiled benignly at the insult. "No offense, but what I do with the money is entirely my affair."

"Of course it is. But I can't help but wonder."

"It doesn't go for food," he answered with finality in his voice.

"Well . . . I was wondering if you could use more."

His eyes narrowing, Matthew said, "What are you talking about?"

Mr. Woodruff grinned. "You're doing such an outstanding job that I would like to add another quid to your salary every month."

It was an offer that made his dreams of paying off his debts and becoming a student again even more accessible, but Matthew knew enough about the man in front of him to suspect a catch. "And what do I have to do to earn this extra quid? Murder someone?"

"I do so like your sense of humor," the man across from him said with a chuckle; then his tone turned serious. "I have been feeling regrets about not visiting my aunt Helene, and I would like to remedy that situation."

Clearly, Matthew hadn't heard correctly. "Excuse me?"

"It was beastly of me to hire someone to impersonate me.

Not that you aren't doing a splendid job of it," he added hastily. "But she's part of my family, and I've come to realize how important that is."

"Are you saying that you don't want me to pose as you anymore?"

"I'm not saying that at all," Woodruff said. "It's too late to change that . . . not without confessing, of course, which would only serve to hurt her."

*You don't care one bit about whether she's hurt,* Matthew thought. The catch was there somewhere . . . he just had to wait for it to manifest itself. "Then what did you have in mind?" he asked, playing along for the moment.

Mr. Woodruff smiled. "I would like to accompany you tomorrow, as one of your friends from Pembroke."

"Impossible!"

"And why is that? My aunt already believes you're her nephew. What's she going to do . . . suddenly realize that she's been mistaken?"

"It could happen."

Mr. Woodruff shook his head. "She *wants* to believe that you're her dear Gregory, and nothing will convince her otherwise." Resting his elbows on the table, he said, "Now, what time does Aunt Helene send the carriage for you?"

Matthew caught a glint in Woodruff's eye and knew with dreaded certainty what was going on in his mind. Leveling his gaze at the man, Matthew said, "This hasn't anything to do with your aunt Helene at all."

"Why, whatever do you mean?"

"This has to do with Miss Burke, doesn't it? How did you find out?"

Slapping himself lightly upon the forehead, the man across

from him gave a wide grin. *"That's* her name—of course! And her first name . . . isn't it Deborah?"

Just the idea of her name upon this cad's lips made Matthew curl his hands into fists upon the table. The motion was not lost upon Mr. Woodruff.

"I do understand your keeping the information about my aunt's houseguest from me," he said with a knowing grin. "How could any man help but become infatuated with her?"

Matthew didn't bother to deny it, for he knew that the look in his eyes would prove him a liar. "She's not your kind."

"Oh, but I would like the opportunity to find out."

The waiter returned with the dishes of food, but Matthew's appetite had left him. Gregory Woodruff had his mind set upon meeting Deborah, and men like him were experts in getting what they wanted. Then a sudden memory brought a ray of hope. What had Deborah said about the man at the Cambridge station?

*She called him "odious."*

Woodruff could flirt all he wanted to, but Deborah Burke would be able to see through him as clearly as through work-house soup. His appetite restored, he picked up his fork and began to work upon his first entree, a platter of spiced beef with dumplings. From across the table, Mr. Woodruff eyed him curiously.

"Your disposition seems to have changed, all of a sudden. May I know why?"

*Why not tell him?* Then he would see how useless all this would be and perhaps reconsider. "As I recall, Miss Burke described her chance meeting with you," Matthew said, wiping his mouth with his napkin. "I believe she wasn't as impressed with you as you think she was."

Mr. Woodruff pushed aside his plate of oxtail stew. "I didn't ask for your opinion, Mr. Phelps. I want you to take me with you when you visit my aunt this Sunday."

"Absolutely not."

Woodruff shrugged. "Either you'll agree or I'll be waiting at her door when you get there."

"And what if I tell your aunt Helene who you really are?"

"How do you propose to do that without indicting yourself?"

A picture came into Matthew's mind of Deborah and Miss Knight seated in the drawing room, outrage and hurt in their expressions. *He's trying to manipulate you,* he thought. *He has just as much to lose if you confess.* But when he said as much, Woodruff gave a wry smile and shook his head.

"I'm afraid not, Phelps. You see, if you do confess, my father will call me on the carpet, perhaps even purchase a commission for me in the army, and everyone in my family will be put out with me for some time. I don't relish any of that happening, to be honest."

He pointed a finger at Matthew. "But you, my friend, will go to prison. That is where people are sent who knowingly practice fraud, you know. And I don't think your Mr. Cornell would be eager to help you, considering you've been in a shady business deal with a client."

Matthew could only gape at the man across from him, speechless, while a smile spread across Woodruff's face.

"I take it you've decided to become reasonable?"

"What is your plan?" Matthew said in a dead voice.

Mr. Woodruff leaned forward on his elbows, his forehead furrowed in concentration. "Well . . . the first step is, you'll need to practice calling me by another name. Fred Tarleton." He smiled. "We're old friends."

"It won't work," Matthew told him while a bit of hope rose in his chest. "Miss Burke has already asked me if I was acquainted with the man from the station."

"She did?"

"She said that he was from Walesby, and I told her I didn't know him. Now, how am I going to tell her that we're old friends?"

"You can't," Mr. Woodruff agreed, nodding. Presently he snapped his fingers. "But you *can* tell her that we share the same staircase at Pembroke. When we discovered just recently that we were from the same town, we became fast friends."

"Fast friends," Matthew echoed flatly.

"May I serve you some more coffee, sir?" the waiter asked, coming over to the table with a steaming pewter pot. Mr. Woodruff held out his cup, but Matthew shook his head.

"Would you mind wrapping up the steak-and-kidney pie?" he asked, motioning toward his other untouched entree.

"Leaving?" Mr. Woodruff asked after the waiter had gone with the dish. "We should make sure that our stories match before Sunday."

"You mean our lies, don't you?"

Mr. Woodruff shrugged. "Whatever you take it to mean."

"I don't want to memorize any more facts," Matthew said bitterly. "You say whatever you like Sunday, and I'll sit there like a coward and resist the urge to give you the thrashing that you deserve."

"Careful, now . . . ," Mr. Woodruff said with a warning look.

"Or you'll what?" Matthew growled back.

The waiter brought over a bundle wrapped in heavy brown paper. Matthew took it from his hands and pushed out his chair. "Your aunt Helene's liveryman fetches me at the corner of Pembroke and Trumpington at two," he told him. "If you're not there, I'll assume you have some decency after all. By the way, I'll take that extra quid every month."

Leaving the café, Matthew turned to the south instead of taking his customary route home. He walked along, staring at the passing doorways until he came to a dark alley. The wretch who'd almost had a hand chewed off by Royce was still there, taking advantage of a few last opportunities to beg. Trying not to inhale, Matthew bent down and tucked the warm bundle into the man's arms.

"Huh?" asked the man, blinking his eyes as if waking from a sleep. "What's 'is?"

"Supper," Matthew replied, then turned his steps in the opposite direction.

Later in his flat, he lay on his bed with his hands behind his head and stared up at the ceiling. How long had it been since he had prayed? *Not since William died,* he thought. Why would God care to listen now after having been ignored for so long? Besides, what good were the prayers of a liar? *And a thief,* he reminded himself. *You stole the trust of two innocent people.*

Warm tears trickled down both sides of his face, and he moved a hand to wipe them with the corner of his sheet. "Lord God," he prayed in a voice barely above a whisper, not even sure if his words reached any higher than the ceiling. "I've been involved in a terrible thing, and I don't know how to undo it without hurting the people I care most about."

He realized then that he had no idea what he should ask God to do. He only knew that he needed help, so he wiped his eyes again and said, "Help me, Lord. Please."

# 14

YOU know . . . your Miss Knight likely has some jewelry layin' about, too," Orville said Sunday morning,
as he stood in the doorway of his hovel and turned
the silver-and-jade pillbox over and over in his hands.

Thomas shook his head. "I'm not going up into her room."

"Rich woman like that might have some diamonds and
such," the man wheedled. "Don't you want to see that yer
mum gets special treatment?"

The mention of his mother brought an ache to his chest,
but he shook his head again. "I can't take jewelry from her."

"Then get out of here, brat!" Orville said, punctuating his
command with an oath that would sear the ears of the rowdi-
est sailor. He slammed the door, and Thomas turned away,
relieved that his vile duty was over for this week.

As he walked down past rows of crumbling tenements, he
wondered how long it would take to receive a reply from the
letter he had posted Wednesday to the sanatorium in Northampton. How grateful he had been to receive the address from
Mr. Gregory! If only he had trusted the man earlier, he told
himself, he would already know by now if Orville was indeed
telling the truth.

A shudder racked his shoulders. If Orville was lying, that meant only one thing. He pushed the thought out of his mind. No use thinking about that until he was forced to do so. As he walked on, he tried to decide where he should spend the rest of the morning. A warm spell had come through yesterday, and there would likely be punts upon the river to watch. Or he could go farther south, to the branch of the Cam where Newnham Mill sat. Perhaps a barge would be there, unloading fat sacks of corn.

While he was trying to decide, Thomas found himself walking closer and closer to Market Street. When he became aware of his direction, he thought, *It can't hurt to listen to the music.* But he would stand behind the crowd this time so that he wouldn't be carried along into a place where he didn't want to go.

The band was assembling, and a small crowd had gathered when he arrived in front of the building with the Salvation Army banner. This time he noticed another woman had joined them. She was young and pretty like Miss Burke and held no instrument.

Soon the band began playing, and the young woman took a step forward and began to sing:

> *"We walk by faith and not by sight;*
> *No gracious words we hear*
> *From him who spake as man ne'er spake,*
> *But we believe him near."*

Her voice was sweet, and she smiled often. Reluctantly, Thomas turned and worked his way to the back of the group of onlookers. Still he listened.

> *"We may not touch his hands and side,*
> *Nor follow where he trod;*
> *But in his promise we rejoice,*
> *And cry, 'My Lord and God!'"*

The little band played, and the woman sang four songs, then two more when someone in the crowd asked for them. Thomas wished that he had the nerve to squeeze through the crowd again and ask the lady with the smiling eyes for another song. There was something soothing, yet troubling, about the music. It sounded like home, and family, and love, yet it reminded him that he had none of these.

When the announcement was made about services and food inside, he turned to leave. He stopped when he felt a touch upon his shoulder.

"Wouldn't you like to stay? There is food inside."

Thomas turned to face the young woman who had been singing and was stricken with bashfulness. "Not hungry," he mumbled.

"Then come have some food for the soul." She held out her hand. "I'm Evangeline Booth."

"Thomas Sully," he mumbled, shaking her hand. He glanced at the people pressing to get inside the door. "You work there?"

She laughed. "My father and I work at the London mission. But we visit the others as they're established. You see, my father founded the Salvation Army."

He didn't know what he was expected to say, so he came out with, "You sing pretty."

Again she laughed. "I'll be singing some more inside, Thomas. Why don't you stay?"

*There probably won't be any grain barges today,* he told himself. And even though there was a nice warmth in the air, the river Cam would still be cold. *No punts on the water, either.* "Well, maybe for a little while," he muttered.

He sat in the very back row so that he could leave whenever he was ready. An older man was standing up on the platform this time, and Thomas wondered if he were the young woman's father. There was a resemblance, although the lines of the man's face were more severe. Still, he had the same smiling eyes, and Thomas settled into his back-row bench and listened.

"'My sheep hear my voice, and I know them, and they follow me,'" the man read from a black Bible.

"'And I give unto them eternal life; and they shall never perish, neither shall any man pluck them out of my hand. My Father, which gave them to me, is greater than all, and no man is able to pluck them out of my Father's hand.'"

Thomas leaned forward. On the wall in the servants' hall at Miss Knight's was a framed portrait of a lamb being held by a kind-looking man carrying a bent staff. Underneath were some phrases having to do with the Lord being a shepherd. He had always felt drawn to that picture whenever he joined the others for meals in that room.

"'I am the good shepherd,'" the man read on. "'The good shepherd giveth his life for the sheep.'"

*His life?* Of course Thomas had gathered from listening to prayers around the supper table that we were to be grateful to Jesus for dying for us. But the *why* of it all had escaped his understanding.

His ears perked up when the man up front lowered his book and said, "No matter what you've done in the past, be it adultery or robbery . . . or even murder, Jesus wants to be *your* good shepherd."

*My good shepherd?* It made little sense that Jesus would be interested in anyone who stole and had never even had a father. Thomas listened as the man went on to describe the Son of God's death upon a cross and his coming to life three days later.

"He allowed himself to die and then came back to life

again, so that you would see that there is nothing to fear from death. And he would like nothing more than to cleanse you with his precious blood, so that you may stand blameless before his Father in heaven."

The thought of standing blameless before anyone, and especially God, was too much for Thomas's comprehension. He glanced at the faces around him and found most watching the preacher with rapt attention, some wiping their eyes with handkerchiefs or the backs of sleeves. Their expressions seemed to mirror how he was feeling. *How wonderful it would be if this was true!*

Then someone began playing a violin, and the young woman with the sweet voice walked up to the front.

"Come every soul by sin oppressed," she sang.

Thomas didn't exactly know what *oppressed* meant, but it sounded exactly like what his sin was doing to him.

"There's mercy with the Lord."

How could he even ask for mercy, when he would likely steal again next week?

"And he will surely give you rest . . ."

*Rest,* Thomas thought. What did it feel like to rest? It had been so long.

"By trusting in his word."

He wanted to trust, so much, and to join the others who were filtering toward the front. The man at the platform spoke again, as the violin continued to play softly. "My friend . . . if you're thinking of waiting until sin no longer has a grip upon you, then you'll never be saved. Come to Jesus and allow him to help you loosen those bonds of sin."

*I want to,* Thomas explained to the preacher silently, for it seemed now that the man could read his very thoughts, could see the struggle going on inside of him. A picture came to his mind of Orville turning the pillbox over and over in his hands, of himself slipping through the dark to steal. The room suddenly became unbearably warm, and his hands, gripping the sides of his bench, began to sweat. *I have to leave,* he thought, as a wave of nausea coursed through him. Grateful that he was in the back row, he slipped away and was through the door before anyone could ask him to stay.

~

That afternoon in his private room at Pembroke Hall, Gregory Woodruff stood at the wall mirror and rubbed several drops of Brooke's Elegant Hair Dressing for Gentlemen briskly through his dark hair with both hands. He picked up his comb from his dresser and asked himself again why he felt so driven to meet the woman who was his aunt's houseguest. True, she was beautiful, but there were other beautiful women in Cambridge—and most were far less snooty than Miss Burke.

Phelps's words had stung him Thursday night, even though he would have undergone torture rather than allow the clerk to know it. *She disliked me at the depot because I was too forward. My fault.* He knew better now. Women of Miss Burke's sort were only interested in men who were too cowed to do anything but tiptoe around a woman's delicate sensibilities—boys who spent too much of their childhoods under the care of nursemaids and nannies and didn't know how to be men.

After straightening his cravat, he drew back his lips and checked his teeth in the mirror until satisfied that he had cleaned them thoroughly. He then practiced different smiles—some showing teeth, some close-lipped—studying his reflection from all angles to see which made him appear most like the "harmlessly roguish" and "charming though unaware of it" persona he wished to project.

*One day she'll beg me to love her.* He knew he could win her heart. True, it was going to take some work, but he looked forward to the challenge. No woman had the right to look down her nose at him the way she had at the depot, no matter how forward he had acted. He would prove to himself once again that his good looks and charm were irresistible to even the most high-minded of women.

~

Matthew exhaled heavily at the sight of Gregory Woodruff coming across the Pembroke College lawn. Clad in a well-cut, double-breasted navy jacket and gray trousers, he looked every inch the son of a country squire, from the derby to the pipe peeking from his breast coat pocket.

"Good afternoon to you, Phelps," Woodruff said when he was closer. He frowned down at one of his white sleeve cuffs and held out his wrist. "Be a good man, will you, and fasten the cuff? Isn't it frustrating how something always goes awry when you want to look your best?"

"Yes," Matthew replied as he pulled the gold button back through the opening and fastened it. "So, you haven't come to your senses, have you?"

A trio of young women passed by on the footway, parasols lifted above their bonnets. Mr. Woodruff smiled at them while touching the brim of his derby. "Why, I never left my senses."

"Well, you've wasted your time dressing up. I've changed my mind."

"I beg your pardon?"

"You can't come with me."

"You don't say?" Mr. Woodruff gave him a benign smile, as if dealing with a temperamental child. "Didn't we go through all this last night?"

"I'm ashamed that I allowed you to talk me into it last night," Matthew said, standing his ground. "And I've got enough to be ashamed for already. I'm sure you can find something else to do today."

The aristocratic lines of Woodruff's face hardened. "You forget that I'm the one who hired you."

With a shake of the head, Matthew answered, "I've not forgotten, but until you decide to dismiss me, *I'm* Gregory Woodruff at your aunt's house. And you, 'Mr. Tarleton,' are not invited."

For several seconds the real Mr. Woodruff stood there with a smoldering fury in his blue eyes, as if weighing the consequences of striking him. Matthew stared back, hoping that he would. But then the man surprised him by giving a resigned shrug. "Obviously you have me at a disadvantage."

His posture was so defeated that Matthew almost took pity on him. "I apologize that you dressed up for nothing. I wasn't sure if you'd want me to contact you here, or I would have looked you up this morning."

"Oh, don't concern yourself about me," Mr. Woodruff replied. He straightened the lapel of his coat. "A good set of clothes is never wasted."

Still not quite believing that the man had given in so easily, Matthew watched him turn and walk down the busy footway of Pembroke Street toward the Botanical Gardens. The man cut an elegant figure, drawing glances from more than one woman he passed. Strange, that someone like him would have such a profound effect upon Matthew's life. What was sup-

posed to be a couple of hours every Sunday afternoon now
consumed a good portion of his waking thoughts and had
given him many a restless night's sleep. He had even fallen in
love as a result of those visits, although it was a love doomed
to smolder in his heart in secret.

*What will come of all this?* he wondered. With each visit
to Miss Knight's, he added to his house of cards. How long
before it collapsed under its own weight?

His melancholy thoughts were put aside when Mr. Henry
pulled up beside him in the trap. *There wouldn't have been room
for him anyway,* Matthew told himself wryly as he climbed
aboard to sit next to the driver.

"Sorry I'm a bit late, Mr. Woodruff," Mr. Henry said in
his gravelly voice. "Pleasant Sunday weather brings out every
carriage in the city."

"It would seem so, wouldn't it?" Matthew said, eyeing the
congestion of vehicles moving up Trumpington Street.

"And how is the day treating you?"

Matthew glanced over his shoulder. "Better now."

Now that he didn't have to worry about Gregory Woodruff
making an appearance, he sat back and wondered if Deborah
was still angry with him over his behavior at the concert Tuesday night. He had been so tempted to confess everything after
he saw the hurt in her eyes. She would have understood then
why he'd backed away. Of course, she would have hated him,
too, but at least she would have known that he hadn't suddenly found her lacking.

But she would leave his life forever if she knew the truth,
and he would just as soon tear his heart out of his chest as
cause that to happen.

~

"Fourteen Park Parade," Gregory Woodruff told the driver
as he swung into a hackney cab. "You'll have to take the back
way up Queen's Road to get there, but there's a half crown
extra if you take less than ten minutes."

The driver spat out a wad of tobacco and lifted the reins to
a powerful-looking black Irish draft horse. "Bessie'll make it
there in five."

Gregory braced his feet on the floorboard and gripped the
sides of his seat for dear life when the cab made a right turn
onto Silver Street and then another onto Queen's Road. But
Queen's Road, on the outskirts of town, was far less choked
with vehicles than Trinity Street had been, and the driver
made good his promise. After Gregory stepped down from the
carriage and paid the man, he had to stand still for a second or
two until his equilibrium returned and he could take the steps
leading to his aunt Helene's portico.

A homely looking maid with ginger-colored hair answered
the door, and Gregory immediately began to pour on the
charm. "Good afternoon, miss," he said, lifting his hat and
giving her one of his best smiles. "My name is Fred Tarleton.
Is it possible that I might pay a call upon Miss Knight?"

The maid looked unsure and glanced over her shoulder
before replying, "Does she know you, Mr. Tarleton?"

"Well, not directly." He pretended to fumble in his waistcoat pocket. "I left in such a hurry that I forgot my cards. But
I share a staircase with her nephew, Gregory Woodruff, at
Pembroke College." Lowering his voice in a confidential
manner, he said, "Gregory invited me to come along with him
today, but I had an appointment with one of my tutors and

didn't see how I could make it. Fortunately, the appointment was canceled . . . but I missed catching up with Gregory."

He gazed past the maid into the empty entrance hall. "Has he shown up yet?"

By this time the maid was favoring him with a smile. "Not yet, sir, but come on inside, and I'll show you up to Miss Knight. No doubt Mr. Gregory will be pleased as punch you could make it after all."

"Oh, I'm sure of that," the real Gregory answered, handing her his hat as he stepped through the doorway.

He had thought that he wouldn't remember the inside of his aunt's house, having visited it only once when he was two or three years old. But as he followed the maid up the staircase, the smooth carved oak of the banister felt familiar to his hand, and he hesitated for a half second at the sight of his father and mother's wedding portrait above the wainscoting.

On the next floor, the maid paused at a door facing the front of the house and turned to give him a grave smile. "Mr. Gregory *has* told you that Miss Knight is blind, hasn't he?"

"He has," Woodruff answered solemnly, thinking how odd it was to hear his name spoken while referring to another person. "But is there anything else I should know?"

She put her hand on the doorknob. "Just be sure you don't yell at her. Some people think they have to when they first meet her, but she ain't deaf."

He nodded and followed the maid into the room. His aunt sat alone with her back to the fireplace, her lined face raised in his direction with an expression of pleased expectancy. "Gregory?"

His throat tightened at the thought of his aunt feeling so affectionate toward a stranger he'd paid to deceive her. But he

239

rationalized that as long as she was happy, it didn't really matter who was responsible for the happiness.

"No, missus. This here is Mr. Tarleton," the maid said, motioning for him to go closer and take her hand. "He's a friend of Gregory's."

"Indeed?" Still smiling, Aunt Helene lifted her chin.

"Fred Tarleton," he said and walked closer to take her frail hand. "Gregory invited me, but it appears that I've gotten here too early."

"Oh, not too early, Mr. Tarleton," Aunt Helene said, smiling. "And I'm happy that Gregory invited a friend."


Avis was all smiles as she held open the door for Matthew. "Miss Knight is in the sitting room now," she said after they had exchanged greetings, "and Miss Burke is on her way down."

Matthew returned the smile and handed her his hat and muffler. As had been his practice since his second visit, he climbed the staircase alone to the drawing room on the next floor. The door was open, and he walked in just in time to see Gregory Woodruff standing in front of Miss Knight's chair with her hand clasped in his.

"Oh, here he is now," Bethina said when she spotted him just inside the doorway. "Good day, Mr. Gregory. Your friend made it here after all."

The real Gregory Woodruff turned to grin at him. "Well, you finally decided to show up, old chap!"

Once the disorientation wore off, Matthew took a step closer, aware that he could feel the veins throbbing in his temples. "How did you . . . ?"

"My meeting with old Henson was canceled at the last minute," Mr. Woodruff went on in a lighthearted manner. "I tried to catch up with you, but you'd already left."

Matthew heard a footstep behind him and turned to see Deborah entering the room. She looked lovely in a gray dress with narrow burgundy stripes, her hair drawn back in a thick coil, with little pearls at her ears. For a fraction of a second, he thought about how wonderful it had felt to kiss her, but he pushed the thought from his mind as soon as it had come. "Hello, Gregory," she said, avoiding his eyes, but then caught sight of Mr. Woodruff and froze.

"Deborah?" Miss Knight said, her face in their direction. "Gregory?"

"I'm here, Miss Knight," Deborah told her. This time her eyes met Matthew's with an expression of bewilderment.

*I'm sorry,* he tried to signal back with his own eyes.

Her mouth set in a grim line, Deborah walked over to touch her hostess's arm. The real Gregory straightened, and for once, something like nervousness flitted across his expression.

It left as quickly as it had come, for with practiced warmth, he said, "I was just asking your aunt to forgive me for imposing upon her hospitality."

Miss Knight smiled. "And I was telling Mr. Tarleton how happy we are to have him here. Any friend of my nephew's is most welcome." She turned her face in Matthew's direction. "Would you bring up another chair, Gregory?"

"I don't believe Mr. Tarleton planned to stay the afternoon, Aunt Helene," Matthew said with a meaningful glance at Mr. Woodruff. "He's quite busy with his studies. The end of the term is just around the corner, you know."

"Oh, but I can spare the time for a visit," Mr. Woodruff countered, his smile as angelic as a schoolboy's. Leaning down

241

to his aunt again, he added, "But only if you're positive that it's no imposition."

Miss Knight assured him that he was welcome, so there was nothing for Matthew to do but fetch another chair from the fireplace. He set it down facing Miss Knight's right, so that Mr. Woodruff would be on the opposite side of Deborah, with himself in the middle. But when he looked up to offer the chair to Mr. Woodruff, he discovered the man had already seated himself . . . in *his* chair.

Grinding his teeth, Matthew sat down in the extra chair and looked over at Deborah, now seated on Mr. Woodruff's right side. She sat rigid on the edge of her seat, her expression unreadable. Just a fortnight ago she had expressed relief that he didn't know the "odious" person from Walesby, and now here he was, bringing that same person to call. Matthew couldn't very well say that he had no idea Fred Tarleton was the same man because she *had* told him that the man was from Walesby. How many men from the same small town could there be at Pembroke College?

There was no way to explain himself out of that, so he sat down, stared at the chimneypiece behind Miss Knight's chair, and wished himself a hundred miles away.

"Are you at Pembroke with Gregory, Mr. Tarleton?" Miss Knight asked, her expression as trusting as usual.

"We even share a staircase, but only this week did we realize we both came from Walesby," he said, his eyes shining from the wonder of it. "Imagine, growing up in the same place and never meeting! But then Gregory here was sent away for his schooling, and I went to school in the village."

Then, with a stroke of audacity that left Matthew speechless, Mr. Woodruff sent an apologetic glance to Deborah and said, "The reason I begged Gregory to allow me to come along is that I wanted to apologize to Miss Burke for making a fool of myself upon our first meeting. When Gregory told me about your houseguest, I thought it a stroke of good fortune, for I had despaired of an opportunity to ever make up for my inexcusable behavior."

Deborah shot a questioning look at Matthew and gave the real Mr. Woodruff a tentative nod. "I'm sure you meant well," she said with absolutely no warmth in her voice.

"Ah, but that's where you're mistaken . . . although it pains me to admit it." Mr. Woodruff wore a convincing expression of self-loathing. Lifting a hand in a helpless gesture, he said, "How can I explain? I was so full of myself that day. Going off to Cambridge. Out to make my mark upon the world!"

His blue eyes lowered to stare humbly down at the carpet. "Only when I arrived at the university, I discovered there were hundreds just like me and that I was quite low in the pecking order."

Deborah's face softened, just a bit, at this display of candor. "I sometimes struggle with those feelings myself."

"You?" He shook his head. "I find that impossible to believe, Miss Burke."

"Oh, but that's one of the pitfalls of the performing arts," she told him, her green eyes serious. "You have to have confidence in yourself, or you'll never be able to walk out onstage. But confidence and conceit seem to be only a fine line apart, and sometimes I discover that I've stepped over that line."

Miss Knight clucked her tongue lightly and said, "You're too modest, Deborah. *I've* never detected any conceit in your character."

243

"That's because you see only the best in everyone," Deborah told her affectionately.

The elderly woman waved away the compliment. "Come now, I can be just as critical as the next person."

"Somehow I find that impossible to believe," Mr. Woodruff said with that same warmth he had displayed when meeting the old woman. Crossing one knee over the other, he said, "If you'll forgive my bluntness, I would wager—if I were a gambling man—that you would be hard-pressed to remember the last time you were critical of anyone."

Miss Knight sent an amused smile in his direction and said, "How long have you known me, Mr. Tarleton?"

"Well, not very long, I admit."

"So how can you make that assumption about my character?"

"Because your character is written all over your face, if you'll pardon the cliché." Settling back easily in the cushions of his chair, Mr. Woodruff added, "So now I suppose I'm presenting you with a challenge. When *was* the last time you were critical of anyone, Miss Knight?"

*Tell him it's none of his business,* Matthew urged under his breath. He understood Woodruff's strategy and, in spite of his dislike for the man, had to admit it was nothing short of genius. The cad had obviously figured out that the way to Deborah's heart was through solicitous attention to others, chiefly Miss Knight. *He doesn't care one whit about his aunt. . . . He's just trying to impress Deborah.*

To his disappointment, Miss Knight answered after a thoughtful pause, "I was convinced that Mr. Disraeli was foolish to buy shares in the Suez Canal. But look how wrong I turned out to be."

"And that was in 1876, if my grammar schooling wasn't wasted." Mr. Woodruff exchanged quick smiles with Deborah. "Seven years ago, Miss Knight?"

"Oh, but I was extremely critical of him to anyone who would listen, may God rest his soul." Miss Knight was obviously embarrassed but just as obviously pleased with the young man she thought to be her nephew's friend.

Bethina appeared with the tray, and Mr. Woodruff was on his feet before Matthew could sit up in his chair. "Here, let me help you with that table," he said to the maid, who blushed and thanked him.

Then, in another stroke of genius, Mr. Woodruff grew quiet during tea, as if he realized he had dominated the conversation long enough. He answered Miss Knight's and even Deborah's questions with a bashful reluctance that could fool even the most sharp-witted observer. And when his aunt told him of Deborah's opportunity to audition in Venice, he responded with quiet congratulations, telling her that he envied anyone with the tenacity to pursue her dreams.

When the time came for Matthew to read from *Treasure Island,* Mr. Woodruff, who had likely never read a book for pleasure in his life, sat back against his chair with his hands clasped behind his head and his eyes half closed, as if imagining the scenes that the words painted. He was quite convincing as a book lover, but Matthew glanced up from the page once and caught Mr. Woodruff shifting his eyes to the clock on the mantel, a fleeting expression of boredom upon his face. They locked eyes, briefly, and Woodruff gave him a lightning-quick look that conveyed the message, *Haven't you read long enough?*

Matthew glanced at Miss Knight and Deborah. The two wore their usual expressions of relaxed attentiveness, so he read on with animation until the clock chimed six, and Miss Knight apologized for not stopping him an hour ago. "I was so caught up in the story that I lost track of time again, dear," she said, with Deborah nodding her head in agreement. "Let me send word to Mrs. Reeves that you'll stay for supper."

"Thank you, Aunt Helene, but I'm afraid we'll have to pass this time," Matthew was quick to reply as he shot to his feet. "Fred and I each have a beast of a paper to finish tonight."

"Actually, it isn't *that* . . . ," Mr. Woodruff began, but Matthew turned around and gave him a chummy grin.

"Now, Fred, your very words to me this morning were that we should give ourselves enough time to work, remember?"

"Oh, dear." Miss Knight's hand touched her cheek. "And I've kept you so long."

Matthew turned to her and took her hand. "Please don't concern yourself. It was our pleasure." It was a relief to speak at least a word of truth for a change, for he did enjoy reading to the two women. And the opportunity to torment Woodruff had made it even more pleasurable.

"The story *was* quite fascinating," Mr. Woodruff agreed. He got to his feet reluctantly, while his eyes flitted a murderous glance at Matthew. "I shall have to buy a copy of the book."

"You're welcome to come back with Gregory and join our little reading circle," Miss Knight told him as he leaned down to kiss her hand. "Anytime."

"I hope you don't feel pressured to ask me. I certainly wouldn't want to impose upon your kind hospitality."

"It's no imposition at all."

Mr. Woodruff turned to Deborah, who was now standing. "It was good to make your acquaintance again, Miss Burke," he said simply, shaking her hand in a nonflirtatious manner.

Her posture eased a bit, as if she had been expecting the opposite.

"Thank you," she said simply.

Mr. Henry had the barouche ready so that the two men could ride back together. Once the ringing of the horses' hooves and reverberations of the wheels covered his voice, Mr. Woodruff looked across at Matthew and said, "I know what you were doing back in there, old boy."

Matthew raised an eyebrow. "Reading? How very astute of you."

A smirk crossed the man's face. "You know what I'm talking about. And I know why. It's for the same reason you weren't going to tell me that she's leaving Cambridge soon. You've definitely become smitten with her yourself . . . haven't you?"

"That's none of your business."

"You know there's no future in it . . . you and her," Mr. Woodruff went on, folding his arms and settling back in his seat. "Even if you weren't pretending to be someone else, she's miles above your class."

Although he knew better than to argue, Matthew took the bait. "And what future have you with her? As you said, she's leaving soon. And you can't go on being Fred Tarleton forever."

"I realize that, but that's where we differ, my friend." Woodruff smiled. "I'm not interested in 'forever.' I'll settle for 'as long as it suits me.' Besides, I've only got eight weeks, haven't I?"

"Miss Burke is more perceptive than you think she is. She could never feel anything for someone like you."

"Someone like me?" Mr. Woodruff covered a mock yawn with his gloved hand, but it was obvious that he was taking a cruel delight in baiting Matthew. "Poverty puts such limitations on a courtship, Mr. Phelps, so I'll excuse your ignorance.

You can't possibly be aware of how flowers, jewelry, and expensive little gifts can, over time, change a woman's heart. Why, I might just stay in town over the Christmas holidays. Christmas is such a romantic time, don't you think?"

"Why her?" Matthew persisted. "I'm sure you can have your pick of women."

"That may be so, but the pursuit grows boring when the catch is easy."

Having Deborah referred to as a "catch" was the last straw. Leaning forward suddenly, Matthew stretched out his arms and took hold of both of Mr. Woodruff's lapels.

"Hey, what—?" the man protested, but Matthew pulled him close, so that their faces were only inches apart.

"How welcome do you think you'll be without me next Sunday?" he hissed through his teeth.

"Take your hands off of me!" Woodruff exclaimed, causing Matthew to tighten his grip.

"If you show up there next Sunday, or any Sunday, while Miss Burke is still there, I will tell them that you are no friend of mine, and then I will leave. Do you think they'll ask you to stay and visit?"

Gregory Woodruff glared back, his face red as a brick. "You do that, and I won't pay."

"I don't care. You are going to stay away from that house."

Both men scowled across at each other in the tense silence until Woodruff held up both palms. "Fine, then. I won't go. Now, would you stop wrinkling my coat?"

Matthew let go, and Woodruff sank back into his seat. He brushed at his lapels, his pride obviously injured. After a minute of this he looked up at Matthew. "This is a free country, Phelps," he said carefully. "You can keep me away from that house, but you won't stop me from finding another way to meet her. After all, we *have* been formerly introduced."

~

"Mr. Tarleton was quite pleasant company," Miss Knight remarked over a supper of poached haddock with parsley sauce. "But I wonder if I was too hasty in inviting him to join again."

"Why is that?" Deborah asked.

"At times there seemed to be a hesitancy in your voice when you spoke with him. I wish I had paid more attention to it."

*For a blind person, she observes more than most people,* Deborah thought. "His manners were exemplary, but I suppose our first meeting has me still a little prejudiced against him. It's really not fair of me."

"What happened during your first meeting, if I may ask?"

"Nothing drastic, actually. And he *was* quite helpful." She went on to relate the meeting at the railway station. "But it came to a point where I felt uncomfortable with the way he was looking at me. He made me feel . . . well, ashamed of being a woman, if that makes any sense."

"It makes perfect sense." Miss Knight frowned. "I wish I had known. I wouldn't have invited him back here."

"Oh, but I'm glad you didn't know. It would have been unfair of me to prejudice you against him. And he did apologize for his earlier behavior."

"But you're not sure if he meant it, are you?"

"Let's just say I feel the need to be skeptical until I know him better."

"That may be a wise idea. Give discernment time to work."

"You sound like my father."

"I do? I'll take that as a compliment." Miss Knight sighed. "You know, I've never been one to brood about my blindness, but it is frustrating not to be able to see people's faces. You can tell so much about people's character from their expressions, their eyes particularly."

Deborah had to smile. "If you were any sharper, you would be reading minds."

"Oh, not at all. I make mistakes even now." She leaned forward on her elbow. "Take my nephew, for instance. The first day Gregory called, I felt that something wasn't right about him."

*"Gregory?* You mean it?"

"See what I mean about not being able to see the face? No doubt I would have taken one look in his eyes and instantly formed the opinion that he was the most well-bred young man in England—" she smiled and added—"which I've become certain that he is."

Even though she still brooded inside over what had happened Tuesday evening, Deborah couldn't imagine anyone having anything but favorable thoughts toward Gregory Woodruff. She realized then that, apart from the reading, he had been quieter than usual this afternoon, as if troubled about something. Did he think as often as she did about the brief kiss they had shared?

"My first opinion of Gregory was that he was rather shy," she said. "And often he's that way even now." *Could that be the reason he backed away?*

Miss Knight felt for her fork, which she had accidentally pushed out of the way with her water glass, and Deborah reached over to place it in her hand.

250

"Thank you," her hostess said, expertly using the utensil to pick up the next bit of fish. "For a year or so after I lost my sight, I allowed servants to hover over me as I ate, cutting my portions and buttering my bread. I grew weary of being fed like an infant, so I refused to allow anyone to help me anymore." She smiled. "It must have been a messy sight for a long time."

"But regarding Gregory again," Miss Knight went on, "you mentioned his occasional bashfulness. From what I hear in his voice, it seems that he's afflicted with it chiefly when he's speaking with you. Have you noticed?"

Deborah could almost feel the pressure of his arm against hers as they sat together at the guildhall. "I've noticed."

Miss Knight smiled in her direction. "As I mentioned, Deborah, I've the disadvantage of not being able to read faces. But unless my nephew sits there every Sunday and scowls at you without my knowledge, I would say that he has deep feelings for you."

*I know.* The words came to Deborah's mind at once. She recalled the way he had looked at her, up in the box at the concert, and the light-headedness that had come over her as they kissed. A shiver ran down her neck. What had he said to her afterward? *"I don't deserve to be here with you, Deborah."*

"I have embarrassed you, haven't I?" Miss Knight said, her expression worried.

"Not at all. I just don't know what to think about it." She thought about the weekly journals she had already sent home, how more and more often Gregory's name seemed to crop up. "I am . . . fond of him as well," she admitted. "But as a friend . . . not in a romantic way." The words caught in her throat, and even as she said them, she knew they weren't true.

"And here I am, practically having the two of you engaged."

Miss Knight sighed and felt for Deborah's hand. "Don't allow me . . . or Avis or Bethina . . . to pressure you, dear. I'm selfish enough to want you in our family, but I suppose it's time for me to tend to my crocheting and dominos and allow things to happen naturally . . . if they're to happen at all."

Gently Deborah squeezed her frail hand. "I appreciate your understanding. And I'm honored that you would want me in your family."

They finished the rest of the meal in a companionable silence, and when Bethina came in the dining room to lead Miss Knight up to her bath and bed, Deborah went to her own room to study the Italian words for the role of Rosalie. Yesterday she had found herself humming snatches of tunes from the opera. It was becoming a part of her, as had the other operas she had memorized.

She still hadn't written to her family about Signora Pella wanting her to go to Venice. Why get their hopes up when she still felt so uneasy about it?

*I'll tell the signora that I will take the part only if she and Signor Giuseppe agree to stay away from each other.* But on the heels of that thought came the realization, *They would never agree to that.*

She couldn't prevent their adultery. They could both leave their families tonight and run away together, and it certainly wouldn't be her fault. She *almost* wished that they would and not involve her in their sordid scheme. Bitterness rose in her throat. She was to be used as a smoke screen that Signora Pella and Signor Giuseppe could hide behind with no fear of being sued for divorce.

*Well, I just won't do it,* she thought, swallowing hard. So what if this was a role that most of the sopranos from the Royal Academy of Music would have shaved their heads for?

Posters and playbills, reviews and telegrams would be poor compensation for the sleepless nights her conscience would cause her.

A picture crossed Deborah's mind, then, of the faces of her family and friends when she was forced to return to London. There was no doubt that Signora Pella would immediately drop her as a pupil if she refused to go to Venice.

*But I don't have to tell her right away,* her mind argued. I could still stay in Cambridge for a while. Signora Pella was being well paid for the lessons. And she had to study *something.* What difference did it make if *Isabella* was the teaching tool?

Still, was it right to lead Signora Pella on this way? *I didn't ask her to put me in this position,* Deborah thought. *And God hasn't given me a definite answer yet.* Surely it would be best to wait for that before doing anything rash.

*Lord, please show me what to do,* she found herself praying again. *I'm not strong like my parents—and far less strong than Signora Pella.*

# 15

LATE that night Matthew sat on the edge of his bed with his head cradled in his hands. *Where was your mind?* he asked himself. Why had he allowed Gregory Woodruff to dupe him into going along this afternoon? He could have simply denied knowing "Fred Tarleton" and escorted him to the door. What could Woodruff have done—dismissed him?

How could any man sit there and deceive his dear, helpless aunt the way Woodruff had, with apparently no qualms about it?

*If he's this ruthless with family,* he asked himself, *what will he do to Deborah if he has a chance?*

An ache in his jaw made him aware that he had been clenching his teeth. Things had gone far enough, he decided. No amount of money, no future promise of education, was worth the lie he had been living. And Miss Knight didn't deserve this. Yes, the truth was going to cause her pain, and he hated that thought, but the truth had to be told—immediately. Tomorrow he would go to her house after work and confess everything. Then he would look up Gregory Woodruff at Pembroke and return every shilling he'd been paid.

With his decision came a welcome rush of relief, as if a heavy load had been lifted from his shoulders. But sorrow still gripped him in its vise. By this time tomorrow, Deborah would think even less of him than she did now, and Miss Knight's heart would be broken. Those were the worst consequences of his decision.

The specter of prison didn't frighten him anymore, now that he'd had a chance to give Mr. Woodruff's warning some thought. Matthew had absorbed some knowledge of British law during his three years with Mr. Cornell. Miss Knight would have to be the one to notify the authorities, since the fraud had been perpetrated upon her and in her house. As crushed as she would be upon learning of the deception, Matthew knew in his heart of hearts that it was not in her nature to lift a hand against him.

Mr. Cornell would not be so forgiving. One complaint from Woodruff's father, and he would be sacked. *I can get another job,* he told himself. Maybe not in Cambridge, for he doubted that his employer would give him a character reference. But perhaps it was just as well, for everyone concerned. *At least I'll have a chance of getting back my self-respect . . . one day.*

~

Driven by a hunger that food could not satisfy, Orville Tilton plunged through the darkness down a narrow street flanked by tumbledown houses. Every door he passed stood open, revealing kitchen fires blazing far in the interior, and strange figures moving about.

Finally he reached a door that was closed. His knock was answered by a stocky man in corduroy breeches and gray stockings, his unbuttoned waistcoat revealing a dirty shirt.

"What have ye?" The man spat past Orville into the street. Jack Trumble was his name, and Orville had been doing business with him off and on for years.

Orville reached shaking fingers into his coat pocket and drew out a gold hunting case watch on a fine rope chain. It was a good thing he had never been one to put all of his eggs into one basket. Even though the boy hadn't brought him anything to sell today, he hadn't come to Jack empty-handed. *But I'll box his ears next week,* he thought.

Trumble held the watch and chain up close to inspect it, then smiled. "Th' boy brung ye this?"

Orville shook his head. "I took it off'n one of them college gents last night after he'd been too long at a pub. What's it worth to you?"

"Come on in," the man said. When the door was shut and locked behind them, he motioned with his head toward a chair in a drafty corner of the stark room. "I'll give ye a fiver for it."

*"A fiver!"* Orville shivered and drew his coat closer around his stringy frame. It seemed that he could never get warm these days. "It's worth four times that."

"But not to me. Ye know how it works."

Orville exhaled heavily, then nodded.

"The boy quit comin' over?" Trumble asked while unlocking a cupboard against a wall.

"He was there today, but all he left was some money."

Trumble took a hinged metal box bearing the trademark of Pride of the Kitchen Soap. "Ye think he still believes you took his mum to a sanatorium?"

"He believes anything I tell him," Orville boasted. "I been like a father to the brat." He could hear the sound of coins clinking together in the box, muted somewhat by paper bank notes.

"Ye never told me what you did to her."

"I didn't do nothing." With the thought of Doreen, a vague

feeling of sadness surfaced in Orville's mind, but his main concern was the money that would buy him some more opium. "She was already in a bad way when I hired a boy with a pony cart to take her up to the hospital. They had her last, so's I figgered it was their worry."

"Her name didn't get in the obits?"

"I didn't give 'em her name," Orville said with a sniff. "And she was too sick to tell 'em anything." His teeth began to chatter, and he stared hungrily at the box in Trumble's hands. His hand crept into his pocket, touching the handle of his knife. *He'll get twelve quid for that watch, at least! How much money has he cheated me out of over the years?*

"Here ye go," Trumble said, snapping the lid shut. He waved a five-pound note for Orville to see, then turned around to put the box back into the cupboard. Orville saw his chance and took it, flipping the knife open and springing to his feet with a wiry agility. He was only three feet away when the man turned to face him again. This time Trumble held a pistol in his hand and raised it to point at Orville's face.

"Goin' somewhere?" he said, a grin set wide in his face.

Orville's mouth gaped as he stared down the bore of the pistol. "I . . . I was just . . . ," he stammered, shoving his knife back into his pocket.

"Next time ye try that, make sure ye ain't all trembly," Trumble advised, still pointing the gun. With his other hand he held out a five-pound note by a corner. "And move a little faster, 'cause if you do it again I ain't gonna be so forgivin'."

~

Matthew began his clerical duties the next day as if he were a cog in a machine, automatic and unemotional. He had spent every last ounce of his emotional reserve in the dark hours of last night—all that was left was a shell of a man.

Even Mr. Cornell noticed something amiss, for when he came downstairs after his morning coffee and newspapers, he paused at Matthew's desk and peered owlishly over his spectacles at the stack of completed paperwork.

"How long have you been here, Phelps?" Mr. Cornell asked.

Matthew cleared his throat. "Since six, Mr. Cornell."

"Why so early?"

"I was going to ask if you'd allow me to leave an hour early today."

His employer lifted concerned eyes to Matthew's face. "Feeling ill, are you?"

"Not at all, sir. I've an important call to make, but I don't want to interfere with this person's supper."

Mr. Cornell waved a hand. "Certainly. I know your work will be done no matter what time you leave. You're the most conscientious employee I've ever had."

Matthew thanked him. His employer was generous with compliments upon his work performance, but Matthew was painfully aware that this would likely be the last time. Mrs. Cornell, leading a sullen Royce, passed through the office later on her way to pay some morning calls. As had her husband, she stopped at Matthew's desk and asked if he were feeling ill.

"I'm fine, thank you," he lied.

"Well, I'll have Cook send you down some strong onion soup for lunch," she told him. "It works wonders for Royce, here."

At five minutes past six, Matthew locked up his desk, took his hat and muffler, and left the office. He hailed a hackney on

259

King's Parade so that he could get to Miss Knight's house
as soon as possible. Now that he had decided to confess, he
wanted to get it over with. It occurred to him to wonder,
as the carriage approached Park Parade, if he should speak
to Miss Knight and Deborah separately or together.

*Together,* he decided at once. He had deceived them both
together, and they would certainly need to draw upon each
other's strength when faced with the truth about the monster
they had unwittingly allowed into their lives.

For a fleeting second, as he stood on the portico at the front
of the house, he considered turning around and going back to
the life he'd lived in his "pre-Gregory" days. He could simply
not show up for any more Sunday afternoon visits. What could
Mr. Woodruff do—tie him up and drag him over here? *Ring
the bell,* he told himself. Mrs. Darnell appeared at the door
mildly surprised to find him standing there on the portico.

"Mr. Gregory?"

He clutched his hat in his hands. "Has Miss Knight gone
to supper yet?"

If the housekeeper thought anything strange about his use
of "Miss Knight" instead of "Aunt Helene," her expression
didn't show it. "Why, no sir," she answered, opening the door
wider. "She's upstairs listening to Miss Burke practice her singing lessons. I'm sure they'd be happy to have you join them."

The temptation to turn back became almost overwhelming,
but it was too late. He thanked the housekeeper but kept hold
of his hat and muffler. For the sake of all concerned, it would
be best if he left the house as soon as possible once the deed
was done.

"Oh, by the way, Mr. Gregory," Mrs. Darnell said from
behind him as he started down the hall toward the staircase,

"your Mr. Tarleton sent over a lovely arrangement of red roses today for the missus and a big box of bonbons for Miss Burke."

He turned and offered her a feeble smile. "How kind of him."

At the bottom of the staircase, he could hear music drifting down from the next floor. Piano notes, and a woman's voice, as clear and smooth as water. He moved on leaden feet up the steps, wishing that he could stay there forever and listen to the bittersweet strains of the music. But every note made a fresh wound in his heart.

When he reached the door to the drawing room, he took hold of the knob but leaned his head against the frame, waiting for some miraculous surge of strength that would allow him to go into the room.

"Mr. Gregory?" Mrs. Darnell's voice came from behind him. Matthew turned and focused his bleary eyes upon her.

"Are you all right, sir?"

He nodded, turned the knob, and opened the door. At the piano, Deborah was singing something in Italian to Miss Knight. Bethina and Mr. Henry sat in shield-back chairs with their backs to the door. She looked surprised to see Matthew but finished the last few notes of her song. "Good evening, Gregory," she said after graciously acknowledging the applause of her small audience.

The servants got up from their chairs, and Miss Knight turned her face toward the door. "Gregory is here?"

Stepping into the room, Matthew caught a whiff of sweetness and noticed the red roses, at least three dozen, spilling from a vase on one of the tables. "May I speak with you and Deborah . . . alone?"

"Why, of course you may," she answered as the two servants

slipped out of the room. "Come and sit down. Has something happened at the university?"

He looked at the roses again. "I wish it were that simple."

He told them both the whole story, from the day that Gregory Woodruff walked into Mr. Cornell's law office. His voice choked up twice—once, at the sight of tears on Miss Knight's wrinkled cheeks, and again when he noticed the coldness in Deborah's expression.

When he was finished, he stopped talking and waited. No doubt they had questions, and he owed them answers.

The silence was eventually broken by Miss Knight. "Why would Gregory hire you to take his place?"

Even though she couldn't see him, Matthew couldn't bear to look at her. He stared down at the hat he had balanced upon one knee and considered how to answer. He would have felt more than justified in railing against Gregory Woodruff for his selfishness, but it was time to spare this good woman from even more hurt. Besides, he sat before them no less guilty than Gregory Woodruff.

"Your nephew never really got to know you as a child . . . remember?" Matthew answered with a voice that sounded as hollow as the emptiness in his chest. "And he did mention being afraid that he wouldn't be good company for you."

Again a silence hung heavy over them, until Miss Knight said, "Why?"

"Why?" Matthew cleared his throat. "Perhaps he was unsure of what would be expected of—"

"I'm not asking about Gregory now," the elderly woman cut in. "I'm asking why you agreed to do this."

Matthew raised his head to look at her now. She had wiped

the tears from her face, but the pain was still obvious. "Money, Miss Knight."

"Money," she echoed softly and sadly. "Then you never really cared for me . . . for us?"

Matthew glanced over at Deborah's appraising green eyes and wondered if the lump in his throat would strangle him. "I didn't know either of you when I agreed to do this," he got out. "But if I hadn't grown to care about you, I wouldn't be putting an end to this now."

Finally Deborah spoke, her voice as cold as granite. "Who are you?"

He looked at her again. "My name is Matthew Phelps."

"And why did Gregory change his mind and decide to come here?" Miss Knight asked. But before he could answer, she said in a flat voice, "It was because of Deborah, wasn't it?"

He had to answer truthfully this time, even though it would cause more hurt. "Yes."

"Then he still has no feeling for me."

"I wouldn't say that," Matthew told her. "He chose me to take his place because he wanted someone—" he had started to say *honest,* but the word wouldn't form on his tongue— "who wouldn't steal from you."

He lowered his head again. "I didn't realize, then, that stealing someone's trust is just as wrong as stealing material objects. Or that I would care for you . . . both . . . so much." The emptiness in his heart threatened to overwhelm him, and he got to his feet. "I don't deserve even to ask for your forgiveness. But I want you to know that as soon as I leave here, I'm going to give Mr. Woodruff back all of the money he paid me."

As he turned and walked across the room, he was aware that Deborah's eyes followed him. It struck him that he would never see her again, and he had to fight the compulsion to look at her one last time.

Miss Knight's soft voice stopped him at the door.

"Don't."

Matthew turned around, not quite sure that he'd heard correctly. The older woman's face was set in his direction, her expression unreadable.

"Don't tell Gregory."

"You don't want him to know that I told you?"

She nodded, her lips pressed together.

Stunned at this request, Matthew could only stand there and gape at her.

"I want him to visit next Sunday," Miss Knight said. "As Mr. Tarleton. You must see that he comes with you."

"Aunt . . . ," he began and then clamped his mouth shut over the rest of the name he had called her for weeks. He noticed the look of horror on Deborah's face and said, "Please don't ask me to come back here."

"You must." Her tone was firm, adamant, and with no note of pleading in it. "You may think of some reason to leave once Gregory is inside my house."

Recalling the words he'd had with Woodruff last night, Matthew said, "I'm afraid I've told him not to visit here anymore."

She hesitated in thought and then said, "I will see that he comes. Just make sure that you accompany him, so that he won't be suspicious."

He took another step into the room. "But why?"

"Because I'm asking you," was Miss Knight's reply. "And you owe me that much . . . Mr. Phelps."

~

When the last of his footsteps faded in the hallway, Deborah got up from her chair and knelt on the carpet beside Miss Knight's chair. "I'm so sorry," she whispered, placing a hand over the woman's frail arm.

Miss Knight turned a sad smile in her direction. "It's my fault for being so gullible, dear. My niece has shielded me from any unpleasant news about her family, but I wondered a long time ago why there was no mention of Gregory after he left Owens College. He was her favorite, and her letters were once full of him."

"You mustn't blame yourself. What he did was despicable. What both of them . . ." Her words were left hanging at the thought of Matthew Phelps.

"I'm more sorry for you," Miss Knight said, her sightless eyes glistening. "What happened to me was a prank by a spoiled young man . . . even if he is my nephew. But you cared about him, didn't you?"

Deborah knew to which man she was referring, and she didn't know how to answer. At the moment she hated Matthew Phelps—or so she thought. Why then did she feel as if someone had died? She thought of the three stones he had pressed into her hand. Had the man in the garden ever really existed or the man who could make an old woman smile by reading stories?

"Why are you having Gregory back here Sunday?" she finally asked.

"I believe my nephew requires a lesson in the folly of his actions."

Deborah's eyes grew wide. "You're going to confront him?"

After a thoughtful pause, Miss Knight shook her head. "I don't care for confrontations. But I believe young Gregory needs to experience how it feels to be made a fool of."

"What are you going to do?"

"Nothing drastic, my dear." With her other hand, she covered Deborah's. "I would like you to be here with me, the same as always. Are you up to that?"

Deborah thought of sitting in the same room with the real Gregory Woodruff, and anger burned inside her. "I don't know."

"I understand." Miss Knight nodded, and a terrible sadness came into her voice. "You know, I'm more disappointed in Mr. Phelps than I am in my nephew. I shall miss him very much. And I can only imagine the hurt you are feeling."

"Oh, well," Deborah said with false lightness. "Father warned me about cads. I suppose I thought once I'd spotted one at the railway station, I didn't have to stay on guard."

Miss Knight shook her head. "I cannot think of Mr. Phelps as a cad, Deborah, no matter how he deceived us. It took a good deal of integrity—and not a little courage—to come here and confess."

Mrs. Darnell came into the room to tell them that supper was ready. Although Deborah's appetite was gone, she nonetheless felt relieved at the interruption. The sooner she banished Mr. Phelps from her mind, the better.

They both picked at their suppers of broiled trout and conversed only of painless subjects. Miss Knight told Deborah what Cambridge was like when she was a young woman, and Deborah told about her years of training at the Royal Academy of Music.

Upstairs later, Deborah added a paragraph to her weekly

letter to her family but did not mention Mr. Phelps's visit. She would tell them later, of course. In spite of her resolve not to think about the man, she found herself wondering again how he had fooled them so completely. Only Miss Knight had felt an inkling of doubt, and only for a short while. Now his earlier nervousness made sense. Still, she had to give him credit for that—only someone unaccustomed to telling lies would have had the conscience to become nervous.

As had happened so many times since Tuesday, she thought about the evening they had spent together. *"You don't know anything about me,"* he had said. Now she knew why.

Realizing her mind had strayed into unpleasant territory again, Deborah picked up her copy of *Isabella* and began working on her enunciation. She had foolishly allowed a schoolgirl infatuation to keep her from focusing upon her lessons. *I won't let it happen again.*

~

"You sent for me, Miss Knight?" Mrs. Darnell's voice came from the doorway; then muffled footsteps approached the bed where the older woman lay upon her pillows. She could feel a pleasant warmth upon her cheeks from the lamp that the housekeeper carried.

Helene smiled. "How long have you been with me, Nelda?"

"Oh, goodness. Thirty years?" Helene's hand was scooped up from atop her counterpane and held lightly in Mrs. Darnell's rough one. "I was parlormaid when I came here."

"And you're one of my dearest friends now." Helene swallowed and felt tears gathering in the corner of her eye. "But here I am, getting all sentimental."

267

Mrs. Darnell squeezed her hand gently and said, "What can I do for you, missus? Having trouble sleeping?"

"Oh, I'll sleep fine. But tell me, do you remember the last time Oriel and Edmund brought all of the boys here to visit? It was before I lost my sight."

"Let's see now." There was a *click,* the sound of the lamp being set upon the bedside table. "I do recall that. They were good little ones, as I remember. Didn't trample the flowers in the garden and wiped their feet every time they came into the house."

Helene nodded. "Do you remember Gregory? He was two or three at the time."

"He had to be three, missus, because he could climb the stairs. Why do you ask?"

"I was just wondering. Did the young man who visited with Gregory last Sunday look anything like him? Mr. Tarleton, I mean."

"Why, no," the housekeeper answered. "Well, he had the same coloring as Mr. Gregory, but why would he look like him?"

Letting out a pained sigh, Helene said, "I have to tell you something."

"You do? Does it have anything to do with Mr. Gregory visiting you this evening?"

"Everything, I'm afraid."

She went on to tell the housekeeper what Mr. Phelps had told her. There was a stunned silence when she finished, then the housekeeper exclaimed, "I just can't believe Mr. Gregory . . . I mean, whoever he is . . . would do such a thing! He was such a nice man, even speaking friendly to the servants!"

Grief welled up inside Helene's chest. "He won't be coming here anymore."

"But of course not, after lying to you like that!" Mrs. Darnell's voice softened then. "Is there anything I can do, dear?"

"Yes, there is. Would you ask Mr. Henry to post a wire for me in the morning?"

"Of course, missus. To where?"

Helene drew in a deep breath and was finally able to give just a bit of a smile. "To Walesby."

# 16

*C**HE ascólto?*
*Ah, no! Rimanga nel silènzio avvolto*
*Per or l'arcano affetto . . ."*

Thursday afternoon Deborah's voice rose from deep inside
of her, embracing the notes as if they had been written with
only her in mind. The expression on Signora Pella's face told
her that she was doing more than well, that the two weeks of
intensive practice had not been in vain.

"I wish that Cecilio could listen to you now," the diva said
when the aria was finished. "He will be amazed when . . ."
Her eyes met Deborah's, and her words were left hanging in
the air.

"Again," she finally said, striking a chord upon the piano.

~

"Did you know that the sign outside is hanging by one
chain?" Gregory Woodruff said as he walked through the
doors of Mr. Cornell's law office on Friday afternoon.

"Again?" Matthew looked up from a stack of paperwork.
"Thank you for telling me."

Mr. Woodruff raised an eyebrow. "What? You've nothing

disagreeable to say to me? No sudden urge to lunge for my lapels?"

*Remember your promise to Miss Knight.* "What would be the point? I can't stop you from doing whatever it is you plan to do." Matthew put down his pen, then motioned to the chair in front of the desk. "Would you care to have a seat?"

"I must say your newfound maturity is refreshing," Woodruff said, lowering himself into the chair.

Matthew allowed his sharp retort to die in his throat. "Why are you here?" he said instead.

"Because of this." He leaned forward and handed an envelope over the desk. "It was sent to me by my aunt yesterday. I thought you should see it since, of course, it actually pertains to you."

Pulling a folded sheet of vellum paper from the envelope, Matthew opened it and read:

> *Dearest Gregory,*
>
> *How pleased I was that you invited a friend along last Sunday! Deborah and I found your Mr. Tarleton delightful company, and hope that you will bring him again this Sunday. Please arrange your studies so that you can stay for supper this time, and I'll ask Mrs. Reeves to cook something special for you.*
>
> *With fondest regards,*
>
> *Aunt Helene*

Matthew lowered the page and looked up at Gregory. "Yes?"

"Well, what are you going to say next Sunday when Aunt Helene asks why you didn't bring me along?"

*Don't make this too easy for him, or he'll be suspicious,* Matthew thought. Giving a shrug, he answered, "I'll probably say that Mr. Tarleton sends his regrets but is too bogged down in his studies at present."

"You'll disappoint her. Why, the note practically begs you to invite me along."

"She's just being polite." Before the man across from him could offer any more arguments, Matthew picked up his pen and gave an irritated sigh. "Look, I've work to do. Come along if you wish."

After a moment's hesitation, Woodruff said, "You mean that?"

Matthew sighed. "Your aunt Helene is too good-hearted. And as much as I hate to admit it, she'll probably be disappointed if you don't show." Narrowing his eyes in warning, he added, "But I take the middle chair this time—do you understand?"

After the man was gone, Matthew stared at the door for a minute, wondering if he had just seen Gregory Woodruff for the last time. Surely Miss Knight planned to confront him on Sunday. And whether or not she decided to tell his parents would determine if Mr. Cornell would be dismissing him from his position soon.

*At least he's no more danger to Deborah.* The very thought of her gnawed at the wound inside him. No, she probably hated Gregory Woodruff . . . almost as much as she hated him.

~

Mealtimes at Miss Knight's house were Thomas's favorite times of the day. Even more than the food, he enjoyed the gatherings—always relaxed and unhurried, with much jesting and warm conversation. Mr. Henry and Mr. Darnell always attempted to outdo each other with their stories of the hardships they faced while growing up in "the olden days."

Once the meals were finished, it was a long-standing rule that you had to bring your own plate as well as a platter or bowl from the table down the hall to the kitchen. In the housekeeper's words, "Mrs. Reeves has rheumatism, and Gwen has only two hands . . . and it's easier for the many to do some than for some to do everything."

But when the meal of oxtail stew and Yorkshire pudding was finished on Saturday evening, and some time had been spent hearing about the organ-grinder's trained monkey that Avis had seen while shopping for fruit on Market Street, Mrs. Darnell stood up at the head of the table. "Before you gather the dishes, I've something to say to you," she said, exchanging a somber glance with her husband. "It's rather bad news."

Thomas obeyed numbly, hardly heeding the curious murmurs around him as the others sat up in their chairs. He was dead certain that the theft of some of Miss Knight's treasures had been discovered, and he was just as certain that Mrs. Darnell was about to expose him. He swallowed with difficulty, for it felt as if a hand were closing about his throat. *Oh God . . . please don't let it be about me,* he prayed.

When the murmurs had died down and everyone sat staring up at the housekeeper, she gave them all a sad look. "I appreciate the hard work you've put in to makin' the house and grounds ready for company. The third-story guest room shines, and the terrace hasn't one stray leaf." With a nod to Thomas, she added, "And I've never seen the portico steps as clean as they are now."

Relief flowed through Thomas's every pore, and he finally allowed himself to relax in his chair. *But why does she look so miserable?*

"But the bad news is," the housekeeper went on, pausing to give a weary sigh, "the man you all know as Mr. Gregory is an impostor."

There was a moment of stunned silence, then Bethina shook her head. "That can't be true!"

"I'm afraid it is, Bethina."

"Why, I know the man like he's me own brother!" Mr. Henry exclaimed.

More murmurs and some protests went around the table, and at last Mrs. Darnell cleared her throat. "He has confessed as much to Miss Knight . . . Monday night. She asked me not to speak about it until now."

Mrs. Darnell went on to explain how the impostor, who was actually named Matthew Phelps and worked as a clerk in a solicitor's office, had been hired by the real Mr. Gregory to make the Sunday calls.

"Well, then, where is the real Mr. Gregory?" Bethina's thunderous expression communicated that she would thrash the man if she knew where to find him.

"Most of you met him last Sunday. He introduced himself as a Mr. Tarleton."

After a moment of stunned silence, Mr. Henry declared, "I knew he was a rakeshame the moment I set eyes upon him!"

"And here he's been sendin' flowers all week like some real gentleman!" Avis put in.

Everyone at the table had a comment to make, and after Mrs. Darnell allowed it to go on for a while, she picked up a spoon and tapped it on the side of her water glass.

"Miss Knight is upset that you, as well as herself and Miss Burke, have all been taken in by both men. Their behavior was shameful. But she would like you to know that the real Mr. Gregory is comin' to call tomorrow. . . ."

"Over my rottin' corpse!" declared Mr. Henry.

Mrs. Darnell had to hold up her hand to silence more murmurs of surprise and outrage. When she finally had a chance to go on, she said, "We can't go forbidding Miss Knight's own nephew to visit when she's the one who invited him."

"Well, then, why did she invite him?" Mrs. Reeves asked.

The housekeeper smiled. "I'm going to explain it to you. And the missus asks you for a special favor tomorrow."

~

As Thomas scurried down Milt Street the next morning, he looked up just in time to jump back. "Hey, watch out!" The contents of a chamber pot splashed at his feet.

A woman stuck a haggard face the color of pie dough out the window and laughed. "Look like it's you who oughta be watchin' out!" she shouted back.

*Why do folks have to let themselves get so low?* Thomas thought, moving to the middle of the garbage-strewn street. He could hear an infant's persistent squalling behind one of the doorways that he passed and then an angry male voice ordering the child to be quiet.

Even his own mother had taken a path that eventually led her—and him, until he found a position at Miss Knight's—to living in squalor with men like Orville Tilton. *Will I be like that one day?* he wondered. The silver bonbon dish he had stolen burned through his coat pocket like a hot coal. He supposed he had been well on his way for some time now.

Perhaps the downward spiral was inevitable unless someone were as good as Queen Victoria, Miss Knight, Mrs. Reeves, and the others. Even then, there was a possibility of turning bad, for who could have guessed that the man everyone had thought to be Mr. Gregory would turn out to be a liar? And he had seemed so kind, so concerned about Thomas's welfare, even going to the trouble of finding and delivering the address of Saint Andrew's Way, the sanatorium in Northampton.

His soul still ached with the news. *But the man finally told Miss Knight the truth,* he had to remind himself. *That's more than I've done.*

Every time he knocked upon Orville's door, he held out a fleeting hope that his mother, looking the way she used to look, would answer. That faint hope surged again, only to vanish when Orville stood there squinting down at him.

"Have you heard anything about my mother?" Thomas asked, again keeping to himself the fact that he'd written the sanatorium. *Maybe I'll get a letter from her tomorrow,* he thought, and then swallowed. *If she's still alive.*

"Not so fast, brat," Orville returned, his beady eyes roving over him. "Show me what you brung first, and then we'll talk."

Thomas handed over the dish. "You know, I can't keep this up too much longer. It's starting to look noticeable that some things are missing."

Orville shrugged, too busy inspecting his latest acquisition to pay him any attention. "Oughta fetch six quid easy for this," he said to himself.

"You said we would talk," Thomas reminded him, then repeated his question about his mother.

"Why, yes I have." Orville scratched his sunken chest. "They sent me a letter a couple o'days ago, telling me she was doin' much better . . . but she still needs to stay there awhile. Mebbe six more months or so."

Thomas's eyes widened. "Let me see the letter!"

"Can't." Orville licked his lips and looked away. "I brung it over to a chum's flat so he could read it to me and forgot to get it back."

Thomas suspected he was lying, but he wasn't ready to surrender his last shred of hope. Just because Orville had received no such letter didn't mean that she wasn't there. As he walked away from the flat, he swiped at the tear on his cheek and turned his steps toward Market Street.

The young woman with the smiling eyes and sweet voice wasn't with the band this Sunday, nor was the older man who was probably her father standing at the pulpit. But the preacher who had been up front the first time Thomas walked in to the Salvation Army was there, and that suited him just fine. Any person would do who could show him how to get rid of the ache that lived inside of him.

He sat on the third row this time and could hardly wait until the sermon was over. The preacher read Bible passages from a book called Romans, and although he did not mention sheep and the good shepherd, the message was the same. Even the vilest sinner could come to Jesus and be forgiven. And Thomas wanted forgiveness more than he had ever wanted anything in the world.

When the sermon was over, Thomas was at the front before the pianist could play her second note. The preacher in the dark suit knelt down with him and asked if he would like to accept Jesus Christ, and Thomas answered that if Jesus Christ would truly have him, then he would like to do that very much.

~

"Just out of curiosity . . . how many suits do you own?" Matthew asked Gregory Woodruff when the two met in front of Pembroke College.

The man grinned and brushed one of his blue serge lapels. "You know, I've never thought to count them."

When Mr. Henry arrived in the barouche, Matthew gave him a quick nod, then kept his eyes averted from the man as he climbed aboard. Surely the driver, as well as all of Miss Knight's servants, knew by now what he had done. He winced inside, wondering what young Thomas thought of him, or what Bethina and Avis thought.

*At least I won't be staying,* he told himself, but that thought brought more pain than relief.

"I say, you aren't going to read for hours and hours this time are you?"

Matthew looked at Woodruff and shook his head. "I doubt I'll be reading at all."

Rolling his eyes heavenward, Mr. Woodruff said, "Good to hear that. No offense intended, but it's a dreadful bore to have to listen for that long."

"Well, I don't think you'll be bored today," Matthew assured him. He had no idea what Miss Knight's plan was, but he could almost feel sorry for her nephew. Almost.

Avis met them at the door. Matthew had hoped it would be Gwen, because he knew her the least of Miss Knight's servants. He could see a hint of reproach in the maid's eyes when she took their hats, yet she smiled warmly.

"Mr. Gregory," she said to Matthew. "It's always so good to see you." Turning to the real Mr. Woodruff, she added,

"And you must be Mr. Tarleton . . . why, we've smelled roses through the house all week!"

"Is my . . ." Matthew stopped, unable to say the word. Avis covered for him immediately, motioning toward the staircase. "Your aunt Helene is waiting upstairs. I'll take you to her."

Matthew wondered if this was his time to bow out, but Avis looked straight into his eyes and gave her head a slight shake before leading them both down the hallway. He followed behind Gregory Woodruff, and a wave of envy filled him. For all the trouble that was likely waiting for him upstairs, he still belonged here.

At the bottom of the staircase, Avis finally turned around to face Matthew. "Oh, Mr. Gregory . . . may I speak to you alone for a minute?"

"What?" answered the real Gregory Woodruff. He gave Matthew a quick look of panic and then cleared his throat. "I mean, what do you want with him?"

Pretending not to notice his slip, Avis smiled and motioned for him to go on ahead. "You'll remember the way from last week, won't you, Mr. Tarleton?"

He turned to Matthew, who shrugged his shoulders and tried to look casual. "I'm sure you can get by without my holding your hand for a little while, can't you?" Matthew asked him.

"I'm sure I'll manage," the man snorted sarcastically. He reached for the banister, and when Mr. Woodruff had taken a couple of steps, Avis motioned for Matthew to follow her back to the front door.

"Mr. Henry will take you back to . . . wherever you live," she said, handing over his hat.

She was speaking to him as if he were a stranger, and it

added to his sense of alienation. "Please thank him," Matthew told her, "but I'll walk."

~

Gregory paused at the door to his aunt's drawing room, cupped his hands in front of his mouth and blew into them, making sure his breath was still sweet from the clove he'd chewed earlier. He wondered what was taking Matthew Phelps so long, and what the maid would possibly have to tell him in secret. If she'd been younger and Mr. Phelps wasn't so obviously enamored of Miss Burke, he would have suspected a romantic liaison.

*Oh, well, looks like I get the middle chair again,* he thought as he raised his hand to knock. He paused at the sound of voices engaged in conversation—too low to make out any words, but loud enough so that he could tell that one of the speakers was definitely male. Yet Mr. Phelps was still downstairs, unless he'd crept up some servants' entrance and through another door. Curiosity got the better of him, and he leaned closer to listen.

"Good afternoon, Mr. Tarleton."

Gregory almost jumped back from the door. He turned to find a ginger-haired maid standing there and wondered how she'd come up behind him without his hearing her.

"Good afternoon," he answered, clearing his throat. "I was just about to knock."

"Yes sir." The maid's homely face beamed at him. "Why, I expect Miss Burke will be happy to see you."

He raised an eyebrow. "Miss Burke?"

"Goodness!" she exclaimed, plopping a beefy hand over her mouth.

"Come on, now." Gregory gave her one of his most charming smiles. "Tell me what you meant."

She straightened her apron and looked down at the carpet. "Oh, I mustn't, sir."

"I'll bet a florin would take away your shyness," he said, reaching into his pocket.

The maid shook her head. "Please don't be offering me any money, sir. I only meant that she's gotten dressed up awful fancy today."

Gregory's smile was genuine this time. "Well, we shan't keep her waiting, shall we?"

She reached for the doorknob. "I'll show you in, sir." After the maid had opened the door, she stepped back to allow him to enter first. Now he could hear the male voice again, louder, but he was already in the room before recognition sank in. He stopped and blinked.

"Father?"

"Gregory!" His father was rising from the same chair Matthew Phelps had sat in last week, his smile broad and eyes shining. In the middle chair facing Aunt Helene, his mother had turned to smile warmly at him, and on her right Miss Burke sat with the same strange expression that Aunt Helene was wearing.

Gregory's knees turned to water, but he took another step forward. The maid who had followed him into the room said, "I'll pull over another chair, Mr. Gregory."

He wheeled around to gape at her. Just outside in the hallway she had referred to him as "Mr. Tarleton"! What was going on in this household?

"Are you surprised, dear?" came Aunt Helene's voice from behind him, and he turned back around and faced the group.

There was nothing to do but walk over to where Father stood with a hand outstretched.

"Uh, quite so."

He allowed his father to pump his hand and then leaned down to embrace his mother. They both seemed happy to see him, meaning that Aunt Helene had not yet informed them about his prank. *How did she find out?* he wondered. Then he realized: Mr. Phelps wasn't here. Of course . . .

Gregory had never been interested in fishing, but at the moment he felt like a worm impaled upon a hook, powerless to do anything but wait to be devoured.

"I didn't know you were coming to Cambridge," he said lamely as he sank into the chair the maid had brought over to his father's left, facing Aunt Helene.

His father, back in his chair again, was steepling his fingers over one crossed knee. "We didn't even know we were coming until Tuesday, when we received Aunt Helene's wire."

"Oh . . . nice," he mumbled and looked at his aunt again. The expression on her face had turned into a very recognizable one . . . amusement. And one glance at Miss Burke's face told him that she, too, was enjoying his discomfiture immensely.

"I thought it would be a nice surprise for you," Aunt Helene said innocently. "I insisted that they come see for themselves what you've been up to. Behavior like yours should not go unnoticed."

Gregory could only take shallow breaths now, for his collar felt maddeningly tight. He wondered what idiot had built a fire in the fireplace when the room was so stiflingly hot. A mental portrait flashed across his mind of himself in an army uniform, and the room became warmer still.

"You . . . flatter me, Aunt Helene," he finally said, injecting a hint of pleading into his voice that he hoped would escape his parents' ears. He gave a nervous chuckle and added, "I can see a drastic need for improvement in my behavior."

"I had no idea that modesty was part of the curriculum at Pembroke," Father quipped, taking a briarwood pipe from his coat pocket. He turned to Miss Burke and said, "Don't be concerned, Miss Burke—I gave up smoking ten years ago, but I still enjoy chewing on the stem every so often."

"I wasn't concerned." She smiled back at him.

"I'm surprised that you didn't mention Miss Burke in either of your letters home," Father said, turning to Gregory again. "I should think that so charming a young lady would occupy the first paragraph."

Lifting a hand in a helpless gesture, Gregory said, "I was never very good at letters." He sent a desperate glance in Miss Burke's direction and added, "I didn't feel . . . worthy to mention her."

"Gregory has been so kind as to read to us—Miss Burke and me—every week," Aunt Helene went on. "In fact, we should be finishing up *Treasure Island* today, shouldn't we, dear?"

"I believe so," he replied, eager to agree to anything that would delay the moment when he would be exposed. He would have never thought such a meek old woman would enjoy toying with anyone in such a cruel manner.

"Then we'll do that after tea . . . that is, if your parents would like to hear you."

"I didn't think you were fond of reading," Mother said, studying him as if she weren't sure he was her own son.

"Love it," he muttered.

Aunt Helene nodded. "Why, that means we'll have to have another book ready by next week, Gregory."

Relief and gratitude washed through him like a tonic. If Aunt Helene was planning what he would be expected to read to her in the weeks to come, then surely she didn't intend to tell Mother and Father about his little prank. "Anything you'd like to hear," he said magnanimously.

"You're such a dear." She assumed a thoughtful expression and said, "You know, I read through the Bible several times when I had my sight, and Mrs. Darnell reads a chapter to me every morning with the newspaper. But one can never get enough of God's Word, can one?"

*The Bible!* His parents were watching, and he dredged up as much enthusiasm as was humanly possible. "I have always felt that way."

"Wonderful!" She smiled and went on. "And you have such a commanding voice, Gregory. I can just imagine your bringing the Scriptures to life."

"You can?" Gregory sank just a little lower in his chair. "Why, Aunt Helene, I hardly feel that I could give them the justice they deserve."

"There you are being modest again. We'll begin with Saint Matthew, and when we've finished the New Testament, go back through Genesis and the Old Testament."

*Why . . . the old woman is blackmailing me!* Gregory thought. Nothing in his imagination could be worse than being forced to read the Bible aloud every Sunday. Nothing except the idea of getting shot at during some British campaign in some wretched uncivilized country.

"That sounds like a good idea," he agreed and winced inwardly when his mother gave him a sentimental smile. He wondered where Matthew Phelps had disappeared to, envying the man for not having to be here in this room. But he was still too relieved that his mischief wasn't going to be discussed in front of his parents to think about the revenge he would extract from the clerk.

Gregory dared another look at Miss Burke. She sat there with her hands folded in her lap and a pleasant smile on her face, but when they locked eyes, she flashed him a look of utter contempt. For the first time in his life, Gregory realized that there was one woman whose opinion of him could not be changed with all the flowers and gifts in the world.

"Of course it's tempting to start with the Old Testament," Aunt Helene mused out loud. "I've always enjoyed the book of Joshua. What a courageous man he was, general of the Israelites' army! You young men are so interested in soldiers, army matters, and such. Would you rather we started there, Gregory?"

*She just can't resist one last reminder that my life is in her hands!* Gregory thought. Weren't old people supposed to sit around talking about their rheumatism and the weather? How did this one get to be so feisty? "I like your earlier suggestion, about reading through the New Testament first." He wasn't even sure what the New Testament was, but surely it couldn't make him more uncomfortable than some reminder that he was perilously close to becoming a soldier.

"You're quite right, dear. It is fitting that we should begin there. The Gospels have so much to teach us—even a fine young man like yourself." Aunt Helene clasped her hands together and smiled in the direction of Gregory's father. "I can never thank you enough for suggesting that Gregory visit me, Edmund. And just think . . . three more wonderful years of this!"

The ginger-haired maid and the one who had met Gregory and Mr. Phelps at the terrace door came in with trays, and they all had tea. And then, at Aunt Helene's urging, Miss Burke took the copy of *Treasure Island* from the window-seat cupboard and brought it over to him. With his father holding his pipe and beaming, and his mother looking upon him with pride, he found himself wishing he had really earned such parental approval. He cleared his throat and began to read: "'We made a curious figure, had anyone been there to see us; all in soiled sailor clothes, and all but me armed to the teeth. Silver had two guns slung about him—one before and one behind—besides the great cutlass at his waist, and a pistol in each pocket of his square-tailed coat. . . .'"

After supper was over, everyone returned to the drawing room for a game of dominos and to listen to Miss Burke practice. Her singing voice was as rich as her laugh, and Gregory found himself wishing he had never paid someone else to take his place here. Who knows what might have happened?

*Phelps should have had more sense than to go along with my plan. He took advantage of my desperation.* Now that the shock of finding his parents here was wearing off, he began to give thought to what he should do about the man. One word to Mr. Cornell about his employee's deceptions would cause his position to be terminated. He smiled to himself at the thought of Matthew Phelps, dressed in rags and begging on the street because all professional doors were closed to him.

Then a question dawned upon him. How could he accuse Mr. Phelps without admitting his own part in this folly? He didn't care a whit what Mr. Cornell thought about him, but what would stop the solicitor from writing to his father? *I can't even have the satisfaction of challenging him to a fight,* Gregory thought, recalling the force with which Phelps had grabbed at him in the barouche.

He looked up at Miss Burke. Her face was so beautiful, and her voice so bittersweet to his ears. *At least she hates him as much as she hates me,* he thought. It was the only solace he could find.

The liveryman drove him back toward Pembroke at ten o'clock, well before the locking of the college's gates at eleven. Aunt Helene had invited him to stay the night so that he could have breakfast with his parents, but Gregory had begged off, citing early lectures.

He sat back in the barouche and recalled how, moments ago, his mother and father had walked outside with him to say their farewells. They had laughed at his descriptions of some of his lecturers and fellow underclassmen. Father had even given him a quick embrace—the first Gregory could remember.

He could still feel that embrace, sitting there alone as the pair of horses plodded through the night air. How strange, that he should leave one of the most uncomfortable, disastrous evenings of his life with a sense of well-being.

~

*I have a Father now!* Thomas thought as he lay staring up at the ceiling in his darkened room. He knew it was so, more than he had ever known anything else, for there was a reassuring presence with him. He was not alone anymore.

As what the preacher this morning had called a "child of God," it only seemed natural that Thomas should talk with his new Father before closing his eyes in sleep.

"I'm not going to steal anymore," he promised under his

breath. "Never again. No matter what." A lump came to his throat at the thought of his mother needing money, but he had to tell himself that a God who was big enough to create the world and to save him was big enough to help him with this problem as well.

Relief washed over him with this decision, bringing tears to his eyes, and he wiped them with a corner of his sheet. Yet something was still not right.

Then a voice, inaudible, but very clear came to him. *You must tell the person you've wronged.*

"I can't do that," Thomas whispered, wiping his eyes again.

*You must,* the voice urged again.

"But I'll lose my position here . . . maybe go to prison."

*Whatever happens . . . I will be with you every moment.*

# 17

I'VE been doing something shameful, Miss Knight,"
Thomas said under his breath to his reflection in the mirror
as he pulled a brush through his curly brown hair. He tried
to imagine what her reaction would be. Never had he known
Miss Knight to raise her voice in anger, but he couldn't imagine
her being anything but furious when she learned that so many
of her precious belongings were gone.

"I'm not alone," Thomas repeated to himself. *Even if I go to
prison,* he added silently. He set his brush down on his dresser
and left his room. As he climbed down the steps to the stable
below, he noticed that the two horses, Chester and Prince,
as well as the barouche were gone, even though the sun was
barely up. Come to think of it, he'd been stirred awake briefly
about an hour ago by the sound of someone moving around
in Mr. Henry's room. *Miss Knight's company must be catching an
early train back,* he thought. That was good, for he would ask
for a chance to speak privately with her as soon as he'd helped
clear away the breakfast dishes.

The rest of the servants, save Mr. Henry, were already gathered in the hall when he walked in. Thomas could see the
steam rising from the platters on the sideboard and realized
that he'd dawdled too long at his mirror this morning.

"Sorry I'm late," he said, hurrying to stand behind his chair, and Mrs. Reeves favored him with a smile.

"Not at all, lad. Most of us got up a little earlier so that we could help the missus dress and pack a hamper."

"Pack a hamper?"

"Her and Mr. Gregory's mum and father are takin' a drive over to Newmarket so he can look at some horses," Bethina told him.

A mixture of relief and disappointment washed over him. "Do you know when they'll be back?"

"Pretty late, I expect," Mrs. Darnell answered, then eyed him curiously. "Is anything the matter, Thomas?"

He realized that his hands had a white-knuckled grip on the back of his chair, and he relaxed them. "I just need to talk to Miss Knight."

Mr. Darnell went to the head of the table then, and all heads were bowed for his prayer. Thomas listened along, adding silently, *I won't forget to tell her.*

Two hours later he was sweeping leaves from the bricks of the terrace when Mr. Darnell brought him an envelope. "Never knowed you to get a letter before," the man said affably.

"Guess I'll read it after I'm done with this," Thomas answered back, stuffing the envelope into the pocket of his trousers. It took great restraint, once the man was gone, to finish sweeping the terrace, but Thomas figured that he would be a liar if he didn't do exactly what he'd told Mr. Darnell he was going to do.

When he was finished, he carried the broom to the gardening cottage, sat down on a crate in front of a curtainless window, and tore into the envelope.

*Dear Mr. Sully,*

*Thank you for your inquiry of November 14, 1883. As we are a facility established and operated by the British Royal Navy for the treatment of veteran sailors with chronic diseases, we would have no knowledge as to the whereabouts of your mother.*

There was more to the letter, words expressing hope that he would be successful in locating his mother and such. Thomas skimmed through to the end, just in case some final sentence would tell him that the writer had been mistaken, that the facility did indeed take in an occasional woman patient. But there were no such words, and he rocked back and forth on the crate, clutching the letter to his heart and groaning.

Half an hour later, Mr. Darnell came into the cottage. His mouth dropped open at the sight of Thomas.

"Lad?" the gardener said, walking over to put a hand upon Thomas's shoulder. "Whatever's wrong? Did you get some bad news?"

The back of Thomas's throat was raw now, but he managed to rasp, "Orville was lying."

Thomas couldn't even remember being carried into the house, when he woke up in the middle of a strange bed, he sat up and peered at his surroundings with dry, itchy eyes. "You're in the room Mr. Henry took when his toe was broken," Mrs. Reeves said from the doorway. Gwen stood next to her, holding a bowl that sent wisps of steam into the air.

"How long have I been in here?" he asked, startled at the croaking sound of his own voice.

"Well, lunch has been over for a while," the cook replied. "So I would say about three hours. We've all been taking turns lookin' in on you."

"We made you some beef tea," Gwen said as the two walked into the room. "I'll even feed it to you if you like."

"Three hours?" Thomas threw back his covers and swung his legs over the side of the bed. He looked down at the floor for his shoes, but they were nowhere in sight. "I've got to mulch the flower beds today."

"Not today, you're not," came an authoritative voice from the door, and Mrs. Darnell took a couple of steps into the room. "Mr. Darnell has already taken care of that. Just drink your soup like a good lad, and when you're ready to talk about whatever happened, we'll see what we can do to help you."

Mrs. Darnell stood there while he consumed half of the beef tea under Mrs. Reeves's watchful eye. When the two women left with promises to come back later with more, the housekeeper ordered Thomas to lie back down, then walked over to sit on the side of the bed.

"I had to read your letter, Thomas," she said, tucking the covers under his chin.

His eyes flew open with panic, but the housekeeper's hand upon his shoulder prevented him from springing from the bed. "Where is it?"

"It's in the cupboard there with your shoes. Why didn't you tell us your mother was sick—and you don't even know where she is?"

Tears blurring his vision, he answered, "I can't tell you about that yet, Mrs. Darnell. I have to talk to Miss Knight first."

"All right," she said with a nod. "Then, what can I do to help?"

Thomas glanced at the cupboard against a wall, where his

shoes had been stored. Although he was sure now that his mother was dead and had been dead for weeks, he had to hear what had happened from the last person to have seen her alive. He had to confront Orville.

He turned his face to Mrs. Darnell again. "Please, may I have the rest of the day off? There is someone who . . . knows where my mother is. I have to talk with him."

She looked puzzled by his request. "But you've had a bit of a shock, dear. Shouldn't you save that for tomorrow?"

"I have to know *now*. Please?"

"How about if Mr. Darnell goes along with you?"

The thought was tempting. Even for his age, the head gardener was a good bit stronger than Orville. *But then he would know.* Until he could tell Miss Knight himself, Thomas didn't want anyone else in the house to discover the truth about his mother. *Whatever that might be,* he thought.

Thomas sat up in bed. "It's something Mr. Darnell can't help me with. Please let me go. . . . I'll work twice as hard when I get back."

"No need to do that," Mrs. Darnell said, her brown eyes still worried. "All right, then," she said after a while and wagged a finger in front of his face. "But be back here before dark, or I'll be sending the police to look for you."

He was about to assure her that it wasn't necessary but then on second thought decided that it wasn't a bad idea. Orville had a cruel streak, and there was no telling what he was going to do when confronted.

~

"Oh, Mr. Phelps, dear . . . ," the female voice said in a singing tone as steps sounded louder and louder on the staircase.

Hard at work at his desk, Matthew cringed. *Stay busy, and she'll notice how much work you have in front of you,* he told himself.

"I don't think he heard us, Royce." This time the voice came from the bottom of the staircase. "Our Mr. Phelps works too hard. He needs some fresh air just like you do."

There was no use pretending not to hear her anymore. Matthew reluctantly tore his eyes from the paperwork in front of him and got to his feet. "Good afternoon, Mrs. Cornell."

"Good afternoon, Mr. Phelps." She wore a dress the color of a ripe pumpkin and a hairpiece of brassy copper curls that screamed out against her graying auburn hair. "You forgot to say 'good afternoon' to Royce," she reminded him with a mocking pout on her lips.

"Good afternoon, Royce."

Beaming with pleasure, Mrs. Cornell leaned down and raised Royce up on his hind paws, lifted one forepaw to wave, and spoke for the dog in a high-pitched, childish voice, "And good afternoon to you, sir."

Now that the pleasantries were over, Matthew stood and waited to be assigned some chore involving Royce, for that was obviously why Mrs. Cornell had approached his desk. *Please don't ask me to give him another bath,* Matthew thought. He listened as she told how Royce was going stir-crazy upstairs and how Latimer had already walked the dog once today and now had much to do to help prepare for a dinner party she and her husband were hosting tonight. The little-girl voice returned, and she spoke for the dog again. "Won't you please take me for a walk, Mr. Phelps?"

To Mrs. Cornell—not the dog—Matthew answered, "I'll have to ask Mr. Cornell if I may leave."

"I'll take care of that." She handed over the leash, reminding Matthew not to allow the animal to get dirty. "He needs to stay pretty for our guests this evening. They do so enjoy watching him eat from his own plate at the dining table."

*I'll wager they can't wait,* he thought.

The late November air was as cool and damp as a grotto, but Matthew found it refreshing as he followed the dog up King's Parade. He had awakened this morning with a throbbing headache, following a frustrating night of trying to push thoughts of Deborah Burke from his mind so that he could sleep. Royce seemed to find the air invigorating, for he tugged impatiently on the leash as if to tell him to walk a little faster. Matthew found himself envying the animal.

*All you have to worry about is an occasional flea,* he thought, pulling the animal away from the remains of a dead pigeon on the footway. *You'll never know what it's like to feel shame, and your heart will never be broken.*

~

*Orville's not too bright . . . he could have gotten the name of the town mixed up with another,* Thomas told himself as he turned from Bridge Street to Saint John's Street. *Mother could be alive in some other place.*

Then reason took over. If Orville had been sending the profits from the stolen items to the sanatorium, he would have known the name of the town.

*She's dead,* Thomas told himself. *You have to stop pretending that she's not.*

He continued on, despite the grief that welled up within him. Orville had talked him into stealing, had given him false hopes about Mother, and had caused him to live every day with the terror of being discovered. He feared the man greatly, but he had to find out the truth about her death. Had she suffered? Where was her grave?

By the time the corner of Green Street, the entrance to the slum, was in sight, his heart was racing and his teeth were chattering. He could still remember the savagery with which Orville had once beaten him. *Father, please help me,* he prayed under his breath.

Then he caught sight of a familiar figure in the distance.

~

When he first noticed Thomas weaving through other pedestrians in his direction, Matthew lifted a hand to wave. But he thought better of it and let his arm fall to his side. Surely the boy was aware by now of how he had pretended to be Gregory Woodruff. He was probably out running some errand for Mrs. Darnell and hadn't expected to see him here. Matthew considered turning right just a few steps ahead into Green Street, even though it did lead to a rough area, so that he wouldn't have to look at the hurt and anger that would likely be on the boy's face. But he couldn't run away every time he saw one of them. Besides, Thomas deserved a chance to give him a tongue-lashing if it would make him feel better.

Matthew was stunned when Thomas broke into a run to cover the last few yards between them and even more stunned when the boy threw himself into his arms. "Mr. Gregory!" he sobbed against his shoulder.

Royce looked as confused as Matthew felt and sat down on the bricks of the footway to glower at them both. "Why, what's wrong, Thomas?" Matthew asked, not bothering to correct him about using the wrong name. When the boy continued to sob,

Matthew put an arm around his shoulders. *That's what you get for your little charade,* he thought. *You've broken this child's heart.*

Finally Thomas calmed down enough to blurt out his story—how an opium addict in the slums, a man named Orville, had information relating to his mother's death but had refused to tell him. The relief Matthew felt because he wasn't the cause of the tears was replaced with horror that anyone so young would have to endure what this boy had suffered. He continued to listen, ignoring the passersby, who took a wide berth around the three of them. And he kept a firm grip on the leash, for Royce was pulling at the other end, eager to be on his way.

When Thomas had finally gotten everything out, Matthew took his arm and led him over to an alley between Saint Michael's Church and a chemist's shop, out of the footway traffic. Royce, thinking he was going back home, had to be dragged every step of the way. "The first thing we have to do is go to the police," he told the boy.

"Oh, please no!" Thomas exclaimed, his face blanching. "Orville beat me once almost to death. If you get the police, he'll find me and kill me!"

"But he can't kill you if he's locked up."

The boy shook his head adamantly. "They'll lock me up, too! Maybe in the same place!"

"We'll tell them that this man forced you to steal," Matthew told him. "They have children of their own. . . . They'll understand."

"But I haven't told Miss Knight yet. If they arrest me, she'll find out from the police and not from me." He looked Matthew square in the eyes and said, "I have to tell her myself what I've done. I promised God I would."

There was no talking the boy out of it, and, for a second,

Matthew considered overriding Thomas's objections and going to the police. But he couldn't guarantee that the boy wouldn't be locked up, at least for a while. *You told him he could come to you for help anytime, h*e reminded himself. Well, the boy was doing it now. He had to take his concerns into account.

"I'm going with you, then."

Thomas's eyes opened wide. "You will?"

"Of course I will." Royce pulled at the leash. "But I've got to take the dog back."

That proved to be easier said than done, for Royce wasn't ready for his outing to end. He dug with all four feet into the dirt of the alleyway and growled as Matthew pulled on his leash. "All right, you stubborn tartar . . . I'll drag you if I have to!" Matthew finally growled back, but when he crouched down, Royce stuck out his massive jaw and bared his teeth.

Matthew stood, gave Thomas a helpless look, and then scratched his head. "I suppose we'll have to bring him with us. Anyway, if I take him back to the office, I might have to stay there."

He began to doubt the wisdom of that decision later, when the streets into the slums grew narrower and seedier, and the voices of the impoverished who loitered about grew louder and more profane. Royce, however, seemed to relish the adventure and trotted on ahead with his stub of a tail wagging. They reached a wreck of a ground-floor tenement, and Thomas, after a solemn look at Matthew, raised his hand to knock.

"Wait."

Thomas turned his head. "Sir?"

"Let me go first. You wait out here."

Relief mixed with uncertainty came over the boy's face. "But he won't talk to you."

Matthew recalled how Thomas's voice had wavered as he told how the man had once beaten him almost to death, and his jaw clenched tight with anger.

"Oh, yes, he will." He handed Royce's leash over. "Now, you've got to hold tight, or he'll drag you all over Cambridge."

Anger coursed through Matthew, and the rotting door rattled under his fist as he pounded upon it. Too late he realized he had made a mistake. It wasn't the knock that a thirteen-year-old was capable of making, and snakes such as this Orville person usually lived in fear of an authoritative knock upon the door. *He probably thinks you're the police,* he scolded himself. *He could be halfway out of a window by now.*

Matthew turned to the boy and saw that they had attracted a group of ragged onlookers from one of the doorways behind them. He ignored them and said, "Does another tenement back up against this one?"

"Yes sir."

Matthew let out a relieved breath. There were tenements on each side as well, so Orville had nowhere to go but through the front . . . if indeed he was at home. He knocked again, just as hard. There was no use pretending now.

This time he heard a quick shuffling sound. Thomas leaned closer, having heard it, too, and whispered, "Could be a rat."

"Human or animal?" Matthew whispered back. He went over to the lone window but could only tell through the accumulation of grime that there was darkness on the other side. He tried the knob and found it locked from the inside. Turning to the boy again, he said, "Remember . . . stay out here until I call you. And . . . try to keep the dog clean."

"What are you going to do?"

In answer to his question, Matthew raised his left shoulder

and slammed into the door. After a faint resistance at the knob, it splintered open. He stumbled into a darkened room and immediately was overcome by the nauseating odor of rotting food, rodent feces, and filth. It was easy to see, even in the dim light coming in through the doorway, that nothing human was in this room. Bending to pick up a wooden dowel that lay on the floor next to a broken chair, he stepped carefully over mounds of garbage to another closed door set in the middle of the back wall.

Matthew had seen opium addicts before, emaciated and pitiful, begging on street corners. He was certain that the wretch who lived in this filth would be no match for him physically, but fear of the unknown began to creep over him, causing the back of his neck to break out in a clammy sweat. There was no lock on the second door, just a knob that turned easily in his hand. Barely daring to breathe, Matthew pushed the door open an inch at a time.

Once he had the door open enough to enter the room, he stuck his head in to look behind the door. Satisfied that no one lurked there, he took a couple of steps into the dark room, holding his arms out in front of him so that he wouldn't bump into anything or anybody. He heard a noise, but before he could move, a skeletal arm wrapped around his shoulders, and the point of a knife pressed against the back of his neck, below his right ear. Matthew brought his hands up to grab his captor's left wrist, but when he did so, the knife pressed so hard that it bit into his skin.

It was ludicrous that a creature who felt like an insect on his back could immobilize him so! Matthew tensed himself to swing around, but then a wheezing voice said from behind his ear, "Yer a big man all right, but it's gonna be hard to breathe with a knife stickin' from yer windpipe."

Matthew forced his shoulders to relax, and the pressure of the knife subsided just a little. "Why are you here?" rasped the voice in his ear.

"I came to ask you about Thomas's mother."

"Yer with the police . . . ain't you?"

"No."

"Then who are you?"

*He'll let his guard down soon,* Matthew thought, automatically tensing up again. The sharp pain of the blade brought tears to his eyes and caused him to relax his stance. "I . . . my name is Matthew Phelps. I'm a friend of the boy's."

"You work for the old woman?"

"No." Matthew tried to ease his neck to the left, away from the knife, but the point only pressed harder. He could feel warm blood trickling down his neck into his collar. "I'm just here to find out what happened to the boy's mother. That's all I want."

"Then why did you break down my door?"

"I'll be happy to replace it."

"Liar!" The voice wheezed.

Through the open doorway Matthew suddenly heard movement in the outer room. He could not turn his head to look, but knew that it was Thomas, coming into the house to see what was wrong.

"Stay back!" Matthew warned as loudly as he could without moving, but the footsteps came even closer. "Go get the police!"

"It ain't aginst the law to go after someone who breaks down yer door and tries to sneak up on you," Orville whispered in a warning tone. "Now, you tell that brat to—" His words stopped abruptly, and then came an ear-piercing scream and the sound of the knife clattering to the floor.

"GET HIM OFF ME!" Orville yelled, thrashing about in the darkness.

"He pulled away from me, Mr. Gregory!" Thomas shouted, close at Matthew's side, but his voice was barely audible above Orville's howls.

The growling bulldog, his jaws clamped determinedly, had hold of Orville's leg and was not about to let go. Pressing two fingers against the painful cut on his neck, Matthew bent down to feel for the knife. He found it and snapped it shut, then called out to Royce.

Unfortunately for Orville, Royce wouldn't listen but only growled louder and shook the man's leg. "Find a lamp!" Matthew yelled over the din to Thomas as he tried to take hold of the dog's collar with his hands. It was like trying to move an anvil. Finally the boy had a candle burning, and Matthew retreated to the doorway leading to the front room and clapped his hands.

"Royce! Time for tea!"

In an flash the dog let go of the howling man's leg, trotted to the door, and waited for Matthew to pick up his leash. Matthew hooked the end over the doorknob and walked over to where Orville now sat on the floor, whimpering and clutching his injured leg.

"See if you can find something clean he can put around his leg," Matthew told Thomas, who looked with uncertainty around the room.

"Everything's filthy in here."

With a sigh, Matthew removed his coat and waistcoat and handed them to the boy. "Hold these, please."

"You're not going to give him your shirt, are you?"

"It's already got some of my blood on it," Matthew said as he began to unfasten the buttons. *Why did I have to wear my newest one today?* He threw the shirt over to Orville, who snatched it and tied the sleeves around his bleeding leg. When he had put on his vest and coat again, Matthew approached the man on the floor.

"Now you're going to tell this boy about his mother, or so help me . . ." Matthew allowed his voice to trail off and gave a meaningful nod in Royce's direction. The dog, having been duped out of his tea, seemed to blame Orville, for he was straining at the leash to get back to the man.

"All right!" Orville cried, inching away from his tormentor. Matthew turned to the boy and put a hand upon his shoulder.

"Are you sure you're ready for this?"

Thomas nodded back. "Anything's better than not knowing."

Between self-pitying blubbering and reminding Thomas that he had taken care of his mother to the best of his ability, Orville told how he had not been able to wake her one day from what appeared to be a fitful sleep. By the time the second day had rolled around, he had grown more alarmed and hired a boy to bring her to Saint Luke's Hospital. "I went along with her, too," Orville sniffed, wiping his nose with one of the sleeves. "Only I . . . didn't give 'em her real name. And I slipped away before they could ask me any more questions."

The boy's tears were shining in the lamplight now, but with admirable control he asked the man why he had left her to die alone.

"I didn't want to," Orville replied, wiping his nose again. "But I knew when they found out it was opium they would send fer th' police. I couldn't help her anyway, could I?"

305

After a long silence, Thomas said, "She died there, didn't she?"

Orville nodded with what looked like genuine sorrow on his face.

Thomas looked up at Matthew. "Where does Saint Luke's bury the people who die?"

"The hospital doesn't bury people," Matthew told him gently. "She's likely in the charity yard."

They both turned to Orville again, and he nodded.

"Mary Tilton. That was th' name I gived at th' hospital." After a long sigh, he added in a wavering voice, "It were my mother's name."

~

"I'm sorry about your mother," Matthew told the boy as the two followed Royce away from Orville's tenement.

"I thought I was going to cry," Thomas answered back, his voice heavy with disbelief and disappointment. "I did love her."

"You'll cry later. Trust me."

Thomas didn't speak again until they reached Green Street, and then he said, "Do we have to turn him in to the police?"

"We have to," Matthew replied.

"But he did love my mother . . . in his way."

"He beat you and then forced you to steal—"

"He didn't force me."

"*Forced* you," Matthew said with emphasis. "What boy wouldn't steal if he thought it would save his mother's life?"

"But he's not doing it anymore," Thomas persisted.

"Because he got caught. Trust me, Thomas, if he's allowed to go free, he'll only do the same sort of things to other people, maybe even another young boy. His addiction will make him desperate now that you won't be supplying him with a source of money." Touching the boy's shoulder, Matthew added, "We can't allow that to happen."

Fear replaced the pity on Thomas's face. "But the police?"

"I think I know someone who can help." Matthew gave him a reassuring smile, hoping his optimism was justified. They walked on, and Matthew became aware that he was drawing curious, even indignant stares from passersby. With his left hand he pulled the lapels of his coat together at his neck, wincing when the back of his collar pressed against the cut.

Mrs. Cornell was pacing the carpet when they walked into the front office. Matthew let go of the leash, and with a cry of relief the woman dropped to her knees to throw her arms around the dog's neck. "Oh, my darling!"

Almost immediately she looked up at Matthew, her eyes wide with accusation. "Why . . . he's filthy! And what is that on his jaw?"

"That would be blood, Mrs. Cornell."

"Blood!" A plump hand shot up to her throat. "Where have you taken him?"

Matthew knelt at Royce's side. The animal turned his great head to lick his hand. "It's a long story, ma'am, and we really need to tell it to Mr. Cornell as soon as possible."

He reached over to scratch between the dog's ears. "But I'll be more than happy to give him a bath after we've finished."

Mr. Cornell sat back in his chair and listened while Thomas told him everything. When he was finished, the solicitor gave a thoughtful nod and looked up at Matthew, who sat in a chair next to the boy's.

"I believe we should send for the police right away," he

finally said through his index fingers. "Before this Mr. Tilton decides to up and leave."

"I don't think he's going anywhere for a while," Matthew offered. After exchanging looks with the boy next to him, he added, "Do you think we could wait until tomorrow, after Thomas has had time to tell his employer what he's done?"

"No need to do that. It's a clear case of coercion."

"Then, you don't think Thomas will be arrested?"

Mr. Cornell shook his head. "Inspector Lyle Howard is a good friend. I'll make sure he hears the boy's story." He lifted a warning eyebrow. "But if this Miss Knight decides to bring charges against him, that could change."

The King's College Chapel bells were chiming six o'clock by the time the inspector and his assistant left. They had given assurances that the police had dealt with Orville Tilton before and would have him in custody within the hour. Mrs. Cornell ended up having a servant give Royce his bath, and she waved away the still shirtless Matthew along with Thomas before her guests could arrive and get a look at them.

"Feel better now?" Matthew asked the boy as they stepped out into the brisk air.

Thomas shook his head. "I've still got to tell Miss Knight. She's likely back by now."

There was so much sorrow in Thomas's voice that Matthew found himself offering to accompany him and was ashamed of his relief when the boy turned him down.

"I don't think it would be right to try and make it any easier," Thomas said in a flat voice. "I knew it was wrong every time I did it."

"Well, I'm going to find you a hansom. You're too young to be walking back this late."

"I didn't bring any money with me."

"That's all right—I'll pay."

"Thank you, sir." The boy looked up at him. "We've both been up to no good, haven't we, Mr. Gregory?"

*"Mr. Matthew,"* Matthew corrected, then reached out a hand to tousle the boy's curls. "I believe there's still hope for you, at least."

# 18

RIGHT *arm out in front . . . elbow bent and palm cupped slightly . . . left hand closed and resting at small of waist . . . shoulders square . . . chin up . . .*

Her hair bound up in a towel, Deborah sashayed across her bedroom in a flannel nightgown, while the orchestral music from act 2, scene 3 of *Isabella* played in her head. The audience, represented by her dressing screen, listened in rapt attention as Rosalie wrestled with her conscience over whether or not she should warn her mistress of her French soldier's unfaithfulness.

This was the most challenging part of the whole opera, for its highly ornamented virtuosi passages required an extremely flexible and light voice. She lifted her right arm higher to ponder an imaginary moon—the mantel clock—and closed her eyes, imagining her own voice gliding over the trills and runs as smoothly as a pebble skipping over water.

"Miss Burke?"

Deborah gasped and spun around to look behind her. Avis stood at the door, her eyes lowered but with a decided quirk at a corner of her mouth. "I knocked, but you didn't answer," the maid said soberly.

Both hands on her hips, Deborah leveled a gaze at her. "It's all right, Avis. You can laugh now."

311

"Laugh?" Avis looked up at her with raised eyebrows, as if the thought had never occurred to her. She held up a pair of stockings. "The laundrywoman had these mixed in with Gwen's clothes."

"Thank you." Deborah took a step toward the door to take them, but Avis waved her away and started walking to the rosewood chest of drawers.

"I'll put them away for you."

"Thank you," Deborah repeated, then moved over to her bed to pull down the covers. When she turned back from laying the pillow shams on a nearby chair, she found the maid standing on the other side of the bed.

"I'll help," Avis said, her green eyes darting up for a quick look at her. They pulled down the covers and fluffed up the pillows. "Is there anything else you need?" Avis asked. "Draw you a bath?"

Deborah gave her a curious look and touched the towel wrapped turban-style around her damp hair. "I've already had one, thank you."

"Oh. Of course." With a sigh the maid ambled toward the door but turned back when she was halfway there. "I could comb out your hair for you. Even put it in papers if you'd like."

Hoisting herself onto the foot of the high bed, Deborah nodded at the dressing-table bench. "Why don't you sit down, Avis?"

"Wouldn't you like your hair combed?"

"I'll take care of it." She motioned toward the bench again. "Do you mind?"

Uncertainty passed over the maid's delicate features, but then she shook her head. "No, Miss Burke."

When Avis had pulled out the bench and seated herself,

Deborah asked, "Aren't your duties finished once Miss Knight goes to bed?" She happened to know that Miss Knight had turned in early, having come back weary from her outing with Gregory's parents.

Avis shrugged. "I suppose so."

Deborah folded her arms in front of her. "There is something you want to discuss with me, isn't there?"

"Well . . ." Avis suddenly took great interest in the pattern in the carpet.

"Why do I have a feeling it's about the man who pretended to be Mr. Woodruff?"

Avis looked up at her. "Mr. Phelps, you mean?"

"Yes."

"Well," Avis began again, "Bethina and I have been talking."

*Now there's a surprise,* Deborah thought. "And what might you have been saying?"

Avis let out a doleful sigh. "We tried to think bad of him. We even hated him when we first found out what he did. But we just can't do that anymore."

"I'm sure we'll all be the better for forgetting and forgiving him," Deborah said with an almost clinical detachment. They were obligated to forgive, as Christians, after all.

The maid gave another sigh. "He was so nice . . . he would always ask how we were doin'." With a sober expression, Avis looked up at her and said, "Most people treat servants decent enough, but they still look at us like we don't have anythin' in our minds but cleanin' and bowin'. Especially upper-class people—yourself and Miss Knight excluded, of course."

Deborah closed her eyes in frustration. "He wasn't 'upper-class' people, Avis—and I'm not referring to his profession.

He made fools of all of us just for money." *Just because I've forgiven him doesn't mean I have to like him,* she thought.

"But why did he come here and tell the truth . . . especially knowin' it would make him look so bad? And if he only cared about money, why didn't he ever ask Miss Knight for any? or you?"

"How do you know he didn't?"

"Well, did he?"

Deborah began fiddling with the hem of her nightgown and thought about the man who had put pebbles into her hand in the garden. She had successfully kept that man from her mind all day, and she didn't want to think about him now. "Why are we talking about Mr. Phelps?"

She took a deep breath. "Because when Bethina and I were helping the missus get ready for bed tonight, she said that she was rather going to miss Mr. Phelps's calls, an' that she was ashamed to admit it, but she almost wished he hadn't come here and confessed."

"She'll have Mr. Woodruff," Deborah said. She could not, would never, address him as "Gregory." That name had once meant something to her.

"And how much fun do you think that will be, Miss Burke, with him not even wantin' to be here? The only reason the missus doesn't call off Mr. Gregory's visits is that she feels a responsibility to try an' help him change."

Deborah was very fond of Avis, but her patience had about reached its limit. Covering an exaggerated yawn with her hand, she said, "Is that all you wanted to tell me, Avis?"

"Almost done, miss," Avis said, smiling self-consciously. "I do go on and on sometimes, don't I? But back to Mr. Phelps, well, Bethina said that maybe the missus should invite him for supper sometime. Not on Sundays anymore, of course, but—"

"This is Miss Knight's house," Deborah said, proud of the chilled disinterest she managed to infuse into her voice. "She has the liberty to invite anyone she pleases."

"But she won't, because she thinks you might not be happy about it. That's just what she said, too."

"Are you suggesting that I tell Miss Knight that I could be comfortable around Mr. Phelps again?"

Hope lit up Avis's heart-shaped face. "You *were* fond of him at one time. . . ."

A brief image of warm blue eyes flitted across Deborah's mind, and then she frowned. "That has nothing to do with the present. If Miss Knight invites Mr. Phelps to share a meal, I will be civil to him, for her sake. As I mentioned before, this is her house."

"But she won't invite him unless you tell her that you'd like to see him, too."

Deborah shook her head. "Enough lies have been told to that poor woman. You and Bethina can't expect me to say things that aren't true."

"That's not what we wanted at all."

"Then what *do* you want?"

"We just hoped . . . that it might . . . that you might be *wantin'* to see Mr. Phelps again. We could tell that you both, well, were happy being near each other . . . an' wish you'd give him another chance."

Deborah had to smile at the misery on Avis's face. "I can't believe, after all that's happened, that you two are still plotting to bring us together."

"Not plotting," the maid corrected.

"All right, then . . . hoping. Why is it so important to you?"

Avis sighed and lifted a hand in a helpless gesture. "I've never had a serious beau. Don't know why, but it's something that never happened. Neither has Bethina. It's been nice seein' the two of you grow fond of each other. We wish it could be that way again."

"Well, it can't." Lowering her feet to the floor, Deborah walked over to put an arm around the maid's shoulder in a quick embrace. She finally understood why the two maids, and even Miss Knight, had attempted to push her toward Mr. Phelps a long time ago. *Every life needs a little romance . . . even if it's someone else's.* "But I do appreciate you for caring so much about what happens to me. You've been a good friend."

Avis patted Deborah's hand. "Aye, and so have you. We're goin' to miss you when you go to Venice."

When Avis had gone, Deborah sat down at the dressing table, unwrapped her towel, and began pulling a comb through the ends of her long hair. *When you go to Venice,* Avis had said. Those words, which should bring so much happiness, caused a queasiness in the pit of her stomach.

Sick of the struggle within her, Deborah wished she could talk with someone about this . . . someone who wouldn't be biased strongly toward either side. *That excludes Signora Pella and Miss Knight.* Her eyes wandered over to the three pebbles on her dresser, and she wondered why she hadn't thrown them away.

She could still recall the clarity and logic with which Mr. Phelps had presented his counsel as they sat in the garden and almost wished that she could seek his advice again.

"Almost." She said aloud to the frowning woman in the mirror. *But not enough to risk seeing him again.*

~

"Well, the lad's finally asleep," Nelda Darnell told her husband, who sat in a chair in their bedroom threading new laces through the eyelets of his work boots. She opened their armoire and took her nightgown from a hook on the inside of the door. "Maybe he should stay in that extra room for a while."

"Thet's a good idea," her husband replied. "Did he ever say what he found out?"

"Aye." She shook her head, recalling how Mrs. Reeves had bathed Thomas's face with a wet flannel until he'd finally stopped crying and went to sleep. "His mother's dead for sure. But that's all he'll tell us. He won't even say how she died."

"Why?"

"Says he has to save it all for the missus. But she was already in bed by the time he got back."

"Well, mebbe you'd best let him sleep in as long as he will in the morning. There ain't much that needs doin' in the garden."

"Can't do that," Nelda told her husband, who was now frowning at one end of the bootlace that had come out much longer than the other. "Mr. Gregory's folks leave for the station at eight. Thomas made me promise to wake him if he happened to still be asleep."

"Awful queer, ain't it?" He began loosening the laces in an attempt to make them even again.

"You'd think he was a hundred years old, the way he looked when he got here," Nelda agreed. "And what's even more queer . . . he mumbled something, just before he drifted off to sleep, about Mr. *Gregory* helping him." She shook her head again. "I guess you never know about people. Didn't

317

think he was the sort to go about helping anybody, much less a servant boy."

"God sees the heart, Nelda," her husband reminded her.

~

Thursday morning Matthew Phelps was surprised to see Mr. Henry walk into the office. "Got a message for you from the missus," the liveryman said as the two shook hands over the desk. He pulled an envelope from his coat pocket and handed it over.

"How is Thomas?"

"About the same," Mr. Henry said with a nod. "But he'll get better. He's a mite stronger inside than his years. And he's got every female in the house motherin' him."

Matthew smiled. "It sounds like just what he needs."

When the liveryman was gone, Matthew sat back down and tore open the envelope. It was a letter from Miss Knight, penned, no doubt, by Mrs. Darnell. He straightened it upon his desk and read:

> *Dear Mr. Phelps,*
>
> *Thomas has confessed to having stolen some of my belongings. I feel it is important for you to know that I have forgiven him completely. And I would like to thank you for helping him find out the truth about his poor mother and for protecting him from the person who was causing him to live in such torment.*
>
> *I blame myself, Mr. Phelps, for not being more aware of the lives surrounding me. Had I taken more interest in the child, perhaps he would have come to me with his problem. Be assured that I am remedying that situation, and when Thomas has had some time to*

*recover fully from the shock of what has happened, I intend to speak with him about continuing his schooling.*

*The last time we spoke, Mr. Phelps, was under harsh circumstances. I would like you to know that I bear no ill will against you for what happened. Your visits were a balm to my soul, and I greatly admire the courage it took for you to come to me with the truth.*

*I would be honored if you would be our guest at dinner tomorrow evening. You need not feel uncomfortable about being here, because you are still well thought of by the members of this household, particularly after what you did for Thomas. It will give us the opportunity to begin a new friendship, based upon mutual trust.*

*One additional note: I have divided the rest of my keepsakes among my servants. There is no sense in allowing them to sit in dark cupboards when the people who love me the most can benefit from them.*

*With highest regards,*

*Helene Knight*

Matthew smiled and reread the letter before folding it back up to put in his pocket. And although everything in him urged him to accept the invitation, he took a clean sheet of paper from a desk drawer and hastily penned his regrets. He cared for Miss Knight very much, but there would be time to renew that friendship once Miss Burke was gone. Seeing her was like pulling fresh stitches out of a wound. A person could only do that so many times without bleeding to death.

Lucas would be coming soon with the afternoon deliveries. He sometimes ran errands for Mr. Cornell as well, and

Matthew was sure that the boy would be happy to deliver
his note to Miss Knight's for a couple of shillings. He was
just about to seal the envelope when, almost as an after-
thought, he wrote out a check for the full amount that
Gregory Woodruff had paid him. *Please apply this to
Thomas's education,* he wrote in a postscript. As he sealed
the envelope he thought, *Perhaps he'll even want to be an
engineer one day.*

~

"Mr. Phelps sent his regrets about having supper with us
tomorrow night," Miss Knight told Deborah when she
returned from her music lesson.

"Why?" Deborah asked and then reprimanded herself. *Not
that I really care.* After learning what Mr. Phelps had done for
Thomas, she had reconsidered Avis's request and suggested to
Miss Knight that it might be good for the boy to have some
contact with the man. "Avis and Bethina are quite fond of
him, too," she added, ignoring the fleeting smile on the older
woman's face.

"His letter said perhaps it would be best if he allowed some
time to pass before coming back."

*Meaning . . . after I'm gone,* Deborah mused.

"Are you disappointed, Deborah?"

"Because of Mr. Phelps, you mean? No," Deborah answered.
She took a sip of hot lemon water. "Why should I be?"

The older woman looked uncomfortable. "I had so hoped
that you and he . . . well, I'm sure you know."

*I know.* Touching the older woman's hand, she said, "You
used to encourage my friendship with . . . Mr. Phelps . . .
because you wanted me to be in your family. Now that you've

320

found you two aren't even related, I should think you would
lose all interest in matchmaking."

"Oh, but there is always Gregory." Miss Knight sent a mis-
chievous smile in Deborah's direction but shook her head and
sighed before Deborah could protest. "I suppose I still wish to
think of Mr. Phelps as my nephew."

*That's why it was so easy for him to fool everyone,* Deborah
thought. His acting skills had been lacking, and his nervousness
certainly should have given him away. *But all of us wanted him to
be Gregory Woodruff.* Even Mrs. Darnell, who had actually seen
the real Gregory as a child, had accepted him without question,
not even raising an eyebrow when "Mr. Tarleton" came to call.

"You can still be friends with him," she reassured the
elderly woman.

"And you?"

"You can be friends with me as well," Deborah teased.

"You know what I meant," Miss Knight said with a wistful
smile.

"Of course. Mr. Phelps and I will be friends." *We'll likely
never see each other again, but we'll be great friends,* Deborah
thought cynically.

~

The first day of December fell on Saturday. As soon as Matthew arrived at the office, he prepared for the students who
would be arriving to claim their allowances, Gregory Woodruff included. He had wondered all week what had happened
after he had deserted the man at his aunt Helene's last week.
The revenge he'd expected had never come, for he still had his
position with Mr. Cornell.

*She probably forgave him,* Matthew thought, *just as she forgave me*. Still, it was with some uneasiness that he looked up every time the door was opened.

Woodruff walked in at half-past four, sat down in the chair in front of Matthew's desk, and pulled an envelope from his pocket. "Another directive from my father," he said with great nonchalance. "I'm to receive just enough allowance for the next week."

"Oh." Matthew read the letter, ran his finger down the list of names in the ledger, and penned in the amount. After he had taken the money from the cash box and counted it into the man's hand, he felt compelled to add, "I'm sorry," even though he had told himself over and over that Mr. Woodruff had brought whatever had happened upon himself.

"For what?"

"You're . . . being punished?"

Mr. Woodruff looked puzzled and then glanced down at the envelope on the desk. "Oh, you mean the cut in allowance. Well, you see, old boy, it's just temporary. I've only one week left of university. Holidays . . . remember?"

"I thought you were going to stay here in Cambridge."

"Well, my parents have decided that they miss me at home, so what can I do? They seem to see something worthwhile in me after all, especially since I've been so considerate to Aunt Helene." A corner of his mouth quirked up into a wry smile. "Gullible souls, aren't they?"

"Perhaps not." Matthew stood and held out a hand. "I wish you well."

"Same to you." Mr. Woodruff nodded as he rose from his chair. Matthew watched as he walked across the office and then turned before reaching the foyer. "By the way . . . would you mind calling on Aunt Helene now and then during the holidays? I believe it would mean a lot to her."

"Of course," Matthew answered after a moment's hesitation. *Deborah will probably stay upstairs, anyway.*

~

Without actually planning to do so, Matthew bundled up in an overcoat and muffler on Sunday morning and walked over to the chapel at Trinity College, where he'd once been a student. The worship service would not begin for another hour, but a handful of people were already seated quietly in the pews. He paused just inside the foyer to take off his hat and draw in a deep whiff of the familiar scent of polished oak and lamp oil. As he took a seat in the back, an older gentleman wearing a black robe came out from one of the doors behind the pulpit and went to the organ. Soon the soft strains of Bach's *Mass in B Minor* floated through the sanctuary.

God had drawn him here this morning—Matthew was sure of it. He closed his eyes and listened to the music and felt somehow that Father and Mother and William were watching him at this very moment, their faces radiant with approval that their beloved prodigal had returned. Matthew breathed a contented sigh. It was good to be home.

~

Late that afternoon, Deborah, Gregory Woodruff, and Miss Knight's servants formed a circle around a stone in the charity yard on Grange Road and listened as the vicar from Saint Giles prayed a memorial for Doreen Sully, Thomas's mother. Mrs. Darnell had insisted that Miss Knight stay home, with Avis to attend to her, because of her age and the weather.

A biting early December wind rattled the dried leaves of the trees bordering the cemetery and tousled Thomas's brown curls as he stood solemnly between Mr. Darnell and Mrs. Reeves.

"Why did the stone say 'Mary Tilton'?" Mr. Woodruff asked Deborah quietly when the brief service was over and the group walked back to the barouche and the hired coach. Before answering, Deborah glanced over her shoulder at Thomas, who walked several feet behind them with the head gardener's hand upon his shoulder.

"It was the name her . . . friend used when he took her to the hospital," she whispered. "Your Aunt Helene is going to have another stone made."

Mr. Woodruff glanced back at the boy. There seemed to be genuine sympathy on his sculptured face. "How is he?"

"He's bearing it well," Deborah answered and dropped her voice even lower. "But I did come upon him crying in the garden yesterday. I suppose it's just going to take some time."

Mr. Woodruff lapsed into a thoughtful silence and then said, "I wonder if Aunt Helene would allow me to get the stone."

"But why would you? You hardly know him."

"I've never really done anything for anybody before. Without some ulterior motive, I mean."

"And what is your motive now?" It was a rude question, Deborah knew, but she was acutely aware that Gregory Woodruff would still be pretending to be Fred Tarleton if Mr. Phelps hadn't confessed.

"Why, I'm not quite sure myself," he answered with seeming sincerity. "I don't believe I have one this time, other than feeling the need to do something worthwhile." He gave her a sidelong look. "You don't believe me, do you?"

"I'm sorry. Perhaps one day."

"Fair enough. Besides, on second thought, I do seem to have an ulterior motive after all."

"Yes?" She was a little disappointed but not surprised. "And what is that?"

He shrugged self-consciously and quoted one of the passages from Saint Matthew that he'd read aloud just an hour ago to his aunt in the parlor. "'Blessed are the merciful: for they shall obtain mercy.'"

They walked on in silence, and as seats were being filled in the two carriages, Deborah suddenly looked over her shoulder again.

"Miss Burke?" Mr. Darnell was holding out a hand to help her into the barouche, but she shook her head.

"Thank you, but I believe I'd like to stay here for a while. You go on ahead."

The gardener exchanged concerned glances with his wife, now seated in the barouche. "But how will you get home?"

Deborah gave them a reassuring smile. "I'll hire a hansom. Really, I shan't be too long."

After repeating her reassurances to Bethina and then again to Mrs. Knight and declining Gregory's offer to accompany her, Deborah set out for the charity yard again—this time alone.

For a long time she stared at the newly dug grave and the stone bearing the name *Mary Tilton*. And at last she knew that God had given her an answer.

# 19

*P*LEASE *give me the strength to stay with my convictions,*
Deborah prayed as Merrit led her to Signora Pella's
sitting room. Too riddled with anxiety to sit, she
stood in front of the fireplace and waited for the diva to come
downstairs.

"Good afternoon, Deborah," Signora Pella said five minutes
later as she entered the room. She was dressed in a stunning
gown of dark garnet and wore one of the smiles that had so
often graced her face these past weeks, ever since Cecilio
Giuseppe's visit.

"Good afternoon, signora," Deborah answered, but before
her teacher could go to the piano, she said, "May we speak
first?"

A wariness passed over the diva's face, but she nodded and
walked over to the settee, where Deborah joined her. When
they had seated themselves, Deborah said, "I want you to
know that I appreciate all of the time you've poured into my
lessons. I feel that I've learned more from you these past nine
weeks than in a whole year at the academy."

"You have been an exemplary student," Signora Pella
answered, still smiling but also still wary. "But that is not
what you wished to speak about . . . is it?"

"It's what I wished to say first, because it's important to me that you realize what these lessons have meant to me. But no, it's not the only thing I want to talk with you about."

The smile faded. "Then say what you have to say."

Taking in a deep breath, Deborah said, "I don't want to go to Venice. Not with . . . the way things are between you and Signor Giuseppe. I'm weary of wrestling with my conscience."

Signora Pella raised an eyebrow. "Perhaps it is your common sense you are wrestling with, Deborah. It is imploring you to be reasonable."

"No, I don't think so."

Leaning over to put a hand upon Deborah's sleeve, the diva looked at her with an expression of understanding. "It is so hard to be young, dear one. So many moods to do battle with, especially if you are a woman. And I have put so much pressure on you to learn this part perfectly. Why don't we practice other things today and speak about this again tomorrow . . . yes?"

*She's doing it again!* Deborah thought, feeling her resolve begin to weaken. A story Father had once read aloud to the family from Homer's *Odyssey* suddenly crossed her mind. On their journey home, King Odysseus's men had to cover their ears to keep from being allured by the sirens—sea nymphs whose sweet singing lured mariners to destruction on the rocks surrounding their island. Indeed, now Deborah felt like stopping up her ears with her fingers until she could get out everything she had to say.

"Verdi's *Simon Boccanegra* has some lively arias that might be amusing to try today," Signora Pella went on, starting to get to her feet.

"Wait," Deborah managed.

The diva gave her a long look and then settled back into the cushions of the settee. "Yes?"

"I attended an informal memorial service yesterday for the mother of a thirteen-year-old servant boy."

Signora Pella raised an eyebrow but looked totally disinterested. "Unfortunate. But why do you tell me this?"

"The boy wasn't always a servant. He had a comfortable home once and was able to go to school. I don't know what happened to his father . . . or if he ever knew one, but he did love his mother dearly."

"And what does this have to do with *Isabella?*"

"Everything," Deborah answered, willing herself not to turn away from the diva's intimidating gray eyes. "His mother had a succession of lovers, and one introduced her to opium. Some of her lovers mistreated her son, but she was in too much of a stupor to notice. She lost their home and her business, and the opium eventually killed her."

Deborah thought of Thomas, standing there at the graveside, and shook her head. "It could have all been so different, signora. I'm sure that the boy's mother would have been horrified had she been able to see into their future. But that's what sin does. It draws us in, a little at a time, until it has complete control . . . and then it devours us."

"That is enough of such talk," Signora Pella said flatly, her expression darkening. "I have already told you that you're not to speak about your religion in my house."

"This has nothing to do with religion," Deborah insisted. "It has to do with a responsibility we have to each other. If just *one* home is wrecked because I've compromised my Christian values, I cannot live with that."

The corners of the diva's mouth turned up into a cynical

smile. "I see. And so you, young Deborah Burke, are going
to give up the opera and go on a moral crusade to convince
everyone to live as they should."

"No. I'm an opera performer. I have trained half my life
to be one, and I dream about the day when I can win serious
parts. But God help me, I will never allow myself to be used
as a vehicle for evil. There are already too many Thomases
in the world."

"What do you mean . . . 'too many Thomases'?" Signora
Pella asked with an annoyed frown but shook her head before
Deborah could answer. "You will live to regret this foolish-
ness, Miss Burke."

"I won't if my heart stays in the right place."

"You know what this means, don't you?"

Deborah didn't know, but she could guess. With a knot in
her stomach, she said, "You're not willing to teach me anymore?"

Signora Pella stared at her with burning, reproachful eyes.
"You are going to make me look like a fool in front of Cecilio
Giuseppe, you silly child!"

The rebuke hit its mark, causing tears to sting Deborah's
eyes. She dabbed at them with her fingers and said earnestly,
"I'll win other roles, signora, and put my heart into them. And
it will be your teaching that will help me to make them great."

Obviously unmoved by Deborah's declaration, Signora Pella
got to her feet. "Go back home to your tea parties and needlework circles, Miss Burke," she ordered coldly, waving a deri-
sive hand toward the door. "Amuse your guests in the parlor
with your little songs, but stay away from the stage. You will
*never* have what it takes to be a diva."

~

Mr. Henry ambled toward the trap from the direction of the stables, stopped and squinted in Deborah's direction, then hurried over. "How long have you been waitin', Miss Burke?" he asked as he swung himself up to sit beside her.

"Not long." The truth was, she had no idea how long she had been sitting there in front of Raleigh Manor, only that the cold air felt good against her feverish face.

"You all right, miss?" the liveryman said with a worried stare.

"I'm not sure, Mr. Henry." Grief and humiliation welled up inside her. "I've been told not to come back."

"You have? But why?"

Deborah could only shake her head. "May we just leave now?"

"Hold on tight, then."

He let out a whoop and snapped the reins, urging Prince into a full gallop around the circle and down the carriage drive. Her heart in her throat, Deborah held onto the side of her seat with both hands and did not relax her grip until Mr. Henry slowed the horse to a walk to turn onto Sidgwick Avenue. She felt to make sure her hat was still pinned securely in place, then gaped, uncomprehending, at the driver.

Mr. Henry winked at her. "Figgered we should give 'em a good show."

~

Miss Knight was playing dominos with Mrs. Darnell in the parlor when Deborah peeked in the door.

"Miss Burke?" the housekeeper said before she could ease the door closed again. "You're home early. Are you ill?"

"Deborah's here?" said Miss Knight, sitting up in her chair.

Mrs. Darnell cocked her head to study her as Deborah walked over to their chairs and the marble-topped table. "Have you been cryin', dear?"

"No," she croaked. She wiped her face and blew her nose with the handkerchief she had wadded up in her hand, then sank into the third chair. "A little. I feel like such a child. I can't seem to stop."

"I'm going to fetch you some hot lemon water and let you two talk," the housekeeper said, getting to her feet. Mrs. Darnell stopped to put a hand upon Deborah's shoulder. "Or maybe you'll be wantin' somethin' stronger, just this once? A good cup of tea?"

She started to decline out of habit but then let out a short, humorless laugh. "Why not?"

Mrs. Darnell's skirt swished across the carpet as she walked out of the room. After the door closed behind her, Miss Knight turned her face in Deborah's direction. "I take it you made the decision you spoke about. Are you all right, Deborah?"

"I will be—one day. Do you mind if I tell you about it?"

Lines in the aged face deepened. "If it would help, dear."

"It would." The back of her throat felt raw, but Deborah managed to get everything out. To her relief, Miss Knight didn't appear embarrassed at the mention of Signora Pella's and the composer's adultery but sadly shook her head.

"I'm so sorry, Deborah. But you know you did what was right."

"Yes." Suddenly Deborah felt drained, too weary to hold her head up straight. She pushed herself out of her chair and said, "I just can't think anymore—I need to lie down. Would you apologize to Mrs. Darnell about the tea?"

"She will understand."

"I know." Deborah stopped halfway across the room and turned around again. "Everyone here has been so kind. I will miss all of you."

Miss Knight's expression was one of sad resignation. "I suppose you'll be leaving soon?"

"Yes, soon." Impulsively she walked back over to the elderly woman and gave her a quick embrace. "But we'll always be friends. And I'll come back to visit you."

Upstairs, she slipped out of her dress and threw it over her dressing screen, then crawled under the covers in her shift. As she lay there on her pillow, she thought about how close she had come to giving in to temptation. The battle she had waged with herself had been the toughest she'd ever fought— perhaps if she hadn't had so much time to think about it, she would have lost.

For the first time she could fully sympathize with Matthew Phelps.

~

Early evening twilight had crept into the room by the time she awakened by a knock on the door.

"Come in," she said, raising her head from the pillow.

Avis slipped into the room, a tray in her hands and concern on her face. "We didn't know how long we should let you sleep, but Miss Knight wants me to help you dress for supper."

"I'm not hungry." Deborah allowed her head to sink back into the pillow. "But thank you anyway."

"Oh, but you will be by the time supper comes." The maid's footsteps grew louder until it was obvious that she was standing at the side of the bed. With a sigh, Deborah lifted herself onto

one elbow. Avis smiled and nodded down at the contents of
her tray. "Mrs. Reeves made you a toasted cheese sandwich
to hold you till then. And here's a nice, strong pot of tea."

"But I'm not supposed to . . . ," Deborah began, and then
Signora Pella's parting words came back for a fresh assault.
*"You will never have what it takes to be a diva!"*

What was the use? Covering her legs with her shift, she
swung them over the side of the bed and allowed Avis to put
the tray in her lap. "How did you know?" she asked as the
maid poured the steaming tea into a Wedgwood cup.

"Miss Knight told us." Avis looked up at her with sympathy
in her green eyes. "Mrs. Darnell says you need a little something stronger than lemon water to lift your spirits."

She added milk and sugar to the tea and handed it to her.
For a few seconds, Deborah just held the cup up to her lips
and breathed in the aroma.

"Just what I needed," she said after taking a sip.

"Good." Avis turned and walked over to the armoire
against the wall. "Now, it's threatenin' rain out," she said,
opening both doors and peering at the dresses hanging inside,
"but Mr. Darnell says it'll hold 'til early in the mornin'. Still,
you don't want to be wearin' anything that might ruin, like
satin . . . even with your cloak over it."

"Wait." Deborah closed her eyes for a second, not sure if
it was the tea or Avis's words that were making her feel out
of sync with the rest of the world. "Why are you talking
about rain and satin?"

"Because you're going out for supper," the maid answered
as she pulled out a gown of smoky blue-gray damask. "Let's
see now," she mused, frowning down at the skirt, "I'll need to
press some of the folds out of it while you're havin' your bath."

"I bathed last night," Deborah said, then motioned to the frock thrown over her dressing screen. "And I planned to put that back on. And what do you mean, 'going out for supper'?"

"You're gettin' as bad as me about talking on and on," Avis scolded good-naturedly. "All I know is, the missus says it would be a good evening to go out, since we're not sure how much longer you'll be stayin' with us."

Deborah sighed and laid her sandwich back on its plate. *She's trying to cheer me up again . . . just like she did the last time.* She considered asking Avis to give her regrets to Miss Knight so she could climb back under the covers and sleep until the ache in the pit of her stomach went away.

*I could be on my way home in the morning.* The thought was both comforting and disturbing, for the family had been so proud of her for securing the attention of so great a performer as Signora Pella. *They'll understand,* she thought—but she didn't want understanding. She wanted them to believe in her, believe that she would one day succeed with her dreams. And she wanted so badly to believe in herself. She rubbed both temples and tried to silence the condemning voice. *"Go back home to your tea parties and needlework circles. . . ."*

Deborah blinked and looked up at Avis, standing in front of her. "I've got you a nice hot bath drawing," she said, taking the tray from her lap. "It'll do you good. Now, let's pin up your hair so it won't get wet, and you'll see how much better you're goin' to feel in a little bit."

Suddenly Deborah remembered how much Miss Knight had enjoyed their last outing. How could she even think of hurting the dear woman's feelings after she had shown her such hospitality? She sighed, got to her feet, and stretched.

"But isn't it rather late to be planning to go out?" Deborah said after a glance at the clock. "Miss Knight goes to bed early, and it's almost seven now."

"Let's get your hair pinned up before your bath overflows," Avis replied.

~

"I wish to be left alone," Clarisse Pella said coldly to the trembling servant girl who had dared to inquire for the second time within the hour if she would be joining Lord Raleigh in the dining room later. "And tell Merrit not to send anyone else up here. If I want something to eat, I will ring for it."

When the door had closed behind the maid, Clarisse shifted back around in her chair to the open drawer of her writing desk. She pulled out a small stack of envelopes, all of identical Crown linen. From the top envelope she took out a sheet of matching linen paper, smoothed out the folds, and scanned the contents. She stopped after the third paragraph, then read it again:

> *I have been studying for the past three years, since the age of four-teen, in Paris with Madame Reine Quincey. She has taught many great performers in the past, as you are likely aware, and says that I am her prize pupil. But I have lately become impatient with my progress, and have come to the reluctant conclusion that Madame Quincey's methods are outdated and too conservative. When I found out that you were no longer performing, I felt compelled to implore you to accept me as a student. Your genius is legendary, Lady Raleigh, and I have no doubt that you could guide my career to the heights to which I aspire. I am willing to follow any regimen, no matter how demanding, to become as great a presence on the stage as you once were.*

"We shall see about you, Miss Bellamy," Clarisse murmured as she took a piece of stationery and a pen from the open drawer. "Are you as ambitious as you appear in your letters?" Her lips tightened at the thought of the hours she had wasted upon Deborah Burke. *This time I will make no mistakes in judging character.* Before any potential student ever sang a note, she would be questioned thoroughly about any tedious moral reservations that would cause her to turn up her nose at a role.

But no matter how promising this young woman turned out to be, Clarisse could have no one ready in time to audition for *Isabella*. She sighed and thought of the letter she would have to write Cecilio after she finished the one to Estelle Bellamy. He would rant and rave the next time they met but in truth would easily find someone else to play the role. She wouldn't be spending time with him in Venice, for now she had no excuse to go. But they had always managed to find time to be together through the years. Another opportunity would come.

The thought that caused bitterness to rise to her throat was the realization that her dream of being an influence upon the opera stage, even vicariously, was to be delayed. The paper before her became blurry, and she dabbed at her eyes with the sash of her dressing gown. No matter how hard she grasped for happiness, it seemed to hover like some elusive hummingbird just out of her reach. Even at the peak of her fame, she had felt an emptiness inside during the dark hours of the night.

A movement at the corner of her eye caught her attention, and she glanced at the cheval glass in the corner. The woman who looked back at her was pitiful, ghastly, with splotches of crimson all over her face. Clarisse glared at the reflection for a long time, then turned her face away and wiped her eyes again.

*Your name will be in the history books with other great performers,*

she reminded herself, pressing her lips tight as she picked up
her pen again. *You have sung encores before kings and queens.*
*Young singers all over Europe aspire to have your talent.*

She had accomplished so much during her life. The happiness would come as well one day; she was sure of it. She just
had to keep grasping.

~

Matthew pulled the knit wool of his muffler up over his nose as
soon as he closed the office door behind him. As far as he could
see, dark clouds hovered overhead, turning the evening sky a
dismal gray. *Please let me get home before it starts to rain,* he prayed.
Even an umbrella was of little comfort during a chill night rain.

"Mr. Phelps?"

He turned at the sound of a familiar voice and noticed
for the first time that the horses and barouche waiting in the
street in front of the office belonged to Miss Knight. "Is that
you, Mr. Henry?"

"Aye, it is at that." The man was standing at the side of the
carriage, bundled up in an overcoat, muffler and hat. He took
a step forward. "Miss Knight asks if you would come right
away."

A faint worry crossed his mind. "Is something wrong?"

"Now, I don't know if you should be askin' me that. I was
just told to fetch you, if you're willin' to come."

~

Mrs. Darnell answered his knock at the door, and Matthew
remembered that the circumstances of his last visit had been
less than favorable. Still, the housekeeper smiled warmly.
"So good of you to come, Mr. Phelps."

Matthew gave her a self-conscious smile and glanced past her at the staircase. "Miss Knight . . . how is she?"

Waving a reassuring hand, she said, "Well, Mr. Phelps. She's waiting upstairs for you now." She went with him up to the drawing room, then opened the door to show him in. Miss Knight was seated in her usual chair with the table in front of her, from which Bethina was picking up dishes and putting them onto a tray.

"Do I hear Mr. Phelps?" Miss Knight said, and Mrs. Darnell answered for him.

"He's here, missus."

Bethina paused clearing the table to send a smile to Matthew, leading him to wonder how every person here could be so forgiving. Surely *somebody* in this house held a grudge against him. Then Deborah's face popped into his mind. He had to stop thinking about her!

"Please, come and sit, dear," Miss Knight said. Matthew crossed the room to give her hand a gentle squeeze before sitting in the chair he had once occupied as Gregory Woodruff. It was good to be back in the room that had nurtured so many happy, if guilt-ridden, memories.

"Just ring if you need us," Mrs. Darnell said from the doorway before she and Bethina slipped out of the room. When the door closed behind them, Matthew turned back to Miss Knight and noticed a slight gray pallor to her complexion, as if she had been ill.

"Are you well, Miss Knight?" he asked gravely.

"Very well," she answered, but the smile that she gave him only made her look melancholy.

"Are you sure?"

"I'm sure." Another smile, this one a little more genuine. "And how are you, Mr. Phelps?"

"Very well." He asked about Thomas and was assured that the boy was coping with his loss, then he glanced at the door and said, "Don't you usually take meals in the dining room?" What he really meant, he realized as he asked the question, was, *Where is Deborah?*

"When I haven't company, I prefer a tray up here."

He held his breath. "When you haven't . . . *?*"

"Oh, Deborah is still here. But she's upstairs dressing to go out for dinner."

"I see." Matthew wondered if Gregory Woodruff were taking her out, and he felt some of the old animosity creeping back in. Surely Deborah wouldn't want to go near the man after finding out the whole truth about him. *It's none of your business,* he reminded himself. *You never had any right to her to begin with.* Still, he breathed a quick prayer—*Take care of her, Lord.*

"I have two reasons for asking you here, Mr. Phelps," the elderly woman went on. She stopped then and tilted her head him. "Would you mind terribly if I addressed you as 'Matthew'?"

"Of course not." Relaxing a bit, he said, "In fact, it would please me very much."

"I'm glad. The first reason I asked you here . . . Matthew . . . is to discuss your future."

He wasn't sure if he'd heard correctly. "I beg your pardon?"

"I was going to ask you to come for supper this Sunday so we could talk about this, but it seems now that today would be a better time." After a moment's hesitation, she went on. "I pray you don't take offense, but I asked my nephew Gregory to make some inquiries about you. He tells me that you had to leave the university after your third year because of your brother's illness."

He would have been irritated had anyone else confessed to intruding into his affairs, but how could he feel anything but affection for the woman who had so graciously forgiven him? "I would do it all over again," he said quietly. "And I plan to go back one day."

"I know. That is why you allowed Gregory to talk you into assuming his identity." She held up a hand before he could apologize again. "I'm sorry about your brother, dear. William was his name?"

*I called him "Willie" when I wanted to torment him. Remember that, William?* "Yes," Matthew answered.

Miss Knight's voice, already warm and caring, became even more so. "He was blessed to have a brother such as you. And surely it would please him if you returned to school next term."

"I'm afraid that would be impossible." The Lenten term started in mid-January, just after the Christmas holiday. He would not be financially ready for at least three more years.

"But you've already tested. It should be a simple matter of enrolling again."

Matthew gave a quiet sigh and wished he could make her understand that his finances forbade even the dream of doing so. But if he admitted how deeply his brother's interment had plunged him into debt, it would be tantamount to hinting for a handout. He could never do such a thing. In an effort to bring an end to the subject, he said with gentle firmness, "Next term is out of the question, Miss Knight. But I do appreciate your encouragement."

"It's not only encouragement I'm offering, Matthew," she replied, her voice no less firm. "I would like to sponsor your education. *And* pay off any debts that were incurred because of your brother's treatment. You sent him to a sanatorium, and I know they are expensive."

His heart lurched in his chest, and it took him a moment to recover from the shock before he spoke. "I would feel like the lowest cad in England if I allowed you to do that."

"Why, pray tell? I have much more money than I need. It would give me great pleasure to do it."

"You are exceedingly generous," he told her. "But I just can't accept."

"And I still don't understand why," she persisted. "What is the use of having money if you can't use it to do some good? Isn't that what you did for William?"

"He was my brother, Miss Knight."

"And I still feel that you're part of *my* family."

Matthew savored the sound of those words, for they meant that he belonged here. He got up from his chair and knelt at the side of hers. Picking up one of her frail hands, he held it in both of his. "Just knowing that you've forgiven me . . . that you care enough to make such an offer is sufficient," he said through a throat that was suddenly tight. "But please understand that I cannot allow you to do this."

The elderly woman said nothing, and when he finally looked up at her, a tear was trailing down her withered cheek.

"Miss Knight?"

Her voice was as frail as her hand when she finally answered. "A generous spirit involves more than giving to others, Matthew. Sometimes the utmost generosity can be shown in receiving."

His heart went out to her. "But I've already taken so much from you."

"Not as much as you've given. Won't you please change your mind?"

"It means that much to you?"

Just a bit of hope came into her expression. "It does."

"Then I thank you." Squeezing her hand against his cheek, he allowed the incredible fact to sink in that he would be a student within weeks, with no debt hanging over him. He filled his lungs with air and felt almost giddy. "I'm overwhelmed!"

Five minutes later when Bethina came back into the room, he was still at Miss Knight's side, answering her questions about his earlier days at the university and about his brother, William.

"She'll be on her way downstairs in just a minute," the maid said, grinning again at Matthew.

*Deborah?* he thought with panic, getting to his feet and turning to stare at the door. Was Gregory Woodruff going to meet her in this very room? Did he have time to clear out before having to bear the sight of the two of them together? Turning back to the elderly woman, he said, "I will be grateful for the rest of my life for what you've offered, Miss Knight. But I have to go now."

"Wouldn't you like to stay and speak with Deborah?" Miss Knight asked.

"I—perhaps some other time."

She nodded, as if she understood. "You must allow Mr. Henry to take you home, Matthew. I hear that it's threatening rain."

*Won't she need the carriage?* The question was on Matthew's lips, but of course, if Woodruff were taking her out, he would arrive in a hired carriage. "Yes, thank you." He bent down to give her a quick kiss on the cheek and hurried out of the room.

Mr. Henry was still waiting out front. "No rain yet," the driver commented as he lowered the step at the side of the barouche.

"Thankfully," Matthew replied with a glance at the clouds. His breath formed ghosts of vapor in the air as he talked. "Why are you using the barouche tonight?"

"Oh, felt like giving Prince a little exercise, too."

As Mr. Henry fiddled with the horses' harnesses, Matthew realized that Miss Knight had not had a chance to tell him the second reason she'd asked him to visit.

~

"Here, let's go ahead and bundle up now," Avis said, holding out Deborah's navy wool cloak. She had just finished fastening the one button at the neck when Bethina came into the room for the second time in five minutes.

"Mr. Henry's waiting with the carriage," Bethina said, exchanging a meaningful glance with Avis. "Are we ready?"

"Ready," Deborah answered. She turned to fetch her reticule from the foot of her bed, but Avis was already holding it out to her. The two maids flanked her all the way down two flights of stairs, waving her on when she paused at the second-story landing. "But Miss Knight . . . ," Deborah mumbled, then hurried to catch up with them. Now she understood the haste. Obviously, the older woman was already out there, waiting in the carriage. She winced inside at the thought of the Miss Knight sitting in the cold and wished she'd not dawdled earlier.

~

It seemed that Mr. Henry had to check every piece of leather on each horse, and Matthew wondered why the liveryman hadn't thought to do that while he was inside. He heard a noise to his left and turned to see the front door opening and three female figures stepping out onto the portico, barely illuminated by the amber glow of the gaslights. He could hear Bethina and Avis chattering like magpies. The cloaked figure in the middle looked straight at him and then froze. It was Deborah Burke.

~

From the top step of the portico, Deborah peered out at the waiting carriage. *Matthew Phelps!* For just a fraction of a second a sense of relief washed over her, but then she became irritated at herself for it. *You're leaving*, she reminded herself. A mental picture of his backing away from their kiss came into her mind again. *Besides, he means nothing to you.*

"Why didn't anyone tell me that Mr. Phelps was coming along, too?" she whispered to Avis as the maid urged her down the steps.

"Miss Knight was afraid you wouldn't want to go," Avis whispered from her side. "You won't change your mind, will you?"

*How can I now?* she thought, her teeth on edge with irritation. She walked with the maids out to the street, wondering all the while why she didn't see her hostess in the barouche. Mr. Henry gave her a grin and lowered the step for her. "Miss Knight *is* coming, isn't she?" she said to Bethina. She didn't bother to lower her voice this time.

345

"Here, now," the maid answered. "Let's help you up in there."

Mr. Phelps stood to offer his hand, and Deborah realized as she took it that he seemed as stunned as she felt. "Thank you," she said when he had helped her into the seat facing his. She turned to look at the two maids again, but they were already walking back to the house.

"Are you going to get Miss Knight?" she called to them, and Avis turned around just long enough to wave. Just then Mr. Henry made a clucking noise from his box, and the carriage lurched forward.

# 20

MR. HENRY kept the horses at a steady trot, precluding any effort by Deborah to get his attention. She settled in her seat, drew her cloak tightly about her and watched Thompson's Lane grow longer and longer behind them. Finally she looked across at Mr. Phelps, who stared back at her with a dazed expression.

"I want you to know that I had nothing to do with this," she told him. *On the first London train tomorrow,* she promised herself, *I am going home.*

"Of course you didn't. But I hope you don't think *I* did."

She believed him, even though he had been guilty of duplicity before. Avis and Bethina obviously had not given up on their matchmaking. *And Miss Knight is in on this as well,* she thought. *The maids wouldn't dare engage in such a scheme without her permission.* "Miss Knight found out that I'm leaving." She sighed. "That's why this is happening."

"Leaving? You mean for your audition?"

"No, sooner." She swallowed. "There will be no audition. My lessons are finished."

His mouth gaped open. "What happened?"

As exasperated as she was with the maids and Miss Knight— *Mr. Henry, too,* she thought, for he was part of this— Deborah found that it was a great relief to talk to Matthew. "Signora Pella and I had a difference of opinion. I wish I could tell you more, but . . ."

"I understand, Miss Burke." His blue eyes filled with sympathy. "But surely you don't feel that you've failed, do you?"

Deborah gave another sigh. "My *head* tells me that I haven't. But my heart is in a tumult. I'm so afraid that all of my dreams have been for nothing."

"But Signora Pella can't destroy your dreams."

"And my *head* agrees with you," she said with bitter humor.

He opened his mouth to speak, but the horses slowed abruptly to turn onto Petty Cury. The barouche stopped in front of Sidonie's, and Mr. Henry climbed down.

"This is for you," the liveryman said, handing an envelope to Deborah before bending down to lower the step.

"From Miss Knight?"

"I expect so. 'Course, Mrs. Darnell is the one who gave it to me, and she would be the one who held the pen. You're supposed to read it inside."

Deborah and Mr. Phelps looked at each other. "I'll understand if you'd rather not," he said, though his eyes seemed to beg her to stay.

*You were friends once,* Deborah reminded herself. *And this is the last time you'll see him.* "Do you want to?" she asked.

"Very much so . . . but only if you do."

"Would the two o' you polite people mind settlin' this indoors?" Mr. Henry asked from the side of the carriage. "I'd like to get these horses into a stable so's they don't stand out here in the cold. I'll be back for you in a couple o' hours." To Matthew, he added, "I'm supposed to take you home after we deliver Miss Burke back to Miss Knight's."

The restaurant was not nearly as crowded this time, possibly because of the threatening rain. The same French maître d' directed a young woman to take Deborah's cloak and Mr. Phelps's coat and hat and then led them past tables occupied by well-dressed patrons. The whole place seemed to glow under the soft lights of the chandeliers. "Nice and cozy for young lovers, yes?" he said, smiling indulgently as he placed menus on a table in a snug corner.

Deborah's cheeks flared, and she glanced around the restaurant, certain that every eye in the place was upon her. When she saw that the other patrons either had not heard or did not care, she took the seat that Mr. Phelps was holding out for her. "That was very embarrassing," she whispered.

"I'm mortified myself," he whispered back. She eyed him suspiciously for a fraction of a second, but his blank expression made it unclear whether or not he was joking.

She held up the envelope. "I suppose we should see what's in here." She broke the seal and took out a folded sheet of paper. When she opened it, a five-pound note fluttered down to the tablecloth.

"Oh no," Mr. Phelps groaned. Deborah looked up at him. He had part of his face covered with one hand as he shook his head. "Please give it back to her."

*But do you have enough money?* Deborah wanted to ask him. She doubted a solicitor's clerk made a huge salary. *Should I offer to pay? After all, he was tricked into coming here, just as I was.*

He seemed to read her mind, for he gave her a wry smile. "I can pay for the meal, Miss Burke. I'll draft a check if I have to."

She nodded and said impulsively, "You know, it seems absurd for us to address each other so formally. Do you think we could go back to given names?"

He looked relieved. "I would like that," he answered, "as long as you don't call me Gregory."

Deborah held the letter closer and began to read aloud:

*My dear young friends,*

*Please forgive me for meddling this one last time. I would like to re-pay you in some small measure for the joy you have brought me these past two months, and I pray you will take the money and have a lovely meal. Deborah, my heart grieves for you concerning Signora Pella, but you will be glad of your decision more and more as you grow older. I admire your courage and integrity and will continue to pray that God blesses your music. Matthew, you are a better person than you know, and I am the richer for knowing you. I will be the proudest person in Cambridge when you are awarded your degree.*

*With deepest affection,*

*Helene Knight*

"What does she mean . . . awarded your degree?"

Matthew was still staring at the letter. "Why, she would not have had time to dictate this letter after she spoke with me. She *knew* she could talk me into it!" He looked at Deborah and shook his head in wonder.

"Talked you into what, Matthew?" Deborah persisted.

"Oh, I'm sorry." He told her how Miss Knight had offered to sponsor him at the university and pay off his debts. "I'm sure you know that she's going to send Thomas to school as well."

"She's a most generous woman," Deborah said. "I'm very happy for you."

He looked truly surprised. "You are?"

"Of course. I suppose you'll be giving notice at your office?"

"Why, I haven't even thought of that yet. But yes, I'll have to do that."

A waiter came for their orders, and Deborah and Matthew exchanged sheepish looks, for their menus still lay on the table, unopened. "Why don't you order for both of us?" he said. "I'm not familiar with French cuisine anyway."

Deborah nodded and ordered roasted chicken for both of them without opening the menu. When the waiter was gone, Matthew looked across at her and frowned. "Forgive me, Deborah. Here I am, glowing over my good news when you've had a devastating day."

Her stomach knotted at the memory of Signora Pella's angry words. "She said I would never have what it takes to be a great singer."

"And do you believe her?"

"I don't want to. But she's such an authority in her field. It's like Charles Dickens telling someone he could never be a great writer. Or Wordsworth advising a person to give up poetry."

"That would be intimidating," he agreed. "But why would she recommend you for an audition if she didn't think you had talent?"

"Well . . . she wouldn't."

Folding his arms in front of his chest, Matthew said, "You mustn't think your success is in Signora Pella's hands alone, Deborah. What if she had never been born? Wouldn't you still be as talented as you are now?"

"I suppose I would. But it *was* her performance that influenced me to study opera."

"I know very little about music," he admitted. "But surely the inspiration would have come, just the same. If it had not been Signora Pella up on the stage that day, it would have been some other great singer. Or the inspiration would have come later, during some other performance."

Deborah had never considered that. She mulled it over in her mind. "For years I've linked opera with Clarisse Pella, as if one couldn't exist without the other." She nodded as the concept became clearer. "But operas were being performed for decades before she was ever born."

"And as far as the opera she wanted you to audition for is concerned . . . *Isabella,* is it?"

She nodded again.

"What if *Isabella* had never been written? Do you feel you would never have the opportunity to audition for another role?"

Again, Deborah had allowed emotion to obscure this point. "No, of course not." *She said those things because she was angry and disappointed,* she told herself. *People lash out when they've been hurt.*

She sighed, some of the confusion and worry that had so tormented her having been eased away. Feeling her tensed shoulders relax, she sat back in her seat and smiled across at him. "I still have a chance, haven't I?"

His eyes were shining as he looked across at her. "I would wager my life on it."

A self-conscience silence came over them, and Deborah looked around and pretended great interest in the goings-on of the restaurant. By this time dinner was proceeding briskly at the tables around them. Underclassmen in flannel suits were debating philosophy at the nearest table. At another, matrons in old lace and lorgnettes gossiped. Waiters in dark blue jackets hurried here and there, and a torrent of gourmet dishes flowed out of the kitchen against an eddy of soiled china moving back in.

"Deborah?"

She turned her face to look at him again. This time he wore a worried expression that reminded her of his first visit to Miss Knight's. "Yes?"

"I just . . . well, I would like you to know that my switching places with Gregory Woodruff . . ." He cleared his throat and looked away. "I've never done anything like that before in my life. And I'm more ashamed of it than I can possibly tell you."

The old anger she'd felt at being betrayed attempted to nudge into her thoughts, but then she remembered the kindness with which he'd treated a blind old woman and an orphaned boy. Suddenly she found that she couldn't have hard feelings toward him. She folded her hands together upon the table. "You did put a stop to it."

"Yes," he replied, "but I'm afraid honor wasn't my main reason for doing so."

"What do you mean?"

"You seemed to grow fond of Gregory Woodruff. I was afraid that he . . ."

She had to smile. "Would try to court me?"

He looked away for a second. "Yes."

"Why would that concern you?" she asked, forcing casualness into her voice. It was absurd to ask that question, when she would be leaving Cambridge soon, but she could not stop herself from asking it.

This time he looked straight at her, his expression sadder than she had ever seen it. "You already know why."

"No, I'm sure I don't," she said lightly, irritated at herself for playing such silly games. She should come right out and tell him what had bothered her for three weeks. Even now she shuddered inside at the humiliation. *My head was swimming with . . . affection for you; my heart was about to burst . . . and you backed away and looked at me as if I'd turned into some loathsome creature!*

Deborah looked down at the table and blinked at the sight of two dishes of *poulet à la paprika,* salads, bread plates, and water goblets. She vaguely recalled the waiter returning sometime during their conversation, wishing them *bon appètit.*

"Then I will tell you, Deborah," Matthew said as he pushed his plate to one side and leaned closer again. "Although nothing can come of it, I don't want to spend the rest of my life wishing I'd said something and wondering what your reaction might have been."

She looked at him, wondering at the intensity in his blue eyes.

"I have been in love with you from the first," he said softly. "And just the thought of Gregory Woodruff spending one minute alone with you was more than I could bear."

Deborah's breathing became shallow. This was too much to take in all at once. "If you were in . . . if you felt that way about me, then why . . . ?"

"The night of the concert?"

"Yes."

He gave her a somber nod. "I know that I hurt you."

"It didn't matter," she told him, trying hard to mean it.

"It did to me. But you don't know what it is to find yourself in the middle of a world where you don't belong, all because of your own deviousness. I didn't deserve to have you even look at me . . . much less . . ."

"Don't say that." Weariness overtook her. She had been through too much emotional turmoil lately. She lowered her voice, so as not to provide entertainment for the nearby patrons, and said, "My mother would faint if she heard me being so blunt, Matthew . . . but it was my first kiss. It was wonderful and special, but then you backed away."

He closed his eyes for a moment, and when he opened them again, they glistened with raw pain. "It took every ounce of strength that was in me to back away, Deborah. If you only knew how much."

For just a moment she wanted to reach across the table and touch his cheek again. But what was the use of waking up all those feelings? "It was probably for the best, anyway."

He winced. "Why do you say that?"

"Because I was wrong to take my mind off of my lessons. I'm not a schoolgirl, and yet I acted like one."

~

*She felt something for me that night,* Matthew reminded himself, though her words now seared his soul. He had relived that kiss a thousand times in his daydreams. Even now, three weeks later, he could remember how tenderly her gloved hand had caressed his cheek. Deborah wasn't the type of woman who would kiss a man just for the sake of having something to write in her diary. It had to have meant something.

One part of his heart urged him to give up belaboring the past and settle for an amiable evening of pleasant, safe conversation. *She'll forget about you anyway,* he told himself, *as soon as she's back in her own world.*

But he had learned something today—that prayers could really be answered. How could he have imagined, as he had dressed for work this morning, that within a few weeks he would become a student again? In just two years he would be designing bridges! For the first time since he'd had to leave school, he felt an optimism about the future.

And he had nothing to lose by making her understand just what she meant to him. Emboldened by his feelings for her and by the realization that this could be their last time together, he said, "You weren't acting like a schoolgirl, Deborah." He studied her green eyes, memorizing them for the days ahead when she would be gone. "I believe you felt something for me, too."

She studied the water goblet in front of her. "Something," came her voice, just above a whisper.

The admission gave him courage enough to ask, "Do you feel anything for me now?"

Matthew held his breath in the silence that followed. Finally she looked up at him, her green eyes liquid in the light of the flickering chandeliers. "I have to try for the opera, Matthew. I've studied for so long. I have to find out . . ."

"I know. You have to." The idea of her leaving was almost unthinkable, but he would never ask her to give up her dream. He could still taste the bitterness that had seized him when his own dream of becoming an engineer had been set aside. He wouldn't wish that upon anyone, especially not Deborah.

"At least give me something to live with while you're gone, Deborah," he urged, softly. "Just tell me how you feel."

~

*I love you,* she thought, staring across at the face that was so masculine, yet so tender. How long had she known? Since the evening of the concert? That time they'd sat in the garden? When she heard how he'd rescued Thomas?

But it really didn't matter when those feelings had blossomed because she couldn't tell him about them. It wouldn't be fair to him. Those words implied a commitment that she was not yet ready to make. When the time came for marriage and a family, she wanted to be able to give her whole heart away, without reservation. She took a deep breath and willed her racing pulse to slow down.

"I am very fond of you," she finally said.

She could tell by the slight sag of his shoulders that he was hoping for something more than that. Still, he gave her a little smile. "I suppose I'll have to come to London to hear you sing."

"Oh, dear. I never did sing for you, did I?"

"I heard you on the day that I . . . well, the day I confessed."

"Of course." The evening had been so traumatic, she had forgotten. "You would come to London to see me?"

"Would you want me to?"

"Oh, yes, as often as you will." The thought made her spirits lighter. "You could stay with my family. I would love—" Realizing she had actually said the word, she stopped and stammered, "I mean . . ."

"It's all right, Deborah," he murmured. "I'll settle for that right now. Just remember that I'm a dreamer just like you are—and just as determined."

It was so thoughtful of him to put her at ease in this way, even though she knew his disappointment ran deep. *I'm going to miss him so much,* she thought. Overwhelming emotion took hold of her, and she leaned forward. "Matthew, I'm not going to end up like Signora Pella." Somehow it was important that he understand that.

"I know that, Deborah."

"Are you sure?"

He smiled at her. "Would Signora Pella have given up that audition?"

"No. But Signora Pella wasn't given three stones and a leaf by a very wise person."

"Not wise," he said, shaking his head. "Just a poor bloke so much in love that he couldn't see straight."

Embarrassed, Deborah lowered her eyes, but when she raised them to look at him again, she couldn't help but return his smile. He moved aside his water goblet and stretched out his hand, and she immediately slipped hers into it. They sat there like that for a long time, while he asked her about her years at the academy and she asked him about his family, until a worried voice from the side said, "You found the food unacceptable, sir?"

"Our meal!" Deborah gasped pulling her hand away, then turned to look at the waiter's concerned face.

"I'm sure the food is fine," Matthew told him. He raised a questioning eyebrow at Deborah, and she shook her head. "But neither of us has an appetite right now. Would you mind wrapping it so we can take it with us?"

"Take it with you?" Now the waiter looked offended. "You are going to feed Chef Marselle's creation to a house pet?"

"No." Matthew gave him a reassuring smile. "A person. And I can guarantee you he'll think it's delicious."

# 21

M R. HENRY was waiting when they left the restaurant and lowered the step to the barouche. Enjoy yourselves?" he asked, his words gusting out in a trail of vapor.

"Very much," Matthew answered. He offered his hand to Deborah and helped her onto the seat facing the front. In an act of great willpower, he took the opposite seat for himself. *You've pressured her enough. Give her some time to think.*

He wasn't hurt this time at the relief in her expression, for he was aware that she was struggling with a battle within. That gave him hope. Had she not had deep feelings for him, leaving would be a simple matter of saying good-bye.

"Have you decided when you're going to leave?" he asked her as hoofbeats rang out against the cobblestones under a grayish purple sky.

She gave him a hesitant smile. "Wednesday, I think. I would like to spend tomorrow with Miss Knight, since she's been so kind to me."

*That soon!* His heart sank within him. "That's very thoughtful of you. What about your family—will you wire them?"

"I don't know. I'm afraid they'll worry about me if I do. Perhaps I'll just surprise them."

*She asked me to visit her in London,* he reminded himself
and felt a little better. *That means she wants to see me again.*
"Surprises are nice," he said.

~

The horses pulled the carriage onto King's Parade, moving
north, and soon Matthew turned in his seat and called out to
Mr. Henry to stop. "Be back in a minute." He hopped down
to the street with the package of food under one arm.

Deborah watched, curious, as he walked over to a dark alley
and disappeared, only to come out again almost immediately
without the package. "An old acquaintance of mine," he
explained as he climbed back into the barouche.

"You really are a good man," Deborah told him as the
carriage started moving again.

It was hard to tell in the dim light of the streetlamps, but
it seemed to her that he was blushing. "I don't know how
you can say that, after what—"

"With utmost conviction," she cut in, smiling across at him.
*And I'm going to miss you so much, Matthew Phelps.*

They rode the rest of the way in silence. When the carriage
stopped in front of Miss Knight's house, Henry came around
to lower the step. "I expect you'll want to see Miss Burke to
th' door?" he asked Matthew in his gruff voice. "Won't hurt
to check the harnesses again anyway."

Matthew thanked the driver warmly and offered Deborah
his arm. Together they walked up the steps to the portico. At
the front door he turned to face her. "You know, there are
more engineering firms located in London than anywhere else
in England," he said. Uncertainty filled his expression, as if he

weren't sure she would be pleased. "That is . . . I'll have to work *somewhere* after I've earned my degree."

"London is a good place to live," Deborah responded, suddenly lightheaded. "In fact, I've been thinking about limiting my work to the London theaters. Once I start winning roles, of course."

"You have?" He took both of her hands. "But will that hurt your career?"

"Well, this is one of those 'pebble and leaf' situations, Matthew. When I have a . . . family of my own, I won't want to leave them to go on tour."

"I just hope you won't have regrets later."

"Regrets are for people like Clarisse Pella," Deborah answered, then smiled again. "It can't be so bad to be the most famous performer in Great Britain, as opposed to the most famous in Europe. You can only sing to one audience at a time, anyway."

"You're incredible," he told her. "I wish I could tell you everything in my heart right now. But I've already said so much. I don't want to rush you."

A lump rose in Deborah's throat at the thought that this would be the last time she would see him for a while. But she would still be here tomorrow. . . .

"I'm sure Miss Knight would love to have you come for supper tomorrow. Why don't I ask . . . ?"

He shook his head. "I don't think I could take another good-bye, Deborah. Do you understand?"

She glanced out at the street, where Mr. Henry was still busying himself with the horses. "I suppose you have to go now," she sighed. "He can't keep pretending to check the harnesses forever."

"True," he replied. Instead of moving away, Matthew smiled down at her. "But we still have time."

Deborah could feel her heart pounding in her chest. "Time?"

He brought her hands up to his broad shoulders, then took a step closer and encircled her with his arms. "Time enough to finish that kiss. Do you mind?"

"I will be crushed if you don't," she breathed, lifting her chin.

~

"Are you all right, Miss Burke?" asked Avis ten minutes later after answering Deborah's light knock upon the door. "Your face is red as a beet."

"Is it?" Deborah put a hand up to one cheek. "Why, I suppose it is."

Bethina appeared in the hallway, wearing a dressing gown and a worried expression. "You ain't put out at us, are you, Miss Burke?"

"Put out?" It took a moment for Deborah to realize what she meant. "For tricking me into going out with Mr. Phelps?"

The two servants exchanged guilty looks. "Yes, miss."

"I'm eternally grateful to both of you. And to Miss Knight. I'll have to tell her so in the morning."

Avis let out a relieved sigh and took her cloak. "You had a good time, then?"

"I had a wonderful time." She could still feel her heart pounding. "Wonderful."

"That's good," Bethina said, a beatific smile lighting up herhomely face. "You just needed to spend a bit more time together, that's all. Just like what happened with me second cousin, Nell. Her sister, Rose, locked Nell and th' young man she wouldn't give the time o' day to in a turnip cellar for a couple o' hours. They been married for thirty years now."

"Thirty years, you say?" Impulsively Deborah linked arms with the two women. "You know, I've had a box of bonbons sitting in a drawer for a couple of weeks now. Why don't we all go up to my room and open them up?"

"A party, Miss Burke?" Avis asked as they started moving toward the staircase.

"We'll have a nice little visit," Deborah replied, then smiled at Bethina again. "And I want to hear all about Cousin Nell."

# A Note from the Author

Dear Reader,

In case you're wondering what lies ahead on the pages stored in this author's mind, I see Deborah and Matthew marrying and having five children, and Deborah enjoying a long career in London's Royal Opera House.

I tell you this because my mother took issue with me for not spelling that out. "But you know that's what will happen," I argued. "I gave enough hints."

"I want to see it in writing," she insisted.

And so for Mom, and you if you share her opinion, I'll go the second mile and add that their youngest son George becomes even more famous than Deborah, touring Europe and the United States.

Thank you for reading *Song of a Soul,* the final story in my Victorian Serenade series. May God put a lovely song in your soul, dear reader, and may your footsteps keep time with the beating of his heart.

Warmly,

Lawana Blackwell

# About the Author

Lawana Blackwell is an accomplished novelist whose books have found a strong following. Her books include *The Widow of Larkspur Inn*, *The Courtship of the Vicar's Daughter*, *The Dowry of Miss Lydia Clark*, and *The Maiden of Mayfair*. She and her husband live in Baton Rouge, Louisiana, and are empty nesters who love every opportunity to get together with their three recently married sons and their wives. Besides writing, Lawana enjoys Home and Garden television, vegetarian cooking, and garage sales.

Lawana welcomes letters written to her in care of Tyndale House Author Relations, P.O. Box 80, Wheaton, IL 60187-0080 or by e-mail at lawanablack@yahoo.com.

# Wild Heather

*The village of Otley*
*Yorkshire, England; 1813*

Olivia longed for her fan. She felt hot and annoyed and terribly anxious, yet she had no choice but to stand and engage Mr. Bowden in this meaningless chatter. Was the earth created in six days? How silly! How utterly trivial in comparison with the issue of the moment—the chaos Olivia's brother might be wreaking even now at Chatham Hall.

She willed herself to concentrate. Her mother, who ought to tend to duties in matters that beset the townspeople, was all but unable. No one knew the extent to which the mantle of responsibility had fallen on Olivia's shoulders. And she intended to keep Lady Chatham's condition a secret for as long as possible. Indeed, Olivia would do everything in her power to protect her family's reputation.

"To be sure, Mr. Bowden," she said. "The Chatham family are committed to the good of everyone in Otley."

"But what of this lecture to be given by William Buckland on the fifteenth of the month?" he asked. "You know what that man believes, and his speech can only foment hostilities. Miss Hewes, can you be persuaded to speak to Lady Chatham about the situation?"

"Of course. Yes, indeed—oh, can this be Miss Clementine?" Olivia spotted the golden-haired child peeking out from behind a pew. Gratefully turning away from Mr. Bowden, she knelt on the stone floor to greet the little girl. "What a lovely young lady you are, my dear. And how tall you have grown! I declare, you must be eight years old by now."

"No indeed, madam, for I am barely six." Flushing with pleasure, Clementine Bowden made a curtsy. "Miss Hewes, you must come to Brooking House and see our polliwogs. We have ever so many in our stream."

"Polliwogs." A genuine smile came to Olivia's lips for the first time that morning. "I liked polliwogs once . . . and I believe I should like them still. But I fear I must hurry home at once to my own dear mama."

With that, Olivia attempted to stand. But for some reason, her gown refused to budge. Disconcerted, she straightened, and the fabric suddenly gave way with a loud ripping sound.

"Upon my word!" She looked over her shoulder to discover her hem trapped beneath the heel of a man's large leather boot. "I declare, sir—you are treading upon my gown!"

The man turned, and their eyes met. His were blue . . . the bright and glorious blue of a Yorkshire lake in midsummer. Olivia stared, her lips parting and her breath unmoving as every rational thought in her head, every worry in her heart vanished. She looked into a face that might have been chiseled by a Greek artisan—a noble nose, a jutting chin, a square jaw, and the plane of a cheek so fine and smooth it could have been hewn from marble. Yet the color that suffused the flesh of this face gave it life and beauty and bearing.

Such a man! Such breadth of shoulder, such imposing stature, and such a head of hair . . . warm chestnut curls that tumbled over his ears and brushed his collar as he removed a top hat of the finest beaver.

"Dear madam," he said, and his voice was deep and rich. "I sincerely beg your pardon."

His blue gaze tore from her eyes and fell to her gown. Olivia glanced down, too, and saw the astonishing rent. Great ghosts! The embroidered white lawn fabric of her skirt had ripped cleanly away from the back of her bodice! A button hung by a single thread, and the gathers in her skirt were even now unfolding like accordion pleats.

"Lord Thorne has torn Miss Hewes's gown!" Clementine Bowden exclaimed. "I can see her petticoat!"

The announcement brought cries of dismay from those around her as Olivia snatched her pink shawl and attempted to cover the gap with the length of cashmere. The man reached to assist, but someone stayed his hand.

"This is Miss Hewes!" John Quince said quickly. "Do come away, Lord Thorne."

*Thorne!* As that most hated of names registered in her brain, Olivia dropped the corner of her shawl. She sucked in a shocked gasp, and the lemon drop flew to the back of her throat. Lord Thorne? Could it be? She began to choke. Had she actually looked at a Thorne? Had he looked at her?

"Miss Hewes, I fear you are unwell." Thorne took another step toward her, his hand held out solicitously. "May I assist—"

"No, no!" She backed up, coughing the lemon drop into her palm as she stumbled into the group of stunned onlookers behind her.

"Indeed, I can see I have caused you great distress." He was

surrounded by Thornes—relations, friends, associates . . .
oh, dear!

"Miss Hewes is the daughter of Lady Sophia Chatham,"
Quince sputtered in warning. "I insist, sir, that you—"

"But she is . . . I have torn her—"

"I am well, my lord," Olivia blurted out. "Do not trouble
yourself, I beg you."

"Come, brother!" A man in the Thorne party spoke up.
He was nearly as tall as Lord Thorne but younger. "Miss
Hewes has pardoned you. Leave it at that. We have had
enough trouble from her family to last a lifetime."

The bitter tone slid through Olivia's bones. "Trouble from
*my* family?" she retorted. "What is your meaning in this accusation, sir?"

Not deigning to answer, the younger man took his brother's
elbow and turned away. "Randolph, the ladies await us in the
carriage."

Lord Thorne detached himself and gave Olivia a bow.
"I assure you, madam, I meant you no affront."

"Good morning, sir," Olivia managed while executing
a self-conscious curtsy.

His blue eyes fell upon her once again. She clutched the
sticky lemon drop in her glove and hung suspended in his
gaze. For a moment, she felt certain he would speak again.
Instead, he returned his top hat to his head and followed his
brother through the church door.

**LIKE A RIVER GLORIOUS**
*Rachel was an unwilling partner in deception. Only a miracle would set her free. . . .*

**MEASURES OF GRACE**
*Corrine begins a new life—unaware she is being pursued.*